ZIONSVILLE PUBLIC LIBRARY
W9-CCE-990

The Whole Lie

Also by Steve Ulfelder

Purgatory Chasm

The Whole Lie

STEVE ULFELDER

Minotaur Books

A Thomas Dunne Book

New York

This is a work of fiction. All of the characters, organizations, and events portrayed in this novel are either products of the author's imagination or are used fictitiously.

A THOMAS DUNNE BOOK FOR MINOTAUR BOOKS.
An imprint of St. Martin's Press.

www.thomasdunnebooks.com
www.minotaurbooks.com

Library of Congress Cataloging-in-Publication Data

Ulfelder, Steve.
The whole lie / Steve Ulfelder.—1st ed.
p. cm.
ISBN 978-0-312-60454-7 (hardcover)
ISBN 978-1-4668-0242-1 (e-book)
1. Automobile mechanics—Fiction. 2. Murder—Investigation—Fiction.
I. Title.
PS3621.L435 W47 2012
813'.6—dc22

2012005473

First Edition: May 2012

10 9 8 7 6 5 4 3 2 1

For my parents

ACKNOWLEDGMENTS

This novel came together while my first, *Purgatory Chasm,* came to market, so it's only fair to thank everybody who helped with both books.

Start with literary agent Janet Reid, who's been with me and behind me from the get-go. Then there's Anne Bensson, my editor, who wore out a pencil or two shaping *The Whole Lie* (and I'm glad she did!). The copyediting, design, and publicity experts at Minotaur Books have twice made me look better than I deserve to.

I owe a debt of gratitude to Tatnuck Bookseller in Westborough, Massachusetts, whose knowledgeable staffers are staunch allies. In addition, I'm lucky to live an easy drive from more than a dozen Barnes & Noble stores. These B&Ns have been generous in organizing events and talking up *Purgatory Chasm.*

My wife, Martha Ulfelder, and my kids deserve thanks for putting up with typical writer nonsense: More often than it should, my mood depends on the day's 1,500 words. My family's patience and support mean everything to me.

CHAPTER ONE

When Savvy Kane walked into my shop, I was wrestling the rotted muffler from a Maxima.

It's not a pretty job. Rust flakes, road crud, frozen bolts. Cursing is involved.

As I gave a final twist, the customer door swung open.

I looked.

I looked again.

My jaw dropped.

The muffler dropped.

It weighed thirty pounds, and every one of them landed on my right boot.

Her name was Savannah, but when I'd met her in a biker bar on the south side of Owensboro, Kentucky, all the Harley boys had called her Savvy.

It wasn't hard to see why. She didn't pay for a drink all night. And she drank a lot.

Me too. Back then.

"What the hell," I said, stepping into the customer area.

"Some greeting," she said.

"Close the door," I said.

She stepped close, planning a hug until she saw the grime on my coveralls. I could smell her hair. No change: almost like apples, but not quite.

"You look the same," I said.

"You don't." She took my face in both hands, brushing a fleck of something from my forehead. As she studied me I remembered her eyes: They were a gray that could look blue, green, brown, or nearly black, depending on the light. Depending on her mood.

Savvy thumbed my right cheek. "What happened?"

"Life. And lots of it."

She shook her head. "Death."

"Some of that, too."

Her thumb was still on my cheek when the door whooshed and Charlene walked in.

I froze.

Charlene froze.

Savvy did not freeze. She stroked my cheek again, dropped her hand, turned, squinted, paused a long beat. "Darlene?" she finally said.

"*Char*lene," I said. Quickly.

"Well knock me over," Savvy said.

"Savannah Kane," Charlene said, then curled her lip. "Savvy."

"Are you two . . ." Savvy said.

"Hell yes," I said. Quickly.

"How sweet," Savvy said, then faced Charlene. "Come to keep an eye on your man?"

"On my business," Charlene said. "I own the place."

"Well," I said.

"Or may as well," Charlene said. "I hold the note."

"True enough," I said.

"My my," Savvy said. "Business and pleasure."

We stood there. From the work area, where I ought to be, came an Eagles song on the classic rock station. Then the whir of an air wrench as Floriano Mendes, my friend and only employee, took something off a Honda Pilot.

Savvy said, "Can you spare Mister Goodwrench here for a cup of coffee?"

"Ask him."

"Pretty busy," I said.

"Too busy to chat with an old Barnburner who's got a problem?"

Barnburner. Savvy'd said the magic word, and Charlene knew it as well as I did. Charlene hit me with the ice-blue eyes, a stare that cut deeper than words could. Then she turned and walked to her desk. Didn't say a goddamn thing.

Didn't have to.

A long time ago, in a nineteen-dollar-a-night hotel room outside Paducah, Kentucky, Savannah Kane and I had swapped life stories.

She was born and raised in Virginia's Roanoke Valley. Her father made nozzles for high-quality pressure washers and did well enough so the toughest choice his daughter ever faced was jumping or dressage. She majored in drunk at the University of Virginia, put together a rich girl's cocaine-and-vodka habit. She never sniffed or drank any more than her friends did—but after college, when the friends dumped the cocaine and got jobs, Savvy didn't. Couldn't. That's when her story turned ugly, the way they do.

"Nice little place," she said now, looking around the coffee shop. A girl on hidden speakers sang a slow song. Customers diddled with laptops.

"I like Dunkin' Donuts better," I said, "but this is closer. Where have you been? Why are you back?"

She laughed some. "You still don't beat around the bush. I remember how much I liked that."

I said nothing.

"I stayed put for seven years," she said, "right where you and that weird little guy put me."

"Moe Coover."

"Yes! Such a great name, how'd I forget it?"

"So you've been in Greensboro this whole time?"

"North Carolina." She said it *Noff Caro-LYNE,* exaggerating the accent. "And don't sound so skeptical. I grew fond of the place, believe it or not. You were right about its being the perfect city to get lost in."

"*Moe* was right," I said. "Greensboro was his call. What did you do there?"

"I did just as you recommended. As *Moe* recommended, sorry. Some of this, some of that. McJobs. I waited tables in chain restaurants, stocked shelves at Staples, sold sofas in big furniture stores. Never hung around long enough to get funneled into management." She sipped her coffee, a fancy thing with whipped cream and a cinnamon stick. "Not long enough to get close to anyone."

I sipped too, looked her in the eye. "I don't believe you."

"*Ass*hole!" She hissed it, slapping her coffee to the table.

"It's not in you to work a square job," I said. "Maybe for a month, for giggles. No longer than that. You need action. When you can't find it, you make it."

"If you're so sure about that, why'd you help me run in the first place?"

"You were a Barnburner." My AA group, the ones who saved my life. Savvy'd been a member of the group for a while. It's where she met Charlene. "I help Barnburners. No questions asked."

"You're still running around with that crowd? They must all be a hundred and ten. What kind of super-sexy problems do you solve? Canasta cheating scandals? Misplaced hearing aids?"

I took it, both hands flat on the table. On the hidden speakers, a boy now sang a slow, sad song just like the one before it. Only with a higher voice.

Savvy hadn't changed. She was smarter than you and didn't mind letting you know it. She'd whip you up and down trying to get her way. But if you gave in, she lost respect and dropped you as whatever you were to her: friend, co-conspirator, lover.

Lover.

In her bedroom, I remembered, I'd wanted to do everything, tell everything, *feel* everything in a way I hadn't known before or since.

I felt her hand on mine and snapped to, pissed that she could still read my mind. I was a simpleton to her, always had been.

"Why are you back?" I said. "And since it's been seven years, maybe you can tell me why you needed to disappear."

"Why's your face red? What were you thinking about just now, Conway?"

"Why'd you need to leave all of a sudden? You wouldn't tell me then. I didn't force it. You seemed scared. But it's seven years on."

Savvy cut her eyes left and right, then put both hands in her lap so she could lean way in. With her chin nearly touching the table she said, "I don't remember you being much of a political creature, but you *do* know y'all have a gubernatorial election a week from today. Right?"

"Okay."

"And you know Betsy Tinker has been a lead-pipe cinch from the get-go?"

I said nothing.

"Name ring a bell?" she said. "The sweetheart of Massachusetts? The money, the senator hubby?"

"He died. She took his seat. More money than God."

"Right. The whole world loves Betsy Tinker. Doesn't matter what she says, doesn't matter what her plans are. After this clown of a governor, the one who's on his way out, voters want somebody uncontroversial, somebody *nice*. Three weeks ago, the polls had Tinker up twenty-six among likely voters. Do you pay attention *at all*, Conway?"

"Not to politicians. I keep hoping they'll go away if I ignore them."

"Betsy Tinker's not going anywhere except the corner office. Thomas Wilton, her opponent, is a nothingburger, the Washington Generals."

I smiled. Leave it to Savvy to throw in a Harlem Globetrotters reference. "For a North Carolina gal, you know plenty about Massachusetts politics."

"Tinker's lead has been shrinking," Savvy said. "That's natural.

Nobody wins by twenty-six, not even in Massachusetts. However . . ." she leaned forward even more ". . . there's a problem."

I waited.

"Blackmail threats."

I waited.

"There are, I'm given to understand, issues that could put a very big dent in Tinker's lead."

"Such as."

"Such as me." Her eyes danced as she said it.

"Tell me."

"I have a history with Tinker's running mate, the next *lieutenant* governor," she said. "He's a business guy, a charger. He was supposed to grab the blue-collar votes while Tinker focused on Morrissey Boulevard and Newton and the Berkshires. Any idea who he is, my strapping, not-as-dumb-as-he-wants-you-to-think friend?"

I said nothing.

"Thought not. Nobody gives a rat's ass about the second name on the ticket. Ever heard of Bert Saginaw?"

"Made a mint in fences," I said. "Built himself a palace right here in Framingham."

She mock-applauded me for finally knowing something. Like I said, she's smarter than you and doesn't mind if you know it.

I sipped. "What about him?"

Half a smile played across Savvy's lips. "Bert Saginaw has a little John Edwards problem. And I'm Rielle Hunter." She read my eyes, sighed, put both hands on mine. "I asked you and Moe to disappear me seven years ago because I was pregnant with what the tabloids call a love child."

CHAPTER TWO

Maybe ten seconds passed. "You were pregnant?"

"Everybody figured it out but you."

"Why didn't you tell me?"

"You would have gone crazy jealous on me."

"Bullshit."

"You feel a twinge even now," Savvy said. "Even though Charlene's got a ring through your nose. It might as well be stamped on your forehead."

She was right. "We were close back then," I said. "The way I remember it, we had something intense going. It felt . . . it felt exclusive, that's for sure."

"It was intense, you've got that part right." She brushed my cheek with her fingertips. "Seven years. A long time. Besides, you've got grim little Charlene. She cleaned up nice, I'll give her that. Back then she was a bitty bottle-blond crack ho, was she not? Social Services took her kids away, or am I misremembering?"

"She got her daughters back a long time ago," I said, putting my hand on Savvy's left forearm.

"I always figured you'd wind up with someone," she said, ignoring my hand. "You're a serial monogamist. You work the strong-silent-type routine and you work it well, but at day's end you need a woman to fix your dinner and wash your boxer briefs. What good is Brando-hood without someone to tell you what a cool loner you are?"

"They're eighteen and twelve, and I love them. Charlene built a good business from scratch. I live with her, moved in a while back. We've been through a lot together."

She grabbed my hand with her free one. "You're hurting my arm."

"Yes." I kept the pressure on.

"You're *hurting* me."

"Yes." I held her eyes, held the pressure, watched fear bloom behind the pain.

Finally she said, "I'm sorry, ow, ow, I'm sorry, I'm sure Charlene is the cat's meow, *ow!*"

I released, stood. Left the coffee shop, walked back toward the garage. The smart move would be to work my ass off the rest of the day and clear Savannah Kane from my head. Charlene would be frosty for a few days—who could blame her?—but we'd get past it.

Yup. It'd be a mistake to try to explain. Talking doesn't always work out so well for me. I dig holes. Better to buckle down, work my tail off, let my actions show Charlene that Savvy was nothing to me.

She *was* nothing.

Right?

So why did I catch myself listening for footsteps? Why did I slow when I heard her trotting after me?

She grabbed my arm when I was half a block from the garage. "Some things never change," she said, then held up an index finger and put hands on knees and panted.

"You still smoke," I said. "Old Gold?"

"Seen the price of cigs lately? I smoke whatever's on sale at the gas station." She straightened, caught her breath. "I was thinking, as I staggered after you clutching my ticker, how quickly we fell into the old patterns."

I said nothing.

"Me tormenting you over things you don't know," she said, rubbing the forearm I'd squeezed. "You hurting me back the way that comes naturally to you."

"Charlene and I are a couple," I said, fishing my cell from my pocket, flicking to the photos. "This is her younger daughter Sophie. The older daughter is Jessica, everybody calls her Jesse."

"Cute. Quite a financier you found for the brand-new garage. I kid, Conway, I kid. I admit I wondered where you got the dough to launch this shop. Last I heard, banks weren't loaning mucho dinero to guys with manslaughter two on their resume." Pause. "So I Googled. Why wouldn't I?"

"Why *did* you, though? Why are you here?"

"Brass tacks at last."

"How's this for brass tacks?" I said, riffing, thinking on the fly. "This Bert Saginaw knocked you up. He voted abortion, you voted child support. After all, you weren't getting any younger. You had to play the long game. Saginaw must have looked like an ATM with legs."

She slapped me hard.

I ignored it. "You made do with the child support, but it burned you up. When Saginaw went into politics, you couldn't take it anymore. You had to make a run at the big payday. You're here to squeeze him. Gold Digger One-Oh-One."

Her eyes flashed. "You get in trouble when you try to act smart," she said. "You obviously don't realize Bert's famous for blowing fortunes. He wasn't rich when I was with him, and my child-support checks prove it."

"So you're here to renegotiate. And if talks don't go your way, you parade your kid for the reporters."

She slapped my face again. "I would *never* do such a thing, and you're a prick for saying I would! Max is back home with his . . . in very good care."

We stood. Traffic rolled. My face stung.

"You guessed partly right," Savvy said, and I noticed she'd molded herself to me, breast pressing my arm, thigh on thigh. From face-slap to this in two seconds. Typical. "I did come to renegotiate. But a funny thing happened."

"What?" I said, looking at the Shell station across the street.

"Bert and I hit it off. Rekindled, if you get my drift. And believe it or not, the campaign has kind of . . . adopted me, no, *absorbed* me. I'm part of Team Tinker-Saginaw."

"They're hugging you close til the campaign's over. Then they'll brush you off."

"No. I thought that too at first, but there's more to it. Trust me, I'm part of the sanctum sanctorum."

"What's that?"

"Never mind. It was my idea to get your help. We were talking in the war room last night, and I mentioned the kind of thing you do for Barnburners."

"Saginaw's not a Barnburner."

"But I am."

"I need to get back to work."

"*Please,* Conway. Old times' sake."

I stared across at the Shell. "What were you talking about in this war room?"

"Blackmail."

"Not your blackmail? *Other* blackmail?"

"You bet. Weird, isn't it?"

What was weird, I thought, was the pencil-necked kid staring at us from the Shell. He stood by a red Lumina. He was looking death rays at me. Trying to puff out his chest, but he didn't have much of one.

I wouldn't have noticed him, but the Lumina had North Carolina plates.

Huh.

I filed the car away and took Savvy's elbows. "We had a thing a long time ago. You were a Barnburner. You asked for help, I helped. But you were supposed to vamoose and stay vamoosed." She tried to interrupt, but I shook my head and something in my eyes told her to keep quiet.

"You made your deal, and you'd best stick to it. Here's your smart move: call a cab, go to Logan, and grab the next flight south."

"That's exactly what I'll do," Savvy said.

I said nothing, knew there was more coming.

"All I ask," she said, "is that before I go, you come see Bert in action. He wants to meet you. Just watch him, shake his hand, hear him out. Then give a thumbs-up or a thumbs-down. You won't hear a peep out of me."

I checked my watch, looked at the shop. Between a newspaper feature and some e-coupons, we'd gotten off to a good start. We were hip-deep in boring Japanese cars that needed boring service.

"When?" I finally said.

"Right now! Bert's doing a rally downtown."

I sighed and led her to my truck.

CHAPTER THREE

Now some people," Bert Saginaw said, leaning toward the microphone like he was having a neighborly talk with a pal, "*some* people, even some people whose names are on ballots this year . . ." He waited for hoots and applause that didn't come. "Some people would defund the programs I'm talking about, programs that are helping Framingham bootstrap its way back, programs that help *good* people find *good* jobs at *good* wages . . ." He thumped the podium on each "good," working himself into the Martin Luther King–wannabe rhythm that politicians love.

I stopped listening to the words. People who listen to the words of a man running for office deserve what they get. I looked around instead, knew I'd learn more that way.

Saginaw stood at the top of the steps to the Memorial Building, Framingham's city hall, speaking to maybe a hundred bored citizens.

Framingham's a funny place. A little too big to be a town, a little too small to be a city. Route 9, an east-west road that may be the original strip-mall hell, cuts it in half. North of 9, Framingham's a solid little suburb full of Boston commuters. South of 9, it's more of a has-been city. Railroad tracks, a long-closed GM plant, old-school small industrial, two-family homes. Salvation Army, methadone clinics, halfway houses, oldsters who missed their chance to move out.

And wall to wall Brazilians, some of them legal. Fine by me: Every Brazilian I know works as hard as three of anyone else. If Saturday night knife fights and crazy soccer parades don't bother you, Brazilians make good neighbors.

We were on the south side of town. The Memorial Building squats on a three-way intersection whose rotary screws up traffic all day, every day. The rally was making things worse. Background noise: horn honks, siren-blats from ambulances forcing their way over to the hospital. Behind Saginaw stood a dozen people with signs reading SAGINAW—LT GOV in red, white, and blue.

I'd never seen a sign for a lieutenant governor that didn't mention the candidate for governor. I wondered what Betsy Tinker, his running mate, thought about that.

The sign holders were props for the TV news cameras, nothing more. I recognized a few of them. There was the gal who runs a soup kitchen, the preacher who shows up every time a kid gets shot in the projects, a couple guys with purple union T-shirts. Like that.

One woman behind Saginaw, jammed in with a half-dozen handlers in suits, looked so familiar it bugged me. Sandy hair, squared-off jaw, beet-colored suit that didn't do her any favors. I asked Savvy who she was. "Bert's sister Emily," she said. "Faithful assistant, gal Friday, cast-iron-bitch gatekeeper. Take your pick."

I looked from sister to brother, and saw it. They could just about be twins. Hell, maybe they were. I felt for Emily: The face she shared with her brother, with its compass-arrow nose and its Dudley Do-Right jaw, suited a man more than a woman.

I recognized a bunch of folks around me in the crowd, too. Half of them were Brazilian illegals—their bosses must have shooed them over to make a pretty TV picture.

Add it all up, you came away with an impression of a half-assed rally, a place nobody wanted to be. Except Bert Saginaw.

He was rolling now, wrapping up I hoped, doing dime store MLK until his voice cracked and his fist had to hurt from podium-thumps. Finally, in a nice touch, he snapped a white handkerchief from the breast pocket of his suit and wiped his forehead like he'd worked up a sweat. The crowd waited half a beat too long, wondering if he was finished, then finally clapped. A two-fingers whistle cut through. It was one of the handlers, a twentysomething boy whistling and stomping like he'd just heard the Gettysburg Address.

Savvy leaned into me, her breast pressing my arm. "Warning," she said. "Potential disaster looms."

"What do you mean?"

"Bert's supposed to lead a spontaneous march through town. Pressing babies, kissing flesh, primo telegenic shit. But the adoring masses appear to be sprinting back to work."

"They don't look all that adoring."

"Or that massive. Look. He's pissed."

She was right. Saginaw had continued the man-of-the-people routine by taking his coat off even though it was late-October chilly. He now one-fingered the coat over his left shoulder, leaving his right hand free to wave and shake. But there was nobody to shake with, and the only thing to wave at were illegals' backs as they hustled to their shops or apartments.

Wearing what he probably thought of as a TV grin, but which looked to me like that old *Life* magazine photo of some poor sap riding a rocket sled, Saginaw whispered to handlers. One in particular gave off a boss-man vibe. He was letting Saginaw's rant roll off his back.

I checked my watch. "Well," I said.

"You're not getting off that easy," Savvy said, pulling me by the arm. "I said you need to *meet* him, remember?" We tucked into the hind end of Saginaw's parade, which now consisted of him, his handlers, the two guys with union T-shirts, and a pair of gals I recognized from the Brazilian bakery a block down.

As we crossed Concord Street, Saginaw pretended the cars were honking for him, not at him. Sure enough, the two gals slipped into the bakery—their manager flipped green aprons to them before the door even closed. Now I was three steps behind Saginaw.

You could plunk him down in any town, any state, and nobody'd be surprised when they heard he was running for office. He had that born-winner look. Straw-colored hair cut almost in a Boys' Regular, but not quite, like he'd been using the same barber since he was eight. High forehead, that unapologetic nose, smart blue eyes.

But something was off.

It hit me when I compared Saginaw to the campaign manager he was reaming out. The campaign manager—at least I assumed that was his job—looked a lot like Saginaw, a born winner. But he was a full seven inches taller.

Bert Saginaw was a shrimp.

I looked harder, first at him and then at the manager, and I saw he was a shrimp in an odd way: He had the torso and shoulders of a six-footer, but it looked like someone had sawed four inches out of his legs.

Huh. I'd known guys like that who developed complexes, resentments. A few of them would have been taller but for childhood sicknesses. I wondered if that was Saginaw's deal. Looking at his jacketless back, his expensive shirt that had to be custom made, I saw he had a hell of a V shape. Easy guess: He was a fitness guy, a junkie for it. An overcompensator.

Leading his sad little parade through downtown Framingham, the locals avoiding his smiles mostly out of pity, Bert Saginaw was giving the campaign manager hell. He waved, he shook hands with anybody who wasn't quick enough in clearing out of his way, he maintained the grin/grimace. But he was hissing in the ear of the taller man, occasionally grabbing his upper arm in a way that had to hurt. I caught snippets.

". . . couldn't even round up a couple dozen *teachers,* for Chrissake?" Saginaw said.

". . . Good call. I'll take that bullet," the man said.

". . . Tinker's talking to *three hundred goddamn people* in Brookline right now," Saginaw said.

". . . Worcester promises they'll have 'em hanging from the rafters tomorrow," the man said.

This went on for the better part of a block. Finally, seconds after the last diehard camera crew dropped away—unable to resist the smells from a *churrascuria* that would pile meat on your plate until midnight for $9.95—we came to a mini-caravan just north of a Salvation Army where I'd bunked a long time ago. Leading was a BMW X5 SUV, black. Behind it, a brand-new Chevy Malibu in the same color.

Saginaw made for the right rear door of the BMW, but the campaign manager spoke in his ear and guided him to the Malibu, with sister Emily right behind. The manager and his flunkies doubled back to the SUV. Savvy and I stood on the sidewalk.

"Take shotgun," Saginaw said to Savvy, pointing at me. "I want to talk to this one while we ride."

Me, Emily, and Saginaw made for a tight backseat fit.

"What kind of car is this?" Saginaw said, looking around the gray cloth interior.

"Chevy Malibu," I said, "the new one. Supposed to be pretty decent."

"Piece of shit," he said. "Krall says I have to ride around in American cars during the campaign. Probably after, too."

"Krall?"

"Campaign manager. Costing us a mint, soul of a vampire, but he's been around the block a few times."

"He makes you drive American," I said, "while he rides in your BMW. Pretty ritzy deal for him."

"Good point," Saginaw said, half-laughing. "Am I a sap or what?"

"Way I hear it," I said, "you're nobody's sap. What do you want with me?"

"You were right, Savvy," Saginaw said. "He does have a short tolerance for talk." Then he leaned across and forward, putting a blue-sleeved arm through the gap between the front seats, and twined his fingers in hers.

It wasn't a move I expected from Saginaw. It made him look awkward and needy.

It made him look like he cared about Savvy.

A lot.

Huh.

Meanwhile, sister Emily was looking at her brother's arm like she wanted to cut it off.

Double huh.

"Savannah tells me," Saginaw said, "you're some kinda miracle man for the local AA crowd. Robin Hood for drunks."

"Did she tell you I'm a convicted felon?"

"She mentioned it. Why?"

"I couldn't vote for you even if I wanted to," I said. "So stop blowing smoke up my ass and tell me why I'm here."

Long pause. Saginaw's eyes went stormy.

Then cleared, and he laughed like hell. "You were right!" he said to Savvy, squeezing her hand, still leaning. "You were sure as hell right about this cat."

"So tell him," she said. Annoyed? She worked her hand free of Saginaw's and folded her arms.

"Yes," Emily said. "Tell him."

"You know the gist of the situation," he said after a few seconds.

"Savvy had your kid," I said. "She holed up in North Carolina for a long time, cashing your checks. Now she's back."

"There's more to it."

"She came north to squeeze you for more dough."

"*Ass*hole," Savvy said.

"She's not," Saginaw said.

"Of course she is," Emily said.

"At first, maybe, yeah," Saginaw said. "Not anymore. But *somebody's* squeezing, all right. Somebody's running all sorts of games to push me out of the race."

"Isn't it a little late for that?" I said.

"Not *too* late, not with this state's screwy laws."

"Okay," I said, "you should know. But let's get down to it. I assume you're talking about the guy Betsy Tinker's up against. What's his name?"

"Thomas Wilton," Emily and Savvy said at the same time.

"What I don't get," I said, "is why's this Wilton working on you instead of Tinker?"

The car went quiet.

"Tell him," Emily said.

"Yes, tell him," Savvy said. "In for a dime."

Saginaw leaned forward so he could look across his sister at me. "I'm pretty sure the squeezer is my bosom-buddy running mate. Sweet Betsy Tinker, the next governor of the Commonwealth of Massachusetts."

CHAPTER FOUR

Then it was quiet some more. Savvy broke the silence. "Strange bedfellows," she said.

The driver swung right. I remembered reading about Saginaw's massive house when he built it. The place was in Framingham, but barely: If we'd continued two hundred yards we would have been in Sherborn, one of the swankest towns around.

The driver pushed an overhead button and waited for a wrought-iron gate set between stone pillars to roll open. We eased up blacktop that was technically a driveway but was as wide and well-crowned as most public roads. We burst through a final stand of pines and there was the home of Bert Saginaw, rent-a-fence tycoon.

"Well," I said.

More money than taste was my first thought. I'm not Frank Lloyd Wright, but as I climbed from the Malibu I saw something had gone wrong with the mansion. The place had started as a good-sized stone house, nicely balanced. Then the shit had hit the fan. It looked like each time Saginaw made another ten million, or found a new girlfriend, or tried a new hobby, he'd added a wing to the place. But the wings had nothing to do with the original building, or with each other. So this handsome French (I guessed) home sprouted on one end a Japanese-looking atrium, which sprouted a redbrick gentleman's library, which sprouted a damn indoor squash court, which sprouted something Danish-looking—a deluxe sauna?—with dark vertical siding, which sprouted . . .

Like that. And that was just the side of the house nearest me. The other end of the place, hard to see from where we stood, had its own set of sprouts.

"Wow," I said.

"Wow," Savvy said. Poker face.

Saginaw and Emily jumped from the car. "I'll be there in four minutes!" Saginaw said to his sister, loosening his tie as he strode to the main house.

"I'll be there in three!" she said, sprinting past him.

Savvy and I stood by the car.

"Wow," I said.

"They work out together," she said. "Religiously."

We followed Krall inside.

It looked just the way I'd figured, given the outside. Each section of the building was a perfect version of what it was supposed to be—but had nothing to do with the next section. "We'll wait here," Krall said to Savvy at one point, and he and his flunkies peeled off.

I elbowed Savvy, made a *what the hell?* face.

She knew what I meant. "Rite of passage," she said. "Bert and Em like to show off for newcomers in the gymnasium."

"Why?"

"It's their fave place."

"Weird dude," I said. "Weird house."

"No comment," Savvy said as we walked. We cruised through a room full of pinball machines, then what looked to be a museum for suits of armor and swords and shields, then a full-fledged soda shop plucked straight out of 1956. Savvy clipped through each space, paused at a set of double doors, showed me her best deadpan, and shouldered us in . . .

. . . to a fitness center that would cost yuppies a couple hundred bucks a month in Boston. Blue carpet, mirrored walls, spinning bikes, pro-caliber treadmills and elliptical machines, medicine balls, free-weight area, Pilates area, white-painted Nautilus gear. You name it. Disco-pop blasted. Bert Saginaw, changed already into shorts and a T-shirt, held a pair of boxing trainer's paddle-style gloves and used them to catch the punches of Emily, who was dressed in a hot-pink running shirt and black workout pants that left no doubt she was in great shape.

"Hi! Hi!" she said with a left-right combo. "Hee-hee-hee!" she said, right-right-left. "Hoof! Hoof! *Hoof!*" On the last *Hoof!*, she fired an uppercut from her belt line that looked like it could do some damage.

"All *right*!" Saginaw said, wiggling his hand to show the punch had stung. Then, in what was obviously an old and frequent custom, they both snapped their wrists, flipping their gloves to the floor, and jumped against each other—performing one of those chest-bumping high-fives that were big in the NFL that year.

Emily walked over, water bottle in one hand and sweat towel in the other. "I don't think my rude brother made a proper introduction," she said, sticking out her hand. "Emily Saginaw."

I said my name while she tried to break my hand. She was strong. Hell, if my hand hadn't been twice as big as hers, she might've hurt me. As it stood, she was a mouse trying to judo-flip a cat.

"Fill him in while I do cardio," Saginaw said. He walked off without looking at me, snapped a jump rope from a hook, and began to use it.

Emily led me to a pair of weight benches, nodded at one, sat on the other. I sat and let her look me over. Her face was a little red from the workout, with a tiny sweat sheen, but she still managed to hold herself like a vice principal. She wanted me to feel like I was in a job interview. I wanted to let her know I didn't give a damn about her brother's problems.

"I hear you're not much for politics," she finally said.

"That's right."

"Any particular reason?"

"Anybody who wants to wear a suit and sit in meetings all day is crazy as a shithouse rat. Hard to imagine why you'd trust a bunch like that to run a country."

"Or a state."

"Or a state."

"But even a guy like you must know Betsy Tinker," she said. "She transcends politics around here."

"Her husband was a politician for a long time," I said. "They were rich going back to the *Mayflower* or somesuch. When he died in a car wreck, she took his seat in the Senate."

She nodded. "Won reelection on her own, in a landslide. Adored by all. The Darling of the Bay State." Emily's lip curled when she said that. "Tinker's so damn beloved that she's running as if this is 1796."

I looked a question at her.

"Back then," Emily said, trying to be patient with me and almost pulling it off, " 'twas considered beneath the dignity of a statesman to actually campaign. Pete Krall and some of the Harvard twerps advising Tinker told her to try the same thing. It's a tough sell, but so far she's pulled it off."

"Bert does the roadwork," I said, "while she coasts along."

"Exactly." Emily paused. "The question is, why does she want to be governor in the first place?"

"Why not?"

"She could have held her Senate seat for life. It's the best job in politics. It's an exclusive club, and you only have to run every six years. Best of all, you don't *do* anything. You sit in hearings. You move your mouth on unwatched Sunday morning TV shows."

"Governor's a pretty good job, too," I said.

"Like hell it is. Every time there's a snowstorm, you ride around with a plow-jockey for TV. A flood in Hull? You're up at three in the morning, wading around with the locals, trying to look like you give a damn. You kiss the state cops' behinds, and the teachers', too. And I haven't even gotten to the senior citizens."

"Okay," I said. "I give up. Why does Betsy Tinker want to be governor?"

"If you've already got the money and the power, there's only one reason that makes sense." She leaned toward me. "It's what you do if you want to be president."

"So?"

"So Betsy Bite-My-Bag Tinker will be president over my dead fucking body," Emily Saginaw said, snapping off each word, her face going a deeper red.

Then she slapped a hand across her mouth. If she could have reached out with the other, grabbed the words and stuffed them back inside, she would have.

I smiled and let the moment stretch against the disco-pop and the jump rope's thwap. "Why's that?" I finally said.

"My brother," Emily said, composed again, "will be president someday. Sooner rather than later."

"And two Massachusetts pols grabbing at the same brass ring is a losing proposition."

"For both parties," she said. "Now if you'll pardon me, I'll do a little cardio of my own."

She shot from the bench and bounced toward her brother, grabbing a jump rope on the way. Facing Saginaw, she took a moment to figure out his timing, then got to work in perfect synchronicity.

They faced one another.

They smiled at one another.

They were still skipping and smiling when I left the gym.

"Care for a banana split?" Savvy said as the door closed. "Maybe a nice root beer float?"

She stood behind the counter of Saginaw's bizarre transplanted ice cream shop. Across from her, Krall sipped a drink from one of those classic soda-fountain glasses.

I looked at Savvy. I was poleaxed by the Bert and Emily Show. Didn't know what to say.

"An interesting pair," Krall said without looking up. He was an inch taller than me and thirty pounds lighter but with big shoulders, maybe a former college swimmer. Dark brown hair that should've been cut last week and should've been washed this morning, parted on the left, shaggy over the ears. Brown gunsight eyes that took in everything and gave nothing back. Brown suit that cost more than my truck, brown shoes that cost more than my tires, burnt-orange tie that cost more than a tank of gas.

"These people are going to run the *state*?" I said. "I'd sooner vote for Lobster Boy and the Bearded Lady."

"I've seen worse," Krall said. Guy still wouldn't look up. "Hell, I've put worse in office. And this I assure you, friend: Saginaw's money spends as well as anybody else's."

"You're earning every nickel," I said, and made a little salute to Savvy. "Good-bye and good riddance."

I only made it one step.

"Speaking of money," Savvy said. For the first time I noticed a pale blue check, the big kind from a ledger-style business checkbook. It rested on the counter next to Krall's drink. Savvy pushed it three inches in my direction.

From where I stood I couldn't read it.

"He won't sully himself by looking," Krall said to Savvy. "He'll walk out and never look back. Like the assholes in the action movies."

"Stop it, Pete," Savvy said.

"But those action-movie assholes, they don't owe big money to their girlfriends." He looked me in the eye for the first time, finishing his soda, making a sucking noise with his straw. "Do they?"

My hands made fists.

I made myself turn 90 degrees. I made myself take a step that would lead me out. There was no sense beating up this jerk. *Say good-bye to Krall, to Savvy Kane, to the Saginaws. You can be home, showered, eating dinner with Charlene and Sophie, in thirty minutes.*

I took a step.

"Another thing about these action-movie assholes," Krall said. "They don't work with illegals."

I stopped.

"Pete," Savvy said.

He ignored her. "Your shop is F&C Automotive, right? The F is for Floriano? Floriano Mendes?"

"Pete," Savvy said. "Can you give us a minute?"

While the two of them stared each other down, silently refighting some battle, blood pounded in my head. I wanted to bust up this dumbass room, this jerk Krall.

I made myself breathe instead. In through the nose, out through the mouth. When I finally spoke I spoke carefully, like a college professor. "Floriano's not illegal."

"But his wife Maria is," Krall said, chewing his straw. "Or am I wrong about that?"

I took a step toward him. He flinched.

"Pete!" Savvy said. "Give us a minute."

We watched him walk away. He took his soda.

"I'm sorry," Savvy said, stepping to me, hugging me. "I told him that horse shit wouldn't work on you. I told him it wasn't needed anyway. Obviously, he paid no attention. He's pissed I'm even around."

"What do you mean, 'wasn't needed'?" During her hug, Savvy had let her hands run south to my rear end. Bad idea. I stepped out of the hug, crossed my arms.

Her eyes flitted up, then away. "You know what I mean. We share something."

"You didn't need Krall's flavor of blackmail," I said. "You came at me with your own."

" 'Blackmail' is a kid's word, Conway. A soap-opera word. We share something."

"Pound sand."

"See you tomorrow," she said to my back. "Bert's using the Escutcheon Hotel in Cambridge as his headquarters."

As I walked the long hall to the front door, clenching and unclenching my fists, I heard a crinkle. It was coming from me. I checked my back pockets, damn near smiled in spite of everything: She'd tucked the big blue check in my pocket.

Savannah Goddamn Kane.

Here's the first thing I ever said to her, sixteen years ago: "Ahhhhh-*woooooo*!"

It was something I said when I took quaaludes and drank. Which I did whenever I could find and afford quaaludes. When I couldn't, I just drank. I always did like the loose reel of 'ludes—riding them was like being drunk without the puking, hangovers, and other assorted miseries.

Owensboro, Kentucky. Biker bar called the Shovelhead, just west of State Route 81. You could throw a beer bottle from the parking lot to the main runway of the local airport.

I was fresh off a barge making its way southwest on the Kentucky River. Can't remember much more than that, but I had to be flush to be in a bar in the first place—by then, drinking fortified wine in hobo camps was more my style—so chances are I'd been working on the barge, had bailed out in Owensboro with a week's wages in my pocket.

In addition to three pocket-lint quaaludes I'd bought in the parking lot, I'd treated myself to a triple Wild Turkey and a Bud. I know that because when Savvy bumped my elbow, an honest shot of the bourbon slopped onto the bar, and it was all I could do not to lean over and slurp it up.

She'd spent most of the night ignoring me the way a cat ignores you—licking its leg, pretending it doesn't know you're watching. As she danced and flirted and drank free without ever quite falling into the bikers' knuckle-tat mitts, a word had come to me: *smoky.*

And then here she was: bumping precious whiskey from my glass.

"You look like you just lost your best friend," she said, her back against the bar rail, a longneck Bud of her own in both hands. She had to shout over the Doobie Brothers' "China Grove," which was playing for the third time since I'd come in.

That's when I said: "Ahhhhh-*woooooo*!"

Her mouth twitched. She leaned toward me, locked eyes for a full twenty seconds, and said: "Ahhhhh-*woooooo*!"

It was a pretty fair imitation.

Smoky, I thought. I'm not sure I fell in love right then, exactly, but I fell into a place where I wanted to impress her, take care of her, show her I was a man. *All* man. A *good* man. The stinking, swilling, flea-toting bum who stood before her in a peacoat stolen from a passed-out sailor was not me. This was temporary. This would pass.

I thought all these thoughts just fine, but when I spoke, what came out was, "Temp'rary."

"Pardon me, stud hoss?"

There was so much I wanted to say.

I said: "Ahhhhh-*woooooo*!"

"That much we've ascertained," said the woman whose name I didn't yet know, looking over her shoulder. "Here's my problem, stud hoss. There's a man in this bar who's bothering me. He seems to think I know something I don't know. He keeps buying me beers. Now if he was buying me beers and trying to get me in the sack, I'd be on comfortable terrain. Terrain I can handle dead drunk with my eyes closed."

"Wherrizzy?" I said, looking around.

In the manner of people who've spent their share of time talking to drunks in bars, she knew what I meant. "Past my left shoulder, leaning on the wall next to the Rusty Wallace poster. Don't look too long. I believe he's trying to stare a hole in me."

He sure was. Beefy guy, gimme cap that said SNAP-ON, red face, week's worth of beard that looked wrong on him, down vest over flannel.

"The problem, *my* problem," the woman said, "is near as I can tell, fuzz-face doesn't want to get me in the sack at all. He keeps wanting to *talk*, talk talk talk, and he keeps pulling the talk back around to some people I may know and an episode I may have witnessed."

I said nothing.

"Or may not have, of course."

"Zimacop?" I said.

"He might just be," she said.

"Ifugginkillim."

"That's the spirit," she said, squeezing my bicep through the peacoat. "But tell you what, I'll settle for an escort outside and help finding a lift, even if it's on one of these miserable Harleys. Once I get clear of fuzz-face and the parking lot, I imagine I can make my way."

"Lezgo." I drank what was left of my triple and drained my beer.

"My hero," she said. She batted her eyelashes twice, smiling, and stuck out a tiny hand. "I'm Savannah Kane. They call me Savvy."

As a ZZ Top song kicked in, I towed her toward the bar's front door, a sorry-ass plank job with a mesh window and a Z-brace. I bulled straight ahead, shouldering past a couple of bikers hard enough to raise murmuring in our wake.

I took a look over my shoulder as the door slapped open and we hit fresh air.

Fuzz-face had set his beer on a tall table. He was coming after us, adjusting his cap and working a no-bullshit stride.

I smiled. I wanted to show Savvy Kane how useful I could be.

The soft bing of an incoming text pulled me back as I worked west in rush-hour traffic. It was from Charlene. Randall was dropping by and she'd had a hell of a long day, could I pick up dinner at the barbecue joint we liked?

Sure.

I pulled in, made the order, took a cream soda from the cooler, sat on a stool to wait. A TV in the corner bleated local news. I blocked it out, thought about Savvy Kane and Bert Saginaw.

A man sat next to me. Which was strange, because the joint was three-quarters empty. I hopped my stool away from him some. He didn't notice, far as I could tell. Dug into his baby back ribs.

I sipped.

"It's more or less impossible to escape the glow of the boob tube," the man said after a few minutes.

"They're at gas pumps now," I said.

"Annoying."

"Yup."

That was plenty of conversation for me. I looked at the man from the corner of my eye. He was big in a sloppy way, a high-school-football-player-gone-fat way, with greasy hair too long for a man his—my—age.

The TV news gal launched into a story about a protest at a soldier's funeral. The GOD HATES FAGS people were at it again.

"Freaks," I said. "Gimps, clowns, dipshits."

"You'll find no disagreement here, friend," he said in a smooth voice. Southern? "I myself am a firm believer in minding one's own business."

"Amen." I toasted with cream soda.

"Folks like that," he said, nodding at the TV, "folks who involve theirselves in the business of others . . . well, you just daydream about slicing off their balls and stuffing 'em down their throats. Don't you?"

Whoa.

I said nothing, cut another glance at the man. He looked the same way he would've if he'd made a comment about the weather.

I got lucky: The girl behind the counter called my order number.

"Happy trails, friend," the man said, licking each of his fingers as I rose. "This here's some pretty passable barbecue for this far north."

And my friends wonder why I don't like talking to people.

CHAPTER FIVE

Ah," Randall said, reaching up the right leg of his jeans to unstrap his foot and ankle. "At the end of a long day, that's the ticket right there." He scratched his pantleg, flexed his knee.

"I will never, ever get used to that," said Sophie, Charlene's younger daughter, twelve going on twenty. She looked at the titanium-and-ceramic prosthetic, which Randall had dumped near the sofa the same way a teenager kicks off his sneakers. Which made sense, as the prosthetic's perfectly formed foot was inside a white-and-blue Nike running shoe.

Randall Swale was the son of my parole officer, Luther. We met awhile back, and he'd helped me with a few things. He lost a foot and half a leg in Fallujah, Iraq, three weeks after he got there. He's the smartest guy I know, but he did something dumb that day: kicked a trash can lid. Turned out it housed an IED. Now he walked around on his quarter-million-dollar prosthetic, and ran faster than me when he needed to.

Randall had colleges lined up to give him full-ride academic scholarships. "There would appear," he'd said once with a couple beers in him, "to be a dearth of black, one-legged, veteran, certified geniuses with four-point-oh high school transcripts. Go figure." He talked about the scholarship offers all the time, but had let them slide so far. Sometimes I wondered why. He'd met a nice gal with her own insurance agency. She was five years older than him and head over heels. She was dragging him around New England for leaf-peeping and outlet shopping that fall, which seemed fine by Randall.

We were sofa-flopped in the great room of Charlene's house. Shrewsbury, two towns west of Framingham. Charlene wasn't more than ten feet away, heating up dinner, but between her anger over Savvy, microwave noise, and the little TV she had tuned to the news, she might as well be in the next county.

Randall and I'd been discussing Savvy and Bert Saginaw before Sophie joined us.

I cut my eyes to her.

"Sophie," Randall said, leaning to grab his prosthetic. "Be a good kid and run this out to the front hall for me."

"Hop it out yourself."

They locked eyes, then cracked up. Sophie rose, snatched the prosthetic. "For the record," she said over her shoulder, "I know you're just getting rid of me."

Smart smart smart.

"Don't tell me you're actually planning to help this Saginaw turd," Randall said, leaning in, keeping his voice low.

"Take a look at this before you say that." I pulled the blue check from my back pocket, unfolded and smoothed it, set it on the cream-colored hassock.

Randall's eyes went big, and he made a near-silent whistle. "Who do you have to kill to earn that?"

I tucked away the check. Randall sat with his elbow on his good leg, chin on fist. He squinted. After a while he shook his head. "It still doesn't make sense. You're not a money guy. You're . . . *you*. Somebody offers you dough to do something you don't want to do, you're more likely to make them eat it than you are to take it."

I was ready for that. "Maybe that's why my girlfriend holds the note on my business. Maybe that's not the smart way to play it when you're my age. And your parole has a ways yet to run. And everything you own fits in two dresser drawers."

Did Randall buy it?

Maybe.

Almost.

Probably not.

But if he knew there was more to it than the money, he didn't press. He sighed instead. "What's your move, then?"

"Meet Saginaw tomorrow morning," I said. "See what they want with me."

"Tomorrow morning."

I nodded.

"Which would be," he said, and made a big show of counting on his fingers, "the third day of existence for your nascent business."

"What's nascent?"

"The point is, you're doing it again."

He wanted me to ask what I was doing again.

I didn't ask.

"What you're doing," Randall said as if I'd asked, "you're misdirecting your energy. Lighting into a wild-goose chase just when you've got something worth concentrating on."

I patted my back pocket. "This isn't worth concentrating on?"

"That check's bullshit. It's not what's driving you. Whatever's going on here, it's not about any check." He sighed, slapped his thighs, nodded in Charlene's direction. "What's milady think about your plan?"

"Haven't told her yet."

"Remind me not to be here when that conversation takes place." He raised his voice. "Give me a sec, sweetie, I'll come set the table."

Then Randall hopped to the front hall to fetch his foot.

A few hours later, with Randall gone and the dishes done, I took my second shower since getting home. No matter what coveralls and gloves you wear, deep grease goes with the job. I hadn't felt clean since Sunday night.

I was rinsing shampoo when I heard Charlene slide the curtain a foot and a half and climb in. She said nothing, but pressed her front to my back, wrapped arms around me, worked the Irish Spring from my hand, and took up where I'd left off.

I froze, guilt-racked, Savvy thoughts flooding. I stiffened, but not the way Charlene wanted. Instead I hunched, keeping myself from her as much as I could. She picked up on my hesitation, but not on its cause. "Not to worry," Charlene said. "She's buried in homework and wearing earbuds to boot."

"It's not that," I said. "It's just . . . long day, so much to think about."

"A grand opening deserves a grand reward," she said, giggling as she reached around.

"No!" I said, and twisted away harder than I meant to. "Dammit, now I've got soap in my eyes."

When I opened them again, she was gone.

Charlene Bollinger wobbled into her first Barnburners meeting a little over a decade ago. She was three weeks sober, junkie-pale, weighed maybe ninety. Wore black eye makeup, looked like a raccoon. Tap her on the shoulder, she'd jump a foot. Her daughters—Jesse was eight and Sophie two at the time—had been taken away by the state Department of Social Services.

By then, I had a fair amount of sobriety and had worked my way into the hard core of the Barnburners: an under-the-table group called the Meeting After the Meeting. After Charlene's first night, when the basement of Saint Anne's emptied but for us Meeting After the Meeting types, we all agreed the shaky, pimply gal who looked like she cut her own hair with a butter knife wouldn't last a month.

We were wrong. We were so damn wrong. Charlene Bollinger had strength most of us could only dream about.

Over the next few years, Charlene bootstrapped like crazy. She got sober, stayed sober, got fit, got her girls back. Got a job typing transcripts in Westborough District Court. At work, she saw cases being thrown out for lack of translators. Non-English-speaking bad guys, guilty as sin, were walking. Prosecutors were pissed. The problem was even worse in federal court.

Charlene launched a business out of her living room: transcription and translation. She approached any woman in court who was obviously foreign. Asked can you speak English even a little? Can you read? Can you type? How about your sisters? How about your friends?

After a frustrating start-up year, business took off. Federal prosecutors had all the work Charlene could handle. They paid slow, but they paid big. Taxpayer bucks: Never mind the cost, just get it done.

Around then, Charlene and I started dating. I learned later the match had looked inevitable to all the Barnburners. There was a $250 pool on when I'd finally get around to asking her out. I don't know who took the pot.

We clicked. We dated. We fell in love. Along the way, I learned more about her past. At her low point, Charlene had paid for crack and crank by posing for pictures, she said. That was when the state took her daughters. There had to be more, I knew. But I didn't pressure her to tell me. She didn't. That was okay. There were things about my bad years she didn't know. And doesn't.

We dated. A year passed. Barnburners started a new pool: our wedding date.

Nobody won that pot. I screwed things up. Couldn't stand the happiness, made things hard when they could have been easy. I put Charlene in a spot where she had to dump me or be a chump.

Charlene Bollinger was nobody's chump.

Free of me, she focused on business. With broadband Internet spiderwebbing around the world, her hiring pool went global. She found astonishing workers, overqualified but grateful for the gig, in Namibia, Botswana, Colombia, Panama, Peru, China, South Korea, Azerbaijan, Ukraine. She paid wages that made the employees, nearly all women, local celebrities.

People noticed. Buzz built. Charlene got pressure to go national, franchise, or sell. She chose instead to stay regional, focusing on New England. Reporters liked her single-mom-succeeds-on-own-terms story even without the addict angle, which she hid. Charlene was profiled in local business journals, then local TV, finally in national business mags.

We got back together a few years ago. Since then we've had ups and downs, togethers and aparts. Truth be told, it didn't feel the same, even though I finally moved in a while back. The first time around, we were an *us,* a pair rolling toward marriage. It would have been my second, her first. Sophie and Jesse have different fathers. I was pretty sure Charlene had no idea who those fathers were, but that was one of the things I hadn't asked and she hadn't told.

Things were different in Conway and Charlene Take Two because after I abused her trust during Take One, she'd built herself a good solid shell.

Charlene Bollinger had rough luck with men when she was a junkie. I'd taught her even sober men could be two-timing assholes. If she had a hair trigger for Savannah Kanes showing up at the shop, there was only one jerk to blame.

CHAPTER SIX

"Tell me you're joking, Conway Sax," Charlene said the next morning, cinching the purple towel that ran from her armpits to her thighs. It matched the one she wore turban-style on her head. "I want *so badly* for you to be joking." Two towels for clothes, eight inches shorter than me, standing at her dressing table with little fists on hips—and she made me nervous.

"Savvy's a Barnburner who needs help."

"Ha! She's a slut who took off when she got knocked up by God knows who."

Huh. I hadn't said anything about that. Hell, I hadn't known myself. "You knew she was pregnant?"

Charlene rolled her eyes and glared.

"Everybody knew but me?" I said.

"Of course."

I decided to see how much she really knew. "Who knocked her up?"

She shrugged. "Who has time to make a list that long? A bunch of us Barnburners assumed it was you." Her eyes bored in. "Was it?"

"No."

"But you're going to drop everything on *this* day, the third day of your grand opening week, to run around helping poor little Savvy."

"I guess I am."

"And you're not even helping her, really. You're helping some . . . *politician.*" Her lip curled. Charlene's a small-business owner, feels the same way I do about politicians: Never seen one do anything useful. "What would a shrink say about all this, Conway?"

"That I'd be nuts to turn down a fat check for easy work."

"We've got all the money we need. I've got all the money we need."

"*You've* got all the money."

"A*ha*!" she said. "So that's it. We talked all this through."

I said nothing.

We stood there maybe fifteen seconds. Finally Charlene sighed. "I'll call Floriano. We'll cover for you. I always had a feeling he was going to be the key player in this enterprise." She turned to the mirror and looked at herself until I left.

The Escutcheon Hotel was in Cambridge on Memorial Drive, right across the Charles River from Boston. As I pulled in, I saw the joint was a construction beehive: Trucks, trailers, and heavy equipment crammed into the tight parking lot, guys in orange vests staring up at a ten-story crane, cops drinking coffee and shooting the shit with the orange-vest guys. It looked like they'd put up an office building next to an existing hotel and were tying the two together.

In the hotel lobby, construction chaos disappeared. Quiet, calm. Slate floors, big paintings of blobs. Two security guys in blue blazers, the biggest Middle Eastern dudes I'd ever seen. The setup was almost enough to make me self-conscious about my autumn uniform: Red Wing boots, jeans, flannel shirt.

Almost.

"Help you, sir?" One of the security dudes flowed to me. Polite smile, quiet voice—but he put himself between me and the elevators. And stayed there.

I let him funnel me to the front desk, then said why I'd come, using Savvy's name. A man in a turban who looked like he'd been tried by a thousand con artists and hadn't been taken yet pushed a button, talked into a phone, and said one word to the security dude: "Penthouse."

The word changed everything. As he trotted, half-bowing, across the lobby, the security dude just about offered to give me a piggyback up the stairs. He could've done it, and I'm not small. In the elevator, he used a key card to get me going. He was still bowing and apologizing when the doors closed.

When they opened, Savannah Kane stood before me in a suite you could use for touch football. She wore no makeup, a white terry robe that said *ESCUTCHEON* on the left breast, white slippers with elaborate *E*s.

She said nothing. She stepped to me, kissed me hard, kissed me til my back thunked the closed doors of the elevator.

She was naked beneath the robe.

I started to melt into it. Into her, the room, the robe, the whole deal.

Then something clicked and I bucked her away, wiped my mouth. "Chrissake, Savvy."

"Look who's here," she said. "Vinnie Virtue. What the hell, lover?"

She moved in for another kiss.

I let her, dammit.

And remembered her ways, her bedroom trance. Something had happened there. To her, to me, to both of us. It was always dark enough, but not too. Candles, incense, Old Golds.

She spun us a 180, and then she was kissing me across the suite's white carpet, her hands shoved down the pockets of my pants. We staggered, our height difference making a wipeout inevitable as I tried to crouch and Savvy walked tiptoe, and finally I went over backward, pulling her with me to the bed.

The robe was mostly off now. The bed was the softest one I'd ever been on. The ceiling had a turquoise tapestry tacked to it—an old Savvy habit, she took some gypsy wherever she went. She was more or less naked, and working to get me there, too. It was nice. It was easy.

It was wrong.

Something inside me was grinding like a dump truck's transmission.

There was one way to make the grinding stop.

She must have sensed hesitation, because she kissed me in a way I'd long forgotten. A way I'd never forget.

Oh boy.

Oh hell.

I sighed. Savvy had my shirt unbuttoned. She was tugging at my belt.

Hell.

I sighed again and jackknifed until I was sitting. Savvy thought this was good.

But only for a second or two. I reached, got one hand high on her chest and one beneath her rump, and tossed her over my shoulder to the other side of the massive bed.

"Hey!" she said while I rose, buttoned my shirt, squared myself away.

"Charlene," I said. "And Saginaw, for that matter."

"Jesus!" she said, and unleashed some foul mouth while I found the bathroom and splashed cold water on my face.

When I came out, she wasn't on the bed. I followed my ears, found her watching a man set up a room-service cart in the suite's living room.

"Tip Marco," Savvy said to me. It was Marco's lucky day: All I had was twenties. He bowed his way back to the elevator.

"Delicious delicious delicious," she said, dropping silver covers willy-nilly on the rug to display chicken fingers, a bacon burger, a stack of pancakes. "Mine mine mine."

Memories came at me, things that used to drive me nuts. She ate like a seven-year-old, always had. Cheeseburgers and chicken fingers at quarter of nine. She was a pig, the most careless person I'd ever known—she admitted part of the reason she loved hotels was that not only did the maids have to clean up after you, they weren't allowed to give you dirty looks while they did it.

"Why am I here, Savvy? If it's just to have you jump me, I'm flattered but I'll pass. I'll tear up Saginaw's check and split."

"Delicious," she said, spinning to me in the terry robe, popping a french fry in my mouth. "That will be my word of the day. As far as the check goes, don't flatter yourself, big boy."

I had to laugh at that. Plucked a glass of ice water from the cart, sat in a sofa that felt like a billion feathers.

She took a ketchup bottle from the cart and tried to open it. But it was one of those single-serving jobs with a plastic seal, and she had no real fingernails—she still chewed them, but not when anybody was around—so the bottle gave her trouble.

"You going to take me to Saginaw?" I said.

"All in good time."

While she gnawed at the plastic seal I said, "Who'd you leave your son with, anyway?"

"Max is in good hands."

"Maybe ditching a six-year-old to go blackmailing wasn't your best move, Savannah."

"Oh *really*!" she said, an ugly grin-sneer racking her face. "How old was your boy when you drank your way out of *his* life, hmm? 'Bout the same age as Max, wasn't he?"

There wasn't much I could say to that.

I said nothing.

Savvy looked at the tiny bottle in her hand like she wasn't sure how it got there. Then she fired it at the corner.

Ketchup sprayed like blood.

CHAPTER SEVEN

We were quiet.

"I left Max with his gramma, or close enough," Savvy finally said. "She loves him to death."

She left the room. In a few seconds, the shower began to run.

I took the opportunity to fish her phone from her pocketbook and scan her call and text logs. I felt a little bad about it. But only a little.

I found nothing important. She must delete her logs pretty frequently. Which maybe told me something about Savvy and maybe didn't.

I hesitated, decided what the hell, began looking at her pictures.

There were a few shots of a long-haired boy who had to be Max. Good-looking kid, brown eyes maybe a little wiser, warier, than a six-year-old's ought to be. Or maybe I was imagining that. A bowling party, a last-day-of-school sack race, sleeping on a sofa.

There were also a lot of pictures of some guy. He looked familiar. I tried to place him, couldn't quite. Context said he was Savvy's boyfriend, or had been.

"Young'un," I said out loud. Savvy was ten years younger than me, and the guy had to be ten years younger than her. Chinless and chestless, with curly sand-colored hair that looked like a half-assed perm.

As I clicked through pics slide-show style, the boyfriend came across as half Sherpa, half puppy dog. He was either doing something for Savvy—lugging a microwave oven up apartment stairs, fixing a flat tire on a busy highway, washing dishes in a checked apron—or holding the camera himself to take snaps that seemed to embarrass Savannah Kane. Here was the guy pressing his head to hers in a restaurant, a state park, a Six Flags. He was always holding the phone at arm's length and smiling lovey-dovey. It was obvious Savvy would have preferred to be anywhere else. Her smile was always thin, and her eyes always said, *His idea, not mine.*

When the shower stopped, I set the phone back in her bag.

"Is there a legit reason you called me here?" I said through the bathroom door. Truth be told, I was nervous. Wasn't sure how many Savvy Kane sex-bomb attacks I could fend off. "Why didn't I just go straight to Bert's office?"

As I spoke, the elevator doors binged open.

"There's your legit reason," she said, stepping out in a towel.

Around the corner came Krall.

He looked the room over for three seconds. "For crying out loud, Savannah," he said to both of us and neither of us. He had no accent at all—draw a line from Akron to Omaha, he could be from any town within a hundred miles of the line.

"Old friends," I said. "Nothing happened."

"Yeah."

"Smirk again and I'll break your jaw."

"How's Maria Mendes doing?"

"Say her name again and I'll break your jaw."

"You got it all wrong, Sax," he said, grinning, hands on hips, suit coat pushed back. "Once you take the dough, you don't get to be high and mighty anymore."

He was right about that. I said nothing.

"Sheesh, boys," Savvy said. "Why don't you just whip 'em out and measure right now? Get it over with?" She padded into the bedroom, laughing.

Krall's face was red.

Maybe mine was, too.

"Hell," he said after a while.

"Why am I here?"

"I had my way," he said, "you wouldn't be. But a campaign's a funny thing. The candidate's the king, the rest of us are supplicants. We backstab each other all day long, trying to get the king's ear."

"Savvy's got Saginaw's ear."

"Along with various other body parts. But the worm turns, Sax. I've been around more of these things than I can count, and the worm always turns."

"So you're going with the flow."

"Long as the checks clear, yeah. Savvy talked you up to Bert. Bert thinks you can help him."

"You don't think I can."

"I think my last check cleared. So let's go see Bert." He raised his voice. "Ready when you are, Savvy."

Ten minutes later, as she punched the button for the ninth floor, Savvy said, "This is Bert's hotel now. You did know this, yes?"

I said nothing.

She sighed. "He's putting up the office building next door. It was supposed to serve as headquarters, but it's not finished."

"That I noticed."

"Not even Bert Saginaw can make the Cambridge city council move faster than it wants to," Krall said.

"He was embarrassed at the delay," Savvy said, "so he called the men in Dubai who owned this joint and made a cash offer they couldn't turn down."

"The man's got some serious cake," I said.

"Bet your ass," Krall said.

"Then he cleared out a couple of floors," Savvy said, "and made a temporary HQ."

"And installed you in the penthouse," I said.

"Can you blame him?" she said.

The doors opened.

On a hushed nuthouse.

It was a huge space, maybe sixty feet by a hundred, and most of the walls had been knocked out. Temporary desks were jammed together everywhere, and a long Formica counter ran the width of one window wall. Here and there a ceiling tile had been shunted aside and a snake-nest of black cabling—T-1 lines, I assumed—had been pulled through.

For all the workers. There were dozens, maybe a hundred. They banged away at laptops or worked phones, every damn one of them, and none of them looked up. Aside from a crooked TINKER-SAGINAW banner near a coffee area, this room could be anything: insurance agency, call center, boiler-room stock scam.

"Usually," Krall said, "I'd call this smilin' and dialin'. But I know for a fact most of these are *incoming* calls. When everybody knows you're going to win, the big dollars roll. People want it on the record that they backed you. This is the fun part."

"But you're worried," I said. "Or I wouldn't be here."

His smile tightened. He walked away fast without saying anything. Savvy followed, leading me through the cheerful mess. The workers were young for the most part, and chipper in their little rent-a-desk forts, with smelly takeout cartons piled up and sub-shop menus and laptop bags. Everybody likes being on a winning team.

Down a hall, quick left into a swank suite. I whistled. It reminded me of rooms you saw on TV shows about Las Vegas high-rollers. Marble floors, twelve-foot ceilings, sliders to a good-sized patio, animal-skin rugs, sinks and bars and doors everywhere.

"Sax!" Saginaw spread his arms as he said it, crossing the room in a Joe Politician suit that couldn't quite hide his bowlegs, his strange proportions. "Not bad for a college dropout, huh?" He caught Krall's eye and jerked his head toward the door. "Pete, Savvy. Ten minutes, 'kay?"

They left. Saginaw sat on a long sofa, nodded. I took the other end. It was like sitting in a pat of melting butter.

I said, "Nice."

Saginaw said nothing for a while. Then he put a finger to his lips, cat-walked to the door, set his ear against it, and whipped it open. Looked both ways, closed it, sat again.

"Paranoid," I said.

"Bet your sweet ass," he said. "I don't trust a goddamn one of 'em. Especially Krall."

"You don't trust the guy who's running your campaign."

"Know anything about him?"

I shook my head.

"Pete Krall would like you to think he's a big man in his world," Saginaw said, leaning forward. "Truth is, he was a minor-leaguer on his best day. And his best day was a long time ago. Sure, he helped a couple South American guys win reelection, but those were banana republics. Places where Maximum Leader wins ninety-eight percent of the vote, and the next day two percent of the houses get torched. You know?"

"So why's he running the show? You and Tinker are both loaded."

"It was Tinker's call," he said. "She waited too long, playing the reluctant-politician bit. By the time she jumped in, the heavy hitters were under contract. Besides, she was supposed to win in a walkover. Didn't think she needed the best."

"Does he know what he's doing?"

"Not really. Ever see an NFL coach on the sidelines, and you could tell from his eyes he had no friggin' idea what was going on out there? He was just hoping for the best?"

"Wade Phillips," I said.

Saginaw laughed big, actually slapped his thigh. "I like it! Yeah, when you see Krall in action you get that Wade Phillips vibe. Krall needs a big win to salvage his career."

We were quiet awhile.

"You going to tell me why I'm here?" I finally said.

"Today's Wednesday," Saginaw said, not looking at me. "That makes tomorrow Dirt Drop Day."

I said nothing.

He shifted, looked me in the eye. "Old campaign tradition, they tell me. It's when the other guys throw their last, best, worst dirty trick at you. Thursday's the perfect day because it jams up the news cycle all weekend, doesn't give you much of a chance to come back."

"What's their dirty trick for you?" I said.

"Tomorrow . . . meaning tonight, really, 'cause the newspapers release all the good stuff early on the Web . . . the *Globe*'s gonna run a story about me. It's embarrassing, but it's not fatal. It'll trim a bunch of points off our lead, but it won't cost us the election."

"So what's the problem?"

Long pause. "The problem," he finally said, "is *another* set of pics."

CHAPTER EIGHT

Let me get this straight," Randall said on the other end of the line. "Saginaw knows of not one but two, count 'em, *two* sets of photos that could potentially sink him?"

"And Tinker, of course. Reading between the lines, it seemed what scared him most was the idea of pulling her down with him." I jumped on the brakes to avoid a pair of college kids sauntering across the street. I was on my way from Cambridge to Winthrop. Two miles as the crow flies, but one of those can't-get-there-from-here drives.

"Talk about renaming oneself mud," Randall said. "Obviously, the Tinker people tried to vet Saginaw before selecting him as her running mate."

"Yup."

"Also obviously, he lied through his teeth."

"Now it's biting him in the tail."

"It always does."

"But they never learn."

"How much did he tell you about this second set of blackmail fodder?"

In his Vegas-style suite, Saginaw had said there was one, and only one, copy of each photo. "They used a brand-new digital camera," he'd said. "They printed the shots on a virgin printer, then destroyed all the hardware. Never scanned anything, never e-mailed anything, none of that."

I'd told him that was most likely bullshit—a story to suck him in for the first big payment. Then they'd find more copies so they could keep bleeding him.

"What did Saginaw say to that?" Randall said.

"He was positive that whoever's doing the blackmailing speaks the truth on this."

Long pause. Finally: "Huh."

"I know," I said. "Huh. Guess what he did next?"

Randall waited.

"You know that check they cut me yesterday?"

"Sure."

"He said a matched set is always nice, reached in his pocket, and slipped me another one for the same amount. But this one was a personal check from Hubert Saginaw."

"Tell me you didn't take it."

"Of course I did."

"Why, Conway?"

"Imagine how fast I can pay off Charlene."

"Interesting word choice," he said. "Pay off, rather than pay back."

"What's that supposed to mean?"

"Never mind." He was quiet a full thirty seconds. Then he sighed. "So what's the next move?"

"I'm going to see my pal Moe Coover."

"Who's that?"

"A Barnburner, a real old-timer," I said. "It was Moe helped me move Savvy down to North Carolina."

"And?"

"Moe was like *this* with the state cops for forty years. Dirt was his stock in trade. If it happened in this state and it's worth knowing, Moe knows it."

"Come on now, come on come on come on . . . *fuck* me."

"Thanks, nice to be here," I said, setting down a pair of sandwiches from Royal Roast Beef.

"Shut up a sec," Moe Coover said, a pair of military-spec binoculars pinned to his face. "Logan-SFO seven-five-seven bearing down, full to the gunwales, heavy jumbo all the way." I watched the plane roll straight at us, then peel from the runway all at once, nose up, pulling hard left while its landing gear retracted. The wind worked in our favor, pushing noise away. Moe tracked the plane with his binocs, said again: "Come on now, come on come on come on . . . *fuck* me."

Without leaving the peeling white wicker chair on his enclosed front porch, he flicked the power switches on one broadcast-quality video camera and two still cameras with lenses as long as my forearm. All three were aimed at the runway that ended a hundred and fifty yards from Moe's house.

I'd come to see Moe to compare notes on Savvy and learn more about Saginaw. In-person was best—Moe was past the age for long telephone conversations.

Besides, it'd been too long. Moe's mom had died what, four years ago? It was around then he'd started rooting for plane crashes, saying he was going to make a killing with high-quality pics and vids.

For a while, we Barnburners had assumed he was joking.

We'd been wrong. Moe pulled away from the group, especially after a couple of fender-benders made him stop driving at night. Barnburners dropped in on Moe now and then, and always reported back that he was sharp as a tack. But something in him broke when his mom died. I felt shame for not visiting myself until I needed info.

Moe kicked a second chair, indicating I should sit, and checked his watch. "If they don't wreck before the landing gear's stowed," he said, "there's a ninety-nine-point-eight-eight percent chance they won't wreck at all." He squinted at a black digital watch that looked big as a Frisbee on his thin wrist. "Now talk. You got thirteen minutes 'til the next busy stretch."

His head reminded me more than ever of a walnut. He wore a sweatshirt that said BERRY THE BEARS. He also wore blue jeans that were oversized in a way that hinted at a diaper beneath. Big deal: He could wear ladies' underpants on his head without cutting my respect for him one bit.

Moe Coover, who had to be eighty-five now, was an original Barnburner. There weren't more than three or four left.

Short history lesson: After World War II, a couple million Moe Coovers streamed back to the U.S. They'd been raised Depression poor. Then they'd served two, three, or four years fighting in jungles or hedgerows. A lot of them had passed the time stuffing entrails back inside their pals, policing up arms and legs on day-after battlefields, watching each other burn to death in downed airplanes.

So it shouldn't have surprised anyone that when these vets were back Stateside, while some set down their rifles and started families, others drank. Drank like fish, matter of fact, and raised mucho hell—and got paid for it, twenty bucks a week for a year, GI Bill moolah. "Goddamn dream come true," Moe had told a bunch of us years ago. "Twenty bucks a week? Back then that was a roof over your head, three hots a day, and drink yourself blind every night. With enough left over to go see a whore on Saturday."

Meanwhile, this oddball group called Alcoholics Anonymous, launched in Ohio before the war, was gaining traction. Guys just like Moe, guys who for years couldn't get out of bed without a bracer, were walking around clear-eyed and employed, swearing by this AA. "I didn't trust it," Moe said. "It smelled like a racket. It smelled like a tub-thumper's trap."

But one Saturday, the promise of free eats lured him to a traveling AA road show—he still has a picture of himself with Bill W and Doctor Bob, claims he's turned down an offer of ten grand for the snap—and, like a lot of us since, Moe Coover heard something that clicked.

He sobered up April 28, 1946. Two nights later, he helped pull together the first meeting of an AA group that would become the Barnburners.

I was here now because Moe eventually wangled himself a plush civilian job with the Massachusetts State Police, running the staties' entire fleet. That brought power—the various barracks and subagencies were always competing for the newest vehicles—and smart-cookie Moe took his power in the form of knowledge. His specialty: buried bodies, closeted skeletons. If a trooper scored a blowjob from a drunk-and-disorderly teenager, badged his way out of a DUI in some burg at three A.M., or bagged a few law-abiding citizens to meet his speeding-ticket quota, Moe knew about it. He had eyes and ears from Pittsfield to Provincetown.

In Massachusetts, the state police swing a big club: They can and have run governors out of office. And for thirty-five years, Moe Coover was the most powerful man on the staties' payroll. He didn't look so powerful now, this little no-eyebrows man, probably wearing a diaper, staring me down. But in his day, he'd been something.

He said, "Savvy Kane, huh?" Just like that. Typical Moe. I hadn't seen him for two, three years, hadn't been to this house since his mother's wake. Had spent three minutes on the phone asking him to dust off his Rolodex and dig dirt. "I had a feeling we hadn't seen the last of that one."

"Why's that?"

"You knocked her up, didn't you?"

"I didn't," I said. "But everybody seems to think I did."

"How's Charlene?"

Moe Coover missed nothing.

I said nothing.

A jet took off, ripping over our heads, shaking the porch. "FedEx plane," he said. "Pay it no mind. Those things never wreck, and even if they did there'd be no money in it."

"Mother Teresa sends her regards."

"Mother Teresa's dead. Me too, soon enough. Let's skip the bullshit, Conway." He leaned toward me. "Let's say it wasn't you knocked up Savvy, and I believe it wasn't, or at least you *think* it wasn't, 'cause you never could lie worth shit. In that case, the proud papa's got to be Bert Saginaw, and *that,* amigo, is a very big deal."

"Let me make sure you're saying what I think you're saying."

"I'm saying it all right. Back then, just before we moved Savvy, she was banging him while she was banging you. Get over it. Hell, even if he's just the *alleged* proud papa it's a very big deal."

"You're taking giant steps."

"Don't insult me. I haven't talked with you in three years. You call me out of the blue, you ask about Savvy Kane. 'Oh by the way,' you also ask, 'I'd like to learn a little about this Bert Saginaw and his hatchet man Krall, if you get a chance.' You're clever like an eight-year-old angling for another cookie, Conway. It's what we like about you."

What the hell was I supposed to say to that? The people who love you are the people who know all your moves.

I hate that about people.

"Okay, you're smarter than me. It's not a small club," I said, shrugging surrender. "What'd you learn about Saginaw?"

"I learned, for maybe the ten thousandth time, that Fitzgerald may be the most misunderstood man in history."

"Who the *hell*?"

"F. Scott Fitzgerald," Moe said, leaning back, the big rush to photograph a plane crash gone now. Fine by me if he needed to be smug: It meant he had something juicy for me. He was savoring it.

"He was a writer, right?"

"And Jerry Rice was a football player," Moe said. "And Ali was a fighter."

I waited.

A small jet rattled the porch. Moe didn't even look up. "Fitzgerald wrote this line," he said. "'There are no second acts in American lives.'"

Moe looked to see if that meant anything to me. It didn't. He puffed his cheeks out, frustrated. "Everybody misses it," he said. "They quote Fitzgerald like he meant there are no second *chances*. When a politician gets caught with a whore or a baseball player beats up his wife, the newspaper hacks and talking heads trot out the line to mean the schmuck is finished, kaput."

"That's dead wrong," I said. "It's the opposite. A pro football player can gut a koala bear in broad daylight. If he's any good, somebody'll still sign him."

"Exactly!" Moe pounded his armrest. "Fitzgerald was talking about Act One and Act Two in a formal way, like in plays and novels. In Act One, the players get their intro, the problem is set up."

"What happens in Act Two?"

From the way he smiled, I knew it was the right question.

"Depth," Moe said. "Complexity, conflicting paths, difficult choices."

We sat quietly.

Noise built. A US Airways jumbo jet rocked the house as it took off.

"You missed one," I said.

"You've got me all engrossed," he said, looking at the big watch. "You prick."

"Just tell me about Saginaw," I said. "No more writers. I'm beggin'."

CHAPTER NINE

He jerked a thumb at the runway behind his shoulder. "If I miss my big payday bullshitting about Hubert Saginaw," he said, "You're a frigging dead man. What do you know already?"

"Just that he made and blew two fortunes, then finally figured out how to hang onto his dough."

"Fair enough. He dropped out of college twenty-five years ago. Sold some kind of high-tech flooring, European stuff. Did great for a while, then got too big for his britches. The Swiss parent company dropped him like a hot potato. Then, in the nineties, he went to San Francisco and scored big with a software company, like every other asshole out there."

"And?"

"Made a paper fortune that dried up and blew away one day. Just like every other asshole out there."

"Then what?"

Moe shrugged. "Little of this, little of that. I hear he tried the motivational-speaker racket. Didn't make any real money, but it's where he got a taste for public speaking. Decided he'd make a dandy politician if he ever got the chance."

"How'd he end up in Framingham?"

Moe shrugged. "Everybody ends up somewhere. Funny thing is,

Saginaw credits a Dunkin' Donuts in Framingham for starting his fence company. The one near the Ashland border, you've been there a thousand times."

So had Moe—before he stopped coming to Barnburners meetings. I didn't say that. Instead I gestured for more on the fence business. Moe settled in and told it.

You had to hand it to Saginaw: After the software company fiasco, his wound licking hadn't lasted long. Each morning at five o'clock, on his way to the gym for a two-hour workout, he stopped for coffee and a bagel. And each morning, he spotted four or five guys farting around in the donut store while their big-ass flatbed trucks idled outside, burning diesel and their employer's time. From the trucks and uniforms, Saginaw learned the guys worked for a rental-fence operation headquartered a mile and a half from the apartment he and his then-wife shared.

Saginaw wondered if the boss knew his employees blew forty-five minutes every morning in Dunkin' Donuts. He began talking to the guys, doing a little friendly corporate espionage.

The way it worked, he learned, outfits doing construction and events rented fences. All kinds of fences, with chain link far and away the most popular. It was an easy business to get into but a tough one to make real money at: You wound up spending all your revenue to maintain your fleet and hire new assholes to take over for the old assholes who were constantly being convicted, deported, or sliced up in bars.

Bert Saginaw decided to jump in.

Three months after first noticing the Dunkin' Donuts slackers, Saginaw talked his mom into remortgaging her house. He used the dough to buy the very company that employed the slackers—it turned out to be a mom-and-pop outfit run by a sixty-eight-year-old guy who already had one foot in Naples, Florida, and pounced on Saginaw's first offer.

Moe sat.

I waited. The smell of the roast beef sandwiches I'd brought was driving me nuts—I hadn't eaten much of anything today. But Moe made no move for them.

"Well?" I said.

"Well what?"

"What happened next?"

"Like the man said, happy families are all alike." He shrugged. "Happy businesses, too. Saginaw made money, bought more mom-and-pop fence-rental outfits, made some more. After a while he started manufacturing fencing himself. Which these days means he flies to China a couple times a year and they make the fences for him. Been at it ten, twelve years now, made himself a pile. Way I heard it, the sister was Saginaw's secret weapon."

"Emily?"

"Yup. She took one of those super-quick MBA programs at Northeastern. Tore the place up, did so well there was no point in grading her. By the time Saginaw's fence rentals picked up steam, Emily was running all the day-to-day biz and most of the strategic stuff to boot. Sharp as a tack."

"He's into more than rentals now," I said. "He's gone into contracting, putting up buildings himself."

Moe nodded. "Big-time stuff, too. Office parks and downtown midrises. Lot of money there. I guess Saginaw looked at the dimwits he was renting fences to and decided he could do a better job."

We sat. Two planes took off, rattling Moe's windows. Neither of us looked up. I stared at the Royal Roast Beef sammies.

Moe leaned, smiled. "What I gave you so far, it's the Wikipedia stuff, the stuff you could've found on your own. But I still got sources, and one of 'em gave me something good."

I waited.

"Something that might tie into a political campaign."

I waited.

"Hell," Moe said. "You're not gonna beg, are you? I shoulda known."

I waited.

He leaned even farther, elbows on knees. "Saginaw posed for some pictures once."

"He didn't pose, to hear him tell it. He got set up."

He shook his head. "Nothing like that. Weird pictures. 'The Jesus pictures,' my guy called 'em."

"What the hell does that mean?"

"According to my guy, you'll find out soon. Whole goddamn state will."

We sat. Planes took off every minute or so.

Moe said, "I know why you're doing this."

"Sure you do," I said. "I told you about the checks, the dough these people spend without thinking twice."

He shook his head. "I know why you're *really* doing it. I know why you can't say no to Savvy Kane."

I said nothing.

"You were close to her when she was a Barnburner," Moe said. "But *me* and her got close, too."

I said nothing.

Sixteen years ago. Biker bar parking lot, Owensboro, Kentucky. I walked Savvy along. Beard-and-vest followed.

Actually, "parking lot" is generous. It was a dirt path no more than forty yards long that dumped into a service road for the airport. On either side of the dirt, decades of motorcycles had flattened and mostly killed the grass. It looked like the custom was to ride toward the bar for the evening's drinking, turn your bike to face the road, and walk it backward into a parking slot. That way, riders didn't have to do any backing and filling after six hours and sixteen beers: They were already pointed the right way.

There's one other thing worth saying. This happened long enough ago so that Harley-Davidsons hadn't become jokes, toys for fat babyboomers. The bikes in this lot were old iron—Hardtails and Softails, mostly, though I thought I spotted a couple of Sportsters—stripped of bullshit ornamentation and most anything that added weight. There were no fairings, no whitewalls, no five-thousand-dollar tangerine paint jobs. These were old-school choppers built and ridden hard by outlaw bikers.

Except for one motorcycle that had drawn a small crowd of beer-in-hand guys wearing leather vests with club colors.

It was a goddamn Triumph Bonneville. There wasn't much light out here, but the British bike seemed factory fresh, though it had to be twenty years old. In a lot full of road-grungy Harleys, it looked like a Tiffany lampshade in a steel mill.

Night air, adrenaline, and a need to impress Savvy Kane had knocked the worst of the 'lude-buzz from me. I was still in no shape to talk, but I could think a little. And the Triumph struck me as the kind of bike a cop might ride to a biker bar, thinking it—and he—would fit right in. Especially if that cop believed a gimme cap and a week without shaving could make him look like a Hell's Angel.

I tugged Savvy toward it.

Behind us: "Hey."

"What are you doing?" Savvy said.

I knew the Triumph was old enough so it wouldn't have a key. If I could kick-start it, we were all set.

I trotted the last few steps to the bike, threw a leg over, hit the choke, threw all my weight down on the starter.

Nothing but a popcorn-fart.

"Hey!" said the cop, sprinting.

Damn. Had to be something other than a choke on the old bike. I finger-felt, found it: a fuel-line petcock. I opened it.

"The fuck you doin', bro?" a very tall biker said as I tried again and got at least a hint of a start. "You messing with another man's bike?"

I chinned in the direction of the cop, who was no more than ten feet away now. He was tugging at the rear of his pants, probably trying to pull his gun. "Hizzacop," I said.

"He's a cop," Savvy said.

"I grokked him, sister," the tall biker said. "I'm fluent in quaalude."

Then two things happened at once: The Triumph turned over, making a sweet, balanced sound that was nothing like the V-Twin blat of a Harley. And the tall biker stuck his left arm straight out, clotheslining the charging cop.

Here's something I'll never forget about Savannah Kane: She didn't step onto the Bonneville's seat—she *jumped* on, legs in flying V formation, grabbing me tight just as I popped the bike into first gear and spit dirt all the way to the street. I hooked a left, glanced back, saw the knot of bikers closing around the poleaxed cop.

Like I said, this happened a long time ago. Undercover cops sniffing after drug busts were not popular with Harley guys. And Harley guys were serious men. I almost felt sorry for the cop.

We sat on Moe's porch. Planes took off. Planes landed. I noticed a little blue-and-white teapot on a wicker table rattled just before each one. Like a five-second warning. Wondered if Moe even noticed the rattle anymore. Probably not.

I caught him looking at his watch.

"Moe," I said.

He raised eyebrows.

I held up both hands, made a show of looking around. "What are you doing, Moe?"

"I'm tryna make in one swell foop what I used to make bit by bit at the dog track."

"Moe, it's *me* here. Cut the shit."

Because it'd been a few years since he came to Barnburners meetings, he'd probably forgotten how much I knew about him. His mom didn't leave Moe a lot, but the house was free and clear, and even when it's in a Logan flight path, Boston Harbor real estate isn't cheap. And the state cops were no slouches when it came to pensions: Since the day he retired, Moe'd been pulling down half the highest salary he ever earned on the job. No divorce, no kids, no mortgage—Moe Coover's claim that he needed to make a plane-crash score was ridiculous.

So what was it? What was really going on?

We had a staredown, each knowing more or less what the other was thinking.

A drunk like me was always going to assume one thing. A drunk like Moe knew it. Switch us up, him in the visitor's chair and me waiting for a plane crash, and he'd be wondering, too.

He said it before I could ask. "I'm sober, Conway. Jesus, I'm sober how long now . . . once you get a half-century, do you even need to keep track?"

"What I was wondering," I said, "is drugs. Pills."

"Go fuck yourself."

"Doctors these days," I said, "they're kids. An oldster like you drops in, says he's feeling blue, they'll prescribe a happy pill like *that*. They hand out pills like candy corn."

"Go."

"Did you visit the doc and come home with a bottle of happy pills, Moe?"

"Go."

"You want to find a meeting somewhere?"

"Get out, Conway." Chin in hand, dead voice, unable to meet my eyes. "Just get the hell out."

CHAPTER TEN

You wouldn't believe how hard it is to tail a guy. It's not like TV at all.

Barnburner duties had taught me the only way to follow a car was to stick your nose right up his back bumper, make sure you got through the same lights he did, and hope like hell he wasn't paying attention.

Which, I'd also learned, he never was. That was the good news. Even guys with warrants, guys with a rock of cocaine in the cup holder, and guys headed for their exes' homes with ball-bats in the backseat never tipped to the fact they were being followed. It just never crossed their minds, far as I could tell.

I guess I was no smarter than the ball-bat guys and the cocaine guys, because after leaving Moe's I doodled through Winthrop into East Boston without noticing the forest-green Ford Expedition.

Hunger saved me. Hunger and the fact I'd left two Royal Roast Beef sandwiches untouched at Moe's place. Deluxes with horseradish and a large order of curly fries. As I drove I cursed Moe, who'd hit that old-man phase where he no longer ate or slept, for ignoring them.

Rolling west on East Boston's main drag, I thought about grabbing another sandwich and fries to make up for the ones I'd abandoned. I sat at a red light, staring at Royal Roast Beef & Seafood kitty-corner to my right. My wallet said no: Go straight, funnel into the Ted Williams Tunnel, shoot under Boston Harbor, and make a fast run west. Back to Charlene's, where the food was free.

My stomach said hang a right and eat.

While my wallet fought my stomach, my eyeballs ignored the Expedition that was riding my ass.

The light went green. My stomach won. As usual. I grabbed the quick right turn.

Talk about dumb luck.

I heard commotion behind me, checked the mirror. The Expedition had started through the intersection, then stopped dead. It was now fighting across two lanes of traffic to follow me into the parking lot. The driver had jammed himself in an awkward wedge and was trying to straighten out his wheel. He was having a tough time of it because pissed-off locals were leaning on their horns and not giving him room.

Even with all this, my stomach would have betrayed me if the Expedition's driver had played it cool. I rolled into Royal's lot and headed for a parking spot—just in time to see the desperate SUV chirp its tires, free itself from the traffic mess, and bounce over the curb to join me in the lot.

"Shit," I said out loud, *finally* figuring out the deal. I sat for maybe three seconds smelling fried clams and roast beef and delicious curly fries. The whole day was shaping up as a conspiracy to keep me from eating a damn meal.

I got a decent look at the driver, who wasn't more than thirty feet dead ahead.

I knew him.

But where from?

Click: The guy who'd sat next to me in the barbecue joint. The weird guy. He'd crowded me, had started a conversation out of nowhere. What was it he'd said? *Folks who involve theirselves in the business of others . . . slice their balls off and stuff 'em down their throats.*

Jesus. Had he followed me from Moe's?

Had he followed me *to* Moe's?

Who was he? Who sent him?

Option: Jump out, trot over, and pull him out.

Problem: He'd just lock the doors, flip me off, and drive away.

Option: Ram him.

Problem: What the hell for? From the looks of his bumper cover, he was no stranger to contact. In fact, it looked like he enjoyed it. The bumper was misshapen and gouged, its two-tone green-and-gold all chipped up. And if I hit him hard enough for airbags to deploy, a half-dozen looky-loos would call the cops.

Option: Park and eat a sandwich.

Problem: I wasn't hungry anymore. Was pissed off instead. Pissed that I'd led some clown to Moe Coover's house, pissed that I'd been so easy to tail. When you came down to it, I was mostly pissed that Savvy Kane had walked into my shop and screwed everything up just when I was doing okay for a change.

One option left.

I took off.

Dropped the tranny in drive and bounced over the low curb into the street. Got lucky: The curb could have peeled back my oil pan and banged up my custom exhaust, but it didn't. Behind me, the Expedition slammed over the curb and never even knew it was there. Tall truck, high ground clearance, thick-sidewall tires. If we got into city-warfare driving, vacant lots and speed bumps and more curbs, he'd have the edge.

I thought this through as I hammered west on Bennington Street. Kept one eye on the rearview, saw the Expedition come around a corner like a cow on ice skates.

Decided to see what the big ugly dude in the big ugly SUV wanted.

I slowed, let him pull within four car-lengths. Then I spun a quick right onto a typical Eastie residential street: narrow, cars parked on both sides, triple-decker houses stuffed right next to each other.

I took it slow. Wouldn't do me much good to run over a kid in here.

The question: Was the Expedition running a loose tail, or would he truly come after me?

Answer: loose tail. As I chugged through tight streets, the guy had plenty of chances to ram me, even pin me against a car if that was his job. He didn't. Stayed behind me instead, never more than five car lengths back.

I took rights, circling back to the main drag. What kind of guy, when he knows he's been made like that, hangs on your bumper? Why not throw in the towel, motor off, and come at me again another time?

He might be a flunky, an order-taker. And not a smart one. His boss had said follow that car or else—and he was, by God, even when the tail turned sour.

Or he might be a nutcase.

From what he'd shown me in the barbecue joint, that seemed like the smart bet.

But who *was* he?

I knew how to find out.

I hit Route 1-A, took it to the new section of Route 90—the Mass Turnpike extension that was part of the Big Dig boondoggle—and, in light traffic, used my rearview to learn more about the Expedition.

Like me, he used a FAST LANE transponder to zip through tollbooths. But whereas mine, like most everybody else's, was Velcro'd high on the windshield, the guy in the Expedition had to fumble his from the center console at each toll, then aim it at the electronic reader.

Which might mean he'd stolen the transponder from another vehicle. Or might mean nothing.

As we dipped into the Ted Williams Tunnel, lit up bright as day, I learned more. No state inspection sticker in the lower right corner of the windshield, so it wasn't a Massachusetts vehicle. And no front license plate on that chewed-up bumper to help me figure out what state it *was* from.

We cleared the tunnel. I hit the throttle.

The Expedition disappeared.

He tried to stay with me, but there were just enough curves and dips on this chunk of the Pike to make him uncomfortable when our speed topped a hundred. I kept my foot in it and pulled away.

After the exit for Cambridge and Brighton, there was a long flat stretch. I looked ahead and to the right, hoping for help.

Got some, in the form of a bus smoking along in the slow lane.

I dove in front of the bus and matched its speed, keeping an eye on my side-view mirror. In thirty seconds I spotted the Expedition, honking along, still thinking he could catch me.

I eyeballed the breakdown lane—clear—and watched the green SUV and timed everything just right.

As the Expedition drew level with me, I slashed into the breakdown lane and tapped the brakes. The bus threw me one pissed-off honk and kept moving, shielding me from the driver of the SUV.

I rolled into the gas, checked mirrors, cut back into the slow lane, looked ahead and to my left.

There he was. Green Expedition with gold bumpers, highballing along, trying like hell to catch a glimpse of me.

He was looking in the wrong direction.

I might have smiled.

But not for long.

I sat a full two hundred yards behind the Expedition. I could afford to. Knew where the exits were, knew a squirt of throttle would pull me to him anytime I wanted. There were a bunch of cars between us. One of them was a sensible-shoes Nissan Sentra in that boring silver-gold color.

In the light traffic, it soon became clear the Sentra was tailing the SUV. It darted lane to lane whenever he did, rode his bumper too close, then too far—an amateur-hour tail-job.

"You gotta be kidding me," I said out loud. Racked my brain. Had I seen a Sentra in Winthrop? Eastie? In the tunnel?

No. I was sure. So the car had picked up the Expedition somewhere on the Pike.

I thought all this through as our weird little caravan trundled through the tolls at Route 128, the Sentra crowding the SUV, me giving them both plenty of room.

As we pulled away from the tolls, I drew level with the Sentra. Took a good look.

Then another.

I damn near swerved.

"You gotta be kidding me," I said again.

Savvy Kane was driving the Sentra.

CHAPTER ELEVEN

What the *hell*?

I dropped back, wrote down license numbers, and thought. Thought about the mystery man in the Expedition. Thought about Savannah Kane in a car she got God knew where, following the mystery man.

Mostly what I thought was that I was in over my head.

Especially when I realized the Expedition wore a Massachusetts license plate. I'd already seen it didn't have a state inspection sticker. What did that mean? Out-of-state truck with a stolen plate?

A text came in just as I watched the Expedition take the Framingham exit, Savvy following. I glanced at the text:

Please come home 911

From Sophie.

I'd taught her to tag texts with 911 only in emergencies. She'd never done it before.

Hell.

I had two seconds to decide: Hang on to Savvy and the mystery man? Or stay on the Pike and see what Sophie needed?

I canceled my turn signal, headed west. To Sophie.

I swung into Charlene's driveway, hopped out, trotted up the steps sifting keys and worrying about Sophie. Thought I heard something, stopped, listened.

"Saaave me! *Saaaaaaaave* me!" From around back.

Sophie's voice.

Back down the steps in one leap, around the house at a dead sprint. It's not a big place, but it's built into a hillside, so I was pounding uphill the whole time.

"*Saaaaaaaaaave* meeeeee!"

Scrambling uphill, a nightmare run—like the bad dream where you need to move fast but are up to your hips in muck.

As I cleared the back corner, I heard her more clearly and it all made sense.

"*Daaaaaaay*-vee! Where *are* you, Davey?"

Jesus. My ears had played tricks. My head, too, I guess.

She was patrolling the deck in fluffy boots, pink sweatpants, a T-shirt I'd given her that read FLATOUT.

"You should have a sweatshirt," I said.

Sophie ignored me, yelled some more. "Daaaay-vee!" She rattled a bag of kitty treats the way I'd showed her. "Would you like a *treat*, Davey? Who wants a treat?" I could see her breath. I could see her trying not to cry.

My older cat Davey was about fifteen. Dale, the other one, was ten. Take cats that age to a shelter, you might as well gas them yourself and cut out the middleman.

When Charlene and I had talked over the idea of my moving in, we'd sidestepped the cat question as long as we could. Charlene didn't like animals one bit, and didn't mind telling you so.

Give her credit, though: Either she understood it was a battle she couldn't win, or she knew how much the cats meant to me. Especially Davey. He'd been about all I had for a while, when things got truly bad for me. Before I found the Barnburners.

The night before I moved in she'd said, "What do you think about putting the litter box in the basement? You can install one of those kitty doors." She'd said it real casual. But it hadn't been. It cost her something to say it. It was a classy move.

Davey, being a cat, had repaid Charlene by turning into a pain in the ass. Furious at moving, living in a house for the first time—with me he'd lived in a series of rented rooms, then apartments—he spent our first week in Shrewsbury behind the powder-room toilet, hissing at anybody who came near. He stopped letting me trim his nails, and he used them to destroy a living-room sofa that cost more than some cars I've owned. Every once in a while he dropped a turd wherever he was standing, then looked you in the eye and walked away.

He also started escaping. He'd been an indoor cat nearly all his life, but he turned into goddamn Houdini: silently appearing when a neighbor or UPS guy rang the bell, flitting through your legs and down the steps and into the bushes, and good luck catching him.

I didn't get worried until the first time he spent a night outside. The next morning, he was happy enough to come in and show off the chipmunk he'd killed. For a while there, Davey's midnight murder sprees had been funny.

But it was fall, and nighttime temps dropped near freezing. And there were fisher cats and foxes and coyotes in this neighborhood—you saw them in broad daylight sometimes—and it wasn't funny anymore.

And this time, Davey had been gone two nights running.

And I was pretty sure he was dead.

And that would wipe out Sophie. The day I'd moved in, with the cats as a pot-sweetener, had been the best day of her life. She told me so. She was finally part of a genuine family, with pets and everything. We were all pretty beat-up in our own ways, and we were sketchy as to how this family deal was supposed to work. But we were a legit family nonetheless.

Lately, Charlene and I hadn't been doing so hot. Hard to say why, though there were times I admitted to myself that having my girlfriend bankroll my business didn't feel right. Made me resentful. Then I felt ashamed of resenting someone who was just helping out.

Charlene and I had an unspoken agreement not to discuss all this. We were pretty good at not talking about things.

The problem was, Sophie was too smart to hide things from. So maybe it wasn't just Davey she was worried about.

"Cats know how to take care of themselves," I said, taking off my jacket, setting it on her shoulders while she rattled the treat bag. I left my arm across her shoulders.

Cold and stiff, she resisted the hug.

Then she didn't.

Sophie dropped the bag and put her arms around my middle and cried.

She cried so hard.

I made noises and kissed the top of her head and rubbed her back to warm her.

When Sophie was all cried out, the sun was just an orange slice above treetops. I put our backs to the wall. We slid down until we were sitting on the deck. We looked at the orange slice.

Sophie lifted my arm from her shoulders—gently, like she was worried my feelings would be hurt—and wiped her eyes and nose on my jacket.

We watched the sun drop away. Then we watched our breath.

"He was such a good guy," I said.

"*Is* such a good guy."

"Remember taking him for walks?"

She half-laughed, half-snuffled. "He thought he was a dog."

I smiled. One year, I'd gone to a Yankee Swap–style Christmas party and had come home with a useless nylon dog-walking rig. I tossed it in my truck and forgot about it until Sophie, nine at the time, asked what it was for. When I explained, she said it looked like a good fit for Davey. We laughed, but one thing led to another and soon we had the poor growling guy trussed up in this silly red harness. We took him outside . . .

. . . and damned if he didn't love it. He took to it right away, and suddenly he wanted to go for walks all the time. Sophie and I couldn't believe it. We became neighborhood characters who took our cat for a walk around the block every day, earning smiles and honks as the black cat paced ahead, sniffing like a bloodhound, tail-dancing all the way.

But after a week of this, Sophie discovered the drawback. Rounding a corner, she and Davey came face to face with a neighbor's high-strung dog. I forget which breed—the kind that looks like a dirty mop-head. Mutual sniffing turned into a fight, and Sophie learned the hard way that when a cat fights, you can't break things up with a leash-tug and a bop on the nose. She tried to heft Davey and wound up with a claw piercing her lower lip. Through and through, as the cops say about bullet wounds: in and out. Davey was more or less hanging off her face.

Nine-one-one. A ride to the hospital. Two stitches. A visit from Framingham Animal Control. The works. It took some tap dancing to keep Davey out of the gas chamber. And since all this happened on my watch, in my old neighborhood, in which it wasn't a great idea for a nine-year-old to be walking around the block by herself, Charlene had been good and pissed.

As far as taking Davey for walks, that had been that.

Sophie had to be recalling this, too, because she touched her lip where she would have a tiny scar forever.

"Did you come to get your stuff?" she finally said.

"Huh? *What?* 'Course not."

"It's just a matter of time." Dead voice that hurt my heart.

I said nothing.

"Why, Conway?"

"Why what?"

"Why can't you *do* it?"

I decided to stop playing dumb. Thought awhile, trying for a good answer. Or at least an honest one.

Couldn't find it. "I always fuh . . . I always screw it up, don't I?"

"It's all here," she said, waving her arms to include everything. "*We're* all here. Everything you say you want."

"I *do* want it. Your mom. You. All of it."

"No," she said, shaking her head. "There's something you want more. There must be. Otherwise, why would you fuck it up?"

Four and a half hours later, I parked outside St. Anne's, home of the Barnburners. I was way late for the scheduled open meeting we called the Civilian Hour, but the important stuff—the Meeting After the Meeting—was still in session.

That was good. Sort of. I had news to break. It'd been one hell of a four and a half hours.

I rubbed my eyes. Tired. Didn't want to climb from the truck. Didn't want to think.

Everybody stared as I made my way to the front of the basement meeting room. Mary Giarusso scribbled in her notebook, as always. Carlos Q, a nasty Colombian who wouldn't speak to anybody with less than a year of sobriety, sat looking bored with his meaty arms folded. There was Chester Bagley in his laugh-out-loud toupee, the biker dude with a cobweb tattoo on his neck, the Brazilian gal who spoke perfect English but never opened her mouth unless we needed a translator. There were three or four others whose names I couldn't be sure of—the cast changes, and a corner of my brain reminded me I hadn't been coming around enough lately.

Maybe that was why the other Barnburners' stares felt ugly.

I *knew* why Charlene's felt ugly.

When I sobered up for the last time, more than a decade ago, I was white-knuckling it and getting ready to backslide for the hundredth time when I stumbled into a Barnburners meeting. I saw right away they were different: serious people, serious AA, no posers or excuse-makers need apply. Knowing there was something extra, something different about this group, I hung around until they let me into the Meeting After the Meeting. Which, it turned out, was where they did some hardcore work that stemmed from the Barnburners' heritage as a post–World War II biker gang.

Barnburners stood up for each other. No exceptions, no mercy. If you were in the group and anyone—your ex, your boss, a bookie, anybody with a score to settle—gave you a hard time, the Barnburners had your back.

I'd spent a long time bouncing around hobo camps, county jails, rail yards, the streets. I'd learned skills.

The skills came in handy.

Cut to the chase: The Barnburners saved my life. The debt dies when I die. I do what's needed. No exceptions.

I don't always enjoy it.

Tough. I chose it. I make no excuses.

"You need a new watch, Conway?" said Butch Feeley, the closest thing there was to a boss of the Meeting After the Meeting.

"Sorry." I sat on a folding chair. "When you hear this, I think you'll forgive me. Some of you remember Savvy Kane from way back."

"Oh for God's sake," Charlene said.

"She ain't no Barnburner," Carlos Q said. "She been gone like ten years."

"Seven," I said. "Barnburner once, Barnburner always. Am I right, Butch?"

"Wellllllll," Butch said, shifting. "There are Barnburners and then there are *Barnburners*. I think we all know which kind she was."

"Barnburner once, Barnburner always," I said. "How many times have I heard the words, Butch? How many times have I heard them from *you*?"

Butch felt the weight. "She *did* work her way in here," he said, meaning the Meeting After the Meeting, which wasn't an easy crowd to break into. "And did some good work while she was around."

"Savvy Kane is back in town, running around and backstabbing people as usual," Charlene said. "She found Conway like *that*"—snapping her fingers—"and made big sexy eyes at him and played the Barnburner card. Now he's going to help her with whatever her latest scheme is."

Dead quiet. All eyes on Charlene, Charlene's eyes on me.

"And he's going to *do* it," she said, her voice about breaking. Mary put a hand on Charlene's forearm, but Charlene shrugged it away. "He's going to forget about his family, his business, his . . . sobriety to help the little slut. All in the name of his idiotic Barnburner code."

Dead quiet.

"Tell me I'm wrong, Conway."

"You're wrong."

Eyes swung my way.

"Savvy Kane is dead," I said.

CHAPTER TWELVE

Here's what happened between Charlene's house and the Meeting After the Meeting:

I'd talked Sophie into leaving a bowl of cat treats on the deck and going inside to warm up.

Then I'd driven around some. It's how I think. It's what I do. It's especially what I do when I ought to be doing something else. Like stopping by my own garage to work a few hours.

I'd been noodling east on Route 135 when a call came in. I didn't recognize the number, but the area code was local. Picked up.

It was Emily Saginaw. "Can you come to Cambridge immediately?" she said. She spoke fast, biting off each word.

"What for?"

"There's been a development. There are police. Bert would like you here."

I didn't give a damn what Bert wanted. Started to sound off about what his checks did and did not pay for, but Emily's breathing on the other end of the line made me skip that. Instead: "What development? Tell me."

Long pause. "Savannah Kane is dead."

"Bullshit. I saw her what, three hours ago. Maybe less."

"You saw her today? Then you really must come to the Escutcheon. I'm sure the police will want to speak with you."

Did they ever. Forty-five minutes after the call, I was in a room down the hall from Bert Saginaw's Vegas suite. He must have offered the cops the room as a temporary HQ. There were two state police detectives: a Chinese-looking guy older than me with loose bags beneath his eyes and the smell of a smoker, and a pretty young woman who never said a word, taking notes like there'd be a test later.

The Chinese-looking guy was named Wu, and he was no more Chinese than I was. He actually had a pretty brutal Boston accent, which I'd never heard out of a guy who looked like that.

"Where'd you grow up?" I said. "Curious."

"Quincy. South Shore." *South SHO-ah*. He jerked his thumb in a direction he must have figured was south. "Tell me one more time, will you? About when and where you saw Kane on the Pike."

I told him again. Had told him everything, starting at Moe Coover's place, twice already. Had told it all, told it straight.

Almost.

After a quick battle in my head, I held back about the mystery man in the green Expedition, about the mismatch between the SUV's missing inspection sticker and its Massachusetts plate.

Why?

Partly con's instinct. Never tell everything. Keep a hole card.

But there was another reason, I admitted to myself.

If the mystery man had killed Savvy, I didn't want the cops tracking him down.

Wanted to take care of that myself.

I tried to come to grips with it. Savannah Kane was dead.

As I retold my story, Wu surprised me and the other cop by flopping onto one of the hotel room's queen-size beds. He laced his fingers behind his head and looked at the ceiling and listened.

I wasn't used to talking with cops in non-suspect mode. But by the time I'd arrived here, Wu had pulled the electronic toll records for my truck. Given the time they found Savvy's body, he knew I'd been too far west to kill her.

When I finished, the room went quiet.

"Tell me what happened, Wu," I said after a while. "I deserve that. I knew her."

He sat up, scooched back, tapped his cheek while he looked at me. Then nodded once. "You know the CambridgeSide Galleria mall? Right next to the Museum of Science there?" *THAY-uh*. That accent.

"Not really," I said.

"Well, it's where Cambridge butts up against Charlestown. The Monsignor O'Brien Highway divides 'em."

"Okay."

"Cambridge, being Cambridge and all, won't let Saginaw's heavy equipment sit here overnight while he works on the hotel. Every evening, the crew has to blow an hour hauling the gear to a staging site. And every morning, they blow an hour hauling it back."

"That's dumb."

Wu shrugged. "Maybe the Harvard kids faint at the sight of a front-end loader, who knows. Point being, the staging area's a vacant lot in Charlestown right across the road from the Galleria."

"And?"

"And that's where the body was found."

I said nothing.

Savannah Kane.

I said I'd help her.

I said I wouldn't betray her.

Not again.

Not this time.

Now she was a body. *The* body, to Wu.

He must have been watching me close, because when he spoke again he sounded damn near sympathetic. "You knew her. Well?"

"Once." Long pause. "How'd she die?"

"Fell off an air conditioner. Landed bad, broke her neck."

"What do you mean, fell off an air conditioner?"

"Industrial unit. The size of a rail car, a full story tall."

"But what was she doing on it? Hell, what was she doing *there*? In Charlestown? Makes no sense."

"Tell me about it."

"What is it to you? To you cops, I mean. Accident or murder?"

"Homicide investigation for now," Wu said. "But it's shaping up like an accident. No evidence to the contrary. Nobody saw nothing."

"What about fingerprints? Footprints?"

"All that good *C.S.I.* shit?" He shrugged, half-smiled. "Construction guys in and out of there all day. Then kids at night, drinking, screwing around."

Now was the time to give up the Expedition guy.

I said nothing. Put my head in my hands.

No way. No damn way is Savannah Kane dead.

I'd seen her at her worst. I'd seen her at her best. I'd never seen anybody more alive.

Sixteen years ago, Owensboro, Kentucky. We took that Triumph Bonneville and flew from the cop and the bikers. We went on a tear, me and Savvy.

South to Bowling Green, where we bought scissors, a disposable razor, and hair dye at a Flying J truck stop. Savvy had me choose the dye.

"Don't matter to me," I said. "I'm shaving my head."

"Pick for me then."

I looked at the rack. I chose black.

"But my hair's black *now.*"

"Make it blacker."

She laughed.

Man did I like that laugh.

We slipped into a coin-operated shower together. We cut and dyed her hair, shaved mine, got good and clean.

Then we made love.

It'd been awhile for me. Whiskey, speed, and road-bum paranoia had pushed sex low on my priorities totem pole.

Savannah Kane pushed it back to the top.

And how.

Once I got going, it seemed neither of us could stop. Used up most of the hot water at the Flying J before we staggered out of the shower.

"Will you do something for me, Conway?" Savvy said as we walked through rows of big rigs toward the bike, holding hands like we were at the prom.

"Anything." I meant it.

She slipped a small wad from the back pocket of her jeans, tucked it in my fist. "You want to dig us up a little something?"

I knew what she meant. "Up or down?" I said. "Asleep or awake?"

"Either way," she said. "I just need . . . *something*. Anything. Big old place like this, somebody must be holding."

Off I went.

I scored.

We gobbled truck-stop speed. We gassed up the bike. We slashed west.

When false dawn hit, we were outside Paducah. Even behind shitty speed and occasional slugs from a pint of Wild Turkey, we understood that a motorcycle stolen from a working cop would be a big damn deal. I pulled into a motel that looked to have sufficiently low standards, paid nineteen of Savvy's dollars for a room around back, and trundled the Bonneville right in the door.

"Heh," I said, killing the bike.

"Sleepy," Savvy said. She launched herself from the bike to the sagging bed, and I swear she was asleep before she landed, truck-stop speed be damned.

Not me: I felt like I'd be awake three eyeball-jangling days.

I sighed, set the Triumph on its kickstand, stretched, grabbed a towel from the bathroom. It was as big as a wanted poster and not much thicker. Just for something to do, I set about cleaning the bike.

Checked fluid levels, wiped bugs from the headlight, then began to polish.

What a beautiful machine. It was a T120, which made it damn old, but it'd been restored by an amateur who knew what he was doing and loved the bike. Only some lumpiness in the seat made it look less than factory-perfect.

The lumpy seat bugged me. I began working the leather cover, trying to get the padding beneath to set just right. (Why? Mechanic's instinct and shitty speed. I shouldn't have to say more.) I kneaded it this way and that but couldn't get the padding quite right. I grew frustrated, grabbed the cover with both hands, tried to roll it back so I could reset the padding.

I rolled it back all right.

And found out why everything was slightly off.

My mouth made an O.

After a minute or two I tried to wake Savannah. It wasn't easy—she'd begun a little kitty-cat snore already. I had to rock her pretty hard.

"Whumpf? Humph?" she said, blinking, finally focusing on me. "The *fuck*, dude?"

"You need to take a look at this." I pointed.

She blinked a few more times. Hard to blame her. It's not every day you wake up in a motel outside Paducah with a motorcycle eight inches from your feet.

Then she spotted it. She took in a sharp breath. "Dude." She flipped around, crawled to the foot of the bed, pressed a thick clear plastic bag, then another. "Is this? Are these?"

"It is," I said. "They are."

Four plastic-wrapped packets of hundred-dollar bills.

And four of cocaine.

After the Barnburner meeting, Charlene followed me to her place. Her one-car garage is full of junk, so we both park in the driveway. I leaned on my fender, waited for her to climb from her Volvo SUV.

She did, then came around and leaned on *her* fender. We faced each other, our toes no more than a foot apart, each with arms folded across our chests. Our breath-clouds collided.

"It's hard to know how to feel," Charlene said. "All the way here I practiced saying 'I'm sorry Savvy is gone.' I couldn't do it. I couldn't sell it even to myself."

"I get it."

"No you don't," she said. A little too sharp, a little too quick. "You *love* her, Conway. Some little part, some little corner of you loves her. She was something to you that I can't be. You never talk about it, because you never talk about anything, but . . ."

I wanted to admit Charlene was right, at least partly. But I didn't want it to hurt when I said it. I couldn't figure out how to do both.

So I said nothing.

"What was she to you?" Charlene said. "What corner of you does she own? How can I own it?"

She was pleading, or damn near. I'd never heard her do that.

Quiet.

"We didn't . . . do anything," I said. "Not this time, I mean. She wanted to, but we didn't."

Charlene flicked a hand. "I know. You wouldn't have been able to hide it."

Jesus, *everybody* read me like a book.

"Savvy didn't own any part of me," I said. "I'm here. I'm with you." I moved to hold her.

But Charlene took both my elbows, kept the hug at bay. "Prove it," she said. "Come to work tomorrow. Come to the shop at seven-thirty on the dot, fix cars all day, shoot the breeze with Floriano. Be kind and serious but a little funny, the way you are when you're relaxed." Pause. "The way you *were*."

Her voice, her eyes, her hands on my arms told me how much it meant to her.

"I can't," I said.

Charlene set me loose.

"She was a Barnburner," I said. "And I already took the money."

I said that last bit to nobody. Charlene was already halfway up the front steps, sobbing, keening something at the same time. It sounded like, "I knew it, I *knew* it."

But I may not have heard correctly.

I didn't even want to think about Savvy while Charlene lay awake next to me. Wasn't sure why that felt wrong, but it did. So I waited, staring at the ceiling until her breathing went slow and deep and settled right at the edge of a snore.

Then I let my head go where it needed to go. Which was not a good place. *Because you are a joke, a goddamn unfunny joke. Square up. Face it.*

I faced it. Charlene and Randall had seen right through me: Savvy and the Bert Saginaw circus had come along at a perfect time. They'd provided me a little vacation from growing up and buckling down. And they'd fed me money that served as an excuse. A lame excuse, an excuse nobody who knew me bought, but an excuse.

While I'd been diddling around here and there, Savvy'd been killed.

Accident? Bullshit. Savannah Kane was more likely to fly to the moon than to find herself in a Charlestown construction site. Somebody'd manipulated her there.

Why?

It had something to do with blackmail. Had to.

So who was worried about blackmail, and might be happy enough with Savvy gone?

Bert Saginaw. Or his campaign, anyway.

Figure out the blackmail, figure out who killed Savvy.

Simple.

But not easy.

Figure out the blackmail, figure out who killed Savvy.

I tried using it to fall asleep, repeating it in my head, forcing my breathing to slow.

It didn't work, not for a long time. It just made me think about Savannah Kane. I'd loved her. And how. A pointless, screw-'em-all love that had left a hole in me for a long time. Forever. Charlene sensed it, even if she could never understand it.

Hell, I didn't understand it myself.

I didn't understand a lot of things.

CHAPTER THIRTEEN

Did you *see* this?" Sophie said the next morning, Thursday. She spun her laptop to face me, polished off her cereal, and set the bowl on the floor for Dale to lick. Then she stepped to the granite counter and read the Post-it her mother had left.

Charlene had been gone when I woke up at five thirty. That wasn't unusual—she's a flat-out workaholic and happy to admit it—so there was a chance Sophie hadn't picked up on our fight the previous night.

On the other hand, there was a better chance she had. Hard to slip anything past Sophie. Especially household tension.

Boston.com was up on her laptop. The headline wasn't any bigger than one you'd use the day after World War III. It read:

SAGINAW PHOTOS STIR OUTRAGE
Candidate compared self to Christ during business price war; eager to do "Chain Link Jesus" shoot, editor recalls

In the pic, Saginaw was crucified on his own fencing.

Really.

"Holy shit," I said. "Pardon my French. They warned me."

"Who warned you?"

"Saginaw himself, kind of. And my pal Moe. But . . . *jeez.*"

"Yeah, jeez."

I clicked the pic to see a bigger version. Technically, it was a stunner: Shot in a field somewhere with a filter that made blues and grays dominate, it gave the impression you were looking at a bruise. I remembered a Minnesota tornado—the sky had been those colors before hell broke loose.

The angle: very low, the photographer belly-crawling to get lots of that bruise-blue sky as a backdrop.

Bert Saginaw had dressed up as Jesus Christ. He'd let somebody shoot *pictures* of him that way. The section of chain link he was stretched out on bore a small but readable sign:

SAGINAW FENCE CO.
FRAMINGHAM, MA

They'd gone the whole nine yards. He wore only a raggy loincloth. His muscles rippled and stretched. It was easy to imagine how proud he'd been in particular of his abs and his lats, the lats showcased by outstretched arms.

I didn't know what tricks they'd used to get his feet off the ground, but they dangled just the way you'd expect.

Saginaw had even tilted his neck just right, looking down, patience and enduring in his eyes. He'd been *into* this photo. He'd gotten *off* on it.

As I turned on my cell, I looked at Sophie. "They'll get creamed for this."

"And how," she said. "You might say they'll get crucified, har har."

My phone began pinging like crazy with texts that had come in while it was shut down.

They were all from Krall or Saginaw. I didn't even read them. It was pretty clear what they were about.

"Looks like you've got a full day ahead," Sophie said, swooping up her bowl and setting it in the sink. "Speaking of which, what do you think about the new tech?"

I looked up. "What new tech?"

"The one mom and Floriano hired," she said, shouldering her vintage Boris Badenov backpack. "Tory, I think the name is."

"Never heard of him."

"He's not a him," she said. "He's a her."

I stiff-armed my new motto—*figure out the blackmail, figure out who killed Savvy*—and barrel-assed down Route 9 to Charlene's office in Westborough. Slammed my truck's door, steamed across a porch that ran the width of the building, shouldered the sticky front door, slammed it, too, made for Charlene's suite.

The office was in a converted Victorian that was painted three colors—all of them period-correct, all of them ugly. Charlene split the downstairs with a pair of shrinks who owned the building and lived upstairs. Everybody who worked beneath the roof was female. I always felt out of place and out of scale here.

Charlene could afford more impressive headquarters in any of a half-dozen nearby office parks. But for the same reason she stuck with her little Shrewsbury house, she kept her staff fishing-line-thin and clung to the Victorian. I thought she ought to move—was pretty sure stubbornness had cost her some opportunities. We'd argued about it, but *she* was underwriting *my* new business, so at some point I'd realized my best bet was to shut up.

Besides, I had to admit Charlene's low-overhead style meant her company was pure value, no frippery or debt in sight. She'd recently turned down a cash offer of $8 million and change from her biggest national competitor.

I whipped open the suite door. Joy, typing away while looking at a stack of forms, smiled big and said hello.

"She here?" I said.

Something in my voice made Joy stop typing and really look at me. "Is everything all right, Conway?" Raising her voice just a little, alerting Charlene behind her heavy four-panel office door.

Joy Cleburne wore her hair straightened and pulled back. The hair was pure black except for a white streak directly over each ear. Damnedest thing. She spent her first fifteen years fearing her father's belt, the next ten fearing her husband's, and another five smoking cocaine to forget them both. Then she cleaned up and pulled her life together. She was Charlene's first hire, Employee Number Two. Her salary was exactly a dollar a year less than Charlene's, which was damn healthy, and she was one of the few who owned points in the company. She could and had run the operation for long stretches while Charlene wooed clients and recruited translators.

Joy had always been kind to me, but I didn't kid myself: She'd set me on fire before she'd let me so much as raise my voice to Charlene.

Charlene slipped from her office. Her clothes—black pointy shoes, black pants, black jacket, light-blue blouse—and the way she closed the door told me there was a client or prospect inside.

"Who the hell's this new tech you hired without telling me?" I said.

"Can we talk outside?"

"I shouldn't have to learn this stuff from Sophie."

"Can we talk outside, please?" She said it with exaggerated quiet, like a few lemon-puss teachers I had in school. The trick had pissed me off then. Still did. But I fought the red mist, the urge to break something just to be a jerk.

As Charlene whisked past Joy's desk, a look passed between them that pissed me off more. In a glance that lasted less than a second, they fired woman-messages back and forth:

Here we go again.

Is everything okay?

I can handle him.

Why does he get like this?

Tell me about it.

Is he worth it?

We'll see.

Charlene elbow-steered me outside to the broad porch, and I hated the feeling I was being handled, hated how obvious it was she and Joy had talked me over before now.

"You should have called, Conway."

"Just tell me if it's true."

"Of course it is. Floriano and I had a tech lined up because we suspected you'd run off and do what you do. Victoria's local, she's ASE certified, and she's young. Which equals cheap."

"But we *didn't* need her! It's a two-lift shop, and we've got two techs."

"Do we?" She folded her arms as she said it. "So you're saying I can count on you, what with the passing of Ms. Kane?"

I said nothing. Started to talk, stopped, started, stopped. "I can't just drop it."

"Of course you can."

"We covered this last night. It's a Barnburner thing. You know how that goes. You know what it means."

"I do," Charlene said. "That's my point." Then she turned on one pointy shoe and pushed through the door.

It opened right up for her. It didn't stick at all. She must know the trick.

CHAPTER FOURTEEN

Randall's phone rang through to voice mail the first two times I called. But I knew his ring tone—*We had joy, we had fun, we had seasons in the sun*, the old bubblegum song that caught on as his Army unit's motto—would annoy him into picking up sooner or later.

"Sorry," I said when he did.

"Umph," he said.

"I'm parked outside Charlene's office," I said. "I just picked a fight, and I feel like a shitheel."

"Mmmph."

"And now I'm sensing you're not alone, and I'm feeling like even more of a shitheel."

My phone made its incoming-call chirp. I looked at the screen. Krall.

"Gotta pick up the other line," I said. "What I need you to do, I need you to research Bert Saginaw. They say he blew a couple fortunes before this one stuck. Find out how he made them, how he lost them. 'Kay?"

"Who's on the other line?"

"Krall, the campaign manager."

"You still working for Saginaw? After what happened to Savannah Kane?"

The question surprised me. I thought Randall knew me better than that. "*Hell* no I'm not working for them," I said, "if I ever was."

"You've got two checks from the man in your billfold."

"Sure do," I said. "But as of yesterday afternoon, I'm working to find out who killed Savvy Kane. Barnburner once, Barnburner always."

"And if the path leads straight to Bert Saginaw's front door?"

"Wouldn't surprise me at all. Look, I really need to take this other call."

I clicked over.

"Where the *fuck* are you?" Krall said. "Where the *fuck* have you been? How many *fucking* messages do I need to leave?"

"I'm in my truck. I'm coming to Cambridge to meet with you and figure out what comes next. But if you keep fuckity-fucking me, I might just pick you up by your throat and pound on you once I get there."

Krall took a deep breath that just about sounded like a sob. "I'm sorry, okay? Long night into a long morning. Into a long day, no doubt."

"Thanks to Chain Link Jesus."

"Drudge put the pics up at nine thirty last night. We've been all hands on deck ever since."

"Where'd those shots *come* from?"

"Tell you later."

"They take you by surprise?"

"We knew about them, and deep down I guess we figured they'd come out. But you get in a groove. You tell yourself maybe you got lucky this time. Know what I mean?"

I said nothing.

"Our internals, our eyes and ears, all the anecdotal stuff," he said, "it's brutal. The Catholics, the oldsters, and all the people who never liked Bert but had a hard time putting their finger on why . . . well, they can frigging well put their finger on the reason now. Our numbers are dropping through the floor."

"Go figure."

"Reason for this morning's messages, there's a big change in plans. Tinker and Saginaw are doing tag-team rallies all day. Maybe she can drag him up. We're not sure, but we've got to try *something*."

"Doesn't that torpedo Tinker's too-dignified-to-campaign strategy?"

"Bet your ass. But it can work in our favor, too. We're hoping Betsy Tinker Coming Down from the Mountain pushes Chain Link Jesus out of the news cycle. Or at least aside." Big sigh. "Like I say, we've got to try *something*."

"Where do I come in?"

"This morning, we're doing our first rally since the Jesus pics. Why don't you come on up?"

"What good will I do Saginaw there?"

"Search me, but it was Bert's idea. And it's his nickel."

I thought about that. Decided a rally was as good a place to be as any. Randall would do his usual ultra-thorough job researching Saginaw, and I could get my first look at this Betsy Tinker. "Where are you?" I said.

"Know where Braxton is?"

Fifteen minutes later I exited I-495, drove west and south on back roads. This was apple country: hills, orchards, farm stands. Nice. Finally hit Braxton, found its newish high school, parked in a nearly full lot. The best parking spots had been swiped by vans from all the local TV stations plus Fox News and CNN.

When I entered the gym, I got my first taste of big-time politics. Uniformed state troopers flanked the double doors. One of them saw something in me he didn't like. Next thing I knew I was being elbow-walked toward a trailer serving as a mobile command post. That was bad: I figured I was in for a credential search and a serious pat down. And once my record came up, I'd be bounced or held.

"Sax!"

I'd lucked out: It was Krall. He nodded thanks to the trooper, who dropped my elbow but didn't like doing it. Then Krall speed-walked us inside the school, fishing out a purple badge on a lanyard, telling me to wear it. "Just in time," he said at the back of the gym, talking into my ear as a local poo-bah did the world's longest introduction of Betsy Tinker. "Herself is about to descend from the heavens. The people love her."

He was right about that. The gym was packed, the roll-out bleachers SRO, plenty of homemade signs waving (CLASS AT LAST, WE LOVE YOU BETS), the Braxton Bulldogs marching band taking floor space, the media penned off to one side.

The local poo-bah couldn't decide whether he was introducing AC/DC or the pope, so he covered both. About the time even his wife was ready to give him the hook, he finally ran out of dumb things to say and waved an arm at a side door.

In came Betsy Tinker, followed by Saginaw and a few flunkies.

From the way people talked about her, I'd expected a cross between the queen of England and Aunt Bea. This woman was not that. Though, I decided as she walked and smiled and waved, she did have a royalty vibe about her. In a good way. The gracious, gliding way.

She couldn't be ten years older than me. Fit, pretty, shortish hair that wasn't gray or silver or blond—but was somehow all three. She smiled at everyone, and though she seemed to make time for them all, she never stopped moving. That was a skill shared by natural politicians and NASCAR drivers.

Tinker stepped to a miked podium; the others stood in line behind her and to her right, their rear ends brushing one of those hanging pads that prevent basketball players from slamming into cinder blocks.

The gym went crazy. Bleachers vibrated. Signs waved. Krall grinned, hands on hips, soaking it in. The band played a song I was pretty sure was supposed to go with the president of the United States. Nobody seemed to mind.

It was hard to decide whether Betsy Tinker was a natural at milking the moment, or just surprised by the intensity of it all. She stood, smiled, waved.

Applause rolled, faded, returned. Each time the ruckus came close to settling, some dimwit would yell, "We love you, Betsy!" the way dimwits always do nowadays, and the applause would heat up again.

Finally, the gym went quiet. "I'm Betsy Tinker," she said into the microphone. Perfect pause. "And you must be the great unwashed."

The place went nuts again, this time with laughter that built to a standing ovation. "That's my line!" Krall said into my ear, grabbing my arm like he wanted to break it. "I knew it would kill. I *knew* it!" Then he pointed all the way across the gym at one of the flunkies, who grinned and made a big thumbs-up.

After that it was all downhill. Not because Tinker did anything wrong, but because she stopped being a folk hero and became a politician giving a stump speech. The magician's reveal was over.

I watched Saginaw. His face and body language didn't give away much. He smiled and clapped when he was supposed to, just like everybody else in the gym. Once in a while he cut his eyes in various directions. When he spotted me next to Krall, he froze for a second or two.

Then the speech was over—after only fourteen minutes, and God bless Tinker for that—and people got enthusiastic again as the pols and flunkies walked out the same door they'd walked in, media in hot pursuit.

"What do you think?" Krall said.

"Who cares what I think?"

"I do. You're my one-man focus group."

"I think your strategy of stashing her was smart," I said. "The more you trot her out, the more people will see she's just another politician pissing in their ear."

"For what it's worth, I think you're right. Obviously our hand has been forced. Look on the bright side. Nobody was hollering at Chain Link Jesus up there. People don't want to be rude with sweet Betsy

Tinker around." He nodded and chewed a thumbnail, talking to himself now. "What we do, we do a handful more of these gigs, say two a day. Run out the clock that way, wait for the polls to settle. And nobody can say Betsy was afraid to face the public. Speaking of which, let's go see how she does with the hacks." He turned and moved away through the crowd.

I started to follow, but felt looked-at. I don't know how to describe it better—I just felt eyes on me. I've learned not to ignore the feeling, so I spun.

And saw Vic Lacross maybe twenty feet to my right.

Double take. *Vic Lacross*?

He used to be a state police detective. We'd met a few years back when a young Barnburner got shotgunned. Lacross had turned out to be the kind of cop I could work with: not quite straight, not quite dirty. Played everything his own way. I'd heard it bit him in the ass, that he wasn't a cop anymore.

His hair was still a 1974 bowl cut. He wore it that way to cover his missing ear. Acne craters still dominated his face. Maybe his crow's feet were deeper.

Maybe mine were, too.

I wanted to make my way over, but the crowd was flowing against me, and Krall said my name. So I turned and moved away.

Vic Lacross. Huh.

I pulled my cell and shot Sophie a text asking for a quick Google on Victor Lacross, former statie. She texted back right away: *Will do, mom'll be thrilled I'm yr accomplice.*

It was packed in here, and the locals hadn't thought through their traffic flow. The double doors Tinker and company had used to exit the gym were becoming a crush zone. The TV people had zipped through the same doors, and that had signaled the looky-loos and fame-sniffers that this, and only this, was the place to be, the other three sets of double doors be damned.

The bottleneck grew nasty. Looking over people's heads, I saw why. Just outside the doors, a wing of the school teed away and a concrete patio formed a natural stage. Tinker, Saginaw, and their handlers had stopped there. So had the reporters, and a handful of staties to boot. Now the crowd, Tinker's great unwashed, was trying to press its way through the same doors, and there was nowhere to go.

A toddler cried. Then another. Nervous parents began lifting small kids. Folks up front tried to make the staties understand there was a problem, but the troopers were doing their human-cordon thing. I swiveled my head: Behind me, people were getting the message and drifting to other doors. There was no threat of a Europe-style soccer riot, but we were sure looking at an ugly scrum.

No more than thirty feet dead ahead, on that concrete patio, an oblivious Betsy Tinker talked, gesturing with her hands the way politicians do. The sun was climbing, but it was still chilly—I could see her breath. People were gravitating to her from across the parking lot and ballfields: sweaters, fleeces, a few parkas . . .

. . . raincoats?

Yes. Two people had materialized, stepped from the woods maybe. A man and a woman. They looked like kids to me, but these days that's true of anybody under thirty.

They wore secret-agent-style trench coats. Tan, belted.

There was no rain. There was no threat of rain. There hadn't been rain for a week.

CHAPTER FIFTEEN

The man and woman in raincoats also wore identical shades, the heavy black ones that always remind me of old-time movie stars. I'd heard they were hip again, for boys and girls alike.

"Hey," I said, wriggling toward the doors.

"Cool your jets, Ace," a man said. I thought about slapping him, then saw he had a hand on the shoulder of a ten-year-old.

The trench coat twins' hands were jammed in their pockets. They were walking straight, paralleling the wing of the school. They used the same gait though the man was four inches taller, and they looked neither left nor right.

"Hey!" I said. "Trooper!"

None of the cops turned.

I wriggled through the crowd some more. People continued to wise up and drop away from the sides of the pack, so it was getting easier to move. A couple of women called me names beneath their breath. The trench coat pair were still forty feet from Betsy Tinker, but they were moving fast and nobody, including the staties, seemed to notice them.

"Trooper!" My wriggle turned into a full-on thrash. I hollered the word over and over as I neared the door. They all ignored me.

The trench coat twins were thirty feet away from Betsy Tinker. Hands in pockets, grim expressions, marching.

"Trooper!" I busted to the doors and finally, *finally,* one turned.

It was the one who'd grabbed me when I first got here. The one who didn't like my looks.

Shit.

"That's far enough, pallie," he said, making a tight little smile when he recognized me. He was short but wide, big chest, big traps, like so many state cops. His name board said OBSITNICK.

"Over there—" I started to say, pointing. But he bodied up to me. Even with three dozen witnesses standing right there, he had a move nobody could spot: He squeezed my upper arms and pulled me toward him in a weird little hug. To anybody else, it'd look like I'd charged him and he'd been forced to absorb me with his body. They couldn't see he was squeezing my arms, pressing with his thumbs . . . doing his damnedest to hurt me, and *enjoying* it. "Easy there, sir," he said, his voice no different than the fifteen times a shift he asked for license and registration. But the tight smile gave him away: The little prick was having a good time.

The trench coat twins were twenty feet from Betsy Tinker. A print reporter noticed them, gave them an annoyed look, did a double take. The male trench coat stalled. The female did not. She was moving her hand in her coat pocket, the way you would to put your finger on the trigger of a gun.

Or of a bomb.

I stood watching, held up by a jerk cop fifteen feet away from the mess. I needed to move *now.* Fighting pain, I pretended to fall against the statie. It forced him to let go, to wrap my waist.

I raised my right boot as high as I could.

I slammed it to his left instep.

His eyes crossed. He released my waist.

I didn't have room for a decent punch. Instead: grabbed a handful of love handle just above his Sam Browne belt, gave it one hell of a sharp twist. Felt things tear. He would bleed beneath his skin for a day or so.

Good.

He made a noise like a mouse in a cat's mouth and stepped back. I busted through.

Everything slowed then.

"There!" I hollered, pointing at the trench coat twins. "Them!"

The male trench coat, the one who'd faltered once already, spun and took off.

I took off after him.

The woman never took her eyes from Betsy Tinker. The right hand came out of her coat pocket. Her pinched face went savage, and she began to holler something. Just as I flashed past, focused on the man, I heard a beating-laundry sound. Whatever she'd started to say stopped. Something hit my hair.

Running full speed, I touched my head.

Blood.

I ran. I focused on the man, thirty yards ahead and moving well. His trench coat tails flapped. He wore trail-running shoes and long, thick socks. Like he'd prepped for this getaway. Huh.

He hit the woods. I was closing, but not quickly. We crunched through fallen leaves, the man knowing every twist and turn, and I flashed back to my own high school days: This would be the path kids ducked down to smoke a cigarette or a doobie, or to bail out of school after lunch. This would be the path the vice principal patrolled once in a while, making surprise busts.

Closing. I was twenty yards behind.

The man took a left. I did, too, and saw we'd popped from the path onto a packed-dirt road, high-crowned. A corner of my head guessed it would serve as both access to the high school sports fields and a fire road for the woods to my right.

The man was fading, panicking. His gait, which had been fluid on the path he knew well, grew choppy and spastic. He looked over his shoulder every four strides.

Me, I could go all day. Running in work boots feels ridiculous at first, but once you build a head of steam, they almost work in your favor, their weight pulling your feet along.

Twelve yards, ten, eight. He was flailing. That was good. I had to assume that whatever his girlfriend had been clutching, gun or bomb, he had one too—but as long as he kept whipping his arms around like a kindergarten puppet, he couldn't grab for it.

Six yards. He breathed like a train leaving a mountain station. I clomped, felt the first sweat-trickle at the small of my back.

When I got within three yards, I decided to end it. Exploded for a few fast strides, reached for the collar of his trench coat, jerked down and toward me.

It wiped him out, as I'd hoped.

What I hadn't planned on: The trench coat slipped off his arms, came away in my grasp.

Underneath it, he was naked but for the socks and shoes. So much for my suicide bomb theory.

What the hell?

It took me a bunch of strides to whoa down my heavy boots. When I did, and turned to walk back to the man, he lay in a fetal position clutching his side.

I made my way to him, catching my breath. I stood over him, set hands on knees. "What the hell?"

He was crying.

That pissed me off.

I kicked him in the back. Not hard. I just wanted to un-fetal him.

It worked. He grabbed for his back like a little girl. He mewled. He cried and panted and looked at the sky.

He had something written on his chest: *FURDER.*

Written in red. Lipstick? Blood?

I faked another kick just to keep him still and quiet. Then I rifled the pockets of the trench coat.

What I found: an oversized vial of blood, corked with a black rubber stopper.

I held it up, looked at the man. "What the *hell,* pal?"

"Furder is murder," he said.

I looked at him maybe fifteen seconds. Finally I said, "You gotta be shitting me."

"Gold," Krall said. "Pure goddamn gold."

The school gym had been taken over by the staties.

"The girl had bigger balls than the guy," one trooper said to another.

I leaned on a folding table while Krall rattled on about how perfectly things had played out. "From an optics standpoint only, of course," he added, trying not to drool on himself.

What I pieced together: Betsy Tinker wore fur coats once in a while, and her late husband had always voted not to cut funding for programs the animal-rights types hated. So a pair of local coffeehouse heroes, ten years out of Braxton High and still living in mom's basement, had hatched a plan to toss vials of blood on Tinker while the cameras rolled. Then they would strip to reveal the big FURDER IS MURDER message. The sound I'd heard as I took off after the guy, and the blood I'd felt on my head, had resulted from a cop tackling the trench coat woman as she cocked her arm to splatter Betsy Tinker.

"Pitiful and confused," said a tall state cop who seemed to be the boss man, leaning next to me and folding his arms.

"Dipshits," I said.

"The male Rosa Parks claims you worked him over while he was down."

"I kicked him once," I said. "He'll live."

"He will at that. Funny thing," the cop said, looking at me, "the only real injury here is to one of my guys. Busted foot."

"Obsitnick," I said.

"Know anything about that?"

I said nothing for a while. Finally I turned, met the cop's gaze. He was an inch taller than me. Silver hair just this side of a buzz cut. Didn't have the workout muscles favored by most staties. Instead he moved like a guy who'd been a good small-college tight end, but had been relieved to lose twenty-five pounds when he graduated.

"Just a guess," I said. "Obsitnick has a history. Bully-boy stuff, but hard to pin down. Always has an explanation, always quick with his side of the story."

"You've got a ways to go on your parole."

"Yes."

"Manslaughter. Heavy stuff."

"Yes. Can I go?"

He jerked a thumb to say *beat it*.

I pushed off the table, started for the parking lot.

Before the Tinker-Saginaw circus had pulled out of Braxton High, a flunky had told me Betsy Tinker would like to express her gratitude. I told the kid it would have to wait—I had things to do.

When he realized he'd have to deliver bad news to the boss, his lip quivered. He looked like a dog that just piddled on the floor. I clapped him on the shoulder harder than I needed to. I may have told him to grow a pair. Then I felt bad for the flunky—knew I was mostly annoyed at the Furder is Murder numbskulls. But Jesus, how old do they need to be these days before they're *men*?

Checked my cell as I crossed the parking lot. Text from Sophie: *Victor Lacross left state police 3 yrs ago, not sure why but he is suing to get full pension. Owns lacrossresearch.com domain, a 1-page website with e-mail address and the word RESEARCH.*

The contact info for Lacross's domain was an office address in a part of Framingham I knew well. If it was the building I was picturing, it was a shithole.

I thanked Sophie, asked if Davey had shown. She texted back a frowny face.

RESEARCH. It could mean a lot of things.

Huh.

Vic Lacross wasn't a guy who would just happen to be at a political speech up in Braxton. Mental note: Look him up. Maybe we could help each other.

CHAPTER SIXTEEN

Working south on 495, I took calls from Krall, Emily Saginaw, and finally Bert Saginaw himself. The theme: Betsy Tinker wanted *very much* to thank me for rescuing her from a tube of blood. *In person.*

Undercurrent: What Betsy wanted, Betsy got. And the toadies around her weren't used to explaining why she couldn't have it right away.

She lived on Beacon Hill. Of course. I plugged the address into my GPS, hopped on the Mass Pike east, and thought.

Mostly I thought about the big sloppy guy in the green Expedition. He'd followed me, Savvy had followed him. A couple hours later, she was dead. I knew most of the players, but not him. Who the hell was he?

Thinking about being followed made me check my mirrors.

Then again.

"I'll be damned," I said out loud.

There was a red Lumina two cars behind me.

Things came back. Things clicked. The day Savvy showed up at my shop, I'd spotted a red Lumina with North Carolina plates. A geek had stood by the car staring hate-rays at me.

But what really clicked was this: The Lumina kid was also the kid featured in Savvy's cell phone pics.

The one who sure as hell seemed like a boyfriend. Or at least a boyfriend wannabe.

"I'll be damned," I said again. This was good. Looked like Betsy Tinker would have to wait awhile longer.

I pulled into the next rest area. The Lumina followed. I parked but left my truck running, watched the Lumina back into a slot forty feet away. Amateur hour.

I backed out of my parking space and covered the forty feet quickly, left my passenger door half a foot from the Lumina's nose, killed my truck, opened my door.

Give the kid credit: He spent just a second or two paralyzed. Then, quicker than I would have guessed, he was up and out of the Lumina, coming at me as I went at him. We wound up toe to toe. He was two inches shorter than me and fifty pounds lighter, but he surprised me with an index finger to my chest. "What did you *do*?"

I grabbed the finger and was ready to twist it—but didn't. Dropped it instead. "Who are you?"

"What did you do?" the kid said again, shaking all over. "Why ain't you arrested?" He said it *hain't* in the North Carolina way I remembered from my NASCAR run. He shoved my chest with both hands. It was a nice try, but my feet didn't budge.

"I saw pictures of you on her phone. What were you to Savvy? Boyfriend?"

"I'm her fiancé, or was," he said, lips and jaw quivering. "I am Blaine Lee from Level Cross, North Carolina, and if the Yankee-ass police up here can't take care of business, I'll take care of it myself."

"I'm after the same thing you are, kid. I . . . cared about her. A long time ago."

"Not that long," he said. "I saw you two the other day."

"You said your name's Blaine?"

He nodded.

"I didn't kill her, Blaine. Cops would love to say I did, but they cleared me. Think I'd be walking around otherwise?"

He stood and panted at me, his adrenaline fading.

"For what it's worth," I said, "I told her to forget Saginaw and head back home. To her kid. And to you, I guess."

"Then I guess she listened to you about the same as she listened to me. Which ain't much."

Look at him there, leaning at me, ready for whatever came next. No chest, no chin, blondish hair in a poodly near-mullet. Boxed in and outweighed, but unafraid.

You make a snap judgment. You trust yourself. You hope you're right.

"How about I park my truck and we talk?" I said.

"That'd be fine, sir."

I smiled as I climbed into the F-150. *Sir.*

"How long were you and Savvy together?" I said a minute later when Blaine joined me.

"Nearly a year."

"And it was serious?"

"As a Fort Worth bar fight, sir. I pestered her to marry me and let me adopt Max for six months or more, and I guess I finally wore her down, 'cause she said yes."

"But she came up here. What changed her mind?"

"Bert Motherfucking Saginaw, pardon my French. She read he was running for office. It got under her skin and stayed there."

"You knew about her past."

"I knew *all* about it," he said, staring at me to let me know exactly what that meant. "Sir."

"What'd you do, follow her up?"

Blaine nodded. "Savannah swore she just wanted to shake some money out of him, but he went and fell for her *again* soon as she knocked on his door."

"There's something about her."

"I guess there sure is."

We each looked through my windshield, thinking our thoughts.

"Was," I finally said.

"Was," he said.

"Cops know about you yet? Chinese-looking detective maybe, name of Wu?"

"No, sir. I can be pretty clever when I need to be."

"They'll want to talk with you."

"Why's that?"

"You're the boyfriend. You're the first guy they look at. But it's even worse than that. You're a jealous boyfriend, a dumped boyfriend." *Which is why you should be looking at him yourself,* I thought. But I wasn't buying it. Let the cops waste their time crossing Blaine Lee off their suspect list. He was crossed off mine already.

"I was not dumped!"

"Suit yourself." I shrugged, thought awhile. "What do you do down in Level Cross?"

Blaine smiled. Had good teeth except for one brown one that looked like an Indian-corn kernel. "I'm an installer at Best Buy in Greensboro. It's how we met. She wanted satellite radio."

More quiet.

"What are we going to do?" Blaine said.

"You truly ought to head home. I think Savvy said her son is with your folks?"

"My folks. Yes, sir, he is." He seemed to sneer on *folks*. But maybe I imagined it. Why the sneer? Worth keeping in mind.

"It's a hell of a thing, what happened to his mom. Go home. Be there for Max."

"I guess maybe I will." Long silence. Blaine set a hand on the door handle and left it there. I could tell there was more on his mind. "Are you really the Conway Sax ran Busch Grand National back in the day?"

Racing is North Carolina's state religion.

"Sure," I said.

"You raced Mark Martin, Jeff Gordon, Davey Allison, all them boys."

"Sure."

"You *beat* 'em."

"A few times."

"Your ticket was stamped for Cup, but you drank instead. So Savannah said."

"She was right."

"I saw in a magazine where Jeff Gordon earned thirty-two million last year."

"I didn't do quite that well," I said. "Hop out, Blaine. Drive home to your folks and your job and your boy."

He swallowed. What an Adam's apple on the kid. "I guess I will."

He had one foot out the door when I said, "Hey."

Blaine turned.

"This'll sound strange," I said, "but did you bring anybody up here with you? Guy my age, going to fat? Sloppy-looking, brown hair kind of long? Bombing around in a green Ford Expedition?"

Did Blaine's eyes and jaw tighten? Or did I imagine that?

"Reason I ask," I said, "he had your accent. Tarheel through and through."

"Can't say he sounds familiar," Blaine said. "But I will think on it."

Huh. How much thinking could it take?

I followed him back onto the Pike, stayed behind the Lumina, did some thinking myself. Blaine Lee sure didn't strike me as a man who'd snapped his girlfriend's neck yesterday. But the thing about really good liars is that they're really good liars.

He took the exit for I-95 south. I kept rolling west, to an appointment with Betsy Tinker that I was now good and late for.

Blaine Lee.

Huh.

An idea hit me. The cops must not have connected Blaine to Savvy yet. Otherwise, he wouldn't be driving around. So why not make the connection for them? That way, if I was dead wrong and he *had* killed her, they could nail him. And if he hadn't? Hell, better to have the cops focusing on him than on me. More elbow room.

I fished in the F-150's center console, came out with the business card Wu had given me. His first name was Credence. Go figure. I dialed. He picked up on half a ring, said his name.

"This is Conway Sax."

"I know."

"Savvy Kane gets her neck snapped in Charlestown," I said, "and eight hours later the *Globe* has creepy pics of the pol she was messing around with. You feeling the pressure? Brass breathing down your neck?"

"You're wasting my time," Wu said. "Got anything for me?"

"Do you know about Savvy's boyfriend?"

He sighed, paused, seemed ready to hang up. "Saginaw. No shit."

"No," I said. "Her other boyfriend, her *real* boyfriend. You must've seen pics of him on her phone. He wanted to marry her. She came north instead to put the squeeze on Saginaw."

Pause. But a short one. "Tell me more."

"Blaine Lee from Level Cross, Enn-Cee. Chevy Lumina, red, North Carolina plates." I said the plate number. "He just got on Ninety-five south. He'll be in Rhode Island in fifteen minutes."

"No he won't." Click.

Sorry, Blaine.

I drove. I thought. Bert Saginaw, me, Blaine Lee. Savvy Kane never had much trouble getting men to do what she wanted them to do.

Sixteen years ago, Paducah motel. Savvy and I spent forty hours there, the Triumph at the foot of the bed, and we were wide awake, cocaine awake, every second. We counted our hundreds over and over again, sorting and stacking them the way kids do pennies. We had eight thousand dollars. All the money in the world. Bonnie and Clyde money. We talked Mexico. Savvy had been to Cuernavaca and wanted to go back.

When the Haitian maid knocked on the door, we slipped her a pair of the hundies and sent her for food, booze, and cigarettes. Savvy swore by Old Golds, and I found I liked them too.

Two cartons of Old Golds, two pints of Wild Turkey, a bucket of fried chicken, and a brick of cocaine. No need to screw around cutting lines: Just lick your thumb, jam it in the coke, sniff for all you're worth, then rub your gums.

We ate. We drank. We smoked. We screwed. We stayed naked.

We fell in love.

You can laugh. You can scoff. But by midnight we were stripped naked in more ways than one. Exhausted, punchy, wanting to sleep but unable to keep our thumbs out of the coke.

We talked.

We spooned and talked all night long.

Life stories, dreams, daydreams, nightmares.

We told it all.

By sunup, I knew everything there was to know about Vinton, Virginia, where Savvy'd grown up. She felt the same way about my hometown, Mankato, Minnesota. I knew her family, her pets, her school, her tormentors. Her demons.

And she knew mine.

"Savvy?" I said into her neck at six thirty or so, traffic just starting to pick up outside.

"Mmmm."

"Who is he?"

"Who's who?"

"Who's the cop?"

"I dunno. James."

"What kind of deal was he talking about? In the bar?"

"Sleep," she said. In a few seconds I heard the kitty-cat snore.

I slipped the lit Old Gold from her fingers, put it out on the nightstand, wondered why she was lying.

Krall's flunkies had said I should just pull up to the front door—the future governor of Massachusetts was expecting me. Good thing: I sure as hell wasn't going to find a parking space here on Beacon Hill.

I idled at the address, looking up and down a long row of red-brick town houses. Cream-colored trim and black shutters, as far as you could see, both sides of the street. In the center: a little park wrapped by a wrought-iron fence. Carpet of grass in the park, not a fallen leaf in sight. Neighborhood like this, they probably had a guy running around all day catching the leaves in a trash bag. Two women walked dogs smaller than my cats. Hired help, I assumed, because each wore a plastic poopy-glove on her free hand.

"Are you Mr. Sax?" a man's voice said. I turned left, saw a guy who seemed familiar—either because I knew him or because he looked exactly like a sawed-off Ernest Borgnine. Even had the big split between his front teeth. "Conway!" he said, reaching through my rolled-down window to shake. He saw I was drawing a blank. "I'm a friend of Bill's," he said, not seeming offended that I didn't quite know him. "I'm a regular with the High Steppers in Natick. We've visited you Barnburners at Saint Anne's many a time."

Small click. "Shep?" I said. "You the one tells the story about the family of possums lived under the bar?"

"That's me! I've worked here seventeen years now."

"I figured from the getup." He looked like a bellhop from a 1946 movie, right up to the navy-and-gold hat. "But I thought you were a contractor."

"I am. A contractor with one customer. There's always a project needs doing . . ." he waved at the building behind him ". . . and you can't beat the pay."

"Hope she lets you change clothes when you're working. Be a shame to dirty up that uniform."

"Yeah yeah yeah, I've heard all the jokes. And yeah, I'm a driver and even a butler, kinda, when there's no *real* work to do. But it's a good living and she's a good boss, believe me." He looked me over. "You're the Mr. Sax come to see Miz Tinker? No offense, but you should've worn a suit coat. I'm supposed to park your car . . . truck, but I can run upstairs and grab you one. Say the word."

"You're dressed nice enough for both of us, Shep." I clapped his shoulder as I stepped from the truck, looked at the marble steps and six-panel door before me. "Which apartment's hers?"

"*Apartment?*" Shep had been halfway into my idling truck, but he climbed out and grabbed my sleeve, pointing, his voice a harsh whisper. "Jesus Christ, she owns from there . . . all the way down to there! Something like fifteen thousand square feet in Louisburg Square. You need to know who you're dealing with, my friend."

"Big coin."

"The biggest."

As I climbed the steps I remembered something about Shep, something a lot less funny than the possums under the bar: He'd lost his wife and kid in a house fire five, six years ago. The kid had been in his twenties but had never moved out—retarded, maybe, or just unable to hack it. A rough break. We'd all passed the hat for Shep a few times. I wondered if he lived here now. Had to be rooms for the hired help.

CHAPTER SEVENTEEN

Five minutes later I was sitting in a parlor with pale pink walls, pale pink floor-length drapes, and a tiny fireplace with a tiny fire that smelled like tiny apples. I half-expected the little man from the Monopoly board to walk in.

Instead: Elizabeth Tinker. I had the presence of mind to stand. Too fast—damn near knocked my chair over with the backs of my thighs. Even up close she looked much younger than I knew she was, rich, and fit. She wore blue jeans, God bless her. Had likely changed into them after a huddle with the maid who showed me in. Another victory for the great unwashed.

"Miz Tinker," I said, feeling oafish and oversized even in a room with nine-foot ceilings.

"Betsy," she said, shaking my hand, looking me in the eye though it probably hurt her neck. Short little thing. "May I call you Conway?"

I said she could. These politicians, the good ones anyway, make you feel like you're the most important person in the world. You know it's artificial, that in forty-five seconds they'll be doing the same routine for someone else, but you like it anyway. I wondered what the trick was.

We sat. A different maid showed up with a tray. Soon I was drinking coffee from a cup whose handle my pinkie didn't fit through.

"I'm given to understand you're a man of few words and fast action," she said. Then she leaned far enough to put a hand on my forearm. "So I'll belay my politician's instincts and keep this short. Thank you, thank you, thank you."

"You're welcome."

She leaned back. "Pete Krall says you're doing good work for the campaign."

"Mostly," I said, "for Bert Saginaw."

Something passed across her eyes. Anger? Worry? Hard to say. She was a pro—it passed quickly. "Yes, well," she said. "What's good for Bert is good for me, I daresay."

I took a deep breath. *Time to screw with these people.* "For now."

"Pardon?"

"The way I hear it," I said, "the plan is to drag you across the finish line, then move you aside. You must know Bert Saginaw doesn't want to be a pissant lieutenant governor."

It got to her, I could see from narrowed eyes and flared nostrils. "Drag *me* across the finish line? Good Lord, Mr. Sax. Conway. I invite you here to thank you, in person, for your derring-do. And you respond by hurling warmed-over rumors from the *Herald*?"

I said nothing.

"It is entirely possible Bert Saginaw has his eye on the governorship," she said. "No man worth his salt would be after less, and whatever else you want to say about Bert, he is . . . he is indeed . . . a competitor, of the sharp-elbowed genus."

A young guy in a uniform just like Shep's came in, waited for his boss to nod, crossed the room silently, punched up the apple-wood fire, and left.

"It may be hard for you to grasp this given your proximity to Bert and his sister and their acolytes," Tinker said. "But what Bert Saginaw wants and what Bert Saginaw gets will turn out to be very different things."

"I brought it up," I said, "to throw you for a loop."

"And?"

"I didn't throw you far."

She laughed a little and looked over my shoulder, where I knew there was a fancy table clock. I wondered how much time I had before the polite bum's rush.

"Speaking of Bert," Tinker said, "he and I are speaking to a group of teachers in Holyoke this evening. It's quite a long drive."

There it was. I didn't have much time.

"The reason I wanted to throw you for a loop," I said, "was Savannah Kane."

"Bert's paramour. A former flame rekindled."

"A former flame of mine, too."

Raised eyebrows told me I'd finally surprised Betsy Tinker, at least a little. "Do tell."

"Somebody killed her yesterday."

"I heard, and I'm sorry. I'm given to understand the case is being investigated with vigor, and that her death was likely an accident."

"What if Bert Saginaw killed her?"

"Be careful what you say, please."

"No. What if he killed her, or had it done? The whole reason she showed up was blackmail. What if she was blackmailing him over those weird Jesus pics? What if she leaked them to the *Globe,* then told him out of spite?"

"If she did," Tinker said, "and I don't believe it for a moment, but stipulating that for argument's sake, it's impossible to conceive a more indiscreet murder."

"By the time somebody's good and ready to kill," I said, "discretion is pretty much out the window."

"You say that with conviction," she said. "Even personal experience, I daresay."

She raised one index finger in a *just a minute* gesture. I turned. Shep had silently appeared in the doorway. Sheesh, the rugs here were thick. I'm not easy to sneak up on.

"What is it you hope to gain," Tinker said, "by informing me of Bert's history with the tragic Ms. Kane, not to mention your own?"

"I'm going to find out who killed Savvy Kane." I felt a hint of red mist as I said it. Clouding my eyes, clogging my brain.

"As previously mentioned, I'm told the police are investigating."

"Sure. But cops are big fans of the path of least resistance."

"My."

"And rich folks can put up a lot of resistance."

Behind me, Shep cleared his throat. "We should get on the road soon."

"Rich folks," Tinker said, "such as those who use pocket change to buy Cambridge hotels?"

"And those who own a full block on Beacon Hill."

"We should get on the road soon," Shep said, touching my elbow.

Part of me, the red-mist part, wanted to spin and slug. But there was no sense taking anything out on Shep.

I left the room. Behind me, an apple-wood knot popped.

It took two different maids to show me out.

Forty minutes later, at about five thirty, I backed my truck against a chain-link fence that separated a busted-tarmac parking lot from the east-west railroad tracks.

This was the wrong side of those tracks.

It was the section of Framingham I knew well: methadone clinics, halfway houses, two- and three-deckers overflowing with illegals. I'd done some good work down here for Barnburners who found themselves in a pinch. I'd busted people up down here. Most of them deserved it.

I looked at Lacross Security World Headquarters. It was a dump: an old warehouse subdivided into a couple dozen offices, a martial arts studio that seemed legit, and a modeling agency that did not. In the parking lot were a couple of Accords with rusted-out wheel wells, an ugly GM bomber from the '70s—closest you'd find to a classic car down here—and a snack truck with its logo painted over. From where I sat I got an eyeful of moms fetching their kiddies from martial arts. They rolled up in sixty-thousand-dollar SUVs. Funny world.

A train rattled west behind me, happy commuters headed home.

I waited, watched, thought. Why talk to Vic Lacross? Why take a chance busting into his place? Hard to say. It was a dumb risk: Getting popped for B&E would send me back for more state time at MCI Cedar Junction, even if I *was* pals with my parole officer's son.

But.

Lacross wasn't a guy who hung around political rallies for yuks. And his half-assed little Web site hinted at dirty tricks. What were they calling it these days? Oppo research. There was a reason he'd been at that high school gym in Braxton. It was a thread I needed to tug. Maybe the thread led back to Saginaw's blackmail problem.

And maybe the blackmail and Savvy's death were connected.

When Lacross helped me with a thing a few years back, he'd been a hard guy to figure out. He was a homicide detective for the staties then, which placed him high on the cop totem pole, but he didn't have CAREERIST HACK stamped on his forehead like most of those guys.

Lacross told a funny story about how he started out as a hostage negotiator. His first gig was a half-assed bank robbery out in Sterling, two meth heads holding a teller hostage. Rookie Lacross, trained in all the latest psychological mumbo-jumbo, expert on defusing tense situations, strolled in and told the punks he was going to blow their fucking heads off. One of them took a wild swing with a straight razor and amputated Lacross's ear.

Lacross blew their fucking heads off.

The hostage was unharmed.

Lacross's bosses were not pleased with his bedside manner. No more hostage negotiator. He grew his black hair into a Pete Rose bowl cut to cover the missing ear.

With a first impression like that, he must have been damn good to work his way up to detective. But by the time I knew him, Lacross seemed half-dirty. My vibe: He loved the investigating part of his job but didn't feel duty bound to hand the dirt to his bosses and prosecutors. He was a freelancer at heart.

Me too.

To my right, the sun dropped. I got cold. I texted Sophie that I wouldn't be home for dinner. She texted back: *K. Miss u.* And another frowny face. Why had I texted Sophie instead of Charlene? I tried not to think about that.

At quarter of six I was hungry, cold, and cranky enough so that B&E seemed like a good plan. Followed a little Hispanic guy into what passed for a lobby, waited for him to unlock the staircase door, stuck my foot in it while I figured out which suite Lacross rented.

The Hispanic guy saw me just fine. But it wasn't the kind of neighborhood or building where tenants brace a stranger. It was the kind where they hustle to get the hell away from him.

Upstairs, in a hall that smelled like ammonia and mouse turds, I found Lacross's door. Cursed when I saw a dead bolt above the crappy knob-lock. But smiled when I checked: The dead bolt hadn't been thrown. You can tell by how much the door rattles. People go to the hassle of buying and installing their own dead bolt, but then they lose the key or get lazy.

I stood very close to the knob and gripped it with both hands—if you'd watched me from behind you'd have thought I was taking a leak on it—and twisted one way, then the other. Once, twice, gauging the metal fatigue, torqueing against it, up on tiptoes for leverage—

The lock snapped. Just like that.

It ain't rocket science.

The office was bigger than I expected, a full twenty by twenty. At the far end, the original warehouse-style windows could have been cool, a yuppie selling point, if the frames hadn't needed paint and a third of the panes hadn't been cracked. Desk, chair, lamp, filing cabinet, yard-sale rug, futon with a Mexican blanket puddled at one end, dorm-size fridge, microwave. Atop the microwave: Pop-Tarts, ramen noodles.

Home sweet home.

I cracked a box of Pop-Tarts, took one, squatted before the filing cabinet.

And heard a click.

Not a doorknob click. That particular knob would never click again.

No, I heard the *shift-click* of a round being chambered.

Hell.

"Fuckin' Sax," Lacross said.

CHAPTER EIGHTEEN

First Shep, now Lacross. Two guys had sneaked up on me in the past hour. The grease-monkey life was making me soft.

I rose and turned.

"Stop," he said. He had an ugly little semiautomatic on me, a nine-millimeter something or other. "Show me the hands and open the . . . you stole a man's *Pop-Tart*? I've seen people do some shitty things in my time . . ."

"Starving," I said, spreading my jacket to show I had no gun, then waving the Pop-Tart. "And brown sugar cinnamon. It's my favorite."

"It's everybody's favorite. Sit on the bed."

I did. Lacross wore black boots, black slacks, a black fake-leather car coat. He sat in the desk chair, set his gun within easy reach even though we both knew he wouldn't need it.

We looked at each other maybe ten seconds.

"I'm a regular world-beater," he said, spreading his arms. "I'm kickin' ass up here."

"Why'd they throw you off the staties?"

He waved a hand, ignored the question. "You're here 'cause you spotted me at the Tinker thing. You're a hero. A dumb fuckin' hero."

"Why were you there?"

He slipped a card from his shirt pocket and flipped it to me, but it didn't tell me anything new. "I know," I said. "Research. That mean what I think it means?"

"Political stuff."

"Oppo research. Dirty tricks."

"Sure." He shrugged.

"How's the pay?"

"Better'n you'd think from my, ah, situation here." Pause. "Three divorces."

"Say no more."

"I'm working against your pal Tinker, working for Wilton."

"I figured."

"And it's the screwiest thing, Sax."

I waited.

"I don't think Wilton wants to win."

"Why?"

"I've worked three or four of these elections now," he said, "and Wilton's people are pros, but they're doing everything wrong. They send me down blind alleys. When I *tell* 'em they're blind alleys, they get pissy. They tell me shut up and cash your check. And when I *do* dig up something half-decent, they don't use it. Hell, I had the Jesus pics three weeks ago."

"What happened?"

"When I passed 'em along, Wilton's top advisor patted me on the head, but the pics disappeared. The *Globe* got 'em from another source."

"So what's going on?"

"I think Thomas Wilton got pushed into running by the country-club boys, the yacht-club boys. I don't think he wants to govern anything bigger than a gin and tonic, and I think the best moment of his life'll come Tuesday night when he makes his concession speech at the Copley."

Huh.

We sat. A west-east train rattled the office windows.

"That was pretty loose of me," Lacross said when the train was gone.

"What was?"

"What I just blabbed to you, about my own client maybe not really trying. Something like that gets out, it's firing-offense loose. It's you'll-never-work-in-this-town-again loose."

"So?" I said. But I knew where he was going.

"So what have you got for *me,* Sax? Spill it. You saw me at the rally. Whoopy-doo. Takes more than that to make a man pull a B&E. 'Specially when he's still on paper."

So he knew about my parole. "Keeping tabs?" I said.

"On everything and everybody."

I knew I shouldn't tell Lacross any more than I needed to. He wasn't a guy you could ever trust. On the other hand, he was more or less an honest thief, like me. Aren't many of us left. And he sure had come through with dirt on his own client. I decided to take a chance.

"Tinker and Saginaw have this whole damn soap opera going," I said. "Everybody hates everybody, everybody's screwing everybody. I can't say a whole lot about it, but there's blackmail."

"The Jesus pics."

"There's more."

"Worse?"

"Yup." I paused. "Somebody got killed." I told him a bare-bones version of Savvy. Left out the personal stuff, but the way he looked at me said he knew there was more.

"Huh," Lacross said when I finished. "Cops sticking with the accident scenario?"

"So far."

"You're not buying it. You think she was killed. Over the blackmail."

"I had to look at Wilton, had to see if he was the blackmailer," I said. "Especially when I figured out you were working for him."

He nodded. "I get it."

"But when you tell me Wilton's not even trying, it fits. It makes sense. Everything about this blackmail deal feels . . . personal. It feels like an inside thing."

"You take a look at Saginaw's ex?" I must have looked surprised when Lacross said it, because he half-smiled. "Oppo research, remember."

"Haven't talked with her yet," I said, "but I will. That's the vibe I'm talking about, that brand of meanness."

"These other pics," Lacross said. "Are they bad enough so Wilton might actually win?"

"I haven't seen them," I said. "But judging by how nervous Saginaw seemed, and stacked on top of the Jesus pics, it's a possibility."

Lacross whistled, nodded. "Well, I can make your life a little easier. No goddamn way is Wilton behind any of this. Trust me. If I'm wrong, I'll wear a pair of his pants all week. They're green with blue whales."

"Bullshit."

"My mouth to God's ear." He looked at his watch. "I need you to scram now. Got some useless oppo research to do."

I rose, started to leave. But thought of something: If Lacross was trailing around after Team Tinker-Saginaw . . . "A guy's been tailing me," I said.

"Green Expedition. I wondered if you'd made him yet."

"Who is he?"

"Wish I knew. I made him about a week ago, told my bosses there was a dude trailing around after Saginaw, sometimes Tinker. They told me not to worry my pretty head."

"If I give you his plate number, can you run it?"

"Already did."

"And?"

"And unless that big ugly dude is Dinah Wannamaker of Ludlow, Mass., the plate's stolen. What the smart guys do, they hit an airport parking garage, find a car just like theirs, and swipe the plates. The vic spots her missing plate, thinks it got knocked off in a parking lot, gets a duplicate. I know guys been running around three years on plates like that."

Huh. That could work. And anybody smart enough to pull it off was also smart enough to pop a FAST LANE transponder out of any unlocked car in a parking lot, which would explain why the Expedition dude had a transponder that wasn't Velcro'd to his windshield.

But why had he done the plate-and-transponder bit in the first place? "Any way you could take a harder look?" I said. "Maybe visit Wannamaker, imply you're still with the staties?"

"That's a hell of a risk." Lacross shrugged. "And Wilton's checks clear."

"Three divorces," I said.

"Yup."

I sighed. "You should throw your dead bolt."

"I guess so."

"Thanks for the info," I said, crossing the room. "It helps."

"Hey Sax?"

I turned.

"You can take the rest of the Pop-Tart," Lacross said. "I'm not gonna shoot you over it."

"If memory serves, Lacross had something to do with your little stay at MCI Cedar Junction," Randall said thirty minutes later, wiping away a tear. "How far do you trust him?"

"That was a long time ago," I said. "And he was just doing his job. The DA was the one who was really on the warpath. If anybody hosed me, it was her." I blew my nose into a napkin.

I didn't have a cold, and Randall wasn't feeling weepy. We were in the Chicken Bone Saloon, just a couple hundred yards from Lacross's office. The Chicken Bone is a dive. It's a blues bar. It serves the best wings in the state. It's perfect.

What we do, we order eighteen wings in garlic blaze sauce, which'll take the bugs off your windshield, and eighteen in thermonuclear sauce, which is about what it sounds like. Only hotter. We have the waitress mix 'em all up, and then we play roulette to see who gets what. Randall was having a tough run: three thermonuclears in a row. I'll attest that if a black man eats enough hot wings, you can watch his face turn red.

"Did you get the skinny on Bert Saginaw?" I said. Someone behind the bar turned up a Lucinda Williams record.

"Of course," he said, dunking a celery stick in as much ranch dressing as it would carry. "But you go first, while I wait for my heart rate to recede."

"No sympathy. At least you can wash yours down with beer."

"I'll drink to that."

While he did, I started to fill him in.

It took a while. As I worked through my day, its fullness surprised even me. By the time I was done we had a basket full of bones, my lips were numb, and Randall had about finished his second beer.

"That's a hell of a day," he said.

"Packed," I said. "Tell me what it means."

"Gee thanks." But he looked down at his lap and began twiddling his thumbs. He actually twiddles them, but only when he's thinking. I looked at the Chicken Bone's stage, which wasn't much bigger than a Ping-Pong table, and wondered how the hell the band that was trundling its gear through the door would make it all fit.

"Question," he finally said. "Let's say Bert Saginaw *didn't* kill Savvy. Who benefits if Saginaw looks bad?"

"Thomas Wilton."

"But you stipulated Lacross as a reliable source," Randall said, "and he says Wilton would just as soon lose."

"What about Betsy Tinker, then? They tell me she can still be elected with or without Saginaw. And it looks like she hates his guts and he hates hers."

"*He* hates her guts? Or Sister Emily hates her guts?"

"Same thing. They're a team, those two."

Randall grunted, either because he was unconvinced or because he'd just ripped into yet another thermonuclear wing. "Anyway," he said, "can you picture Betsy Tinker tossing a woman from a trailer-sized A/C unit in Charlestown? In broad daylight?"

"Of course not. Someone who works for her, though."

"That's worth looking at, but . . . it's hard to make the risk/reward work for a billionaire lady." Randall paused. "Keep it simple, Conway. Blaine Lee."

"I didn't get that vibe."

"Vibe, schmibe. Anyway, we'll know soon enough. The state cops have him in the hot box right now."

"They do?"

"You didn't hear? It was on the radio. They picked him up down in Attleboro, beelining south."

"Nice work, Wu."

"What?"

"Never mind."

"What's bothering me . . ." Randall said.

"The guy in the green Expedition," I said.

"So maybe that's your tomorrow project right there."

"I guess." I reached for a curly fry. "Tell me about Bert Saginaw."

"I will, but first I have to ask: Why the curiosity about him?"

"The more I know," I said, "the more I know."

"Do you believe he's behind Savvy's murder?"

"I haven't run into anybody with a stronger motive. And even if Saginaw had nothing to do with it, there's a chance his background'll point us in a direction."

Randall considered that, then made a *what the hell* nod. Or maybe he was clearing his sinuses. He organized his thoughts, tented his fingers. Charlene says he'll be a college professor someday. I don't disagree.

CHAPTER NINETEEN

Hubert Saginaw was born in 1955 in Fort Morgan, Colorado, to a failed inventor and a nurse. Dad, Paul Saginaw, was smart as a whip and had made a little money during the Depression when he patented a clever locking mechanism for livestock gates.

But he made only a *little* money; the patent boosted his ego in a dangerous way, and Paul would spend the rest of his life handing out pricey business cards with his name over the single word INVENTOR. The sum total he made off his latch probably didn't pay for the supply of cards. By the time Hubert and his two sisters were old enough to understand, Paul was a wet-eyed dreamer who spent all day messing around in his basement "lab" and explaining to the kids that no matter how hard they tried, The Man would always screw them out of what was rightfully theirs.

Mom—Marion Saginaw nee Hartline from over in Hillrose—was the workhorse and the paycheck. She worked in the local hospital, one of those nurses who was liked by doctors but not patients. Marion didn't give a rat's behind who liked her: She had three kids and a useless husband to support. Wake up, get the kids off to school, work a shift, fetch groceries at the IGA on the way home (because Thomas Alva Goddamn Edison was too busy in the basement to be bothered with shopping), pull dinner together, listen to Thomas Alva

Goddamn Edison whine while they ate, supervise homework, and maybe, just *maybe,* treat herself to a knock of so-so Scotch in the bathtub before falling into bed.

"Whatever it is you want me to know about Saginaw," I said, "you're sure taking the long way around to it."

"Getting there," Randall said, pushing up imaginary glasses on the bridge of his nose. He was digging the storyteller bit, the professor bit, and I've learned to let Randall do things his way.

Bert Saginaw wasn't an especially good student, so it surprised the hell out of everybody—his parents, his teachers, and the guidance counselor who'd been pointing him at local voke schools—when he was accepted at Oberlin College in Ohio. It turned out he'd taken his father's rants about getting screwed by The Man, written them up in the form of an application essay, and impressed somebody in the elite school's admissions office.

In late August of '73, armed with a duffel bag, a stack of student loans and ten twenties his mother stuffed in his shirt pocket—warning him he was on his own other than that—Bert Saginaw hitchhiked from Fort Morgan to Oberlin.

I didn't know much about college, but I doubted many kids thumbed twelve hundred miles to their freshman dorm.

"Some family, huh?" Randall said, reading my thoughts.

I took a guess. "Was that it? He never saw his parents again, and good riddance?"

"Hell no. The inventor dad croaked fifteen years ago, but mom's still around. Saginaw put her in a high-end nursing home out in Concord. The older sister is out of the picture, been teaching school in Hawaii forever. But Emily's been with Saginaw his whole career, ups and downs. When he ran companies she was always his admin, his bodyguard, his . . . *wall.* You wanted to talk to Bert, you talked to Emily first. Period. She couldn't be scared, couldn't be bullied, thought her big brother walked on water."

"I picked up on that."

"She's now a *highly valued* special advisor to the campaign." Randall smiled. "That's newspaper lingo for 'queen-sized pain in the ass.' I scanned the political blogs, and even when Tinker-Saginaw was looking unbeatable, anonymous advisors were threatening to quit over Emily's daily goofball ideas. Nothing's good enough for her brother, that's what it comes down to. Naturally, Bert lets her get away with it all. Sorry about the sidebar."

Saginaw lasted less than a year at Oberlin. He was vague about what happened; most likely he just couldn't keep up at the high-octane college and flunked out.

But he didn't walk away empty-handed: His last act before vacating the campus, he would say a hundred times in later interviews, was to peel up a section of flooring from a lab in Kettering Hall, Oberlin's science building. That floor was made up of thick rubber sections—chocolate in color, six inches square in size—that interlocked like a kid's toy. The idea was that if you dropped a test tube or beaker on the stuff, it wouldn't shatter.

Bert had grown fascinated with the flooring. It was the most comfortable stuff he'd ever stood on, it was easy to install, and you cleaned it with a push broom. Why wasn't this flooring *everywhere*? He'd asked his Basic Chemistry prof, who'd shrugged and said he'd heard it was Swiss in origin and was all the rage in Europe.

Long story short: Bert Saginaw declined to hitchhike back to Colorado. Instead, he wrote a letter to his sister Emily and asked her in turn to write this Swiss company to see if they had a Midwest distributor.

They did not.

Three months later, they did. CushionAire Enterprises, based in Elyria, Ohio, consisted of Bert on the sales end and Emily, who'd been looking for a chance to escape Fort Morgan, handling everything else.

Randall paused.

"And?" I said.

"And Bert Saginaw was—is—one hell of a salesman."

"I've seen him give a speech," I said. "Tell you the truth, I wasn't that impressed."

"See if this impresses you," Randall said. "In fiscal '75, CushionAire did thirty-four million in revenue. Let's guesstimate a twenty percent profit margin, because he had no real competition and Euro-stuff was very hip back then. That means he put almost seven mil in his pocket. That was a lot of money back then."

"Back then?"

He waved a hand, made a *pffft* sound, told more.

For five or six years, floors in a big swath of the upper Midwest turned chocolate-brown and comfy to stand on. It was all Bert Saginaw's doing. He was young, he was driven, and he was hyper-charismatic in a strange, charmless way. If he'd been born ten years later, Randall said, he would have carved out a career as an infomercial pitchman. "One of these jokers who starts out on late-night TV, and pretty soon he's a celebrity unto his own damn self for no reason anybody can figure out."

"He *is* a politician," I said. "Isn't that pretty much the same thing?"

"Har har." CushionAire hit the skids when the Swiss parent company told Saginaw it was time to push south into the Tennessee Valley and west into the Great Plains. The expansion made it impossible for the Saginaws to run the business as a brother-sister operation. They soon learned Bert, like a star jock who makes a lousy coach, was no good at training salesmen. His brilliance was deep in the gut, and when he tried to explain it the trainees grew frustrated while Bert grew mean. Emily wasn't much better at hiring and training the human resources, accounting, and support staff needed to grow a business.

"What happened?" I said.

"The Swiss company pulled an end-run," Randall said. "They licensed new regional distributors, letting Saginaw keep the upper Midwest. The problem was, that market was saturated already. Even in the seventies, you could only convince so many people to throw out their rugs and glue ugly brown rubber to their floors."

Bert and Emily flailed another eighteen months before folding up CushionAire. Then they spent fifteen years in the wilderness—launching businesses that didn't pan out, investing in sketchy franchises that went under. Slowly they became clones of their father. They convinced each other CushionAire had been the *one,* had been *theirs,* and that they'd been screwed out of their fortune by The Man.

"We're deep into the nineties now," Randall said. "Got a guess as to how Bert Saginaw made his next score?"

"That decade kind of passed me by, but Moe said something about software."

"Bingo."

Silicon Valley. A company that made software for testing the software they used to build software. "Or something like that," Randall said, waving a hand to indicate neither of us had a chance in hell at understanding what the operation actually did.

While stumbling after yet another half-baked franchise idea, Saginaw met some University of Chicago geeks who'd developed software, which even they considered boring, to double-check the code in their Computer Science projects. Instinctive as ever, and curious about the West Coast venture capital bonanza the business magazines were talking about, Bert smelled opportunity. He cashed in his last goodwill chits for a loan of a hundred grand, impressed the geeks with the dough, installed himself as CEO/CFO, and moved the circus to a rented place in Cupertino, California, that served the next year as a frat house–HQ combo while the geeks wrote code and Saginaw pounded pavement.

He scored in '96, after Netscape showed everybody just how silly these stock valuations could be.

"What's Netscape?" I said.

"Sheesh," Randall said, "you *were* out of it back then. Never mind."

The University of Chicago geeks' software would never be as sexy as Netscape or Amazon, but it was a nice little tool for building complex Web sites. And in 1996, a nice little tool could and did win you $2 million in first-round venture funding, followed by $5 million eight months later, with the big carrot dangling out there eighteen months off: the initial public offering that made everybody rich.

Randall said, "Guess what happened?"

I thought. "Was Emily involved with this company, too?"

"You bet," he said, smiling, knowing I'd sussed it out. "Executive assistant to president, CEO, and CFO Hubert Saginaw."

"They crapped the bed again," I said. "They couldn't handle the growth."

"Indeed. But this time there was another factor."

I waited.

"The VCs," he said. "Venture capitalists. Sharks like you've never seen. They'll rip your heart from your chest, show it to you while it's still beating, and get you to sign it over before you fall."

The waitress brought our tab. Without looking at it, we each tossed a twenty on the table.

Bert Saginaw's problem in Silicon Valley was that he considered himself a peer of the venture capital guys. Like them, he was in his early forties. Like them, he had no particular passion for this tech nonsense, but rather for big money. Like them, he was babysitting a bunch of twentysomething geeks who spoke a different language.

The venture capitalists saw Bert Saginaw in a different light. Had they known he considered himself their peer, they would have laughed themselves sick. Where they were California-fit in that tall, rangy way, he was a bandy-legged deadlift-and-bench-press guy. His Dockers, his weird hard-sell charisma, his strawlike hair that ran shaggy because he didn't cut it often enough . . . none of it worked in that time and place. He drove a Pontiac, he thought vegan was a planet on *Star Trek*, he thought Napa was an auto-parts store.

He was, in short, a mark.

"All of this would have been forgiven," Randall said as we rose and stepped past the band to the parking lot, "had not Bert Saginaw committed the ultimate Silicon Valley gaffe: On the day he walked into the venture firm's Palo Alto office to sign for the five million dollars that would lead to the IPO that would make everybody rich, he actually asked the lawyers in the glass-walled room for advice."

They were, of course, corporate counsel. A woman and a man,

neither yet thirty, both dressed in black slacks and pale blue shirts. They must have been experienced, because they managed not to break out in laughter while urging him to sign.

"Oof," I said.

"He signed himself out," Randall said. "He signed himself poor. The way the VCs see it, anybody who doesn't bring his own lawyer to the table deserves whatever he gets."

"How did Saginaw's geeks do?"

"A year later, they were all millionaires. On paper. *Five* years later, they were all flat broke. Thus do bubbles burst."

"Once again," I said, "Saginaw and his sister earned the chance to remind each other they'd been screwed by The Man."

"Yes. They believe with rock-solid confidence . . . no, it's more than that, it's *fervor* . . . that the world has screwed them over not once but twice."

"And they'll never get screwed again."

"Never."

"Even if that means . . ." I made a question with my eyebrows.

"Who can say?" Randall said.

"Huh."

We were quiet for a minute. Finally I said, "How'd you learn all this in a day?"

"Googlepedia, mostly. Are you headed for Charlene's?"

"Sure." But I paused before I said it, and knew Randall picked up on the pause.

"Good," he said. "You should." He pulled his car key, pressed its unlock button. I saw the interior light go on in the slick little Hyundai he'd recently bought. The car was parked as far from the Chicken Bone's door as you could get and still be in the lot.

"You could park in a handicapped spot once in a while," I said, waving at the vacant ones right in front of us. "You've got the plates, and it's nothing to be ashamed of."

"Right you are," Randall said, but not before staring at me a full five seconds. "Nothing to be ashamed of at all."

Then he pocketed his car key, clapped twice, bent double at the waist, and flipped into a handstand.

Then he walked the twenty yards to his Hyundai.

On his hands.

I was still laughing when he tooted his horn twice and pulled out.

CHAPTER TWENTY

Any sign of Davey?"

It was the first thing I said when I stepped into Charlene's great room.

"No," she said, handing me a tall glass of bubbly water topped with cranberry juice. It's my favorite drink. "And we nearly lost Sophie, too. She spent the afternoon clomping around the woods looking for him. My darling backyard neighbor called the cops. Said he thought it was a prowler, but he knew damn well who it was."

"Where is she now?"

"Bathtub. I chased her up there."

"Why?"

But as I said it, a few things sank in. Charlene had straightened up the room, plumped the sofa pillows. The flat-screen was tuned to a jazz station, and the lights were dim.

So was I. There was something big going on here, and I'd been too wing-stuffed and Savvy-focused to notice.

I looked at Charlene's face, saw her seeing me figure things out. She smiled. She looked sad. "Sit," she said.

"We never talk," she said a few seconds later. We were both on the big sectional. I leaned back. Charlene sat Indian style on the next cushion. She'd showered. She wore a tiny black T-shirt over blue sweatpants that said COLONIALS down one leg.

"Well," I said.

She shook her head. "It's *me* who never talks."

"It is?"

"I make fun of your strong silent type routine, but . . . yes. When it comes to the important things, I'm as guilty as you. We skim. We glide. We get by. Days pass."

I said nothing.

"You don't send big-baby signals the way most men do," Charlene said. "So I forget sometimes."

"Forget what?"

"I forget about the B side of manly-man manliness."

"What's the B side? What are you talking about?"

"The sentimentality, the . . . fragility."

We said nothing for a while. We listened to a slow saxophone.

I decided not to play dumb and make her connect every dot. "Except for the one parole job at the GMC dealership," I said, "I haven't made an honest living since I got out."

"Thank you."

"For what?"

"For knowing where I was going." She lightly raked my cheek with a couple of nails.

"What kind of man," I said, ducking away from the nails, "lives off his girlfriend? What kind of man smiles every month while she pays the mortgage?"

"The answer to that is 'most of them, if they get half a chance.' Sad but true."

"Not me."

"No shit, Sherlock." Charlene smiled. Still looked sad, though. "The way you're expressing the unhappiness isn't doing either of us much good."

"I just want to pay you back."

"No," she said, shaking her head. "You want to *have paid* me back. It's different. You *are* paying me back, starting this month, on the schedule we set up. Impatience is the problem."

"It'll take years."

"What did I just say?"

I swallowed. Hard. "Impatience."

"Men pay their debts," she said. "Look at it that way."

Another song came on. This one had words. About a girl from Ipanema.

"What did you mean before?" I said. "About men being the sentimental ones?"

"There's not much room for sentiment when you're a woman, or a poor one anyway," Charlene said. "Less when you're . . . when you're a . . ."

I waited.

"When you're a whore," she said, rasp-whispering it, eyes locked on the wall now.

"Hell," I said. She'd never used the word before. Not to me. I put my arms around her. I wrapped her up, held her, felt her buck and heave when she began to cry.

Charlene cried hard while a girl sang about the girl from Ipanema. I said "Hey" and "Hell" and "Well" and stroked her hair. I kept my arms around her, let her soak the shoulder of my shirt with snot and tears.

Time passed. Songs played on the TV.

Charlene pushed off, rose, hid her face, pit-patted down the hall to the bathroom.

She was back in five minutes. She stood before me, tears gone, makeup gone, sorrow gone, tiny fists on hips. "One promise, Conway," she said. "One thing. It's *the* one thing. It's all I ask. What have I ever asked?"

I sat. I looked up at her. I wanted to go along. I wanted to so bad.

But my chest went hard.

"*One* thing," Charlene said. "*One* promise."

A jazz song flared, annoyed her. She grabbed the clicker, turned, flipped off the TV.

Then it was quiet.

My mouth was dry. I swallowed.

"She was a Barnburner," I said.

Three seconds later, I was alone in the room.

As Charlene stomped up the stairs, I killed the lights. I hit my knees. I prayed.

I prayed so hard.

I prayed things wouldn't get worse.

While I tried to sleep, they did.

Somebody killed Blaine Lee.

CHAPTER TWENTY-ONE

It's an early household. Sophie's middle-school bus comes at ten of seven, and she needs mucho bathroom time to do whatever girls do in there. I wake up at five every morning no matter what—wish I didn't, but I do—and Charlene can't wait to get to the office.

So the next morning, Friday, at six twenty, Charlene was dressed and gone, Sophie was primping upstairs, and I was news-surfing on my laptop. I clicked over to the *Metrowest Daily News* Web site.

The line above the pic read WESTBOROUGH PIKE FATALITY. The photo was one you've seen a hundred times: heavy-duty tow truck winching a totaled car from the woods off a highway. In this case, the car was red and the highway was Route 90, the Massachusetts Turnpike.

The car, whose hind end was being dragged onto the road by a wrecker that wore BLACKSTONE VALLEY SALVAGE stickers, had an out-of-state license plate. I squinted behind my drugstore reading glasses and leaned in.

North Carolina plates.

Silent alarm in my head. I squinted harder, spotted the Lumina badge on the left side of the trunk.

There was no real news story—just a long caption under the photo. Mass Pike eastbound, one thirty in the morning, one-car accident.

One fatality, male, police withholding the identity until they notified family.

"Blaine." I said it out loud. I called Wu, the state cop, not caring what time it was. No answer. Left voice mail.

The staties must have questioned Blaine and failed to turn up anything good. So they cut him loose. A few hours later, he was dead.

Today's plan had been to smoke out the unknown guy in the green Expedition, but that would have to wait: I needed to find out what happened to Blaine Lee. Hollered a good-bye up the stairs.

Forty-five minutes later I stood between two ranch houses that had the state's busiest highway in their backyards. The day had turned up cold, but there was no wind and the sun felt good on my face. I wore black Dickies work pants and a gray Dickies work shirt, and my left arm crooked a long aluminum clipboard with a legal pad attached.

When a sixty-something-year-old man stepped from the front door of the house to my left, I didn't even look at him. I made notes instead. Let him think whatever he wanted to think. Let him stew.

He glanced at my F-150. It's plain-Jane white, an old landscaper's long-bed. No frills. It may be the last vehicle in America with hand-cranking windows. Just for kicks, I'd recently swapped in a Mustang's V8 and automatic transmission. While I was at it, I'd lowered the suspension some and dug up a set of wider-than-stock black steel wheels. Now the truck handled better than any pickup had a right to.

I'd left it idling in the street, facing the wrong way, flashers on, to lay down an *I'm-with-the-state-so-I'm-a-rude-prick* vibe.

The truck, the clipboard, the Dickies and my attitude all worked. The man—gray stubble, white sweater, berry-colored pants—didn't like me standing on his property ignoring him. He worked up the stones to cross his yard.

As he did, I dotted a final imaginary *i* harder than I needed to and pretended to notice him for the first time. I gestured with my pen. "Did you cut the chain link fence, sir?"

He swung his head toward the back of his yard, which ended in the wooded embankment that rose to the highway. Then he swung back. "Hell no I didn't!"

"Because that fence belongs to the people in the form of the Mass Highway Department and the federal Department of Transportation, sir. And somebody's going to have to repair the people's fence."

"Jumpin' Jiminy!" he said, his face going red, his voice stronger than I would've guessed. "The staties cut the fence to get to the wreck!"

"What wreck is that?"

He goggled. "Jesus H. Jumpin' Jehosophat, aren't you *here* about the wreck?"

"Wrecks aren't my department, sir. Fences are my department. Can you tell me which state trooper cut the fence? A badge or barracks number would be helpful. Otherwise . . ." I stood with pen poised.

"Otherwise *what*?"

Behind the man's shoulder, someone raised a sticky window. I pictured his wife leaning to hear the commotion, fretful, a woman with a highway thirty feet behind her kitchen.

He pointed. "Look, pal. Middle of the night last night, a car came off the road right there. Crouch some and you can see where the guardrail's all effed up, pardon my French. The car angled down the bank and hit that elm hard, can you see it? Shook the house, I kid you not. Mother dialed nine-one-one and I lit up the floods. Had 'em installed a few years back, see 'em on the back corner there? Mother wanted the lights because when you're this close to the Pike, you never know what kind of crazies are gonna come around. This is the first time I've needed 'em, and they worked great, lit the place like daylight. One red car buried in that elm, one dead kid. Next thing I know, two staties are driving a cruiser right through my side yard with an ambulance on their tail. A statie took one look up the hill, dug around in his trunk, came out with a big set of bolt cutters, and *that,* partner, is what happened to your goddamn fence! Pardon my French."

I pursed my lips, though the move didn't come naturally to me, trying to look like a bureaucrat caught with his pants down. Made a *hold on* gesture with one index finger, pulled my cell, scrolled through my call list, made a face. "*Now* they tell me," I said. "I'd call it a morning wasted, but the clock starts when they tell me to roll, so I just made two hours' time and a half taking a nice drive."

He was staring at me.

"Fact it was a statie makes it a whole 'nother thing, whole 'nother asshole's problem," I said. "Sometimes they're slow getting the word out."

"Well, I'm . . . I didn't mean to be . . ."

"No sweat," I said, waving off the apology. The jerk bureaucrat was gone; now I was a guy getting money for nothing, happy as a pig in shit. I gestured with the clipboard. "Between the cruisers and the ambulance, they tore up your yard pretty good, huh? I could give you the compensation form for that, the two-forty-six B, but like I said, the staties have their own process. Hell of a crash, huh? And just the one guy?"

"Sure was. Red Chevy, an old heap. Like I told the other guy, they just about needed a shovel to get the kid out."

"Other guy?"

He smiled for the first time, showing the brownest teeth I'd seen in ten years. "Sheesh, the left hand really doesn't know what the right hand's doing, does it? The investigator who showed up not half an hour after the wreck. He sure wanted to take a look at that car, but the staties were already swarming it. So he interviewed me instead."

"If he was an investigator, why didn't he just wade right in?"

"Well . . ." The man squinted. "That's a good question, now you ask it. I got the feeling he wasn't with the staties. Was with somebody else instead, and couldn't do jack sh . . . couldn't do a darn thing about the car til they were done with it. Pardon my French."

Time to take a chance. "Big guy, running to fat maybe? Longish hair? Drove a green Ford Expedition?"

His face lit up. "Yes sir, yes indeed! I couldn't tell you the exact color of the SUV, but it was dark. And you described the, uh, the investigator." He said the last word like a question. The old man was getting nervous, wondering if he'd screwed up. His nerves were making him suspicious.

"I know him all right," I said. *Who is this goddamn guy?*

Something in the old-timer had changed—his stance, his body language. I'd pushed my luck. One more question about the wreck would be one too many. So I asked instead where I could get a good cup of coffee around here, said he and the missus should get some shut-eye, and split.

Headed for Blackstone Valley Salvage, the towing operation that had hauled Blaine's Lumina away. I knew Blackstone Valley Salvage. Knew it well.

I pulled in just before nine and eyeballed the wrecks that had been dropped outside the gates to be pulled apart or crushed by Mikey Guttman, owner of Blackstone Valley Salvage.

We go back. Mikey's dad used to sell motors to a race team *my* dad worked for. I didn't learn about the connection until I bumped into the dad at an AA meeting. Boy, did he have some stories about the way they used to run around together.

Mikey's dad made it out. He had fifteen years' sobriety when I met him.

He was sad when I told him my father's story was different.

Mikey Guttman was about my age and had inherited a perfectly round face, beefiness that seemed like fat if you weren't looking hard enough, and the drunk's gene. He and his dad went to meetings together. I'm not jealous by nature, but that struck me as pretty cool. I'd taken my dad to one AA meeting. But only one.

Two years ago, Mikey's dad died behind the wheel of his favorite Matsushita forklift. Massive heart attack. We were all happy for him: twenty-plus years sober, died working at the company he built.

Mikey hadn't slacked off. Blackstone Valley Salvage was ringed by the longest white fence I'd ever seen. There was brand-new signage, fresh gravel out front where the wreckers pulled in, a used-car superstore for a neighbor.

Mikey and I called each other once in a while, pissing and moaning the small-business blues, so I knew the backstory. Launched when this was a farm village, the salvage yard had a full three hundred yards of frontage on Main Street. The town had grown up around it, had become one of these edge-city suburbs. Panera Bread, Barnes & Noble, Whole Foods. Like that.

The commuters who paid $650,000 for their four-bedroom colonials weren't thrilled that a junkyard owned the biggest footprint on Main Street. Some of them combed the zoning laws and the environmental regs and the traffic studies looking for a way to put the Guttmans under. Like his father before him, Mikey went to all the town meetings and smiled big and silently told his neighbors to pound sand. He could afford to jump through whatever hoops they set in front of him: He owned the property free and clear. He was making big money, much of which came from a no-bid contract with the Massachusetts Turnpike Authority.

Which was why I was here.

Blackstone Valley Salvage wasn't especially near the Mass Pike—I could take you to a half-dozen junkyards that are closer—but every abandoned, seized, or crashed vehicle found on a thirty-five-mile stretch of that highway was, by rule, hauled to the Guttman place.

And those wrecks were hauled by the Guttmans' fleet of tow trucks and flatbeds.

Talk about a license to print money.

If you had a dozen lawyers and enough patience, you could track the sweetheart contract back to the time when Mikey Guttman's dad and Moe Coover were AA buddies—the state police work *very* closely with the Turnpike Authority.

See how Massachusetts works?

Lucky timing: As I crunched to a gravel stop, Mikey stepped from the cinder-block office building and moved toward a new black-cherry-colored F-350 Crew Cab that had to cost fifty grand.

I said, "Clocking out to play eighteen holes?"

"Conway!" Moon face, big happy smile. "What the hell, brother? A round of golf sounds just about right, the bullshit I'm dealing with. Come see my new toy. It's cool as hell. It's also busted. Again."

We hopped into his truck, which I complimented, and thumped down dirt paths straight as city streets that were lined by stacks of dead cars. In less than three minutes we pulled up at what looked like the world's biggest sewing machine on a flatbed trailer. In the center of the sewing machine was a sort of mouth, and in the mouth was an old Buick Roadmaster cocked at an ugly angle. One man was trying to unwedge the Buick with a forklift. He wasn't having much luck. Another man looked on, occasionally pressing buttons on what must be a remote control unit.

"Frick and Frack got their tit in a wringer right now," Mikey said, "but it's a sweet new crusher from Granutech. Once we get the hang of it we can use it to bale four cars at a time, and it's so quiet my pain-in-the-ass neighbors haven't even griped."

He killed the F-350. We hopped out. Mikey got his workers' attention and made a throat-slashing gesture. They stopped what they were doing. Mikey hopped on the forklift himself and took a long look at the Buick. Ninety seconds later, it was straightened out. In another thirty it was about the size of your living-room sofa.

What happened next was, along with the no-bid Mass Pike deal, the key to Blackstone Valley Salvage's success. Instead of telling the workers what assholes they were, or making some do-I-gotta-do-everything-around-here crack, Mikey called a huddle at the hydraulic controls. He let the guys tell him what had gone wrong, then made a few suggestions, mostly talking with his hands. I smiled at that: Race drivers talk the same way.

"They'll figure it out," he said as we thumped back to the office. "We've only had it three weeks."

While he'd made a lot of concessions and improvements his father would have cussed at, Mikey had left one thing alone: The office at Blackstone Valley Salvage was still a single six hundred-square-foot building built from cinder blocks the father himself had buttered and stacked. There was a counter, a computer, a couple of mismatched teacher desks, a picture window looking out on the main yard, and not much else.

That's how it works in a small business, or a strong one, anyway. The office was ragged, but it was functional—so Mikey pumped his money elsewhere.

He could afford to upgrade the office if he ever chose to, that was for sure. I'd heard he did $12 million gross revenue. The closest he ever came to bragging was one night at a poker game. College was the subject, and Mikey said none of his kids would ever worry about student loans, that was for goddamn sure. One was at Brown, one finishing up at Duke, the oldest at medical school in Illinois.

Mikey Guttman was doing okay.

Alice, the older-than-dirt admin, wasn't in yet, so it was just the two of us in the office. Mikey brought me a black coffee. After five minutes, we'd run through all the small talk we had.

"Well," Mikey said, sipping coffee.

"Favor," I said.

"Aha," he said.

"I know," I said.

"The casual drop-in," he said. "Not your thing."

"No."

"What then?"

"Red Lumina. One-car wreck on the Pike, early this morning."

Mikey's face went cloudy. That's rare. "Yeah," he said, stretching the word.

"Any way I can get a look at that one?"

"Want to maybe tell me why?"

"No."

"Huh," he said, and used his right foot to start a slow spin in his chair. He must have done it a lot, because he spun exactly 360 degrees.

When he stopped, he was looking at me a different way. A thoughtful way. This wasn't a pie-faced kid who'd lucked into his daddy's company. This was a full-grown man whose small business was thriving in tough circumstances.

"I've pulled nineteen cars off the Pike in the past week," Mikey said. "That's pretty typical. Year to date, let's round it off and say I've hauled eight hundred vehicles off my little golden stretch of roadway, okay?"

He waited for me to say something.

I didn't.

"Of that eight hundred, the state cops have shown interest in about twenty. Usually they're just looking for booze bottles to make a DUI case."

"The staties went through the car? Already?"

"Worse," Mikey said. "Some asshole *claiming* to be a statie."

CHAPTER TWENTY-TWO

I said, "*What?*"

"Or 'investigator,' anyway," Mikey said. "That's what he called himself. Bullied the kid working the overnight. The kid's new. Should've called me, but he didn't want to wake me up."

"And the guy was intimidating. Kind of fat, but plenty big. Long hair, Southern accent."

"Yup."

"Did he have his look at the car?"

"Yeah. Which is bad. We got a little shed where we hold cars the cops want to investigate. Keep 'em out of the rain, you know? Letting an impersonator in there to tear a car apart . . . it's bad."

I said nothing.

"Who *is* he, Conway?"

I said nothing.

Mikey sighed. "So you want the favor but you won't tell me jack shit. That Lumina's generating a lot of heat."

"I get it." I began to rise.

"Did I say no?"

I sat.

Mikey said, "Is this one of those wild-ass Conway missions I hear about from time to time? Saving idiots from their idiotic selves?"

Mikey and I ran in the same circles, but he wasn't a Barnburner. It's the Barnburners I trust. It's the Barnburners I'm loyal to. So there wasn't much I could say.

"Don't believe everything you hear."

"I don't," he said. "But I hear a lot, and if a tenth of it's true . . ." He stood and leaned heavily, both hands on his cheap desk. "I'm gonna skip my round of golf today, same as every day, to help those boys figure out the new crusher." He checked his watch. "We'll be down back for an hour, easy. Alice'll be in around ten. You should be gone by then."

He straightened and left the office without turning.

On his desk, where his right hand had rested while he leaned, sat a Schlage key the color of an old penny.

Six minutes later I put on my work gloves, tucked a flashlight under my armpit, turned the key, and opened the door of a cheapo sheet-steel building the size of a three-car garage. At some point, the door had been sealed by one of those heavy-duty stickers: MASSACHUSETTS STATE POLICE CRIME SCENE DO NOT ENTER REMOVE OR DEFACE. The kid working Mikey's overnight shift must have put the sticker on—procedure, I figured, for any vehicle that was hauled inside. But the big mystery man who'd beaten me here had slit it.

Inside: pea-gravel under foot, smell of power-steering fluid, one lonely fluorescent overhead.

Nothing about the Lumina's front end surprised me. The nose was destroyed from slicing through a guardrail and center-punching a tree. Radiator collapsed, transverse engine moved back a full six inches, unit-body warped, windshield smashed on the driver's side by Blaine's head. I knew if I flashlighted the cracks I'd see his hair and matted blood. So I didn't.

I walked around the car slowly. There wasn't much to see until I reached the left rear corner. "I'll be damned," I said out loud, and squatted.

Aft of the wheel well, the bumper cover and quarter panel were banged up. Deep dent, chewed-up plastic, shattered taillight.

I closed my eyes, pulled up memories to be sure. Any chance this damage had been here before the crash, and I hadn't noticed it? Thought about Blaine standing at his car in the gas station lot, Blaine pulling into a parking space after he followed me.

Hell no. There'd been no damage. Most days I couldn't tell you what color shirt I was wearing, but I *always* noticed busted-up cars.

Blaine had been crashed out. Wrecked on purpose. Murdered. No surprise: just confirmation.

Cops call it a California Stop or a PIT Maneuver, for Police Intervention Technique. But there's nothing tricky or technical about wrecking a guy. You pull alongside him, lay your right front on his left rear, and turn right. He loses the back end of his car and spins. Period. The cops need to make it sound fancy and scientific, but go to your local bullring dirt track and you'll see racers PIT Maneuvering each other twice a lap, all night long.

I looked closer.

In the bumper gouges and quarter-panel scratches, I saw two colors of paint: forest green and gold.

Like the Ford Expedition that was turning up everywhere. Two-tone, the pimped-out Eddie Bauer model.

The SUV had killed Blaine Lee. But who the hell was the driver? And why the hell had Savvy Kane been following him before she was killed?

Checked my watch. I needed to be out of here, with the key back in the office, in fifteen minutes. I rose, knees popping, and looked in the open driver's window.

Jesus.

Mikey'd told me the guy went through the car pretty well. It was an understatement. He'd torn the thing apart. The headliner was slashed. The dashboard vents, popular spots to stash drugs, had been busted out. Ditto the center console and ashtray. Even the plastic trim hiding the windshield pillars had been pried apart, the cavities inspected.

Whoever he was, the guy had tried very hard to find something in this shitbox.

What?

And had he found it?

Whether he had or not, I doubted there was much worth looking for now.

Damn.

I climbed out, stretched, decided to call it a wrap.

But what the hell. I opened the rear door, climbed in, sat, looked around. It was torn apart back here, too. Door panels slashed, carpeting cut—he'd made big Xs, then peeled back the resulting flaps—hell, even the backs of the front seats were gouged, gray vinyl torn and peeled.

I sighed and made a move to climb out.

And felt the seat give.

And not in a normal way. There was a small click as I transferred my weight. I finished rising, stood on gravel next to the open car door, pushed the seat with both hands.

Click.

Huh. I climbed back in and knelt on the Lumina's floorboard, facing the rear seat. Tight fit: The front seats had been pushed way back.

The bean counters who run car companies today don't use a screw or a nut if they can help it. (The Germans are the exception, and I guess that's why I love 'em.) This goes double for interiors. You'd be amazed at how much stuff inside your Acura or Infiniti just snaps together like Legos.

I spread my arms to the far corners of the Lumina's backseat, ran my hands down the gritty back where the pennies and Life Savers end up, felt around for clips.

Bingo: My right hand found one. I finger-felt, figured it out, released it. That side of the seat cushion rose a half-inch.

My left hand found a clip, too. As I'd expected, this one wasn't closed properly; I didn't have to release it. Whoever'd snapped it shut last had done a bad job, had left the seat springy.

I tilted the seat up.

Beneath it: stamped metal, wires for the fuel pump, sand, gum wrappers.

Also a manila envelope, eleven inches by fourteen. Sealed.

I set my flashlight where the car seat had been, pulled my multi-tool, slit the top of the envelope, shook it.

Big pictures.

Color pictures.

Naked pictures.

Well well well.

Into the envelope went the pics. Into my jacket went the envelope.

Down came the seat.

Three minutes later, the Schlage key was on Mikey's desk and I was in my truck.

CHAPTER TWENTY-THREE

I knew just what to do with the pictures.

When Floriano had sold me the F-150, I'd been in the middle of something that required a gun.

I don't have much use for guns. For every time a gun helps a man out of a jam, guns screw up fifty guys. Maybe they get a quick ride to jail because they had to be a big *pistolero*. Or maybe they blow a toe off. Or maybe they get shot in a bar fight that would have ended in nothing more than a good beating except that some jerk had a piece.

At the time, though, I'd been working something hot, and I needed a semiauto where I could get at it. So I'd used sheet metal, rivets, and a piano hinge to rig a hidey-hole between the frame rail and rocker panel of my truck. Had stuffed a handful of giant Ziploc bags and zip ties in to secure whatever I was stashing.

The gun was long gone, tossed in the Hopkinton Reservoir at three o'clock one morning. But the hidey-hole was still there, baggies and all.

To make the big envelope fit I had to fold it in half, then roll it up. Into a Ziploc it went, then into the stash.

I pulled away from Blackstone Valley Salvage feeling pretty good about myself. Feeling smug, feeling smart.

Then a hundred questions hit me, and I didn't feel so smart anymore. Called Randall. Straight to voice mail. Told him to call me.

Saw a text had come in while I was dialing. From Charlene: *Tower Hill 4:00?*

I texted back one letter: *K*. Smiled as I did it. Tower Hill was our place, our spot, even if thinking of it that way made me feel like Harry High School. It was a good place to work through whatever bad spell we were in, to get back on track.

Drove east on back roads, shuffling all the questions raised by the pictures. Told myself I was driving slowly, aimlessly, because I needed to speak with Randall about our next move.

Then the truth hit me and my shoulders dropped an inch.

I once heard a rule of thumb for dealing with people: The thing you don't want to do is always the right thing, always the thing you *ought* to do.

The rule stuck with me for a simple reason: It works. Its truth makes it a pain in the neck, though. Once you learn it, you'll never again buy your own bullshit excuse for not apologizing, or for letting something go unsaid, or for letting a grudge simmer.

Or for not calling a family that just lost a son.

Information had three Lees in Level Cross, North Carolina. I took down all three numbers. Tried Vernon and Margery first. The names just felt right.

And were, I knew two seconds after a woman picked up. Even eight hundred miles away, filtered through satellites and towers and sine waves, she sounded like she wore an anvil on each shoulder.

"Is this Margery Lee?" I said. "Blaine's mother?"

"Yes sir, this is." Background noise told me she wasn't alone. It was easy to picture a small house, a lot of family, casseroles. Everybody brings a casserole.

I told her who I was. "I'm up here in Massachusetts, and I was sorry to hear about Blaine. I didn't know him well, just met him the other night, but he struck me as a good kid."

"I do thank you for that."

"I know Max meant a lot to him. Max and Savvy both."

Long pause. "Max meant the world to him," she finally said.

"Time like this, it's good he has you and Mr. Lee."

"When will Mr. Lee be coming back home, sir? Maybe you all know more than I do. Your state police are nice as can be, but it can be difficult getting information."

"Pardon?"

"I assume Vernon is . . . making arrangements, doing what-all needs to be done?"

"Not sure I understand you, ma'am."

There was a pause as Margery Lee realized I didn't know things she'd assumed I knew.

"My husband Vernon is up there, too," she finally said. "Trying to keep Blaine out of trouble. Working on a project with Savannah."

Holy shit.

"Oh sure," I said, trying to be smooth. "Vernon. Big fella in the big green SUV."

"So you know him." Her voice fluttered as she spoke. Was Margery Lee nervous about her husband? Scared of him, maybe?

"I do," I said. "I do know him."

Quiet.

"Was there anything else, sir?" Margery Lee finally said. "Because I've got a houseful of hungry family and a confused little boy, and I'm afraid there's much that needs tending to."

Anvils on her shoulders.

I said again I was sorry. Clicked off.

My heart rate was up. My breathing was shallow.

Mystery man: Vernon Lee. Blaine's *father*?

But Vernon's SUV had spun Blaine off the Mass Pike. Had killed him.

And when I'd described Vernon to a tee, Blaine had claimed not to know anything about him.

But the stolen plates on the Expedition fit. Vernon must have thought North Carolina plates would make him stand out. So he'd swapped a stolen Massachusetts plate, had grabbed a toll transponder while he was at it. It wasn't a perfect plan—the lack of a state inspection sticker could give him away to a sharp cop—but it was damn good.

Some family. *Man,* did I want to talk with Randall.

I sighed and called Moe again, just to check in. Had called the night before. He hadn't picked up.

He didn't pick up now.

Huh.

Randall called me back. Phew. Said he'd slept in Bellingham at his insurance lady's place. I asked him to meet me in twenty minutes.

He made it to the Honeydew Donuts in Hopedale just after I did. We grabbed coffees, sat in a booth.

Randall nodded at the envelope, which held a loose tube shape. *"Que es?"*

I flipped the envelope, pressed it, smoothed it. Looked over my shoulder. Slid pics across the table.

It was quiet for twenty seconds. "Oh my," Randall finally said.

"Yeah," I said, sliding the shots back into the envelope, tucking the envelope in my flannel shirt.

"Know what you've got there?" he said.

I waited.

"An election lost. A political future derailed."

"Yeah," I said, "but I don't care about that."

His eyebrows made a question.

"What I care about," I said, "is who killed Savvy Kane."

Randall blew on his coffee. Then he sipped. Then again. "Of course," he finally said. "Mister One-Track."

"Blaine Lee and Savvy stashed those pics in Blaine's car." I explained how and where I'd found them.

"Unless Savvy stashed them herself," Randall said. "From what you've told me, she used Blaine as it suited her. She might've hidden the pics in his car without telling him."

"I thought about that," I said, shaking my head, "but it doesn't work. Blaine was a stereo installer. Those guys know car interiors like nobody's business. It would've been his idea to tuck the pics under the seat."

He nodded, buying it. "Blaine and Savvy held the blackmail bait. How'd they come across it?"

"Don't know yet."

"Okay, TBD. However they got it, they had it. Somebody wanted it badly. Savvy and Blaine are dead. So the finger points back at Tinker-Saginaw."

"Maybe. Are you ready for an insane twist?"

Sigh. "Why not?"

"I told you about the mystery man in the green Expedition."

"Yes?"

Randall almost spit coffee when I told him about Vernon. He made me go through my phone conversation with Margery Lee line by line.

"Huh," he said when I finished. "Got any ideas? Because I feel like my head's been turned inside out."

"Savvy, Blaine, and this Vernon," I said. "Living small in North Carolina, feeling poor, *tasting* Bert Saginaw's dough. They come north to work an angle. The partnership falls apart, the way those things always do. Why? Who knows? Maybe the boys didn't like the way Savvy cozied up to Saginaw. Or maybe Blaine and Savvy planned to double-cross Vernon all along."

"She was capable of all that?"

"Hell yes," I said, no hesitation at all. "Savvy was driving this bus."

"Off a cliff she drove it. Sorry. Not funny. Keep going."

"What if Savvy got a look at those dirty pictures, saw her opening, and tried using them to chisel Saginaw? Without telling Vernon or Blaine?"

"Huh. A blackmail handle that didn't expose her little boy, is that what you're getting at?"

"Or herself. Which, tell you the truth, might have been more important to her."

"Charmer."

We were quiet awhile.

Randall finally said, "You're saying she made her play, and Saginaw killed her over the photos?"

I shrugged. "Someone working for him, more likely. But yeah. Then Blaine panicked. Kid was crazy about Savvy. Plus he was in over his head, and he knew it. So he took off with the pics stashed in his car."

"Vernon freaks out," Randall said. "Savvy already hosed him over the *initial* blackmail play, the love-child deal. Now she's dead. For argument's sake, let's say the Saginaw campaign murdered her. Vernon's meal ticket: dead. The pictures give him a second chance at the Bert Saginaw lottery, and now *that* opportunity's slipping away. You can see how desperate he'd be. But . . ."

I knew what he was thinking. "Could a man freak out enough," I said, "to kill his own son?"

"Could he?"

I thought about Vernon Lee in the barbecue joint. I thought about the red mist. "Hell yes," I said. "Besides, I'd bet he didn't intend to kill Blaine. Just wanted to keep him from hightailing south. Have a friendly chat with him."

"Father of the year," Randall said, and thought awhile. "I didn't get much of a look at these much-killed-over photos. Am I to assume they feature Mr. Hubert Saginaw and Ms. Savannah Kane? From back in the day?"

"Well, no."

"What? Who, then?"

"I don't know."

"Explain."

I explained.

When I finished, he held his head in both hands. "That doesn't help your theory, though it doesn't extinguish it. The question remains: How did Team North Carolina obtain the pictures in the first place?"

"I don't know. But you know who might?"

"Who?"

"Margery Lee. Blaine's mom, Vernon's wife."

"She might at that," he said. "Something's rotten in . . . where was it again?"

"Level Cross. Birthplace of Richard Petty. You'll love it there."

He froze, cardboard cup halfway to his lips, as the reason for the meeting sank in. I might have smiled. It's not often I can surprise Randall Swale.

"Come on," he said.

"I could use the help," I said. "Flying's not a good idea for me, you know that. And I'm slammed. I need to talk with Saginaw's ex, just to keep Saginaw thinking I'm working for him. Then I'll show my face at the Escutcheon, for the same reason. And I'm worried about my pal Moe. Vernon tailed me there, and now Moe's not picking up his phone. Need to check on him."

I expected Randall to kid around more before agreeing to head for the airport. But when I finished ticking off reasons on my fingers, he was staring at me with calm brown eyes. "Someday," he said, "you'll have to tell me exactly what Savannah Kane was to you."

Sixteen years ago, Paducah. When night fell, I backed the Bonneville from the hotel room and we took off. The bike's seat was more comfortable now that it wasn't stuffed with money. "South or west?" I hollered over my shoulder to Savvy as we hit top gear. "Either one gets us out of state in an hour."

"Surprise me."

I aimed south for Tennessee.

Getting the hell out of Kentucky was job one. No cop—no *straight* cop—would stash money and cocaine in a motorcycle seat. So Savvy's pal was either some freak poser who wasn't a cop at all or, more likely, a dirty cop.

Dirty cops: cop resources, cop buddies, crook's worldview.

Dirty cops scared me.

Heat slipped from the air as we rode south. Pines against the night sky seemed blacker than black, somehow. Savvy's chin bounced on my shoulder as she dozed.

Union City, Tennessee: I found the part of town I wanted, slow-rolled the streets. I was looking for a junkie or car thief willing to trade his four wheels for my two. It was okay if he lied to me about who owned the car and where he got it—I would lie right back about the Triumph.

No luck. Either it was too early in the evening, or Union City didn't feature the type of degenerate I needed. When a cop in a Winn-Dixie parking lot spotlighted me—out of boredom, I thought at the time, as he didn't even put his Caprice in drive—paranoia hit. I stayed under the speed limit all the way to the city line, then opened the throttle and angled southwest on I-51. We'd spend twenty minutes slicing through Missouri, then hit Arkansas.

We would have made it, too. But I got lazy. I-51 became I-155, and when we neared the Mississippi, I just rolled across the bridge near Boothspoint like I was Fred Familyman with the missus riding shotgun and the littl'uns snoozing in back.

The staties lit me up when I was halfway across, humming past a clever sign that made some sort of pun about leaving Tennessee (Y'all Come Back Now)/welcome to Missouri (Set and Stay Awhile).

Troopers from both states, who must have been hiding and expecting us, came haul-assing up the bridge, closing on me like crazy.

Instinct took over: I pinned the Triumph's throttle, waking Savannah.

The throttle didn't stay pinned for long. When I cleared the bridge's midpoint, I saw a roadblock at its end that would have been over the top in the *Blues Brothers* movie. Had to be a dozen cruisers down there. Like I said, that was the problem with a dirty cop: crook desperation, cop resources. Maybe the Union City cops had a BOLO on the Triumph.

"Hell," I said, kicking the bike out of gear and coasting to drop speed without being run over by the hungry staties.

Savvy began to pound me on the back. "Don't slow, don't slow!" she screamed, thumping my back on each *slow*. "I did *not* make you for a pussy, dude. Go go *go*!"

"Go where?" I pointed, braking as we neared the welcoming committee.

"*Go* fucking *go* you pussy, you faggot, *go*!"

She was rocking now like she wanted to toss herself off the bike. If I hadn't been a drunk, coked-up, motorcycle-stealing derelict myself, I might have wondered what was wrong with Savannah Kane. I might have wondered what a tough broad like her was so scared of.

But at that moment, stopping the Triumph without catching a load from one of the dozen pump-action police-spec shotguns aimed my way was all I could handle. The problem was that all the staties were yelling at once, and most were yelling to put my hands in the air, motherfucker, put 'em in the *air*. Which wouldn't be smart for a man driving a motorcycle. But that's what they were shouting.

Finally, with sirens whining and shotguns cocking and Savvy screaming and state troopers hollering, I got the Triumph whoaed up.

The dirty cop who owned it wasn't but three feet away. He stood at the sharp end of the cop-wedge, arms folded across his down vest. He'd lost the gimme cap but not the half-assed beard.

I looked at him.

He looked at me.

I patted his motorcycle's hot gas tank. "She pulls left just a little," I said.

He took one step and hit me with a right that knocked me off and out.

Bert Saginaw's ex lived in Cambridge. Initially, I'd wanted to talk with her because the blackmail shakedown felt ugly and personal, and from what I understood that summed up the divorce.

But that had been before Savvy died. Now I had a different idea: Maybe the ex could tell me something about the pictures. About

Saginaw's operation. About just how heavy he was willing to get to climb that ladder. *Figure out the blackmail, figure out who killed Savvy.*

I called Moe while I drove. No answer. Spent the rest of the twenty-minute ride calling a half-dozen Barnburners, trying to find someone who'd drop by and check on him.

No takers.

I grew pissed as I listened to their cheeseball excuses. They had doctor appointments, meetings, kids in town, grandkids too. I remembered a time when any Barnburner would drop anything to help any other Barnburner.

I sighed. Or did I? Had it ever been like that for anybody but me?

Finally, I made it to Cambridge. Among the Priuses and Minis, my F-150 was a mastodon. Lucked into a parking spot, walked.

I was looking for an address on the right side of the street, but something to my left—a vibe—made my head swivel that way.

A black dude leaned on the hood of a British racing green Jaguar XJ6. Shaved head. Shades. Turtleneck and jeans that he wore like a seal wears its skin. He was perfectly still, perfectly relaxed. He looked down the slight hill toward Massachusetts Avenue, the main drag. Maybe he was waiting for somebody. Or maybe not. He didn't turn my way, didn't acknowledge me.

But he knew I was there.

I finally spotted a house with the right street number. Looked over my shoulder a few times as I made my way toward it. I wasn't sure why, but it seemed like a good idea to know where that dude was. At all times.

"Katherine Saginaw?" I said a minute later.

It startled her. She dropped her key ring, then leaned to fetch it so quickly that she banged her head on the doorjamb. "Ouch," she said, rubbing her head and finally turning. "What?"

"Sorry about that. Ms. Saginaw?"

"It's Katherine Stoll now, or Katy. And why are you here? As if I didn't know." She quickstepped down the seven steps of the antique colonial's front porch as she said it—annoyed, not intimidated. "I need to get to class," she said, glancing at her watch. She wore beat-up running shoes, jeans and a green hoodie that said LESLEY—but the watch was a chunky men's Jaeger LeCoultre that cost eight grand if it cost a nickel.

"Like to talk to you for a sec," I said as she began a fast walk that would, in thirty seconds or so, dump us into Mass Ave.

The black dude and his Jag were gone.

CHAPTER TWENTY-FOUR

No offense," she said, looking up, hoping to catch a green so she could cross Mass Ave without stopping, "but you might as well have I'M FROM BERT stamped on your forehead. I have no old business with Bert, and God knows I decline to have any *new* business with him, and my seminar starts in . . . three minutes, and so away I go."

She caught her light. Mass Ave traffic had done what it does: come to a grudging, honking, crosswalk-blocking stop that was never more than six inches shy of gridlock.

"What I'd like to talk about," I said to Katy Stoll's back as she strode away, "is pictures of Bert."

"Old Chain Link Jesus? That train has left the station, my friend."

"Not those," I said. "Other pictures. Dirty pictures."

It worked. She stopped, stood dead still, turned. The light changed before she could make it back to the sidewalk. A Toyota Echo with flower stickers on its doors honked at her.

"In here," she said, pointing at a coffee place called Veni Vidi Beanie.

Sitting at a table not much bigger than a stool, I watched her order, then wait for, her VentiGrande-half-caff-Colombo-Mumbazo-latte-lighto-creamo. Or somesuch. I sipped a water. Its label said Mother Nature considered it an honor and a privilege to contribute this particular half-liter of purity to the cause of human enlightenment. A portion of the purchase price would be used to knit sweaters for tree-people.

Cambridge.

Katy Stoll reminded me of one of those brave actresses who hadn't set up a tab with a plastic surgeon the day she turned forty. Stoll was clearly a rich woman who took good care of herself—but she hadn't made a career of it. Longish brown hair parted (sort of) in the middle. Honest brown eyes, lips that were thin but not in a grim way, just-right crow's feet. I tried not to look at her rear end—I was pretty sure you could get arrested for that in Cambridge—but failed.

Like I said, she took good care of herself.

The crow's feet reminded me of Charlene.

I set that aside, focused on Katy as she sat.

"I assume that's the blackmail fodder?" she said, chinning at the manila envelope that just about covered the table. "And who are *you*?"

I said my name. "You jumped to blackmail pretty quick there. Care to say why?"

"Don't patronize me, Mr. Sax."

"Conway."

"I'm not a child, *Con*way. Five days before an election, what could dirty pictures, as you call them, indicate *other* than blackmail?"

She had me there. I tapped the envelope. "The photos are of Bert and somebody else."

"Who?"

"Hard to say."

"Because?"

"Whoever he's doing it with is . . ." I spread my arms, looked around the tiny coffee shop. "I could use a little more privacy to explain. What are you smiling at?"

" 'Doing it'," she said. "Very high school. Possibly endearing."

She blew on her coffee, looked at me, smiling eyes framed by pretty crow's feet. There was a better term. Charlene had drilled me on it the first time I said something—something nice, I thought—about hers. What the hell was that term?

I remembered. "Laugh lines," I said, snapping my fingers.

"Pardon me?"

"Never mind. How about that privacy? Aren't you curious?"

"Of course I am. But first, why are you inflicting this on me? You work for the campaign people, I assume? For Peter Krall? Did I not make it sufficiently clear that for the duration, I am the very model of a modern pol's ex-wife?"

"I needed to see if you were behind these."

"I'm not."

"I know. Had that figured out before we hit Mass Ave."

"In that case, the question again rears its ugly head. *Why?*"

"Habit. You always check the ex."

"Whose habit? You're not a policeman. Are you ex-police?"

"Hell no. The way I heard it, your divorce got ugly and stayed ugly."

"Don't they all?"

"Yes," I said. "They do."

"Aha," she said, toasting me, maybe looking at me a little closer. "Common ground. Tell me about yours."

"Long time ago."

"Children?"

"A boy. He stayed with her."

"Of course he did."

"It was the right move. I was a drunk."

"Of course you were."

"I'm not anymore."

"Be still my heart," she said. "Look. It's been years. I escaped an un-marriage and Bert's freaky mansion in Framingham. He was not ungenerous, I'll give him that. I'm not looking to squeeze additional shekels out of him, and I have no desire for the fifteen minutes of tabloid fame to which I am entitled. So whatever's going on in those photos has nothing to do with me." She rose and swirled her coffee.

I thought I'd lost her.

I wondered how she'd taken control of things.

I liked her.

This Katy Stoll wasn't going to do a damn thing she didn't want to do.

"But," she finally said, sighing, "curiosity killed the cat. Let's head back to my place. You'll find sufficient privacy there."

Checking her watch while I rose and drained my water, she sighed. "Looks like no class for me."

"That makes two of us," I said.

Three minutes later, she keyed the door she'd banged her head on and led me up.

The dark staircase with two 90-degree corners didn't prepare me for her home: Nearly every wall, including load-bearing ones, had been ripped out, turning what looked from the outside like a vanilla colonial into a massive loft. Light came in from all sides. A black-iron spiral stairway led to what I assumed was her sleeping area.

"A complete gut job, courtesy of Bert," she said, sitting on one of two identical white sofas that faced each other across a low table. "I rent the downstairs to two Syrians who pay a full year's rent each January first, bless their hearts."

I was admiring the way the loads that used to be borne by walls had been transferred to a few handsome posts. I was also running numbers in my head.

"Million five for the building, another seven hundred for the gut job?" I said as I sat across from her, tossing the envelope on the table.

"I'm proud to say I have no idea. As I mentioned, Bert did not skimp."

"Still doesn't," I said. "You wouldn't believe what he's paying me to tag along with the campaign for a week."

She sipped what was left of her coffee.

I said nothing.

The envelope sat between us.

A breeze caused a tree branch to scratch a window.

"Well," Katy said.

"Well," I said.

She leaned, unclasped, opened, sat back.

"Aha," she said. "The, ah, the other party's face has been covered by a red dot."

"It's more than that if you look close," I said. "Underneath the dot, her whole head's been scratched away. No way in hell to figure out who she is."

"But these are just prints," Katy said. "What about the negatives? Oops, I date myself. Everything's digital now. What about the original images?"

"The way I hear it," I said, "these are the only copies. Somebody snapped the shots and banged them out on a fresh-bought printer. Then they destroyed the camera and printer."

"You'd be a piss-poor blackmailer to do it that way, wouldn't you?"

"Yes," I said. "Piss poor."

She caught me smiling. "If the woman in the photos can't be identified," she said, "what do you want from me?"

"Her *face* can't be ID'd," I said. "But do you see anything else that might help? In the room? Maybe in the woman's, ah, shape?"

She flipped through a half-dozen shots. "She's no spring chicken, is she? Bert would screw anything in a skirt, but he favored younger Implant Barbie types. And Lady Red Dot is certainly not one of those."

"That's what I thought. Anything else?"

"Oy, look at Bert go, with his famous Elvis lip-curl. He put her through her paces, didn't he?"

"Like he was going for a record."

She laughed. "The room is very generic, too."

It sure was. The pictures hadn't been shot in a hotel room the way you might expect, but in somebody's home. In a bedroom, and a decent one—queen-size bed, two big shades-drawn windows, mid-size flat-screen TV on the wall, highboy dresser in what looked like cherry—but not a master bedroom. It was too impersonal for that. It looked more like the primo guest bedroom in a rich man's place.

I said, "Any chance it's a bedroom at the Framingham house?"

"It's been so long . . ." Katy squinted. "No, I don't think so. Not from my time, anyway. We didn't have any bedrooms with windows laid out that way."

"Look at the high angle. I think they were shot through a peephole up near the ceiling. Maybe a dummy light fixture."

"Whatever you say." Her face was red. I realized mine was, too.

"I can't help you," Katy Stoll said.

"You did, though, in a way. Consider yourself eliminated as a suspect."

"There it is again, the policeman talk. Which loops back to my question, which remains unanswered even now. Why are you here? What is your role?"

I said nothing.

"Are you one of Krall's functionaries? No, that's the wrong word. One of his operatives?"

"Hell no." I finger-traced the envelope's clasp. I didn't meet Katy's eyes. Knew I shouldn't say much of anything to her. But wanted to. Decided to. "Somebody I knew got killed. I'm going to find out why. And by who."

"And this person was . . . someone to you? Something?" Katy's voice was different. Kinder.

"She was something, all right."

I rose faster than I meant to. Strode through the big open room and clattered down the stairs louder than I meant to.

Savvy Kane was the one I betrayed. The last one.

Sixteen years ago, it had taken James Sebelius four days to break me.

That was the cop's name, it turned out. He was with the Kentucky Bureau of Investigation, and he was dirty as hell. He told me these things in a county jail in the middle of the woods somewhere. "If I take you to KBI in Frankfort," he said the second day, cleaning his fingernails with a four-inch knife, "we got ourselves an official investigation." He said it *OH-ficial,* not bothering to look at me curled on the floor, shaking and sweating. "We do it this way instead here in my buddy's cozy old jail, what we got is a nice little chat, nice little just-us conversation."

Sebelius hadn't spoken with me my first day in the cell. I spent the day thinking he was clever as hell, letting me get sick, letting me start a nice case of the DTs.

If he was clever, it was by accident: It turned out he'd spent the first day focusing on Savannah Kane.

Because she was his girlfriend.

Had I suspected that? Sure. But when he told me, with a big smile on his face, he got my attention. I paused in mid-wretch, stared his way. The stainless-steel toilet felt cool on my cheek.

"Old Savvy forgot to tell you 'bout that aspect, didn't she? Miz Savannah is my intended, or was, as our future is looking less rosy by the minute."

Sebelius, who'd been sitting on the cell's only bunk, rose, stepped to me, dropped to a knee, wrinkled his nose against my smell. "I'm gonna fuck her up good, Sax. She's a tough one, don't respond to an honest beating in the hoped-for fashion. Well, let's just see how she responds to a nickel up in Pewee Valley."

I said nothing. If you don't know that sweat can burn and freeze at the same time, you've never been sick the way I was sick.

He moved his face close to mine. "What you do, Sax, you blame the whole goddamn mess on her. The theft of my beloved Triumph, the big-ass drug deal that netted all that money and cocaine, the whole enchilada. We clean you up and buy you a suit. You testify, I ain't gonna lie and say you don't have to. But you'll be clear of Kentucky by the end of the month, which I believe both you and I would enjoy, and you will be a free . . . fucking . . . man. How 'bout it?"

I turned my head 90 degrees to get a whiff of the toilet bowl. That was all it took.

Then I turned to him again, finger-beckoned, waited for him to lean close.

Then I vomited on James Sebelius.

I might have smiled while I did it.

But not for long. He beat me unconscious.

Day three: More of the same except that he stayed out of puking range, using his cowboy boots more than his fists. Three visits, three beatings. I could tell the sheriff who ran the jail didn't like it. He must have owed Sebelius a lot to let it go on.

And on.

And if you want the truth, I wasn't opposed to the beatings. They took my mind off the DTs, the sickness, the eyeball-shrinking horror of withdrawal. To feel the toe of a boot in my kidney, the heel of a boot on my knee, was to *feel*.

Sometime between day three and day four, James Sebelius wised up.

It was a gray morning, and he whistled into the cell slapping a folder on his thigh. I flopped from the bunk, which by gentlemen's agreement belonged to him when he came to beat me, and scrabbled to the toilet corner.

But he didn't kick me. Instead he sat like a schoolteacher and opened the folder. Made a big show of running his finger up and down pages, *Hmmming* and *Ah-haing.*

"Your wife," Sebelius finally said. "She to whom you took a solemn vow shortly before vamoosing to drink and drug your worthless life away. Remember her?"

I said nothing. But the world had tipped. The folder was more powerful than any cowboy boot. I knew I was done, and I guess he knew, too—but he would draw this out, would take a victory lap.

"Your wife, way up there in Becket, Massachusetts? I got bad news, Sax. She's a terrible momma, she is."

"She's *not,*" I said. "Don't."

"Don't what? Don't inform you she's a terrible ole momma, neglecting your fine son when she ain't outright abusing him?"

"Sebelius," I said, dragging myself upright for the first time in thirty hours. I had no particular fondness for my ex-wife—still don't—but she was one hell of a mother. It was the main reason she'd left me. "Don't drag her in. Please."

He shook his head and made an Mmm-mmm-*mmm* sound. "Not the way I see it, stud hoss. I got suspicions, see? And when a man's got suspicions, a man's got to *air* those suspicions. 'Specially a sworn officer of the court such as myself. So what I feel an urgent need to do, I feel an urgent need to pick up the phone and dial whatever you call it up there . . ." He flipped through pages, squinted. ". . . shit but it's a mouthful. Department of Social Services, comma, Department of Children and Families, comma, Child Abuse and Neglect. I feel a need to air my suspicions. Your little boy, your little preschool boy, he'll get pulled out of his rotten momma's home. Neighbors'll watch. Local rag'll put it in the Police Log. You know how it goes."

"Please. Don't. She doesn't deserve it. My *kid* doesn't deserve it. If I had a white flag I'd wave it."

"In that case." The folder snapped shut. Sebelius eye-locked me. "You'll clean your miserable ass up. You'll get a suit and a haircut to make you look like less of a vile drug addict. You'll testify exactly the way I tell you to testify." He slapped his thighs and rose. "You'll put poor old Savannah Kane away for at least five years. Then you'll stick out your thumb and clear the hell out of my state and never look back. We got a deal?" Standing over me, he extended his right hand.

I hesitated, then reached to shake.

He pulled back the right and moved to punch me with the left.

I flinched hard enough to bang my head on the wall behind me.

But Sebelius had been faking. He knew the flinch was more humiliating than the punch.

As his cowboy boots clicked away for the final time, I rested my cheek on the stainless toilet and cried.

CHAPTER TWENTY-FIVE

They sent *you* to haul me upstairs?" I said in the lobby of the Escutcheon. "How'd you come to be low man on the totem pole?"

Emily Saginaw said nothing.

"Or should I say low *girl* on the totem pole? That's it, isn't it?"

Her face went red as she card-swiped and punched the button for the ninth floor.

"Funny how it works when you're the only woman," I said. "You may be the smartest person in the room, but you get stuck taking notes and fetching people from the lobby. You get all the to-dos. What are to-dos called these days? There's a phrase. My girlfriend told me . . ."

"Action items," she said as we passed the fourth floor. Ghost of a smile? "If I told you how many action items I cross off every day."

"But you never clear the list," I said.

We stepped from the elevator. Emily led me through the main room for workers and phone-bank volunteers, the room I'd seen buzzing the other day.

It wasn't buzzing so much.

Maybe a third of the workers were occupied. Another third sat at their desks, arms folded, headsets on, waiting for calls. The rest clotted around coffeemakers and water coolers, talking low. In AA meetings, you hear more than enough layoff stories. The vibe today made me think of employees standing around waiting for the ax to fall.

"Chain Link Jesus fallout?" I said as we crossed to double frosted-glass doors.

"You'll hear in a moment," she said. "Short answer? Hell yes."

The frosted doors opened to a conference room dominated by an ash table shaped like the world's biggest surfboard. Damn thing had to be twenty-five feet long. At the far end, to my left, light flooded from a window-wall.

Around the table slouched Saginaw, Krall, and two top flunkies somebody had called boy-wonder pollsters. The room was flat. Silent. Airless. Everybody stared at laptops.

"Wish I had happier news," one flunky said, "but we are hosed. We are fucked." He noticed the other flunky snickering. "In fact, we are well and truly *ass*-fucked."

"Ease up on the language," I said. "For the lady's sake."

Head-whip. Narrowed eyes. "Or?"

"Or I'll grab your pencil neck and bounce your face off that wall three times."

I wasn't looking at Emily, but she moved her hand in a way that made me think she covered a smile.

"Lighten up," Saginaw said to me. "The kid's right. This thing's not bottoming out."

"When's the last time," the second flunky said, "the *Times,* the *Post,* and *USA Today* all ran the exact same page-one pic two days running?"

"Drudge is having a goddamn field day," the first flunky said.

Saginaw put his head in his hands, his elbows on the table. Krall just spun his chair back and forth, looking at nothing as he chewed the inside of his mouth.

"Our lead hit single digits in last night's internals," Saginaw said to me. "People are talking momentum. People are invoking Scott Brown."

"God*damn* it, Pete," Emily said, her face redder than I'd seen it before, an anger flood that came from nowhere. "*Do* something!"

I'm the one could do something, I thought. *Could show you some pics that make Chain Link Jesus look tame.* I'd spent the short drive from Katy Stoll's place thinking about my move here. It was tempting to be a hero, produce the dirty pics, and say mission accomplished.

But with the dirty pics off Saginaw's worry list, I'd lose all access to him and Tinker both. I'd lose leverage.

I'd lose my chance to catch Savvy's killer.

Another factor: The con's instinct to play it close. Same reason I'd held Vernon Lee back from Wu. Info is cash. Nobody gets a freebie.

So the photos were rolled up in my truck's hidey-hole.

Saginaw said, "It's not his fault, Em."

"She's right, though," Krall said, rising. "We *do* need to quit crying and get after it. Look, deep down we all knew this day was coming. Let's get past it. Let's change the narrative. You say momentum? You say single digits? I say a seven-point lead the Friday before the election, and I say that's a damn landslide. Now let's go work our plan, work our firewall."

It was a good pep talk. It straightened spines. Krall pounded from the room without looking back, flunkies hot on his trail.

"I hope he can peddle that horse shit to the volunteers," Emily said.

"If he can't, nobody can," Saginaw said.

"Except you," Emily said.

Saginaw half-smiled. "Except me."

"About those Jesus pictures," I said to Saginaw. "What the *hell*?"

He sighed, looked at his sister. "Tell him."

She did.

Condensed version: Saginaw Fence Co. grew large enough to get the attention of the two national chains he was competing with. The chains started a price war. Bert decided to fight back with a public relations war.

"I'm guessing that was a bad idea," I said.

"Instead of hiring professionals," Emily said, "my dear brother got it in his head he could handle this PR battle against a pair of hundred-million-dollar companies, one of which was publicly held, on his own."

"*Definitely* a bad idea," I said.

"It's true what they say about you," Emily said. "You're not that dumb after all."

"Dear diary."

Her eyes crinkled and she went on.

Like all PR newbies, Saginaw thought the whole world would be interested in his piddly-ass problem. He wrote what he considered a pretty decent press release. It was so bad, so full of indignation and one-sidedness and typos and personal insults, that its entertainment potential struck the editor of the *Worcester Free Press,* one of those alternative newspapers you saw tossed on sidewalks outside rock clubs.

The editor drove to Bert Saginaw's home, photographer in tow, to profile Bert Saginaw. Emily didn't like it; she knew it was a setup. But Bert was in red-mist mode over his price war, and the *Free Press* was the only rag that had responded to his press release. He spent a cloudy afternoon doing the full sit-down interview. By the end of the three hours, the editor had everything he needed—including the knowledge that Saginaw was proud of his workout routine and the resulting physique.

After a huddle, the editor and photog hit Bert with the idea. You know how *Rolling Stone* did these amazing cover pics that the entire industry talked about for weeks? Starlets in their panties, rockers covered in blood, shit like that? Well, they had a crazy notion of how to make Saginaw pop, really *pop,* on the cover of the *Worcester Free Press.* The drawback, the editor said—stroking his beard, baiting his trap—was that the idea only worked if Mr. Saginaw was willing to take off his shirt . . .

The photo had run over the headline CHAIN LINK JESUS. The article became an instant classic in alt-journalism circles: This asswipe cartoon capitalist hanging himself in thirty-five hundred well-crafted words.

"Wow," I said when I realized Emily was done. "How long ago was this?"

"Eight years."

I turned to Saginaw. "Like Krall said, you had to know it'd all come out when you ran for office."

"We thought we could overcome it," he said. "It's why I'm playing second fiddle. It's why I hitched a ride with sweet Betsy Tinker."

"We can overcome it," Emily said. "We *will* overcome it."

Saginaw said nothing.

Me too.

After a minute or so, I rose and left.

As I drove to Winthrop to check on Moe, I thought things through. Or tried to.

My phone rang once. It was Wu. "That didn't take long," I said out loud. He must want to talk to me about Blaine Lee. I didn't blame him. I also didn't pick up.

Pulled into Moe's driveway as a 727 screamed past, ducked involuntarily as usual. Wondered how long you had to live here before you stopped doing that.

Up the steps, into the enclosed porch. With the morning sun around back of the house, it was chilly.

Moe's photo gear was set up.

No Moe, though.

I said his name. Nothing.

The door to the house itself hung open. I stepped in and said his name, louder this time, knuckle-rapping door glass.

Nothing.

I stepped inside.

It stank in here.

"Moe?"

Walked through the parlor, through what was supposed to be a dining room but was crammed with junk. The stench worsened as

I walked. I moved slower as I neared the kitchen. Nightmare pace: My legs seemed to work fine, but the doorway refused to draw closer.

"Moe?" I just about whispered it, finally stepped into the kitchen.

The smell—shit, ammonia, maybe something else beneath—nearly knocked me over. I began to breathe through my mouth only. But the ammonia cut through, stinging my throat.

I looked left, around a corner formed by a half-assed pantry.

It took a few seconds to grasp what I was seeing.

My friend Moe Coover, a WWII guy, a Barnburner back when they called themselves Barnstormers, a man who'd shaken hands with AA's founders, lay dead on the floor.

His head was near the oven door.

His hands were held up in the *I surrender* pose, knuckles resting on linoleum that hadn't been updated in fifty years.

His pants were down around his knees, his ridiculous old-man's privates dangling in the open.

His face was covered by his own diaper.

They'd pulled down his pants and torn his diaper off.

They'd smothered him with it. They'd forced his own yellow shit down his throat.

"Moe," I said. "Oh Moe. Oh God. Oh Moe."

I looked down at my hands. They were shaking.

I forced myself to him, forced myself to a knee, forced myself to peel back the diaper, to make sure.

His chest moved.

"Moe?" I said. Set my hand on his chest, felt it fall and rise.

"Moe! It's Conway. *Breathe,* Moe. *Breathe.*" Pulled my cell, dialed 911 as I spoke.

Six minutes later, God bless 'em, the EMTs crash-carted their way in and I eased my way out. By the time the first white-on-black Winthrop police Charger slammed down Moe's block, I was driving around the corner, making my way back to the main drag.

I drove to a drugstore I'd passed on my way in. Parked near the back corner, wobbled over to the Dumpster, puked. Wiped as much shit from my hands as I could, went in the store. Bought water, toothpaste, toothbrush, paper towels, disinfecting wipes. Ignored the clerk's wrinkled nose while I paid. Cleaned up, brushed teeth, climbed back in my truck.

I was shaking. I was colder than I should be. I fired the truck, blasted the heater.

Think it through.

It hadn't been neighborhood creeps who'd attacked Moe: Twenty-five grand worth of kick-ass photo gear sat untouched on his porch.

So look at it square: He'd been attacked because of me. By this fucking Vernon in the green Expedition. Had to be him. *And you led Vernon right to Moe's house the other day because you couldn't spot a goddamn big-ass SUV riding your bumper.*

But what had Vernon wanted from Moe? Had to be information, but what? I pushed puzzle pieces around. Vernon had wiped out Blaine, had smothered Moe . . .

My mouth dropped open.

I looked at my knuckles on the steering wheel. Death-grip white.

Vernon Lee killed Savannah Kane.

I'd been hung up on the Saginaw people because Bert had a lot to lose. But so did Vernon, as far as he was concerned. This was a brass ring like he'd never seen in his low-rent life. And wouldn't again, and he damn well knew it.

Maybe Blaine and Savvy had double-crossed Vernon. Or maybe Blaine had talked Savvy into forgetting about the whole blackmail scam.

Vernon had gone wild. Vernon had gone on a no-holds-barred tear. He'd chucked Savvy off an air-conditioning unit in Charlestown. He'd run his own son through a guardrail, accidentally or not. But all the killing hadn't done him any good: He still hadn't found the blackmail pics. So maybe he was flailing, caught in a red mist of his own. With Blaine and Savvy gone, the nearest target was me. Moe was just a connection. Nothing more.

Vernon Lee killed Savannah Kane.

So face it. This was on my shoulders. This was for me to live with.

This was for me to avenge.

I was still shaking.

But I wasn't cold anymore.

CHAPTER TWENTY-SIX

Sweet hot fury. Warms the belly, makes a man feel limber.

Racers call it the red mist. It shoves aside your judgment, your common sense, everything you know about the laws of physics. When you're watching a race on TV and one driver tries a boneheaded pass, a pass he never had any chance of making, and he wipes out at least two cars, and you ask yourself: *What the hell was he thinking?* The answer is that he wasn't. The red mist took him over, made him stupid. For a few seconds there, the driver didn't care if he lived or died. By God, he was gonna make that pass.

Now here's the problem: One out of a hundred times, you actually pull off a red-mist move. You make a pass that looked impossible, or save what looks like a done-deal spin at 165 mph.

Result: Everybody says you're a wheel man. Everybody says you're a stud.

Which guarantees you'll try ninety-nine more boneheaded red-mist moves.

Ask any racer.

Sweet fury, red mist, was a specialty of mine for a long time. On the track, it helped me build my rep—then helped cost me my ride. Off the track, it saved my life more than once. But it put me in some bad spots, too.

Funny thing: My value to the Barnburners was built around the red-mist days—days when walking into some jerk's home or office, slamming his nose on a counter, and snapping a couple of his fingers for good measure was no harder for me than buying a soda—but the older I got, the less I liked all that. I had to pump myself up, get a good mad on, fake the fury sometimes.

No need to fake now.

What I *did* need was to find him. Vernon Lee of Level Cross.

Which shouldn't be a problem, since he kept finding me.

So drive. Act natural, eyeball the mirror.

I did.

And planned.

I called Mary Giarusso, Barnburner gossip queen, and told her about Moe. I knew she'd pin down which hospital they were taking him to, would bang the jungle drums. The Barnburners would feel guilty about ignoring my earlier calls for help. They'd rally around Moe.

Trundled through a Dunkin' Donuts drive-through. No Vernon. Kept one eye on my mirrors as I slowed for the toll booths at the Ted Williams Tunnel.

Where there were a half-dozen blue-and-gray state police vehicles waiting for me, along with Winthrop, East Boston, and Logan Airport cruisers. Mostly Crown Vics, but a couple of Ford Explorers for good measure, one of them a K-9 unit.

At least ten semiautos were pointed at me.

I didn't even put my truck in park—didn't want to move my hands that much. Instead: I stopped just after the toll booth, wrists on steering wheel, hands up.

The one who opened my door was the one who'd been running the show at Braxton High: tall, silver near–buzz cut, greyhound body. "Detective Wu would like to speak with you," he said. "Check that. Detective Wu would *very much* like to speak with you."

"A K-9 unit?" I said, looking around the concrete canyon we were in. "What'd you think, I was going to run off through a swamp?"

Traffic in both directions was a mess, everybody swivel-heading at the scene. So while two young staties cuffed me and politely elbow-walked me to a cruiser, it wasn't hard for me to spot the green Ford Expedition dropping into the tunnel. Gold trim. Eddie Bauer package. Vernon Lee couldn't have been more than a quarter-mile behind me when I was pulled over.

Hell.

A couple hours later, I walked out of the state police barracks at Logan Airport's Terminal D. The staties had driven my truck here. Wu had said it was a courtesy. Then he'd sat opposite me in a pale-blue cinder block room, yellow legal pad in front of him, and had begun asking questions.

The drugstore clerk near Moe's place had dimed me out. Pretty smart of her, really: A non-local had come in smelling of shit, with puke at the corner of his mouth, and bought all sorts of cleanup supplies just as the neighborhood exploded with sirens. She phoned my license plate to the Winthrop cops.

"Moe Coover was a friend, huh?" Wu had said once I walked him through the basics. "So you called nine-one-one and fled the scene. With friends like you."

"I waited till the EMTs showed up. Wasn't much more for me to do."

"Except maybe hang around awhile and help us do our job."

I said nothing.

"You keep popping up, Sax. You gotta know that bugs a guy like me."

"What's the latest on Savannah Kane?"

"Accidental death by misadventure." Pause. "Unless you got something more to say about it."

I said nothing.

"Persuade me, Sax. I'm persuadable. I'm persuadable as hell."

I said nothing.

Wu's cell, sitting on the table, buzzed with an incoming text. He read it. Then he stepped from the room.

In less than a minute he came in again. Left the door open, stood with his back against it. Made an exaggerated sweep with his right arm.

I looked a question at him.

"Beat it," he said.

It could only mean one thing. "Moe came to," I said. "He described the guy."

"Beat it."

I may have smiled as I walked out. Moe was okay.

In my truck I texted Charlene I'd be a few minutes late for our meeting, then got the hell out of Logan. At the first rest area on the Mass Pike, I climbed from the truck and double-checked my hidey-hole—didn't trust the staties as far as I could throw them. Courtesy, my ass.

But their search hadn't been thorough, and the dirty pics were still there. I climbed back in and hit the throttle.

Tower Hill Botanic Garden is in a town called Boylston, ten minutes north of Charlene's house. They've got indoor hothouses with a zillion kinds of plants. I guess the plants and flowers are rare. Charlene says they are; truth be told, most of 'em don't look like much to me.

To us, it was the location and the grounds that made Tower Hill worth visiting. It sits on a slope that rolls to a big reservoir. Lots of grass, lots of hiking, blazing colors in the fall.

It was dusk when I got there, and the volunteer lady was ready to close up. I only wheedled my way in because the lady knew Charlene was waiting.

Rolling up the drive, I thought about what Tower Hill really meant to us.

It was where we became a couple. It was where we became a family, or tried our level best to, before Charlene's daughter Jesse hit hard times and everything flew apart.

When we first got together, neither of us had a whole lot of experience dating. Experience with the opposite sex? Not a problem. Experience getting to know someone, caring for someone? That's plenty different.

Other than AA commitments, coffee sessions with carloads of Barnburners, and maybe a McBurger here and there, Tower Hill was the first place we went for a date. Charlene had read about it, and the article had lit off a half-buried memory that she'd once enjoyed gardening.

It had been our favorite spot ever since that first date. I remembered standing by a fountain, looking around like a boy at a high school dance, taking her hand. I remembered how nice it felt. It was the first hand I'd held in a long time.

We became grown-ups at Tower Hill. It became our place. We ate in the little café. Charlene signed up for the mailing list. The old ladies who ran the place knew our names, thought we were cute.

One August afternoon a few years back, an old Chinese guy who must have been half mountain goat caught us making love in our secret spot where the tall grass met the trees, a full quarter-mile from any building. Instead of pretending not to see us, he began whacking my ass with his walking stick like we were a pair of mongrels going at it in his front yard. I never saw Charlene laugh so hard, before or since, clutching me with legs and arms as I fended off the walking stick and cursed the Chinaman.

The memory still made me smile as I passed Charlene's Volvo and headed for the big greenhouse where we always met.

Hint one that this would not be a happy meeting: Charlene stood outside the greenhouse. She's chilly by nature, and she was underdressed in a baby-blue cardigan that didn't match her business clothes at all—she must have rummaged through her car for it.

Hint two: Her jiggling, arms-crossed stance as she waited. Charlene is the stillest person I've ever known.

All this slowed my pace. Maybe I even stepped quietly. Maybe part of me knew what was coming before she turned.

I was two feet away when she did. I startled her. She got over it fast.

"You're late," she said.

"I texted," I said.

"Still," she said.

"Aren't you cold?" I said.

"There are people inside," she said. "Walk to the Secret Garden?"

We walked. When I reached for her hand, she used it to adjust her purse strap.

"What gives?" I said.

At the exact same time, she said, "Clearly things are not working."

We stopped walking. We faced each other. The day's last shot of sun slashed past my right shoulder. It caught her hair in a certain way. So did a wind gust. Behind her, tiny burnt-orange leaves sailed from a half-dozen trees. The trees were from someplace special. I couldn't remember where.

"I'll stop," I said.

"Stop what?"

"I'll stop with the Barnburners stuff."

"But you won't," she said, stroking my cheek with the back of a hand. "You won't, will you? Think it through. Tell the truth."

China? Japan? Japan sounded right. They looked like regular trees, regular leaves, but in three-quarter scale. That seemed very Japanese.

"No," I said. "I won't." My throat was dry. I swallowed. "Will I?"

"You won't." She eye-locked me. "Tell me about Savannah Kane."

"You know we had a thing. It was before you and me."

She shook her head, annoyed. "There's more. *Tell* me, Conway. Please."

I looked in Charlene's eyes. They were the color of the ocean in ads for the Bahamas. "I, ah," I said.

She waited.

"I betrayed her."

"Nonsense. Betrayal is impossible for you, it's . . . it's the *opposite* of you."

"I betrayed her."

Charlene waited, knowing there had to be more.

Sixteen years ago, in Kentucky's Franklin County Courthouse, in a thrift-store suit that made me look like a clown who ran a funeral home, I spoke exactly the words James Sebelius had coached me to say. He'd trained me well. I spoke the words so unvaryingly that the judge called both the prosecutor and the exasperated defense lawyer for a little chitchat. I couldn't make out her words, but the judge smelled a rat. No matter. When the defense lawyer asked me slightly different questions, trying to throw me off or expose a lie, I just said my words again.

The judge—it wasn't a jury trial—had no choice but to convict Savannah Kane of Possession of a Controlled Substance Totaling Greater than Two Ounces, Intent to Distribute, and a half-dozen pissant charges Sebelius and his buddies had piled on. Due to Savvy's existing record and state mandatory-sentencing rules, the judge had to send her to the Kentucky Correctional Institution for Women in Pewee Valley for no fewer than sixty-one months.

After the sentence was read, I did slide in two words Sebelius hadn't authorized: *I'm sorry,* mouthed as Savvy stared straight at me with dead eyes.

She saw the words, I knew she did.

"It was before I sobered up," I said. "Savvy was . . . Savvy was the last person I betrayed."

She got it. Her pupils tightened. She again set a hand on my cheek. Left it this time. "Your vow. To yourself. When you got straight. No more betrayal."

I took her hand from my cheek, held it in both of mine.

"And in your mind," Charlene said, "failing to catch her killer is the same as betraying her."

"Again," I said.

"Again," she said. "And that's more important than . . ."

"Than anything."

"Than me."

"No."

"Yes. Face it. Admit it."

Her hand was cold. I rubbed it. I began to speak. Couldn't. Swallowed again. Charlene knew the word I was trying to make before I made it. She was already nodding.

"Sophie," I said.

"It'll be hard," she said.

"It'll kill her," I said.

She whipped her hand from mine. "It will *not*. It will hurt. It will ache. I'll field endless questions. But it will *not* kill her. Man-deprivation is not fatal, despite what men seem to think."

"How about father deprivation?"

It was a big roundhouse slap, not a cheesy little Audrey Hepburn slap. It hurt my neck.

Japan wasn't right. Indonesia? Why couldn't I remember where those trees were from?

The sun dropped so quickly this time of year. Charlene's face was in shadow now. Hands on hips, she shivered with cold or rage or both.

I wanted to take her in. I wanted to envelop her. She'd liked when I did that.

I couldn't do that anymore.

"My cats," I said.

"Yes," she said.

"My stuff," I said.

"Yes," she said.

"Has Davey turned up yet?"

"Not as of this morning," she said.
"Oh hell, Charlene," I said.
"I know," she said.
"Have you told her?" I said.
"No," she said.
"I'm sorry," I said.
"I know," she said.
I put my arms around her.
She resisted.
Then she didn't.
We stood that way a long time.
Her tears soaked my shirt.
Or maybe they were mine.

CHAPTER TWENTY-SEVEN

I hit Massachusetts General Hospital just after seven o'clock. Forcing myself to unwrinkle my nostrils—I hate hospital smell, never have gotten used to it—I stepped into Moe's room. Four beds, four old men, three TVs running. Moe's was turned off.

"Hell," I said, zinging shut the curtain for whatever privacy we could get.

"Hey!" he said. "If you tell me a jet crashed on Runway Four, I'll kick your ass."

I tried to smile. Moe looked so small, so old, so *white*. How was it hospitals leached the color out of everything and everyone?

"Jesus, Moe. If I could say how sorry I am. If I could undo it."

We were quiet awhile. Battling TVs turned up to old-man volume, the smell, the white-on-white of the tape that held a needle in Moe's skinny arm.

Hospitals.

"He asked about you," Moe said. "He, ah . . . he found me on my porch. He said 'let's talk,' picked me up by the collar and the seat of my pants, carried me inside like a sack of oranges. *Big* fucker, Conway. *Strong* fucker."

I waited.

"Inside, he started pounding on me while he asked about you. How did you hook up with Saginaw, what was your lever. Like that."

"Anything else?"

"He had pictures on his mind. Kept asking about the pics, the shots, the *real* ones he called 'em. I said what the hell are you talking about. He got pissed." His voice cracked, shook.

"Take it easy."

But he locked eyes. He wanted me to hear it. "See, when he picked me up to carry me in," he said, "he found my diaper. It disgusted him. Hell, it disgusts *me*. I'd advise you to never get old, but it looks like you're doing okay on that front."

Moe Coover half-laughed. The other half was a sob.

Three TV shows blared. A machine on a rolling cart beeped and booped.

"I guess he decided I wasn't going to tell him about pictures or any other goddamn thing," Moe said, "because he got this look on his face, half amused, half schoolyard-mean. And he reached down my pants and whipped out my diaper like a . . . like a fucking magician pulling a dove from his sleeve . . ."

"Moe."

". . . and he was smiling when he held it over my face, Conway. Smiling and wrinkling his nose, the way you are now. It's the last thing I saw, last thing I thought I'd *ever* see, this guy smearing my diaper over my face and holding it good."

Then Moe began to cry. "I haven't told anybody else," he said. "Not the details. I had to tell you."

I half-rose. I kissed my friend's forehead.

I didn't know what else to do.

I sat.

"I don't know if this helps," I said, "But the dude, Vernon's his name, is done. I'm going to take care of him."

He looked at me maybe fifteen seconds. "Knock it off, Conway. Don't make things worse."

"He killed Savvy, too."

"So let the cops get him."

"Cops don't even know he exists. But I do. Just a matter of tracking him down. And then he's . . . he's all done."

Even now, Moe was sharp. He looked at me hard. "How is it the cops don't know he exists?"

I said nothing.

We sat awhile. At some point I guess I took Moe's hand.

He faded. The beeps and boops on the machine changed rhythm. A nurse came in, checked the IV bag. I could tell she wanted me to leave, but her fussing woke Moe. "Don't worry," he said to the nurse, "I'll chase this asshole out in two minutes."

Her expression said that was ninety seconds too long. But she split.

"What did the others tell you on your way up?" Moe said.

"What others?"

"The Barnburners," he said. He sounded surprised. "They left just before you got here. Want to find you, read you the riot act." He laughed some. "You're in deep shit."

Three minutes later, I stepped from the elevator and looked for signs to the chapel.

Because where else would a group of drunks be?

When I walked in, I nearly laughed. It was Mary Giarusso, Carlos Q, and Butch Feeley. The funny part was that without realizing it, they'd set up the chapel like a Barnburners meeting—three seats at the right front corner of the room, near the altar, arranged kitty-corner so they could see anybody who came in. They'd even found the only three folding chairs in the joint.

"You could've sat in the pews, guys," I said, making my way toward them. "They look pretty comfy."

"Shut up and sit down," Butch said.

Whoa.

I sat in the front pew. It was like facing the parole board again.

"The fuck is wrong with you, man?" said Carlos Q, the Colombian. It came out *The fock is wrong witchoo, mang?* Carlos Q sounded exactly like a bad *Scarface* impression. But as far as I knew, nobody'd ever been dumb enough to tell him so.

"How many meetings have you been to this month?" Mary said.

"It's not a numbers game," I said.

"Hell it's not," Butch said. "Bring the body, the mind follows. Leave the body at home . . ." He shrugged.

I bowed my head. I would take it. I deserved it.

"When's the last time you checked in with your sponsor?" Mary said.

"A while," I said.

"Six weeks!" she said. "Yes, I checked. Don't look at me that way, Conway Sax. I'm *worried* about you."

It was quiet awhile.

"We're all worried," Butch said.

"The things you do, the burdens," Carlos Q said, tapping his shoulders. "Heavy. Maybe too heavy too long."

"No," I said. "I can take the load."

"Then take it," Butch said. "Bear it. Or pass it along to someone who can."

They all rose at once, filing past me on their way out. "Please fold the chairs before you leave," Mary said.

"Yes, ma'am."

"If there was a coffee urn," she said, not liking my tone, "I'd make you clean it. If I could find a mop, and believe you me I looked, I'd make you swab the floors. Do you some good."

Carlos laid a meaty hand on my shoulder. "Serious AA," he said.

"For serious people," I said, completing the Barnburners motto.

Butch came last. "I want you to do ninety meetings in ninety days," he said. "Get you some routine. Get you some humility."

"Yes, sir."

"Don't 'sir' me. I work for a living."

"Yes, sir."

It was an old joke between us. But neither of us smiled this time.

They left me alone.

I knelt.

I tried to pray.

But couldn't.

It happens. It's a bad sign. Means I'm all screwed up in ways I half understand. But only half.

Frustrating.

I hit my knees, steepled my hands.

I tried.

It didn't take.

"Ow," I said. Didn't know why. But the word felt right.

"Ow," I said again.

I shook.

I knelt.

I steepled my hands.

I didn't pray.

I wanted a drink.

I wanted a drink so bad.

Worse than I had since becoming a Barnburner.

I thought about my early Barnburner days.

I'd been sober a few months but was white-knuckling it, marking time until I picked up again. I'd hitched a ride to this meeting at Saint Anne's in Framingham mostly because the car ride would be warm—it was February—and the guy who brought me promised they had better donuts than most meetings.

I'd known right away something was different about this group that called itself the Barnburners. They took no shit. They brooked no foolishness. Anybody who was serious about staying sober was welcome. Anybody who wasn't got the bum's rush.

I liked it. I was curious. I kept coming around until I got invited to the Meeting After the Meeting.

The Meeting After the Meeting was a tough crowd. Words meant shit. Deeds meant everything.

It was the first team I'd ever stuck with, the first group that ever thought I was worth much of anything.

My eyes snapped open. I wasn't about to give up my role now.

But Carlos Q had figured me out. There was weight to everything I did. Maybe it added up gradually. Maybe every ex-boyfriend I beat up, every douchebag boss I set straight, every debt I cancelled sat on my shoulders like a feather.

A ton of feathers weighs a ton.

I folded the three chairs, set them neatly in a corner.

I walked from the chapel shaking only a little.

An hour later I locked my truck, grabbed my duffel and sleeping bag, eyeballed Floriano's house. Sighed.

It was this or the Red Roof Inn.

The sleeping bag, the duffel, and everything in it were twenty minutes old. I'd made a Walmart run rather than drive to Charlene's to fetch gear. The idea of walking into her house, seeing hope on Sophie's face, then wiping out that hope . . . I couldn't stand it. It made me blue.

It made me thirsty.

Cut the shit.

Floriano either heard my truck or looked out the window at the right time: He opened the oak door before I knocked. The door's a beauty, original to the 1895 house. It's flanked by a pair of stained-glass panels, floor to ceiling, that have miraculously survived in this neighborhood. Floriano was once offered thirty grand just for the stained glass by a Back Bay antique dealer. He turned down the offer. Stubborn.

We looked at each other awhile.

"The stain job we did on that door is holding up," I said.

"Was a long time ago," Floriano said.

"That's what I'm saying," I said.

The Mendes house: warm, meat smells left over from the family's typical late dinner, dishwasher hum, homework-done-getting-ready-for-bed vibe.

From the entry I could see the dining room, with identically framed images of Jesus Christ and Ayrton Senna, the best driver Floriano and I ever saw. Senna, a Brazilian, died in a wreck when he was thirty-four.

I nodded at the curved staircase. "Maria?"

"Putting the girls to bed."

"I don't want to be any trouble."

"No trouble, Connie." He didn't quite meet my eye as he said it. "You want a sofa up here? Or the cot downstairs?"

With an assist from his two older sons, who now ran a for-profit recycling outfit that was growing like crazy, Floriano and I had finished the basement long ago. Put in a bathroom, the works.

"Cot's fine," I said.

"Well then," he said, and looked at his hardwood floor. "Long day tomorrow—"

"Long day today—" I said at the exact same time.

My friend finally looked me in the eye. We laughed a little. I thought he was going to say more. But he didn't.

"Cot's fine," I said, stepping to the basement door.

And it was, I thought. Post-shower, in my sleeping bag atop the cot, hands folded behind my head. Ticking off things that had happened that day. A hell of a lot of things.

No wonder I was tired.

I sighed. I rolled off the cot. I hit my knees and steepled my hands like an eight-year-old girl. I tried again to pray.

It didn't take.

I tried. Really. But instead of the relaxed hum and loose thought chains I was looking for, I got Moe pictures. So tiny in his hospital bed, white on white on white.

Savvy Kane pictures. A girl I'd loved, her neck snapped.

Blaine Lee pictures. Blood and hair and scalp jammed in a cracked windshield.

The pictures spun, danced, floated. The pictures became Vernon Lee of Level Cross.

The pictures were stained by red mist.

No wonder I couldn't pray. The pictures were the opposite of prayer.

The pictures made me thirsty.

Cut the shit.

"I'm sorry," I said, whispering it.

I flopped back into the cot.

I lay awake a long time.

My last thought, over and over, when I finally drifted away: *Nobody can say I didn't try.*

CHAPTER TWENTY-EIGHT

Funny things, words. The way their meaning bounces off you—until it doesn't.

In cold blood.

Found myself thinking those words early the next morning, Saturday. Full cup of coffee, full tank of gas.

I cruised.

I trawled.

I trawled for Vernon Lee.

I trawled in cold blood.

Driving east toward Winthrop, toward Moe's house, visor down against a cold hard sunrise, I tried to heat my blood with Moe images, Savvy images. Snapped necks, diaper shit-smears, Vernon the freak who had to be getting off on it all. Maybe he hadn't at first. But he was now.

I wanted red mist.

I didn't get it.

In cold blood.

Driving with one eye on my mirror. Trawling, hoping for the first time ever that I *would* pick up a tail.

Winthrop, Eastie, back through the tunnel, Mass Pike to the Allston/Brighton tolls, sun at my back now, climbing but not yet warming the day. Just driving to places I'd been. Vernon had followed me before. Maybe he'd follow me again.

I didn't know what the hell else to do.

Cold blood.

Barnburner experience could only take me so far, I realized on Mass Ave in Cambridge. Vernon Lee wasn't some gal's meth-head ex who needed a good scaring. He wasn't some third-rate shylock I could rattle with a couple of open-hand slaps.

Vernon Lee was a stone-cold killer, and whatever I was going to do to him I was going to do without a red-mist rage.

Could I?

Cold coffee. An illegal U-turn on Mass Ave. Back to the Pike on-ramp, feeling like a jackass. *Driving around hoping to pick up a tail.* That *was your plan? That was it?*

I wished Randall was around to help me make a better one. Wondered how he was doing down in Level Cross, glanced at the side-view as I merged onto the Pike . . .

. . . and there it was. Green Expedition, gold trim, the Eddie Bauer model.

"Well I'll be damned," I said out loud.

I may have smiled.

I drove. I led Vernon west. He planted himself two hundred yards behind me and stayed there. Did he *want* me to spot him, or was he just stupid?

I didn't care.

Got off the Pike at the Framingham exit. Drove slowly, signaled my turns, stopped looking in the mirror—didn't want to lose him, didn't want to scare him off. I worked my way through the strip-mall ghetto, banged a left on Concord Street, drove south.

Toward my part of Framingham.

I knew exactly where I was leading Vernon.

No more hemming and hawing about cold blood versus red mist. Pack that away. Do what you already decided to do.

Every couple of years, the Framingham powers that be made a

Keystone Kops effort to supercharge the downtown area. The idea—or pipe dream—was to add businesses that weren't check-cashing joints or nail salons, maybe even businesses without a Brazilian flag in the window and a sign reading *PORTUGUES FALADO AQUI*. Framingham was drooling to attract hip restaurants, yuppie lofts, office condos.

The projects had a predictable arc: They always launched with fanfare and tax bucks, and they always dribbled to a close years later when some poor developer lost his shirt after being jerked around by the city.

Eight years ago, one developer who apparently hadn't learned this lesson had agreed to build a five-story concrete parking garage *before* he built the shopping-and-professional arcade it would service.

The garage got built. The arcade was a hole in the ground. The developer tanked.

Framingham.

I thought all this as I hung a left and approached the place, which hulked just off Route 135 near the Natick border. Five stories of ugly, maintained (sort of) at city expense, to service a vacant lot.

For me, right now, it was perfect.

I reached under the bench seat, pulled out a ball cap, grabbed my sunglasses. The garage would have surveillance cams. Some of them might even work. If they did, they'd be set up to grab license numbers. So no way was I pulling in.

Given my plans. The plans I'd made in cold blood.

Instead: I parked on 135, dodged through a hole in the fence made by junkies and thugs who liked to cut from a taco stand to the garage. I walked at a steady pace, not daring to turn and look for Vernon. Had to assume that once I'd sucked him this far, he'd make the full commitment.

I entered the garage, took a right, and sprinted to the first 180-degree turn, where concrete angled up to become Level Two. Dodged behind a post, listened. For maybe the third time in five years, I wished I had a gun. The damn things are like four-wheel drive: You hardly ever want it, but when you want it, you *really* want it.

Heard the gate buzz, heard the Expedition's low rumble as it came my way.

Good.

No stairs; that would ruin my sucker-hole plan. Instead, I double-timed up the ramps. The idea was to keep the SUV far enough back to stay curious, to always wonder if I'd be around the next corner.

Level Three. One of the many foolish things about this garage was that although it was plunked down in the suburbs, it'd been built to city scale for city-sized cars. So even at a walking pace, the Expedition's tires complained as it tracked the tight turns at either end. I maintained my double-time pace, never looking back, hoping Vernon's curiosity would beat out the alarms that ought to be going off in his head.

Level Four. The parked cars, thin to begin with, were nearly non-existent up here, a few wrecks clustered near the elevators.

Level Five: rooftop. Nowhere else to go. Sudden sunlight made me glad for the sunglasses. The wind was a little stronger up here, making a cold day colder.

I ran hard toward the elevator area. Had a general idea what I was looking for, but needed some luck to find it.

Got some. There, propping open a stairwell door: a steel wheel from a car, thirteen inches in diameter, once silver, now mostly rust. I snagged it, skinning my knuckles on the deck, and duckwalked back to the only car on this level: an ancient pigeon-shit-covered Montego.

Squatting, I heard the Expedition's tires gripe their way around the corner, heard hesitation when Vernon didn't see what he expected to: me. He was looking at an empty rooftop, pigeon shit, and the Montego.

While Vernon tipped the throttle and slow-rolled my way, I gripped the steel wheel I planned to use as a weapon and thought about this structure . . . the rest of the story, as the radio guy used to say.

The rest of the story was that the contractor who'd lost his shirt was a friend of a friend, and I got to know him during the project. Hell, I was part of a crew who tried to talk him *out* of the project. We told him how Framingham worked. We pointed out the half-dozen abandoned efforts to yuppify downtown, we made him watch the all-day traffic jams caused by the train tracks, we asked how many big-time retail chains would welcome methadone clinics and bail bondsmen as neighbors.

Poor sap was too much of an optimist to listen. So I watched him piss away the business he'd built, his thrice-mortgaged house, and his kids' college funds putting up the world's least useful and least used garage.

Near the end, he'd wised up some. Not enough, but some. He threw in the towel on quality, for starters—said he was damned if he'd keep doing top-notch work while the planning commission and the zoning board and the banks jerked him around.

He skimped on rebar. He skimped on his mix.

Last time I saw him, he said if I ever parked in his joke of a garage, I'd best skip the top floors. Said a Boy Scout with a penknife could whittle those floors to nothing. Said you hit a main support with a shopping cart, you might bring the whole damn thing down—the concrete was no better'n what you'd buy in a sack at Home Depot.

I heard he was in Corpus Christie lately, working oil rigs when he could.

The Expedition would have doors that locked automatically once you reached five miles an hour. There would be no easy way inside that SUV. That was where my rusty wheel came in.

When he neared the Montego, Vernon slowed even more. He had to be puzzled, wondering where the hell I'd gone. I kept my head down.

The SUV drew level. Its V8 made a nice little whump-whump at idle.

I tightened my grip on the wheel.

The Expedition moved forward. There was nowhere else to go; Vernon was getting set to turn around and drive out.

Time to stop thinking. *Cold blood.*

I rose and stepped from behind the Montego. Hooked a sharp left, flew at the driver's side of the Expedition. When Vernon spotted me from the corner of his eye, he hit the brakes and the SUV's nose dipped.

Perfect.

What happened next happened fast but felt slow. That was a good thing. It used to work the same way when I was driving well: The world just about froze, and it seemed every move I made was the right one.

I stepped toward the driver's door, raised the wheel over my head with both hands, whipped it straight at the window. Needed to smash glass. If I smashed Vernon's head, too, so much the better.

Steel shattered glass, and then my arms, head, and torso were inside the SUV. I got my feet on the running board, but before I could let go of the wheel and claw the lock open, something stung the meat of my right shoulder. *Hard*. And kept stinging.

Vernon was biting me.

I said, "Ow."

Vernon hit the gas.

We picked up speed quick.

Or maybe it just felt that way when you had a steel wheel in your hands, a man's teeth buried in your shoulder, and a slick plastic running board under your boots.

We were moving fast now. I had maybe four seconds to figure this mess out.

I did the easy part first: Let go of the goddamn steel wheel, which dropped into the passenger seat. Then I glanced through the windshield and grabbed the steering wheel, wondering if I had room to turn us around.

No way, not with a Ford Expedition's turning radius. If I yanked the wheel, I'd just pull us into the wall on my side. And I didn't want to do that.

Yet.

Vernon's teeth in my shoulder were getting to be an annoyance. I wriggle-shrugged hard, trying to elbow his face while I did. It worked, although it felt like I left a chunk of shoulder in his mouth. He made an animal sound, an outraged growl.

Dead ahead, the low concrete wall was coming at us. With my head jammed in the steering wheel, I had a close-up of the speedometer. It said 28. Man, had I screwed up: I realized Vernon's plan was to ram the wall, busting my head against the steering wheel, maybe deploying the airbag against my temple as a bonus.

I needed to stop us.

I slapped at the column shifter, heard the engine scream with revs as I knocked us into neutral. It was a start.

I squeezed my torso between Vernon's legs, eeling toward the floor, blindly reaching around in the driver's footwell. We had to be damn close to that wall. My left hand reached, grasped, stabbed.

Got it. I'd found the SUV's emergency brake. I shoved as hard as I could, felt us brake brake brake, the rear wheels locking . . .

. . . we nosed into the wall, and even though my ear slammed the brake pedal, I got very lucky: We tapped just hard enough to blow the airbags. I could tell because one of them hit my hip, hurting like hell.

The Expedition automatically shut down when the bags deployed.

It was quiet the way it's quiet right after it's loud.

But only for a moment: Vernon made his angry-bear noise again, fired the SUV, and popped it in reverse. Then he buried his foot in the throttle. While gassing us backward, *fast,* with his right foot, he tried to kick my head with his left.

A tiny part of my brain gave Vernon some credit: He was tough as hell. There weren't many who could take an airbag in the face, growl like a bear, and keep right on driving.

Moving ass-backward now, really cooking. Vernon's left shoe clipped my ear hard, and I faced facts: I was losing here. Upside down, shoulder-bit, kicked in the head, airbagged in the hip. I was on my way out.

One chance. Whatever was going to happen needed to happen *now*, while we were in reverse. I wriggled and pushed, eeling again but backward this time, needing to pull my head from the damn footwell where Vernon was kicking it.

A second or two before I would have grayed out, I made it: Got myself right-side up. Shook my head to clear it, elbow-smashed Vernon's face and chest a few times. Looked out the passenger window: Holy shit, we were flying. I had to get out, and it was going to hurt.

Wait wait wait, don't give him a chance to brake . . .

There! One final elbow-shot, then I propelled myself out the driver's window. I had a fifth of a second to tell myself to curl into a ball and land well.

Yeah, right. I flopped to concrete like a sack of suet. I hurt everywhere . . .

. . . but not for long, because I looked up in time to watch the green Expedition smash through concrete and drop five stories, a five-thousand-pound anvil.

I rose. I hobbled to the edge. I looked down.

Five stories. A gradual hillside rose to meet this side of the garage, but still: Call it a forty-five-foot drop into weeds and dirt. The SUV had hit ass-first, had continued over onto its roof. Impact had shortened it a full three feet.

The front tires spun slowly.

"For Moe," I said. "For Blaine. For Savannah."

No time to think more, no time to do more. Framingham Police HQ was three minutes away. Time to split.

I didn't allow myself to hurt, didn't allow myself to shake, until I was in my truck and gone three miles.

CHAPTER TWENTY-NINE

Avenged.

It's a cheesy word, a comic book word.

Avenged in cold blood.

The red mist had let me down. It hadn't been there for me to credit, to blame. I'd avenged Savannah Kane, and I'd done it in cold blood. I was a full-grown man; it was all on my shoulders, in my belly.

It felt awful.

Thinking all this as I rolled a slow, counterclockwise loop through Framingham, waiting for the shakes to settle.

That took a while.

Tired. Feeling like somebody'd let the air out of me.

I drove.

When my knuckles finally stopped shaking on the steering wheel, I saw they were flayed. Looked in the mirror.

Didn't look any better than I felt.

Inventory: the flayed knucks. My left hip hurt from the Expedition's airbag. But not as much as my deep-bit shoulder. Add in scrapes and aches all over from jumping to concrete at speed. Face it: I was a wreck.

The kind of wreck cops take a hard look at.

So get off the roads.

Three minutes later, I pulled to the curb outside Floriano's house. I was feeling beneath the porch stairs for his spare key when I heard the front door. Looked up. Maria, wearing the black slacks and white shirt that meant she was catering that day.

"I thought everybody'd be off working," I said when she turned, spotted me, and jumped an inch.

"I leave now." She put a hand over her chest, settling herself—then made a hiss-intake when she got a look at me. "Connie!"

"Four ibus and a shower," I said. "That's all I need."

"Boolsheet," Maria said.

And she took my upper arm and walked me into the house, into the kitchen. She sat me in a ladder-back chair and spoke rapid-fire Portuguese while she ran warm water and fetched a first-aid kit. I'm pretty sure she was telling me I was an asshole.

I didn't have much to say to that.

In any language.

"I call it good."

I said it out loud. My voice: loud, ragged.

I was in Floriano's basement—my new home—forty minutes after Maria had spotted me. She'd done her thing with a washcloth, antiseptic, and gauze. Then she'd tapped her watch and left. I apologized for making her late, but the front door closed before I finished.

Then I undid much of Maria's work by taking the hottest shower I could stand.

Savvy Kane, Moe Coover, Blaine Lee, now Vernon.

I tried to shower them all off.

The hot water quit before I made it.

But when I stepped out and toweled off, it was over. It was goddamn over. A mess, a train wreck, the ugliest thing I'd been a part of—which was saying something—but it was over.

Thinking that, convincing myself, was when *I call it good* hit me. It was a line from my father, Fast Freddy Sax. He used to say it whenever he jerry-rigged something: a bread-bag tie used as a throttle linkage, a leaky pipe wrapped in ten feet of duct tape, a section of cardboard filling a busted windowpane. Fred would step back, look over his hill-billy repair like a master craftsman, and finally say: "I call it good."

By the time I realized Fred was making fun of himself, he was long gone and it was just me and mom in Mankato.

I call it good.

The phrase kept coming back at me, and my belly was hollow. But why? I thought it through, teased it out.

Reason one: post-revenge letdown, a feeling I'm not proud to say I know well. You get your revenge. You want it to make everything right. It never does.

But there was a second reason for the emptiness, I thought as I began to dress. *What is it what is it what is it?*

Had one leg in my jeans when it hit me.

"You ignored yourself," I said out loud. "You ignored your own damn rule."

Figure out the blackmail, figure out who killed Savvy.

I'd figured out who killed Savvy, all right. Maybe not in a way a jury would've bought, or Wu for that matter. But I'd proved it to myself. Vernon had killed Blaine. Vernon had tried to smother Moe. Savvy had been tailing Vernon an hour before she had her neck snapped. Therefore Vernon had killed Savvy. Good enough for me.

But I hadn't figured out the goddamn blackmail.

I sat hard on the cot, still with a single leg in the blue jeans.

Doubt led to doubt. Questions, including two big ones. Who the hell was the red-dot woman sporting around in bed with Bert Saginaw? And how had Savvy come across the pics in the first place?

Randall. Boy, did I need to talk with Randall.

Finished dressing, went upstairs, put on a few Band-Aids. Checked my cell, which had been on silent all morning. It was red-hot with texts and voice mails. From Krall and Emily Saginaw, mostly.

The only text I bothered to read was from Randall: *Arr BOS 3:30p, much to discuss.*

I thought about texting him to take his time, Vernon was all done. Then realized how bad that could look in an interrogation room.

Or a courtroom.

The phone lit up while I was staring at it. Call from Emily Saginaw. What the hell. I picked up.

"Finally," she said. "Where have you been all morning?"

"What do you want?"

"Bert would like a progress report."

"Bert would like a lot of things."

"Bert's paying you a lot of money."

I thought it through. I could tell Saginaw I'd found the pictures. He would think I was Sam Spade. Maybe he'd loosen up, or slip up, and I could learn something.

And until I learned whatever there was to know about these pictures, I couldn't be sure Vernon had been working on his own. Couldn't be sure I'd fully avenged Savvy.

I told Emily I'd be over soon.

"Hold the heavy bag," Bert Saginaw said in his gym twenty minutes later.

"If you show me how," I said.

"You never boxed? You look like you can handle yourself."

"The fights I've been in," I said, "you don't get a chance to bob and weave and jab."

"Why's that?"

" 'Cause you're already dead if you do."

He thought I was joking.

I wanted Saginaw happy and comfortable when I told him about the pictures. And I knew him well enough to understand what that meant: I had to act like a flunky. I held his sweat towel, his water bottle. I held the heavy bag while he punched and kicked it, trying to knock me on my ass and make it look easy.

He didn't knock me on my ass. So maybe my prospects as a flunky weren't so hot after all.

While he worked a military-press machine, I said, "About those pictures."

He stopped. "The Jesus pictures?"

"The other ones, the ones you were so worried about."

"Yeah?"

"I found them. I've got them."

Saginaw rose so fast he whanged his head on a handgrip. "Well?"

"They're what you said they were. You in the sack."

"What about the, ah, the other party?"

"No way to tell who she is." I explained how her face had been scratched and carved away. "So if what you said was true, if I've got the only copies and the camera and printer have been destroyed, you should be in the clear."

"Who'd you show 'em to?"

"Nobody." *Except Randall and your ex-wife, who laughed at your Elvis lip-curl.*

"Nobody? *Nobody* nobody?"

"Nobody."

Bert Saginaw made the biggest grin I'd seen on him, waggled a finger at me. "Conway Sax," he said, laughing some. "Conway Fucking Sax! You're a gentleman and a scholar. Have Krall cut you a bonus check on your way out, and tell him I said make it a good one. And hey. When this election's done, you want a permanent job, a *good* job, you come to me. Got it?"

"Why'd you think Tinker was behind the pics?"

"Never mind that," he said, sitting and ripping off a set of military presses. "That, my friend, is now a moot point."

Ten minutes later, fetching another water bottle, I spotted Emily outside the door. She tapped her watch.

"Your minders want us to wrap up," I said to Saginaw.

"I'm wrapping, I'm wrapping. Never run for office, amigo."

"You convinced me."

"Home stretch," he said while doing tricep pull-downs. "Nonstop campaign from here on in. Emily and Krall say I'm nuts to waste time in the gym. But it clears my head."

I waited for him to ask for the dirty pics. On the drive over, I'd thought about feeding him bullshit, about claiming I'd burned them already. I wasn't willing to let them go until I knew exactly how they'd come to be, and whether they tied in to Savvy's death.

Saginaw didn't even ask for them.

What a dope.

I looked at the door again. Emily: still there. Impatient. To take Saginaw's mind off asking for his pics, I said, "Your sister's giving us dirty looks."

"She's a tough cookie."

"She sure is squared away," I said. "Your secret weapon?"

"Settle down there," he said, panting as he took giant steps around the room. He'd called them walking lunges. "Squared away? Sure, now. But Em's had her ups and downs."

"Like what?"

"Early on she hooked up with a couple of losers," he said. "Swore off men when she was twenty-six or so, and if you'd seen these dregs you wouldn't blame her. Then she latched onto a cult, enviro-creeps in Oregon. Living in trees so the trees couldn't be cut down, all that shit. She did the vegan thing, the India thing, the Holy Roller thing, all of them. Confidentially, she did the booze-and-pills thing." He wrapped up the giant steps, panted, held out a hand.

"I'm guessing she did the AA thing too, then," I said, handing him a towel.

"Threw herself into it like it was another cult, which in my opinion it *is*, no offense."

"No offense."

"Yeah, she was doing three, four meetings a day there," he said, wiping his face. "Queen of the High Steppers, we called her. That was the name of her AA group. But it got old, the way everything does for her."

Me: frozen.

"Earth to Conway," Saginaw said, snapping his fingers. "You there, ace?"

"The High Steppers?"

"Sure," Saginaw said. "The Sunday Morning High Steppers. Six thirty A.M. at a Unitarian church over in Natick."

CHAPTER THIRTY

I damn near got out of the house. Three fast strides across marble and I would have made the front door, but . . .

"Yoo hoo!"

Looked over my shoulder.

It was Krall, half-running down the long hall, holding something above his head.

"You forgot your bonus," he said, and I saw what it was: another big blue check. He turned it so I could read it.

It was for a whole lot of money, double Saginaw's original check. Lower left, in the memo field: *Consulting, Tinker for governor.*

"How'd you know I was supposed to get a bonus?" I said.

"Bert just told me." He tossed his head to indicate the gym behind him, far down the hall.

"Bullshit," I said. "I left the gym twenty seconds ago."

Krall smiled, held the check perfectly still.

"You bug the gym," I said. "Hell, you probably bug the whole house."

But I reached for the check. If Krall wanted to think I was bought and paid for, let him. I knew where the dough was really going.

He didn't let go of the check. Instead, he held up his cell with his other hand. "There's something else you forgot."

I squinted at his cell. Its screen said ICE ERO and a number with a 617 area code.

"Immigration and Customs Enforcement," Krall said, still smiling, finally letting go of the check. "Enforcement and Removal Operations. I know the head of the Boston office. We go back."

Krall was right: I *had* forgotten. One hell of a lot had happened since he'd threatened to deport Maria Mendes.

Red mist. It hadn't been there when I could have used it to kill Vernon Lee, but now it flooded. I stepped back, cocked my right fist, got set to break Krall's jaw. Hoo boy, was I going to enjoy *this* . . .

"In fact, I already called him." Krall said it barely in time to save his jaw. "If I don't call him again, and soon, he unleashes the hounds."

I dropped my fist. I shook. I looked down at the check, which I'd crumpled. "I'm done," I said, knowing how whiny it sounded.

"You're done when I say you're done," he said. "I'd still like to know who's responsible for the pictures you dug up for Bert. Oh, and I'll just take the pictures themselves. If you don't mind."

Maria Mendes. Four kids, four jobs. Letting me stay in her basement. Cleaning my wounds.

Krall thought he had me. He didn't realize I *wanted* to stick around now. *Had* to. Had to dig out the truth about the blackmail pictures.

He also didn't realize the pics were ten yards away in my truck. "They're in a safe place," I said. "I'll get them to you later."

"Soon."

"Don't push your luck."

He squinted at the screen of his phone, which he still held at shoulder level.

He moved his thumb.

"Soon," I said.

"Now you're talking," Krall said. He spun, pocketed the phone, walked away whistling.

Thirty minutes later I was just about at Betsy Tinker's house.

I was glad I'd grilled Saginaw in the gym: While his muscles had broken down under the punishing workout, his guard had dropped, too. And old Chain Link Jesus had finally let something slip.

Emily Saginaw: former High Stepper out of Natick. Quiet, efficient, lived permanently in her brother's shadow. Prone to cults, fads, obsessions. Was on the warpath over Bert's running mate. What had she said, the only time I'd seen her lose control? *Betsy Bite-My-Bag Tinker will be president over my dead fucking body.*

Shep, Tinker's handyman, butler, and driver: longtime High Stepper out of Natick.

It'd be hard to think of an odder pair, an odder set of partners.

But coincidence is for chumps.

I made Beacon Hill at quarter of eleven. Wanted to reach Tinker's place before the next governor left. With loyal Shep, I-been-here-seventeen-years Shep, driving her.

I was too late, two different maids speaking two different flavors of Spanish managed to tell me, mostly by pointing at an itinerary. On her way to Dartmouth, Tinker was hitting a Boy Scout pancake breakfast in Hingham and a cranberry festival in Kingston. And yes, loyal Shep, employee of the year, was today's chauffeur.

Hell.

I returned to the F-150, idled, and thought.

But not for long. It wouldn't be smart to call attention to myself. The cops would take gold-plated care of this neighborhood, you could bet on that.

And I was about to bust into the ten-million-dollar home of Betsy Tinker, the sweetheart (and next governor) of the Bay State.

I dropped the truck in drive.

Three lefts put me in a short, double-wide alley that dead-ended against the redbrick mansion. I tucked behind a pair of black Range Rovers. My truck would blend in here—in icebox white, it could be any contractor's rig.

I strode toward a green-painted wooden door trying to look like a man who knew what he was doing. I had three things going for me. First, Tinker had so many servants and such a big place that nobody seemed to know what everybody was doing. There was probably one boss lady running the staff, but I hadn't seen her yet.

Second, I knew the house at least a little. As I walked, I figured out the screen door would lead to a working kitchen—the smell and a small Dumpster on wheels told me that—and there had to be a flight of stairs nearby that led up to the main floor.

Third, the screen door was propped open by one of those plastic racks of fresh-baked bread and rolls you see outside sub shops in the morning. A regular delivery, and the kitchen help hadn't grabbed it yet.

So I did. Got lucky: The main door behind the screen was unlocked. Hipped it open, took a quick glance around an empty kitchen that looked just like I'd expected, set the bread rack on a stainless-steel counter. Spotted a staircase, made for it.

"Esteban?" a woman said from another room, maybe a pantry.

"Momentito," I said, and cat-footed up the steps.

More luck: It was a back stairway that didn't empty into the public foyer. I didn't even slow down, went up two more flights.

I was looking for servants' quarters.

I was looking for Shep's room.

Wasn't sure exactly what I was looking *for* there—something that would tie him to sister Emily.

Opened a door, stepped into a hall, knew right away I was getting warm: The wide pine boards hadn't been refinished in a hundred years, and the edges of the floral wallpaper curled here and there. I doubted Betsy Tinker had walked this hall since the day she and her late husband closed on the house.

I minimized floor creaks by transferring my weight slowly. Step to a door. Listen. Decide it's empty. Turn the glass knob. Look.

The rooms were nicer than the hall itself. They looked pretty much like hotel rooms, and by the third one I realized that was how they'd been furnished: Tinker's people, probably led by Shep, had clearly bought a truckload of anonymous hotel furniture and art at a distress auction. Between that and newish wall-to-wall, the rooms were damn nice servant quarters. Tinker did okay by her staff.

The first three rooms I checked obviously housed one or two women, so my snooping went quickly. The fourth was getting the rehab treatment—wallpaper half-stripped, ladders around, furniture stacked.

Two minutes later, after a listening break that told me nobody knew I was here, I opened the door to the next room, the final one in this wing. I had my fingers crossed: If this wasn't Shep's, I'd have to backtrack and find another stairway to another wing, and that would be pushing my luck.

I listened, held my breath, turned the knob, pushed . . .

. . . into a room that was even nicer, but more generic, than the rest. Medium-blue textured wallpaper, queen bed to my left, shades-drawn windows dead ahead, highboy and flat-screen to my right. No photos in frames, nothing tacked to a wall, no towel tossed on the floor.

This wasn't a room Shep or anybody else lived in. This was more like a guest room.

Shit.

I started to back out.

Wait.

Queen bed, two windows, midsize flat-screen.

I stepped in. I pulled shut the door. I looked up and to my left.

I saw a cover for a forced-hot-air outlet.

"I'll be damned." I said it out loud.

I stepped, reached up, pulled the cover lightly.

It slid right out.

And not by accident: Each corner held a screw head, but when I flipped the cover I saw the screws themselves had been hacksawed off, their heads epoxied to the cover. Somebody had massaged this piece to make sure it'd pop out smoothly, quietly. Somebody clever. Somebody with tools.

Shep.

I pushed the cover in place, stepped into the hall. Backtracked to the adjacent room I'd already glanced in, the unfinished one. Set the ladder in place, popped out another massaged vent cover, pushed out the first one I'd found.

And there it was. The high-and-looking-down view that'd been used to get dirty pics of Saginaw.

"I'll be damned," I said again.

Confirmed: Shep as the peeping-Tom shooter. Suspicion: Shep was tied in with Emily Saginaw. Was that a reach? Yeah. I was hanging a lot on a High Steppers connection that might mean anything or nothing. But I couldn't picture Shep running a high-stakes blackmail op on his own. And Emily looked a lot more like a potential partner—hell, Shep's potential *boss*—than anybody else around here. It was something to take a hard look at.

Question: If I was right about Emily and Shep, how did they butt up against Team North Carolina? Was I looking at a miniature gang war between two groups looking to crowbar some dough out of Bert Saginaw? Had Savvy switched teams, pissing off Vernon? Was that how she and Blaine had come across the pictures?

Huh.

Rapid-fire Spanish nearly startled me from the ladder. An argument, two girls rat-a-tatting each other. A door slammed. The rat-a-tat kept up while I slid the vent covers in place. I stood near the door of the room, wondering whether I'd get a chance to split or if a pair of arguing maids would bust me.

One girl rat-a-tatted a final barrage at the other. Another door slammed. A shower started. Stomping, stair noises. I counted to thirty, turned the knob. Saw nobody. Walked out and down the way I'd come. In the kitchen, I walked right behind a woman as wide as she was tall. She was stirring soup.

It smelled good.

Boy, did I need Randall right about now. He was so good at figuring out what mattered, at ignoring all the sideshows.

Checked voice mail as I worked toward the Pike. One, from Charlene. I listened, damn near wrecked: She was sobbing, half-coherent, said I damn well better call ASAP.

"Where the *hell* have you been?" she said, hiss-whispering, when I did. Background noise told me she was moving, maybe plowing through a door.

"Slow down. What's up?"

"Your effing cat turned up half-dead on my deck this morning is what's up," she said. "Now Sophie's inconsolable and I get to blow the day at the vet."

"But he's alive?"

Big sigh. "Barely. His flank was ripped open and infected, and he's dehydrated, and his eyes are milky and disgusting . . ." half-sob ". . . how could you do this to us, Conway? How could you leave me such a mess? This isn't *me,* this isn't what I *do.*"

"How's Sophie holding up?"

"Surprisingly well." Like she half-resented it. "You should have seen her, Conway, cradling this raggedy thing in one of those dumb racing sweatshirts you gave her, waking me up, hollering at me to start the car. Florence Effing Feline Nightingale."

"Where are you? That vet on Route Twenty?" I hoped not—we used him for shots and Davey's special food, but I'd never liked the vibe there.

"Of course not," Charlene said. "Nurse Nightingale insisted we take him to Tufts in North Grafton. She said he'd be in better hands here."

"He is. By a long shot."

"I finally got a neighbor to take Sophie home. She didn't want to leave until the anesthetic wears off, but I made her go. They knocked him out to sew him up, and when he comes to they'll have a pretty good idea whether the infection's going to kill him. So this is where I've spent my Saturday morning. In sweatpants. Eating savory vending-machine fare."

"I'm sure Davey apologizes for the inconvenience."

"*Fuck* you!" The harsh hiss-whisper again. "Don't you dare turn this around, don't you dare put the onus on me."

"Remember Moe Coover?"

"Of course."

"He just about got killed yesterday. He's at Mass General."

"What happened?"

"It had to do with me."

Long pause.

"There's a surprise," she finally said. "Nurse Nightingale will keep in touch on the cat thing."

"Davey," I said. "He has a damn name."

"Yes. Of course. Davey."

"I'll head out there now, check on Sophie. I need to clear out my gear anyway."

"No time like the present," Charlene said, and clicked off.

Hell. Emily, Shep, and all the rest would have to wait.

I drove.

CHAPTER THIRTY-ONE

I spent ten minutes telling Sophie what a hero she was, then another ten packing.

The poor kid followed me around the whole time.

Dale was the last thing. I set his cat carrier on the kitchen floor and he trotted right in, chirping.

"He's so mellow," Sophie said. "The opposite of Davey."

"What's the word on Davey?"

"Anesthesia's difficult for small animals. It's more art than science, they say. I bet they'll keep him overnight, but Mom's pushing to bring him home now so she can be done with it."

"She said that?"

"Of course not. But I could tell."

She began to cry as she said it. There on the L-shaped sectional, hands on knees, apologetic little tears slipping down her cheeks. She'd be thirteen soon. Had that tweener look, not quite a girl anymore. Baby fat, though even I knew better than to call it that. Bare feet, aqua toenail polish chipping away.

I went to her. I sat. I put my arm around her. "You remind me of Dale," I said.

"I am the unsqueaky wheel."

"Yup."

"Don't go," she said. And wrapped both arms around my torso, something she never did.

Shame flooded me, floored me, took my wind.

I held Sophie.

"Jesse's gone," she said. "Now you're gone. Dale and Davey, gone. Just me and Mom."

Her voice broke. She cried. She cried hard.

There was so much to say. It was right there. It would all make sense if I just put it together, the way it sat in my head, and explained it. I couldn't un-hurt Sophie, but I could help her *get it* at least a little.

The words died, the way they do. They stayed in my head. Then they unformed.

I rose, prying Sophie's arms.

I fetched a box of tissues.

I kissed the crown of her sweet head.

"I love you," I said.

I took my cat and left.

I thought I was working my way toward Floriano's, to drop my gear and Dale.

I truly thought that.

But felt a pull.

I ignored the pull for a few miles.

Then I didn't.

Some drunks'll tell you it's never a big thing that gets you. When something big happens, they say, you marshal your forces. You rally. People rally around you.

No, they say, it's always a little thing. A stuck vending machine, burnt toast, a fender bender.

Bender.

It was a pull I used to feel all the time.

Savvy, Sophie. Women crying.

Even while I hated myself for blaming a woman and a girl, I felt rationalization warm my belly.

Warm belly.

Now there was a nice feeling. I focused on it.

I knew just where to go.

High-class Asian restaurant, smallish strip mall, Northborough. Charlene and I had been there a bunch of times. She loved it. The place served mostly sushi, but there was enough other stuff so that I could eat, too.

I parked.

I talked to Dale in his cat carrier. Told him I'd be back before the truck cooled down.

Hoped it was true.

Inside, I sat close to the door at the maple bar. My friends never would've guessed I liked this place. They would've pictured me in a honky-tonk, a roadhouse.

Maybe that was why I liked it here.

When Charlene and I had eaten in the dining room, I'd often checked out the bar. It was the calm that appealed to me: tans and browns, a custom-built waterfall in one corner, New Age music from hidden speakers.

Another thing I liked: There was no Keno and no flat-screen pumping college football, which made for a thin Saturday afternoon crowd. There was a couple in a booth twenty feet away, and that was it. The couple's age, body language, and whispers told me they were married. But not to each other. I wished I didn't notice things like that.

"Help you, sport?"

I nearly laughed when the barkeep said it—she was short, with a fireplug-style gymnast body and black hair pulled straight back, and I wondered how much English she spoke. Had she picked up "help you, sport" during a training session? Had she decided it was the customary way for bartenders to greet customers?

"Can you do me a favor?" I said. "Can you fill a highball glass with crushed ice?"

"Glass of ice only?"

"For now."

"Can do, sport." She'd already nailed the nonexpression that cops and good bartenders keep glued to their phiz. In six seconds, I had exactly what I'd asked for on a thick coaster.

I took a look. It was legit crushed ice: the bartender, who knew her trade even if she didn't know much English, had sandwiched cubes between a pair of bar towels, then used something heavy to splinter them.

Good for her. If you're going to do something, do it right.

I pulled my wallet, set three twenties on the bar.

I picked up a shard or two of ice and popped them in my mouth while scanning the bar shelves.

There it was.

Wild Turkey. Kentucky Straight Bourbon Whiskey. One-oh-one proof, with that ugly-but-proud bird strutting across its label.

I stared. I imagined. I remembered.

There's a phenomenon in racing, skiing, any sport really: target fixation. The idea is that your body goes where your eyes go, whether you like it or not. When one car spins out, you'll see another, maybe more than one, follow him in and spin out in the same spot, piling up like cordwood. That's because the second driver comes along, spots the first, and comes down with a case of target fixation.

The cure is to make sure you're always looking where you want to go. Your hands take care of the rest.

Hand wrapped around my cooling glass, I looked at the wall of liquor. Zoomed in on the bourbon again.

What you do, you slow-pour the Wild Turkey over the crushed ice. Not all at once—you pause a couple times to listen. You can hear the whiskey melting the ice shards, the shards bouncing off one another. If you do it right, it's almost a jingle. It's almost a sweet little song.

My breathing had slowed. Everything in this room was clear and distinct and perfect. Barkeep wiping glasses six feet away. Tiny waterfall. Harp music from invisible speakers. Couple in the corner.

Crisp twenties on the bar, new ones, you could slice a finger on them.

The Austin, Nicholls Distilling Company. Lawrenceburg, Kentucky. Established 1855.

You stop pouring a finger's-width from the top of the glass. The room-temperature bourbon melts the ice shards fast. As they melt, the level rises. Water is the only element whose density decreases when it's frozen. Thus ice floats. Thus life is possible.

Thus Wild Turkey. Kentucky Straight Bourbon Whiskey.

Target fixation. My eyes: bourbon-locked. My hand: wrapping the glass.

I did not think about Savannah Kane, her neck snapped in a dirt lot amidst construction gear.

I did not think about Sophie, alone at home, crying on a sofa in bare feet.

I did not think about Davey, coyote-gashed, panting in a hospital cage, waiting to die or live.

I did not think about Dale, the easygoing one, hunched into himself for warmth in my truck, taking whatever he was dealt.

I did not think about Charlene, giving me more chances than I deserved, looking like a chump every time.

More than anything else, I did not think about her.

My hand on the glass grew cold.

In any heat-transfer scenario, cold flows to heat, rather than vice versa. Drop an ice cube in a hot skillet. You think the skillet melts the cube. And it does. First, though, the ice reduces the skillet's temperature. It's simple science, useful when considering the thermal properties of engines, transmissions, and other drivetrain components.

So my hand was cooling.

Shaking, too.

I tried to still it.

I couldn't.

Now the glass was thumping the cardboard coaster beneath. Quickly, regularly, like a dog leg-scratching itself. *Thumpthumpthumpthump-thump.*

The bartender couldn't help but stare.

The couple in the booth craned their necks.

Stubbornness kept me from pulling my hand from the glass.

The hand seemed to belong to somebody else. I watched it like a TV show. *Thumpthumpthumpthumpthump.*

"Everything okay, sport?"

"I'm . . ." *Thumpthumpthumpthumpthump.*

"Maybe you not need no more to drink this day, sport."

"I'm . . ." *Thumpthumpthumpthumpthump.*

I lifted the hand to stop the thumping. The glass stayed with it. The couple stared. Two busboys had materialized from the kitchen. They raised eyebrows at the barkeep.

I flicked my wrist. Heard the glass drop to the bar, but by then I was three steps toward the door.

Twenty seconds later I was in the truck. The interior had gone cold, so it looked like I'd lied to Dale, same way I'd lied to everybody else. I unlatched the cat carrier, held him to me.

"What are we going to do, Dale?" I said over and over to the cat in my lap, my face in his fur. "What are we going to do?"

But I knew.

CHAPTER THIRTY-TWO

Need to leave you again," I said to Dale ten minutes later. "It'll be an hour. Sorry, brother."

Dale chirped and rolled against the ball cap I'd shoved in his carrier so he'd have something that smelled like me.

What a goddamn trouper.

Next to the carrier: my booklet listing every meeting in this half of the state.

I sighed, eyeballed the storefront squeezed between a nail salon and a travel agency that ran people to and from Rio. Downtown Framingham. Two blocks south of Floriano's home, five minutes west of the parking garage where Vernon had died.

The narrow store sold AA books, signs, sayings, bumper stickers. Also JESUS SAVES signs, sayings, bumper stickers. There used to be meetings here every day, but according to my booklet this was the only one left. I wasn't surprised. Five years ago, when I'd last been here, this meeting had been at death's door.

Every group, every meeting is different. They have life cycles: They're formed, maybe they swell, maybe they raise the roof for a few years or a few decades. Then key players die out, and they take the meeting—its heyday, anyway—with them.

But every meeting gives somebody something they need. I was proof, wasn't I? Like this meeting or not, here I was. And here it was.

I reminded myself of all this as I banged on the door. In this neighborhood, they had to lock it.

A hunchback named Lenny turned, squinted, rose, let me in. "Conway!" He whispered it: I was five minutes late, and a chairwoman I didn't recognize was introducing her first speaker.

I sat in back and counted heads. Eleven drunks, squeezed in among the racks of Big Books and step books and testimonials and Bibles and those little silver fish people stick to the trunks of their cars.

I knew six of the drunks just from the backs of their heads.

Tried to listen to the speakers, but my head went where it went. I knew what I was here for. Shame had brought me. Humility would save me.

Maybe.

When the last speaker wrapped, Lenny hopped up with a clear plastic box in his hand. "Chip time!" he said, and I knew it was his big moment, the high point of his week. At the front of the room, he set the box on the counter next to an old-fashioned cash register. Rubbed his hands, peered inside.

The way it works: Some AA groups, not all, pass out coins or chips marking sobriety anniversaries. The chips are motivation for newbies. I never cared for that kind of thing myself. But everybody's different, and you should see the look on some people's faces when they earn their one-year chip.

"One year!" Lenny said, looking around. He held high the bronze-colored disc. "One year, going once . . . twice . . ."

No takers.

He went through the routine again for the six-month chip. A very dark woman with high cheekbones rose and shuffled forward. The other eleven of us clapped and whistled, and the way she bit back a grin as she sat damn near made me smile. Like I said, the looks on some people's faces.

"A month?" Lenny said, raising a silver chip like an auctioneer. "One month of one-day-at-a-time sobriety?"

No takers.

Lenny looked a little blue, resigned to handing out just one chip at this meeting. But he went through the motions, holding up a turquoise disc. "Last one," he said without putting much into it, "most important one. Twenty-nine days, twenty-four hours, or a sincere desire to quit drinking. Anybody?"

I tried to push out of my chair. Couldn't do it at first.

"Anybody?" Lenny said.

I weighed sixteen tons.

"Going once . . . twice . . ."

I pushed off again, making it to my feet this time.

My chair scraped. My heart thundered.

In Framingham—hell, in most of the state—all the hardcore AA types knew about the Barnburners. They knew about the Meeting After the Meeting.

They knew about me.

People turned at the sound of my scraping chair.

People gasped.

My boots were cinder blocks. My legs were pudding. Lenny stood a thousand yards away.

I went to him.

Somebody whispered, "Barnburner." Somebody else said my name. Somebody else choked on a sob.

Lenny: poleaxed, his mouth an O. I put my hand out. He just stood there. I had to reach for his hand. I had to gently pull the chip from it.

I turned.

I faced them all.

"I'm Conway," I said. "I'm an alcoholic and a drug addict."

They were supposed to say hi, but they were stunned. Nobody said a thing.

I wanted to say more, but my lower lip wouldn't let me. I tried once.

Then again. Then I gave up, began walking back to my chair. It was time to close with the Lord's Prayer.

I took a step, then another. Then my legs mutinied and I couldn't go farther. I sank to one knee. One hand clutched my new chip. The other I set over my eyes like a man driving into the sun. I stared at the floor.

I wept.

"Bring it in here," Lenny said.

Still staring at the floor, I listened to more chair scrapes and wondered what was going on.

Then they touched me.

They laid hands on me.

Every one of them. Eleven hands. On my head, back, shoulders, arms. Someone gripped the hand I was using to shield my eyes. I looked up. It was Lenny.

"Whose father?" he said.

It was the signal to begin.

They all started. *"Our father . . ."*

Soon I joined in.

We prayed.

CHAPTER THIRTY-THREE

It was just about full dark ten minutes later when I pulled up at Floriano's. I grabbed the cat carrier, bounced up the stairs and in the front door.

I felt . . . clean but jumbled. Drained and recharged both. I wanted to drink a glass of water, rinse my eyes, and lie on my cot while Dale sniffed around his new home. I wanted to think. I wanted to plan.

All that went out the window when I spotted Randall. Sitting in a chair in the living room, reading a hardcover book. Kid reads like nobody's business.

"Well," I said. "Hell."

He looked me up and down. His eyes paused a beat at the cat carrier. "I tried Charlene's place first," he said.

"Well."

"Yes. Set poor Dale free and I'll tell you about Margery Lee."

Me: rush of paranoia. Didn't I look different to Randall? Didn't I look like a man who'd shamed himself, who'd come *this close* to drinking? Paranoia doubled when I realized my free hand was fingering the twenty-nine-days coin in my pocket. I dropped the coin like it was a spider, let Dale out. He went straight over and sniffed Randall's shoe, the one covering his real foot.

"Floriano and Maria?" I said.

"Upstairs for the night. Why are you antsy? You sent me to Nowheresville, North Carolina, Conway, and you're going to by-God hear the results."

I sat.

"Talk about unlucky in love," Randall said when he was good and ready. I could tell he'd thought his story through. Probably wrote an outline on the plane ride home, or at least nailed one down in his head. He's like that.

"Margery met Vernon Lee the first day of first grade in Level Cross," he said, "and married him the last day of their junior year in high school. She has been owned by him, and those are her words not mine, a full thirty-eight years. She's been beaten down every way you can name."

"No surprise."

"I don't mean he physically beats her. Not anymore, that is. Margery has been fully aware that her man is the boss for many, many decades, if you ask me. She's a ghost, Conway. A skeleton, a shell."

"Losing her son couldn't have helped."

"Exactly. And Blaine was her *only* son, I might add. Her only *child*. Now here's a twist: How would you react if I told you Savvy came north not to squeeze Bert Saginaw, but to *protect* him from being squeezed?"

"Protect him from . . . Vernon?"

"Indeed." Randall's eyes went cloudy. "Once I got Margery going, once I opened her up, it was . . . it was a torrent. She couldn't stop telling me things Vernon's done. I shall quote again. 'He's a corruptor,' Margery Lee did say about her betrothed. 'A befouler, a viper, a ruiner of anything and everything sweet.' "

"He's also dead," I said. "I mention that yet?"

"What?"

I told him about the parking garage, the crash through the wall. I tried to make it breezy.

It didn't come out breezy.

Randall looked at me awhile when I finished. "This explains the various abrasions and the fact you're moving like a constipated octogenarian," he said.

I said nothing.

"But there's more, isn't there?"

I wondered how he saw through me so easily. I'd fibbed about how Vernon came to be following me, had made it sound like I just happened to spot him. Hadn't mentioned trawling. Hadn't explained in-cold-blood versus red mist.

I wanted to tell Randall. I wanted to explain. I wanted him to know it all, to tell me it was okay.

I said nothing.

"There's more," Randall said, "but you won't tell me until you tell me. I get it. Still, just what you *have* told me . . . it's a lot. On your shoulders. It's too much."

I said nothing.

"No ill effects from the gendarmerie?" he asked.

I told him about Wu. "Believe it or not, he hasn't even braced me yet on Vernon."

"That can't be. Savvy Kane dies, her boyfriend dies, her boyfriend's *father* dies, and they haven't even put you in the hot box? Nonsense." Randall stared at nothing for a while. Dale jumped on his chair back, sniffed Randall's head. "Is there any chance," he finally said, "Vernon survived?"

"I watched him fall five stories in a two-ton SUV. It was pretty convincing."

"Huh." He was still skeptical.

"My guess," I said, "the Vernon news is under wraps because it can only hurt Tinker's chances, which are looking worse every hour. Wednesday morning, you'll see a two-inch story about Vernon on page eleven of the *Globe*."

"Huh."

"You're not convinced."

"Where was I?"

"Befouler. Viper."

"Ah yes."

By the time Savannah Kane met Blaine Lee at Best Buy in Greensboro, her son Max was five years old. Blaine went full head-over-heels in a way that maybe Savvy didn't—Margery admitted her son had never had a lot of luck with girls—but from the start, Savvy struck her as a decent sort and a good mother. A good *single* mother, working a succession of nothing jobs, and that wasn't easy.

My face went red. Savvy'd told me this, or had tried to, and I hadn't believed her—to me she was stuck as a biker-bar broad, a gal who hopped on the back of a stolen Triumph Bonneville and went on a speed-fueled tear with a drunk. A gal willing to blackmail her old lover with dirty pictures she somehow stumbled across—and willing to double-cross me, sucking me into an investigation she knew would lead to nothing.

Time for a rethink. Maybe Max had brought Savvy something she'd never experienced: serenity. *Nice time to accept that. Very helpful. She was only murdered two days ago.*

Blaine was both a gentleman and a gentle man, according to his mother. Best of all, he and Max adored each other.

"Blaine popped the question," Randall said. "Savvy said yes."

"Then what?"

"Then they moved in with Blaine's folks. And everything turned to shit."

On paper, it made sense. The idea was for the new little family to live rent-free while saving for a down payment on their own place. Vernon and Margery lived in a run-down but decent three-bedroom ranch house. There was plenty of room.

"Vernon," I said. "What did he do to her?"

"Margery knew it was a bad idea from the start," Randall said. "You see, he was very high on the move-in plan, always talking it up. That made a big blip on Margery's radar, because Vernon never offered to share anything with anybody."

"What did he do to Savvy?"

"He got her in bed," Randall said. "But first he got her . . ."

I pinched the bridge of my nose, anticipating it.

"First he got her drunk," Randall said. He knew it hit me hard. Whatever you thought about Savvy, it was a fact she'd put together a good chunk of sobriety.

Nine years ago, when she'd walked into her first Barnburners meeting—I probably asked her two hundred times how she tracked me down, but she never did say—she'd already been sober four years. Had hooked into the prison AA/NA group in Kentucky. Said they'd saved her life.

That sounded familiar.

Charlene and I'd been aware of each other at the time, circling each other, but not dating. Me and Savvy clicked like *that*. Every night was like the motel room in Kentucky. Hell, I could practically smell grease dripping from that old Triumph Bonneville.

Going through all this—the whispering, the confiding, the planning, the lovemaking—stone-cold sober made it even better.

For me, anyway.

Savvy had grown restless. Savvy had stopped showing up at Barnburners meetings. Then she'd stopped showing up at my apartment. I knew now that was when she started in with Bert Saginaw.

I shook my head clear, focused on Randall. "There wasn't a lot to do in Level Cross," he was saying.

Each morning, Blaine would head off to Best Buy and Savvy would put Max on the kindergarten bus. Three days a week, Margery worked a full shift in the church food pantry. That left Savvy and Vernon alone, watching awful daytime TV shows. Vernon started drinking at ten thirty, as he had for close to three decades.

"After a while," I said, "Savannah drank with him."

He nodded.

Two adults watching trailer-trash TV, drunk by noon. One of them a corruptor, according to his own wife, the other hating herself for drinking. You didn't have to be a genius to see how it went where it went.

Margery had walked in one time, she told Randall, intending to make a quick sandwich. She'd paused in the kitchen, had put an ear to the door of her own bedroom. Had heard Vernon berating Savvy, beating her down with words. He was telling her he'd understood her slutty nature right from the get-go, had seen she was dying to dump the AA nonsense and make it with a *real* man.

"What did Margery do?" I said.

"Margery walked out the kitchen door very quietly," Randall said, "and made it a point to wash the sheets that night. As I said, Vernon beat the life out of her long ago. She's a husk."

By the time Max popped off the bus each afternoon, Savvy was showered and made up and mostly sober. Her son saw something, *felt* something was different about mommy. Margery, who adored Max by then, could see the puzzlement in his eyes, in his attitude. But he handled it the way boys do: He said nothing, kept to himself more, gave Vernon a wide berth. And Blaine, puppy-love Blaine the car-stereo genius, never knew anything, never figured it out.

"Blaine knew more than he let on to his mother," I said. "He had to at least suspect something was rotten. That would explain why he claimed not to know Vernon when I first met him."

Randall nodded. "Possible. Very possible. Hell, he may have been planning to kill the old man."

"The old man beat him to it."

We were quiet awhile.

"Keep going," I finally said. "Savvy must have told Vernon about Bert Saginaw."

"That's how Margery sees it." Randall nodded. "Pillow talk. Savvy let it slip that Max's biological father was a rich man running for office. Vernon got dollar signs in his eyes. He'd been playing short cons for decades, and he didn't mind telling his wife he was plumb wore out by the effort. He and Savvy would make their way up to the People's Republic of Massachusetts and separate Mr. Hubert Saginaw from a sizeable piece of money. Then old Vernon would return home to Level Cross, invest in a nice rocking chair, and declare himself a retired country gentleman."

"And if Savvy refused to go along with the plan," I said, "Vernon would blow the whistle. He'd sit his son down and tell him what a good lay his fiancée was."

"And Max, who was just getting a taste of life with a daddy and a gramma, would be the first casualty."

We were quiet awhile.

"So Savvy *had* to show up on Saginaw's doorstep and make like a gold-digger," I said. "But it was a front. She was really just trying to keep a leash on old Vernon, trying to spare Blaine and Max."

"Which would explain why you saw her following Vernon that day."

I thought. "But why didn't she *tell* me? Why didn't she tell *me*?"

Randall tented his long fingers, looked at them. "Would you have believed her?"

I tried to tell myself the answer was yes.

"No," I finally said.

He nodded.

I sighed.

"There's a problem," I said. "All this only makes sense if the blackmail threat was that Savvy would go public about the kid. Which wasn't the threat at all."

Randall nodded. "Those damn pictures. I spent the plane ride thinking about them."

"I don't know how Savvy and Blaine came across them," I said, "or who Saginaw's buddy from the pics is. But I did learn a few things."

"So you've done something in the last thirty-six hours other than kill a man?"

"It's not funny."

"It's not. Sorry."

I told him. About Katy Stoll and the likely High Steppers link between Emily Saginaw and Shep.

I said nothing about Charlene.

I said nothing about how close I'd come to picking up a few hours ago.

When I finished, Randall whistled. Then frowned. Then twiddled his thumbs.

"The way I see it," he finally said, "you're all done here. Or this close to it. You've figured out Shep snapped the dirty pictures of Saginaw, and you've already done right by Savvy Kane."

"I knew you'd say that."

By way of answer, Randall raised his eyebrows.

"I need to figure out exactly how this blackmail worked," I said. "And exactly who was involved. I'm sick of being jerked around by rich people. I'm sick of hearing bullshit and semi-bullshit and half-truths."

"Whole lies."

"Huh?"

"Old Yiddish saying. 'A half-truth is a whole lie.' "

We were quiet a minute.

I finally said, "Yiddish?"

Randall shrugged.

I'll never figure that kid out.

CHAPTER THIRTY-FOUR

Woke the next morning with Dale purring on my back.

I felt ready. I felt *clean*. Popped up, deposited Dale in the warm spot. He didn't complain.

One good thing about living in a house full of Brazilians: No matter how early a riser you think you are, you never have to worry about waking people up. Even on Sunday, the kitchen and dining room burbled with Portuguese and knife-and-fork clanks. Maria cranked out ham and eggs as fast as she could, trying to keep up with a half-dozen guys—kids, cousins, cousins' cousins—who were fueling up. Her youngest son, who everybody called Dozen for some reason, helped by washing dishes on the fly. For some, Sunday meant a third job. For some it meant a fourth.

Show me a man who works harder than a Brazilian and I'll show you another Brazilian.

Before I could say no, Maria deposited a plate of ham and eggs and a cup of black coffee on the counter in front of me, kissed me on the cheek to boot. I ate standing up, nodded at Floriano as he made for the sink with dirty dishes.

He nodded back.

Awkward. Tuesday, pre-Savvy Kane, we'd been on the same wavelength, gung-ho about the new shop. Now we were in different places.

"How'd the week end up?" I said.

"Was good," he said.

"That's good," I said.

"Yes, good," he said.

Maria watched all this, her mouth becoming a stern line. She fired a dose of Portuguese at Floriano, nodding in my direction a couple times. His face went red as she spoke. Finally he gestured surrender and leaned next to me on the counter.

"The shop took off like *that*," he said, snapping his fingers. "Me and Tory talking about another lift in that third bay. Charlene says maybe we should move to a bigger place. *Already*."

"Wow." The battle inside me: pride at being part of it, embarrassment at not being a bigger part, resentment that Floriano and Charlene got to talk about expansion without me. "Is this what Maria told you to tell me?"

"What she told me to tell you," Floriano said, "is . . . we been friends a long time, Connie. When you finish doing what you're doing, helping your friend, you come back. We'll have a bay for you."

"Obrigado, amigo," I said, whacking his shoulder. Then I winked at Maria, who was doing dishes and pretending not to listen. *"Obrigado, amiga."*

She smiled just a little and nudged Floriano.

"One more thing," he said.

"Yeah?"

"Maria says if you split up with Charlene, you a big dumb jerk."

My plan: Start at Saginaw's place, then find Shep. Needed to nail down the connection between Shep and Emily. I was pretty sure it was there—but what did it mean? How deep did it run?

That was the angle Randall had kept picking at the night before, in Floriano's living room. "You're talking as if it's a lead-pipe cinch," he'd said after we argued awhile, "but I'm not seeing it. Nobody knows AA better than you. Groups turn over all the time, am I right?"

"Sure."

"So Shep and Emily both spent time at this High Steppers group in Natick. Who knows if they ever talked with each other? Hell, who knows if they even overlapped?"

I shook my head. "Shep's been a High Stepper forever. For him, the group's like the Barnburners are for me."

"Okay. So stipulated. But still. Coincidence *does* happen, Conway."

"Are we better off if we call it coincidence?" I said. "Or are we better off if we smell a rat and check it out?"

"Well."

"Figure out the blackmail, figure out who killed Savvy," I said. "That's been my motto. Thought the one would lead to the other, but I screwed up. Got the hard part first—it *seemed* like the hard part, anyway—but the blackmail's just sitting there."

"And until you're satisfied you've figured out the blackmail, you can't be satisfied you've truly figured out the murder."

"Yup."

"Any chance, any chance at all, you can view this as a job well done, thank God you're not in prison, and walk away?"

I stared at him.

"Sorry," Randall said. "Dumb question."

The other thing Randall and I had teased out—something that had bugged me, something even Katy Stoll had commented on—was Saginaw's confidence there was one copy and one copy only of the shots that could torpedo his career. "Why does he think that?" Randall had said.

"I got the vibe he'd been in contact with the blackmailer," I said. "Had gotten the info firsthand."

"Yes, but who believes a blackmailer?"

It was a good point, and the reason I was headed to Saginaw's place early. The idea was to get him alone before the day turned hectic, press him for more info on the blackmailer.

But before I even cleared downtown Framingham, my plan got kicked in the teeth. I was angling southeast when something caught my eye. Looked left, saw flashing headlights in a convenience store parking lot. Kept moving . . .

. . . had that been a black Crown Vic?

Sighed, spun a 180, pulled into the lot.

Vic Lacross.

He'd backed into a slot. I pulled in, put us window to window, rolled mine down. Chilly morning: I watched his breath as he spoke.

"Glad you spotted me," Lacross said. "I put myself between Saginaw's house and where I hoped you were. We shoulda swapped cell numbers."

We took care of that. I said, "What do you want?"

"I *told* you my guy, Wilton, wants no part of winning this thing. Didn't I?"

"Sure."

"You maybe didn't believe me."

I said nothing.

"I take no offense," Lacross said, plucking something from his passenger seat. "Switch us around and you tell me the same thing about your team, I would've thought *you* were full of shit."

I said nothing.

"Wilton's an early riser," Lacross said. "A crack-of-dawn guy. Likes to watch the sun rise over his three-million-dollar slice of Scituate Harbor." He held up a brown envelope, nine inches by twelve. "When he toddled out to his patio this morning, he found this on his favorite chair."

He passed the envelope over.

I rested it on my steering wheel.

I undid the cheapo clasp.

I reached. I pulled. I flipped.

I looked.

At another copy of the dirty pictures.

"I'm on my way to see Saginaw about these," I said. "He swore there was just the one copy. Guess he was wrong."

Then I looked again.

My mouth fell open.

I looked *again*, held a shot close to my face, squinted, made sure. If I'd had a jeweler's loupe, I would've held it over the picture.

There was no red dot.

I flipped.

There were no red dots at all.

Just a woman's face.

My mouth stayed open.

"It's not a Photoshop," Lacross said. "What do you think, uh?"

I couldn't stop looking.

You could see Saginaw's costar clear as day.

There was no doubt.

"When Wilton looked inside," Lacross said, "he didn't know whether to shit or wind his watch. Woke me up, told me to haul ass down there."

"Nobody else has seen these?"

"Not a soul. He gave 'em the hot-potato treatment. Said he didn't care what I did with 'em, but he never wanted to see 'em again or hear about anybody who did. *Now* do you believe Wilton doesn't want to win this thing?"

I looked at the pics again.

And believed.

"Holy shit," I said.

"Have a nice day," Lacross said.

He rolled up his window and drove away, leaving me to goggle at pictures of two adults banging away like barnyard animals.

Bert Saginaw.

And Betsy Tinker.

CHAPTER THIRTY-FIVE

It was a lot to think about. It could overwhelm me if I let it, cause me to lock up, keep me from doing anything productive. Analysis paralysis, Randall called it.

But analyzing things to death had never been my problem—Randall liked to point that out, too, the little bastard—so I kept moving.

Saginaw's place felt like a funeral home. The pollster flunkies huddled in a den, whispering to each other and pointing at their laptops.

"Like a wake in here," I said when Emily clacked around a corner in a sensible tan pantsuit, laptop beneath one arm.

"There's a reason for that." She plucked a *Globe* from a hall table, held it to her chest. Big-ass headline:

GOVERNOR'S RACE NOW VIRTUAL TIE

Below:

New poll shows Wilton within margin of error;
Tinker campaign denies 11th-hour shake-up

"Ouch," I said. There was another headline, DEBATE DEBACLE or somesuch, but she set down the paper before I got much of a look.

"And that's our friendliest poll. The others are *really* ugly. Did you see the undebate last night?"

"The hell's an undebate?"

"I'll show you, but fair warning: Bert's on the warpath. Pete Krall is on the hot seat, and I advise you not to let him off it."

I wondered what she was talking about while she led me up the stairs, down the hall, into an office suite.

Saginaw: campaign-ready in a charcoal suit, light-blue shirt, red tie. He had tossed the suit's jacket across a chair, had rolled up his shirtsleeves. He kept firing a clicker at a flat-screen across the room like he was trying to shoot a hole in it. All the while, he fired commentary too—at Krall, who sat on the couch making no facial expression at all.

Saginaw fast-forwarded. "Here's a softball I could've hit out of the park . . . *if I'd been there!*" Fast-forward. "And here's where I would have hammered this clown on his Beacon Hill lobbying record . . . *if I'd fucking well been there!*" Fast-forward. "And here we have the crowning glory, the moment of pure gold . . . what say we watch it frame by frame, *numbnuts*? With popcorn, extra butter?"

By then, Saginaw was shrieking. A little drool sagged from one corner of his mouth.

I said, "You want to calm down there, Bert? And maybe tell me what's going on?"

The gratitude in Krall's eyes almost made me feel bad for him.

Almost.

The way Saginaw spun told me he hadn't even known Emily and I were there. "Finally," he said, "someone with a set of balls, someone who's not just cruising til his next paycheck." He pointed at Krall. "And last, I might add! Win, lose, or draw, Pete, you have fucked us royally. Your next gig will be with some crackpot running for selectman in Gill. I will see to it personally, boyo."

Saginaw faded as he spoke, energy draining in a way you could truly see. He panted a few seconds, flung the clicker to the floor, and stomped from the room.

I said, "Fill me in."

Krall gulped. All blood had drained from his face. He stood and tried his confident college-swimmer pose, hands on narrow hips, but it wasn't working—he'd been unmanned. "I, ah," he said. "I may have made a mistake last night."

"The Jesus pictures turned Bert into a liability on the campaign trail," Emily said. "Pete made the call to pull him back as of yesterday."

"That doesn't seem like a bad idea."

"It was," she said without looking at Krall. "Several of us tried to tell him so." She plucked the clicker from the floor, aimed, fired. "You see, the one and only debate between the lieutenant governor candidates was supposed to be last night."

"I decided not to send him," Krall said. "I used the old scheduling-conflicts excuse."

"Thus this," Emily said, hitting play.

"Oh," I said.

We watched a few seconds more.

"Oh damn," I said.

Smallish stage. One podium on each side, both tagged SUFFOLK UNIVERSITY. At one podium: a soft, balding guy I'd never seen before, speaking into his microphone. He must be the other lieutenant governor candidate, Wilton's running mate.

Behind the stage-right podium: a cardboard cutout, life-size, of Bert Saginaw. Wearing a Saginaw Fence Co. polo shirt, a half-sneer on his face.

Emily hit the volume, and after a minute or two I figured out what Team Wilton had done. They'd made a comedy routine out of Saginaw's no-show. The opponent would ask a reasonable-sounding question, then cock his ear like he was waiting for Saginaw to answer. After a while, he would mug for the audience, who were eating it up, before rattling off his own position on the question.

"This was on *TV*?" I said.

"When Bert bowed out," Krall said, "Wilton's folks swooped in, bought the time slot, and said they were ready for a debate, as promised. I knew then we were screwed."

We watched some more. Every few questions, a couple of flunkies would come on stage, carry off the life-size cutout of Saginaw—and return with another that was even less flattering. The students would howl.

"Piece de resistance," Emily said after a few minutes, clicker-jockeying.

"Oh no," I said, knowing what was coming.

"Oh yes," she said.

It came, to laughter and applause that shook the camera: Saginaw as Chain Link Jesus. The loin cloth, the sinewy muscles, the torqued torso, the tilted, tragic face. Propped behind the podium.

Hoots. Shrieks of laughter. The auditorium shook.

Krall heel-rubbed his eyes. "Bert watched all night. Made me sit here the whole time."

"I need to talk with him," I said.

"No way," Emily said. "He needs to regroup. Big day today."

"Where is he?"

Neither of them spoke.

"I'll find him," I said, and left. Then stepped back into the room, grabbed Saginaw's jacket, and left again.

It took a while. I walked both wings of the ridiculous house, finally spotting him through a window. He sat on a tiny patio outside a study. I stepped through the door.

Saginaw had his face turned to catch thin sunlight. His arms were folded across his chest. He didn't open his eyes, didn't turn his head.

"Cold day," I said. "And you stomped out of the room in a huff. Then you realized you'd left your jacket, but after that exit you were damned if you were gonna go back in." I soft-tossed the jacket so it landed on his chest. Then I scraped a wrought-iron chair across flag-stone and sat next to him.

Saginaw still hadn't opened his eyes. But he was smiling now. "Good guess about the jacket," he said. "Cold out here." The smile grew broad, became a chuckle as he slipped his arms through the sleeves. "It's hard getting a good mad on."

"It's a young man's game," I said. The words came to my head, flashed: *In cold blood.*

"Remind me why I wanted to be governor," he said.

"*Lieutenant* governor."

"Sure. What the hell am I supposed to do now, Sax? After the humiliation last night?"

"You do what everybody does. You get past it. You put on your coat, make your speeches, shake a few hands." I scraped my chair closer to his, looked around some, pulled the folder that'd been tucked between my T-shirt and my flannel shirt. "But first, you need to look at these."

"Those what I think they are?"

"You tell me."

As it had with me, it took him a half-beat to realize he could see Betsy Tinker's face. "Holy shit. Holy shit. Holy shit." He whispered it. "They were supposed to . . . she said . . ."

Bingo. *She* said. I jumped on it. "What did Emily say?"

"They told her they'd made only the single copy. That they snapped the pics, printed 'em, destroyed the camera and printer. Just like that."

"You believed her."

"We believed *them*, you mean."

"Still haven't put it together?"

"The hell is *that* crack supposed to mean?"

"Your sister's the blackmailer, Saginaw."

He moved quick, I'll give him that. Hit me with a decent right that rocked my chair. Followed with his body, trying to swarm me to my back on the patio. And he damn near did it, and then maybe he could've done a little damage.

Instead: My chair back wedged against the heavy wrought-iron table, which scraped but didn't move far. So as Saginaw tried to get an arm-bar across my throat, all I had to do was reach up and squeeze his.

The move cut both his air and his blood. His eyes went big. The fight went out of him.

Still holding, I stood. I rattled his throat to get his attention, eye-locked him. "Knock it off, you dumb fuck. There are a bunch of people around here I want to hurt. You're not one of them."

Saginaw relaxed. Didn't have much choice.

We righted our chairs. We sat as if nothing had happened.

"Tell me what you think you know," he said, rubbing his Adam's apple.

"The blackmailers have been dealing with Emily all along, right? Everything you told me you got from her?"

"Yeah."

"Thought so," I said. "Something about the amount of detail, and how sure you were that there was just the one set. Emily sold you that bullshit, didn't she?"

"Come on—"

"*Think!* She did, didn't she?"

Saginaw thought.

Then nodded. "She made it sound like a done deal. But why?"

"Blackmail one-oh-one," I said. "The mark needs to believe he can make it go away with one big payout."

"That's not what I mean. *Why?* What's mine is hers." He spread his arms. "All of it. I'd do anything for Em. I do *every*thing for her."

"Not my department," I said. "I'm no shrink. Here's what I need. I'm going to see Tinker next, and I want your sister to come with me. Make her do it, okay?"

"Why?"

"Never mind. Just make it happen. Convince her."

As I stepped back into the house, Saginaw said my name.

I stopped, turned, held open the door.

"About those pictures," he said. "There's, ah, there's a story there."

"It's an old one."

I closed the door behind me.

CHAPTER THIRTY-SIX

"What does Tinker's day look like?" I said to Emily Saginaw, who didn't look thrilled to be riding in my F-150, fifteen minutes later.

She didn't even have to look at her iPad. "There was a Waltham Elks breakfast. That wrapped on schedule, so now she's shaking hands outside Whole Foods in Sudbury. We should catch the tail end of that. Church services in town, then a breast-cancer awareness march on the Common. It's a five-K walk, but she makes a speech, ducks out after a few hundred yards, and shoots over to Arlington where they're breaking ground to expand the town bike path. Want me to keep going?"

"For crying out loud."

"It's the home stretch. And as you know, there's a new sense of urgency."

"And then some," I said. Looked through the windshield, tried for a casual tone. "I imagine Shep's driving her around today?" My plan: Let Emily know I had the goods on Shep, but keep the High Steppers connection to myself. Once she saw the momentum was going against Shep, she'd likely rat him out, tell me a few things I didn't know already.

"I imagine so," Emily said, and if the name fired alarms in her head she hid them well. "But Tinker's got a good-sized staff, and lately they haven't been bending over backward to keep us in the loop. So who knows?"

"Shep's been with her . . . what'd he say, seventeen years?"

Now Emily did stiffen. The truck's vibe changed.

"I really wouldn't know," she said as I hooked left onto Route 20, the main drag in swank Sudbury.

Time for the bomb-drop. "Reason I ask," I said, going for complete deadpan, "it turns out old Shep is behind the dirty pics of Bert."

Dead quiet. Beside me, Emily sat still as a good hunting dog. But there was a giveaway: a tiny cracking sound. She'd broken a freshly manicured thumbnail on her iPad.

"Aren't you going to congratulate me?" I said. "I tracked 'em down. Tinker-Saginaw can rest easy."

Emily regrouped as we rolled north past cute shops and gas stations dressed up as colonial trading posts. Sudbury's that kind of town.

I frowned as if something was just occurring to me. "Shep must have used a cutout whenever he communicated with you, of course. He would've been scared you'd recognize his . . . it *was* you who spoke with the blackmailer, right? Bert said so not twenty minutes ago."

"Of course," she said, composed again, a pro. "And I certainly didn't recognize the voice, not that I know Shep's especially well. But back up a few steps, please. What makes you think he's the one?"

I told her about my look-see at Tinker's house. The dummy heat vent, the ladder in the next room, the way that room was conveniently unfinished so nobody could bunk there.

"You're quite the investigator," Emily said as I sliced into the left-turn-only lane for an upscale strip mall. "Very enterprising. Do I congratulate you on cracking the case? That sounds very . . . very *Magnum, P.I.* It sounds somewhat ridiculous."

I said nothing. Was waiting for her to ask the big questions, the first questions anybody *should* ask: Who was Bert with? And why had he felt the need to get laid in Betsy Tinker's house, of all places?

She didn't ask.

Which told me a lot.

I rolled toward the western end of the strip mall, where a decent-sized crowd stood outside a yuppie grocery store.

I spotted a Range Rover identical to the ones in Betsy Tinker's alley. Parked near it, killed my truck. We stepped out, looked at the knot of people. I heard Betsy Tinker's pure voice over a loudspeaker.

"What will you do?" Emily Saginaw said. "To Shep?"

"First," I said, folding my arms, leaning on my hood, not looking at her, "I'll bust him open. Find out was he working alone or did he have a partner."

Emily didn't have much to say to that.

"Then I'll deal with him," I said. *How, though? That'll be a problem.*

"By having him arrested?"

"We'll see."

"Because if he's arrested . . ."

"I know. That's why we'll have to see." I was annoyed: Emily, no dummy, had picked up on the problem facing me. If I handed Shep over to the cops, a shitstorm would follow. The pics would go public—hell, they'd go *viral*. There was no way around it.

Was that what I wanted? Did I want to splash Betsy Tinker all over the Internet?

"Look," I said, "Tinker's wrapping up, and I need to talk with her. Whyn't you run along and find one of her flunkies to chat with?"

Emily walked toward the knot of people, which was starting to break up. Looked over her shoulder a bunch of times. I'd rattled her good.

It shouldn't have made me happy.

But it did.

The novelty of sweet Betsy Tinker speaking to the great unwashed must have worn off, because there was just one news truck in sight, and no state troopers. There was a local cruiser, white with blue, a bored cop leaning on its door. He looked fourteen years old. More and more of them do to me.

I watched the rally dissolve. Shep, who wore a brown suit instead of his 1946 bellhop uniform, was helping one flunky wrap a microphone cord and shut down an amplifier. Another flunky sat behind a folding table, doling out bumper stickers and flyers. A third circulated through the dispersing crowd, clipboard in hand, buttonholing folks here and there. That would be the bagman, the closer, the one who put the arm on potential donors so Betsy Tinker didn't have to soil herself discussing money.

Dressed exactly as a rich, kind lady on her way to church ought to be dressed, Tinker was working her way toward the Range Rover. Every single person who approached her got the full thirty-second treatment, including a photo if they asked. I could tell they walked away believing they had connected with Betsy Tinker, had expressed their point of view, had persuaded her of something or other.

She even kissed a baby.

When she finally made it over, listening to a flunky who had to be six-four and looked like a vampire, she said hello, maybe a touch puzzled to see me, and asked where Shep was.

"Over there, helping," I said. "Just as well, tell you the truth. Like to talk with you a sec." I opened the left rear door. "In private."

The vampire didn't like it, but Tinker nodded him away.

"Yes?" Tinker said when we were inside.

I leaned forward, pulled the envelope from between my shirts. Then I held it.

Quiet. Those Limeys at Land Rover don't skimp on the soundproofing.

"This won't be easy," I said.

"I'm on my way to church, Mr. Sax. How may I help you?"

Betsy Tinker didn't seem to give much of a damn about the envelope in my hands. She wasn't acting like a woman who knew, or even suspected, she costarred in a batch of raunchy pics.

Deep breath. "Church may have to wait," I said, unclasping the envelope.

Part of me wanted to turn my head as she slipped out the pictures, to give her a few seconds of something like privacy.

But I couldn't do that. I had to see her reaction.

She screamed.

She clapped her free hand across her mouth.

Her eyes went round and bulged in a way I remembered from *Road Runner* cartoons.

Her pale skin turned pale pink, then the deeper pink of her church suit, and finally red like a fire hydrant.

Betsy Tinker hadn't known about these pictures until just now. I would have staked my life on it. Sitting eighteen inches from me, forcing herself to flip through the sheaf, Betsy Tinker was being violated again.

Convinced of this, I did look away. My ears felt hot, and I figured my face was about the same color as hers.

"Oh," she said after a long time. "Oh." The word—more of a moan, really—was muffled by the hand that stayed across her mouth.

Outside the Range Rover, to my right, three skinny boys in skinny pants did skateboard tricks against parking curbs. It was cold, but none of the boys wore coats. The bored cop was watching the skateboarders.

But not really, I realized as he slouched against his cruiser and scanned the parking lot. He was keeping an eye on Betsy Tinker's car without being obvious about it.

He wasn't bored at all. He was a smart young cop.

Good to know.

"My house," Tinker said. "In my *house*. Who's responsible?"

"Shep."

"Nonsense," she said. "Shep's been with me forever."

"Still," I said. I gave her a thirty-second rundown on the unfinished bedroom, the ladder, the removable vent cover. And, in particular, the screw heads with their shafts trimmed off. Filed nice and smooth, epoxied to the cover. That was the craftsman's touch. It pointed to someone who knew his way around the toolbox, who took some pride in his craft.

It pointed at Shep.

While I spoke she looked out the window, seeing the skateboarders but not seeing them. I felt for her—she had to be reliving the night. Had to be considering logistics, the room, the angle.

"Yes," Betsy Tinker finally said. "Yes," she said again, firmer this time. "Good God. Shep."

We were quiet.

Outside my window, one of the skateboarders actually landed a trick for the first time since I'd been watching. Must have surprised himself, because he glided a few feet and fell on his ass. I expected his buddies to laugh. They didn't. Too cool.

"Your business is your business, but I can't help but wonder," I said. "You and Saginaw? Was it . . . engineered? Manipulated?" *By Emily?* I thought but didn't say.

She'd aged twenty years in two minutes, had gone slack and doughy. The spring and smarts had left her face, and I saw what she might look like if she were a secretary or a cafeteria lady instead of a bazillionaire. I tried to think of something good to say.

I couldn't.

So I said nothing for a while.

So did Betsy. She squared up the corners of the pics, dropped them neatly into the envelope, tamped it on her lap. When she tried to refold the clasps, one broke and stabbed her thumb.

"Damn," she said, looking at a blood droplet, popping it in her mouth.

"Metal fatigue," I said.

"To say the least," she said. And laughed. I couldn't figure out why, but she laughed a long while with her thumb in her mouth.

"Bert was . . . is . . . what is the word?" she finally said, now pressing the thumb to the manila envelope in her lap.

I waited.

"Magnetic?" she said. "Forceful? Not quite. *Elemental*, that's it. Bert Saginaw is elemental. If he desires you, he assumes he will have you. You may as well try to hold back the tide as fend him off. This is old-fashioned and politically incorrect, and that's putting it mildly. Bert Saginaw is *macho*. Not in the smirking manner in which the word is used today, mind you. He is truly *macho*."

She swiveled her head and looked hard at me—wondering, I knew, if I understood.

I did.

"To some women," she said, "this trait is both appalling and appealing. And somehow, its appallingness can, in the right circumstances, make it . . . make *him* . . . still more appealing. Is there any chance whatsoever that you can grasp this, Mr. Sax? That you'll permit it as a . . . a mitigating circumstance?"

"Call me Conway. And your business is your business. I said it once. But this much I have to ask: What happened? And when?"

I glanced through the window on Betsy's side. The flunkies had finished shutting down and schmoozing with the high-dollar types, and Shep was ambling this way. I needed to hurry.

CHAPTER THIRTY-SEVEN

Kissinger said power is the ultimate aphrodisiac," Tinker said. "He meant to explain how men who looked like . . . well, who looked like Henry Kissinger managed to attract pert, big-eyed young things. But sauce for the goose, and all that."

I didn't know what the hell she was talking about.

I nodded.

"It happened the evening my people and Bert's people met to engineer our run. The consultants, the courtiers, the mountebanks . . . and Conway, you absolutely would not believe how many of them a well-funded campaign attracts—"

"You're wrong there," I said.

She smiled some. "It was a very heady evening. By the time the aperitifs appeared, they had Bert and me convinced we would breeze to the governorship. And they had *me* convinced that from there it was merely a hop, a skip, and a jump to the Oval Office."

Shep was forty yards from the Range Rover.

"Two manhattans, a bottle of wine, the aforementioned aperitifs, and a foolproof path to glory," Betsy said. "Once the courtiers had been shooed away, Bert Saginaw's arrogant, annoying, irresistible manner caught me just the right way. Or the wrong way."

"And Shep was ready," I said. "Luckiest night of his life."

Shep: twenty yards and closing. He walked like a sailor.

"What now?" Betsy said.

"I need you to trust me three ways."

Her eyebrows made a question.

"First," I said, taking the envelope and tucking it away, "I need to hang on to these awhile."

She said nothing.

"Second," I said, "I need to borrow Shep. You'll have to find another driver."

"Easily done. And third?"

"You know that check you wrote me the other day?"

Betsy's nose wrinkled.

"I want you to write another," I said. "But I want you to times it by three."

She looked at me maybe ten seconds, nose still wrinkled. "*Really,* Conway? That seems out of character. It seems dreary in an unexpected way."

"I could explain," I said, "But I won't. Maybe there's a better reason than the one you're guessing."

She said nothing. Her eyes said I'd lost her.

Tough.

"Have your bagman . . . what did you call them, your courtiers? . . . get the check to me real soon."

Betsy sighed. "Of course."

"Now you go on to church like nothing happened here," I said, "while I have a little talk with Shep."

Seven seconds later I was out the right rear door, around the back of the SUV, and up to the driver's door. Shep was just grabbing its handle.

When you're two feet from the next governor, and you've got an audience of three wise-ass skateboarders and a sharp young cop, you don't just lay a man out with a Sunday punch. No matter how bad you want to.

"Hey-hey, Shep!" I said it loud for the cop's benefit—me and old

Shep, happy members of Team Tinker. I extended my right hand. His eyes told me he knew something smelled rotten, but what were his choices? His boss was right there. He pulled his hand from the door handle and extended it. I gave him one of those strange half-shake/half-hugs that men do these days.

Then I did my level best to break Shep's hand.

I had size, leverage, and surprise on him. In two seconds, his eyes crossed with pain. In two more, his legs began to quiver. Still in half-hug posture with my left arm crooked around his neck, I grabbed his left ear. "I'll tear it off," I said, twisting it some, whispering, a grin plastered to my face. "Climb in my truck or I swear I will tear it the fuck off."

He wobbled toward my truck.

I drove slowly past storefronts until we were out of the cop's sightline. Then I punched the gas, wanting to keep Shep off balance. Thought he might put up a fight, but he was meek as we drove around back of the stores. I drove faster than I needed to on the service road, flew to the back of a Chinese restaurant that wasn't open yet, chirped the tires while stopping, threw the truck in park, ran around to Shep's door. Pulled him out, slapped him six or eight times. Open hands. Humiliating. Like he was a schoolboy and I was a nun. Like I couldn't be bothered to hit him with a closed fist. Like he wasn't man enough to merit that.

"Conway!" he said between slaps. "Conway! What? Why?"

I stopped, faked one last slap—his flinch made for bonus humiliation—pulled the envelope from my shirt. "Here's why." I showed him just enough of one pic. "I found the peephole you set up in Tinker's house, champ. You're Employee of the Month."

Anything I hadn't already slapped or squeezed or threatened out of Shep left him then. He deflated against the side of my truck. He was done.

"Oh," he said.

It stank back here. Maybe there's something smells worse than a Chinese restaurant's Dumpster after a busy Saturday night. But most likely there isn't.

"Why?" I said.

"Seventeen years," he said. "Everything I lost. Everything she's got. Want to know what Tinker said when my house burned down? When my family died?"

"No," I said.

"She said—"

"I said no."

"But she said—"

I did punch him then. In the gut. To shut him up.

I gave him half a minute to catch his breath. "The big question, Shep. Who?"

"Who what?"

"Who've you been working with? You're not ambitious enough to put something like this together. Sure, you set up the shooting blind for the dirty pics, but I'm betting it was mostly the maids used that room. A little fuck pad for the household help. Am I right?"

He said nothing.

Give her up, Shep. If Emily Saginaw had anything *to do with Savvy's murder, dime her out now.*

Frustration. No red mist, no sweet fury. Just mucho frustration.

I slapped him. "And you got your rocks off watching. That's how it started. Am I right?"

He said nothing.

I slapped him again. "Somebody convinced you to use your little peephole for profit, Shep, not just pervert kicks. Who?" Nothing. Slap. *"Who?"*

I saw I'd lost him. You learn to recognize the signs. Shep had curled into himself like a high school sophomore arguing with his father. My little slaps weren't working. If I wanted to stick with the physical route, I was going to have to deliver pain in more serious ways.

Hell, I didn't want to do that.

Plan B.

I put hands on hips, tut-tutted, shook my head, half-laughed. "This is some one-sided loyalty. She didn't have any trouble giving *you* up. No trouble at all."

"She who? I mean, who? Who do you think you mean?"

"Duh," I said. "Emily Saginaw. She fingered you so fast her knuckles cracked."

"Bullshit." But his eyes gave away the game.

"No bullshit," I said, then cemented things with a guess that wasn't really a guess. "She told me everything, starting when she first came around to the High Steppers meetings."

"Oh," he said. "Emily. Oh, Emily."

"Just tell it. Tell your side of it."

He was quiet for a full minute. His eyes went wet.

"It started with the meetings, like she told you," Shep finally said. "Typical stuff. Going on commitments, having coffee. I told her I worked for Tinker, maybe made it seem like I was a big wheel. Maybe I was trying to impress her." Pause. "Maybe I was trying to get in her pants, okay?"

"When was this?"

"Two years ago? Three?"

Huh. That didn't fit. That was ancient history. "Did you date her? Get in her pants, the way you were trying to?"

"Not then. She stopped coming around. All of us High Steppers knew she would. Emily comes across as buttoned-down, very together. When you get to know her, though, you see she's a dabbler. She's done meditation, witchcraft, any religion you can name, goofy diets, all that. AA was just a flavor of the month."

Now it was making sense. "So you didn't see her at the High Steppers for a couple years. Then she started coming around again. And not long ago, right?"

He nodded. "She bumped into me one day. I know what you're thinking, Conway. I'm not stupid. I knew it wasn't coincidence that Emily Saginaw tracked me down. By then, everybody knew Ms. Tinker was running, and the lieutenant governor rumors about Saginaw were hot and heavy. It wasn't hard to figure out Emily had something planned. I knew she was using me some way or another, but . . ." He shrugged.

"You still wanted to get her in bed."

"Sure."

I felt sad all of a sudden. Sad and tired. Knew I had to keep pressing Shep, poor dumb Shep who lost his wife and kid and just wanted to get laid. Money and sex. The only motives. Toss a coin.

"What about your dirty little setup in Tinker's house? Your peeping Tom rig?"

"I, ah."

"You told Emily about it." I thought for a few seconds. "This is important," I said. "Did you tell Emily about the peeping Tom business when you first knew her? Or just recently?"

"When I first knew her," he said. "We were doing sort of a mini Fourth Step during a BS session one night. You know, the Fearless Moral Inventory. Talking about rotten things we'd done while we drank. I, ah, I may have mentioned the peephole then."

"But you weren't drinking when you set it up. You've been sober a hell of a long time."

"I, ah, may have fudged that detail."

The smell back here made me want to puke.

Or maybe it wasn't the smell.

"You were wrong about one thing," he finally said. "It wasn't the *staff* used that room for a fuck pad. It was Betsy Goddamn Tinker, the Bay State Sweetheart herself."

CHAPTER THIRTY-EIGHT

Shep nodded like a bobble-head doll. "After her husband passed, she had me furnish that room. The maids knew better than to go in there except to clean up after."

"After what?"

"Miz Tinker brought guys home once in a while. I won't say they were rough trade, but they sure weren't the same crowd she went to the opera with, get my drift? They were younger guys, oily guys. Car salesmen, hustlers."

I thought about that. Nodded. It fit. Shep wasn't the only one in the house looking to get laid. But the guys who caught Betsy Tinker's eye, the Bert Saginaws of the world, were guys she didn't want to share her Beacon Hill master bedroom with. What would her adoring fans think about these creeps? Not to mention the late senator, watching from blue-blood heaven?

"You wanted to impress Emily," I said. "You spilled Betsy Tinker's dirty little habits. Emily's eyes lit up. It was her idea to get blackmail shots of Tinker."

"Sure. Emily had—*has*—this dumb-ass idea her brother's gonna be president someday. Me, I don't see it, but I played along. The problem was, just when we started cooking up this plan, Miz Tinker stopped taking guys to bed."

"Why?"

He shrugged. "She got tired of banging thirty-five-year-old telemarketers? She hit menopause? Maybe she knew it was a risk she couldn't take once she was running for office?"

"I'm guessing Emily got impatient," I said.

"And how. She said I was missing opportunities, said maybe I'd been lying to her all along. She even, ah, cut me off."

"Cut you off?"

"You know," Shep said. "By then we were sleeping together. Until she cut me off."

I said nothing. Felt tired. Sex and money. The only two motives.

"So when my alarm finally went off—I set up a little sensor in the door to that room, it dials my cell when somebody opens it—I was good and ready to do my thing, believe you me. Hustled into the room next door, set up my ladder, pushed the heater vent out of the way. Then I saw who Miz Tinker was rolling around with, and I don't mind telling you I nearly shit myself. So'd Emily, when I showed her the pictures."

"That should've wrecked her plan," I said. "She couldn't blackmail Tinker without dragging down her brother."

"We talked it over," Shep said. "Emily decided to print two sets of the pics. One would have Saginaw's face scratched out, and the other would have Miz Tinker's face scratched out."

"What was the second set for, the one with Tinker scratched out?"

"Emily said she needed to make sure her brother took her seriously."

I nodded. "There's a hell of a brother-sister power play going on. She's been blackmailing him anonymously, you know."

"I know."

"But why?" I said. "You know Emily better than most. What's going on there?"

"You answered that already," Shep said. "Bert never took Emily seriously, from the first time he called and asked her to trade her life for being his secretary. In his head, she's an assistant. In her head, she's a fifty-fifty partner who makes everything run."

"Saginaw didn't know it was her til I told him, and even then he didn't want to believe it. He tried to fight me over it."

"That was dumb," Shep said.

I checked my watch. We'd been here awhile, and I was worried about the young cop from the parking lot. The way I read him, he'd take a casual swing around this service road before he took off.

It hit me then. "Wait a sec. You said there were two sets. What about *these*?" I tapped the envelope. "Nobody's face is scratched out."

Shep looked like a kid busted by his mom with frosting on his mouth. "That set might've been my idea," he said. "Just in case."

"That's about what I expected," I said. "What I mean, though, why'd you take them to Wilton?"

"Wilton who?"

Sigh. "Thomas Wilton, the guy Tinker's running against."

"*What?* Didn't you find those pics in my room when you were snooping around?"

I gave him the forty-five-second explainer on what I'd found, how I'd never even made it into his room, how the pics had turned up this morning on Wilton's patio.

"I have *no fucking idea* about any of this," Shep said. "I swear to God."

"This line I keep hearing," I said, "about the dirty pics. I keep hearing they were shot with a new camera and printed on a new printer. Then the hardware was destroyed. True?"

"Smashed it all myself out in Miz Tinker's alley," he said, eager as hell. "With a five-pound hammer."

"I'm sick of being lied to. First there was only the one copy. Then there were two. Now there are three. Are any more going to pop up?"

"Absolutely not, on my dear wife's headstone."

I believed him. It was in his eyes, the openness of his face. Shep didn't know what the hell was going on with this third set, the no-red-dots set.

Neither did I.

My head hurt with possibilities. Combos, shakedowns, double-crosses, triple-crosses.

My cell buzzed. Sophie. I didn't pick up. I had things to do.

While I thought about Shep, he did me a favor and read my mind. "What are we going to do here?" he said.

"In about three minutes," I said, "that cop from the parking lot is going to roll through. He had me marked as wrong the second he saw me. What I ought to do, what I *want* to do, is hand you over to that cop. I'd tell him to pass you to a state police detective name of Wu. You'd have a ball, Shep. You'd spend the next two weeks blabbing."

"But?" Shep said, reading my tone, knowing there was hope.

"But cops can't keep their mouths shut any better'n anybody else. I hand you to Wu, then you go to trial. And somehow those pics go public. I've been around too long to see it any other way."

We were quiet awhile.

"I saw this movie," I finally said. "Ancient Greeks, or Romans, or some damn thing. A man got busted for a crime, a big one. Know what they did?"

Shep was all ears.

"They gave him a choice. Death or exile."

"Come on."

"I want you out of Massachusetts by sundown," I said. "I don't care where you end up, long as it's in a different time zone."

Shep looked at me like I had an ear growing from my forehead. "By *sundown*? What are you, Wyatt Fucking Earp?"

"I told you," I said, shaking my head, "the movie was about Greeks. Or maybe Romans. Send me a postcard from wherever you end up. Iowa's nice."

I used my forearm to gently move Shep away from my door. I climbed in.

"In this movie," he said, "you said they had a choice. Death *or* exile. What I want to know, if I tell you to go shit in your wallet, do I get death? Are you really gonna kill me? *Really*, Conway?"

I didn't even look at him as I drove away. I let my reputation do the work.

Checked the message from Sophie. She was incoherent. She babbled three times to call her ASAP, then hung up.

I did. She picked up on half a ring. "He's out!" she said. "He's okay!"

"Who?" Instant regret as I figured out who she meant.

"*Davey.* For God's sake, did you forget about him?"

"Course not. Lot on my mind."

"They're putting a dressing on, and then we're going to spring him. Come out and see."

"Well . . ." Started to say I had a thousand things to do, but she'd clicked off.

I cursed the timing. Not only had I figured out Emily Saginaw was in this mess up to her eyeballs—possibly in on Savvy's murder, even—I'd more or less *told* her so. Who knew what she'd do if I took off?

But.

If you looked at it from another angle, this was a good place to leave her. Without wheels of her own, she'd be forced to tag along with Tinker's people. And when Shep split, she'd likely take it as a sign he was the fall guy.

Yup. Leave her here, thinking she'd pulled it off.

I headed west.

I should have stayed, should have rounded up Emily then and there. Things would've turned out different. Better.

CHAPTER THIRTY-NINE

When I walked into the waiting room at Tufts, Charlene had a credit card in her hand and Sophie had Davey in her lap. She was just about smothering the guy, trying to stroke and kiss and envelop him all at once.

He didn't look like he minded. Purred like a freight train. Maybe his eyes were gummy, and he looked silly because they'd shaved most of his right flank to sew him up, but he was all there. He smelled me, then spotted me, as I squatted before him. His tail made dipsy doodles.

"Conway!" Sophie squealed it when she saw me. Her eyes were wet. She moved to pass Davey over, but I gestured no. He looked happy where he was.

"I hope that cat can sing the 'Star-Spangled Banner,'" Charlene said, holding a credit card receipt in two fingers, "because I need to take him on the road to recoup my investment."

She smiled as she said it. Sort of.

"This place smells like rubbing alcohol and wet dog," I said. "Let's head across the street."

"Is that what I think it is?" Sophie said. "Where'd you *find* it?"

"I found it," I said, passing her the cat leash Davey used to love.

Tufts is in a pretty spot. Old-time farm country, a grassy hill that rolls to a river valley and a set of east-west train tracks. There's a rectangular patch, maybe three acres, ringed by a dog-walking trail.

It was now a cat-walking trail, too, or would be as soon as Sophie got Davey in his harness. I kept a close eye on his shaved flank, but it didn't seem to be bothering him, and Sophie was careful.

Charlene and I stood at the trailhead. Her arms were folded. Mine too. In a typical New England trick, the temp had sunk ten degrees in an hour. Making conversation, Charlene said something about snow on the way. I watched Sophie and Davey bounce down the path.

"I'll pay you back," I said after a while. "For Davey."

"Never mind that."

"I'll pay you back for the shop, too."

"Right." She snorted it.

That pissed me off. I thought about the collection of checks in my wallet. Daydreamed about snapping one out, signing it over to Charlene, and clearing my debt. Just like that.

I could do it.

I wanted to do it.

I didn't do it. That dough was earmarked.

I started to speak, but my tongue tangled up the way it did, and the idea in my head lost its shape like a smoke ring, the way they do.

But this was important. I dragged the idea back, forced myself to speak, didn't allow myself to worry about how smart—or not—I sounded.

"You think money's the problem for *me,*" I said. "You think I can't handle owing money to a girl."

Charlene said nothing. I had her attention, though.

"But that's not it," I said. "The problem is with *you*. Money means more to you than it should."

"It does not!"

"You're a millionaire single mom with two daughters," I said, "and you work seven days a week. My new shop is your second job, your hobby, and you've worked more hours there than most people do at their *first* job."

Charlene: arms folded, mouth working. But no sound coming out.

"It's not about the money for you," I said. "It's about achieving. It's about being useful. Productive. It's about making up for . . . for another time in your life. I get it, but there's a time to throttle back."

Still she said nothing. But her eyes weren't playing offense anymore. She was listening.

"Maybe I should throttle back, too," I said. "Because what I do . . . the Barnburners stuff . . . that's about another time in *my* life."

A train interrupted. Westbound, silver and purple, Commuter Rail they call it. Things grew quiet in the train's wake. When I looked at Charlene she had turned away, was looking down the valley.

That was okay. I'd said my piece, and she'd heard it. The thought had to percolate.

She said, "What's this I hear about you collecting a training-wheels chip at a meeting yesterday?"

I said nothing. Didn't bother to ask how she knew. AA was a small world, and Mary Giarusso had an itchy dialing finger—we called her Switchboard Mary for a reason.

"Did you pick up?" Charlene said.

"No."

"Why the chip, then?"

"It was something I needed." Long pause. "I needed humility. I needed to stop doing everything my way. I didn't pick up, but that was dumb luck. I was out of control. I went to that sushi place in Northborough looking to drink."

"Dumb luck or no, I'm glad you didn't pick up."

Quiet.

"I wish," I finally said.

"You wish what?"

"I wish it was different. I wish *I* was different."

Ice-blue eyes opened all at once. "*I* wish I weren't a sucker," she said.

"You're nobody's sucker."

"That's almost true. I'm a sucker for you, and you know it. You leverage it."

"Not for a long time I haven't. Not the way you're thinking."

Seventy yards off, Sophie cooed and clicked at Davey.

"When we were kids," I said, "didn't people our age—the age we are now—seem *older*?"

"Yes. Because we were young and stupid. And high. What's your point?"

"I thought . . . I thought by the time I was this age, I'd have my mistakes behind me. The big ones, anyway."

"Well, you made a goddamn doozy with Savvy Kane." She wanted to say more, I thought, but her jaw clamped like a bear trap.

"We didn't *do* anything." I hated the whiny tone even as I said it.

"You made a choice," Charlene said. "You chose a dead girl over me."

"Maybe it's not that simple."

"But maybe it is."

We looked down the hill at Sophie and Davey, who were now coming back.

"How is she?" I said.

Charlene smiled some, watching Sophie trot. She held the leash like a dog-show pro, Davey bounding along looking up at her and smiling. I swear, *smiling*.

"She's absolutely devastated. How did you *think* she'd be?"

"Well."

"Yeah, 'Well,'" Charlene said. "It's the innocents who get it. They can handle it the least, and they get it the worst."

"Did you *see* this good boy?" Sophie covered the final few yards, panting. She knelt to undo Davey's harness. He side-flopped to the grass, stretching, rolling. "Conway," Sophie said, "you have *got* to keep taking Davey for walks. He loved it!"

"You're the expert," I said. "I was thinking *you* ought to take him for walks."

"You mean like a dog-walker for cats?" Sophie frowned, looked from me to Charlene and back. Then again. "Well, I suppose it would depend on where you lived . . . and I'd need rides over and back . . . and, you know . . ."

"What I meant," I said, "you ought to keep him. Hang on to him. He's gotten used to your house, and it's a good neighborhood for cat-walking."

"Oh my *God*. Really?"

"Well."

And then it was a wait for Charlene.

A long one.

I held my breath, felt Sophie doing the same. I strained my ears listening for a train, hoping none would come—I didn't want anything to interrupt the moment.

Finally Charlene said, to nobody in particular, "If it doesn't work out, I suppose it's reversible."

"Yes?" Sophie said. "This is a yes?"

Charlene crouched and stroked Davey's belly fur in that awkward way of non-cat-lovers. He sensed the non-love and nipped at her fingers.

But only a little.

"As long as it's reversible," she said. "There's no sense burning bridges."

"No sense burning bridges." Sophie and I said it at the exact same time.

Looking down at Charlene—sweatshirt riding up, jeans gapping, cotton underpants showing just a little, awkward half-crouch/half-squat, white-blond hair, dark roots—I knew I'd never loved her more.

As we split up and I started the drive east to the Escutcheon, I locked the words in my head for hope: *I suppose it's reversible.*

Tinker-Saginaw HQ was humming. As I crossed the space, I could see—feel, really—the intensity had been turned up a notch. Every phone was manned. Every volunteer working those phones had access to a coffeepot and a plate of bagels, and the volunteers manning the coffeepots and bagels thought *they* were as important as anybody else in the room. Like that. The campaign may be in deep shit—news radio had sure made it sound that way—but it hadn't thrown in the towel.

A bearded guy I'd never met hollered my name, sprinted across the room. I asked how he knew me. By way of answer, he passed me an envelope the color of coffee with cream. On the back: an honest-to-God wax seal, purple, with the initials ET. "Governor Tinker's staff wanted to make sure you got this," he said.

"She's not governor yet," I said.

"She will be." He strutted back to his desk like he'd just run the Olympic torch through downtown Boston.

I opened the envelope, looked at the check inside, tucked it in my wallet with the others. Betsy Tinker had come through.

I pushed through the frosted-glass doors of the war room.

And froze.

CHAPTER FORTY

Only the two polling geeks were here. They didn't even look up from their laptops.

"Where is everybody?" I said.

"Campaigning," they said at the same time.

"How about Emily Saginaw?"

"Cam*paign*ing."

"Where?"

They just shrugged.

Feeling dumb for assuming Emily would have come back already, I left the room and began asking where Bert Saginaw was campaigning this afternoon. None of the phone jockeys knew. Everybody told me to ask Amy, gesturing vaguely toward the building's north side.

I never did find Amy, but while knocking on doors I found something else.

Something that gave me an idea.

A printer-copier-fax-machine-scanner. Plugged in, ready to go, in an office whose dust layer told me it was rare for anybody to stray this far from the central area.

"Huh," I said out loud.

I knew how to get Emily Saginaw here.

On the double and on the QT.

I closed the office door. Unplugged the four-in-one machine's telephone line. Took the envelope from the back of my shirt, chose a pic in which it was obvious—oh boy, was it obvious—that neither Tinker nor Saginaw had a red-dot disguise.

I scanned the picture. Used a cord to jack my phone into the scanner. Pressed arrows and menu buttons until I figured out how to get the image to my cell. Did so. Confirmed I had the image on my phone.

Then I picked up the scanner, stepped onto the desk, and dropped the machine to the floor.

Loud loud loud.

Tough shit: I was gambling that any volunteer who heard the racket would be too focused to check.

The drop split most of the scanner's casing from its guts. My boot finished the job. I twisted out the hard drive, stuffed it in my back pocket.

Left the office, confirmed nobody was investigating the noise. Spotted the poll geeks leaving the war room. One of them said something about pad thai.

I entered the war room. Sat in a rolling chair, sent Emily Saginaw a text message.

And a photo.

I looked through the window-wall at the end of the room. The snow Charlene had mentioned was falling. It's hard to take snow seriously the first week of November, but this wasn't one of those fluffy-flakes-here-and-there deals. The sky'd gone good and gray, and the snow seemed to have a head of steam.

And my rear-wheel-drive, light-in-the-back-end F-150 wore summer tires. *Baldish* summer tires.

Great.

Emily called a few minutes later. "What in *God's* name?" she said, semiwhispering. In the background: Bert Saginaw droning about *good* jobs for *good* people, thumping his fist in his bargain-basement MLK imitation.

"You thought you had Shep whipped," I said. "And maybe you

did. But he wasn't too whipped to make his own little copy of the pics and stash them away."

"I have no idea what you're talking about."

I sighed. People lie even when you've got them dead to rights. "Where are you?"

"Dedham."

"Get yourself here to the Escutcheon war room," I said. "I don't care how. Make an excuse. You and me can settle this thing." I left Savvy out on purpose—thought the mention might spook Emily. Better to let her think she could con her way out of the mess.

Emily thought for a few seconds. "It'll take a while in this snow."

"I'm not going anywhere." Click.

I sat and waited and looked out the window. Smiled some, thinking about Savvy Kane and snow. In Virginia, she'd grown up accustomed to one four-inch storm per year, and she thought that was plenty. Had refused to adjust when she moved up here. Never owned anything heavier than an Irish wool sweater, swiped my coat and gloves whenever the temp dropped. I could still see her sliding my work boots, which she could nearly camp out in, through slush on her way to the convenience store for Old Golds and coffee and a newspaper.

She was something.

I wondered what to do about Emily Saginaw. And stopped smiling. Couldn't tell her to leave town, as I had Shep.

Take her to the cops?

Wait until after the election, *then* take her to the cops?

No and no, for the same reason I hadn't hauled Shep to Wu: Betsy Tinker would be hurt more than anybody. The dirty pics would be everywhere. Tinker didn't deserve that. She was a rich lady who felt entitled to a whole hell of a lot, but she hadn't done anything worse than hop in the sack with guys she wasn't proud to associate with.

When in doubt, call Randall.

"Make it good and make it short," he said when he picked up. "I am cuddling by a fire with a beautiful woman. A California Cabernet, some Wes Montgomery, and a dandy view of the season's first nor'easter." Background: jazz guitar, giggling.

"Here's the problem," I said. I explained.

Once I got started, the music volume dropped and the giggling faded. When Randall spoke, he sounded different—had gone to a smaller room, maybe, to be alone. "Here's what I *don't* want you to do," he said in a harsh half-whisper. "Don't do anything stupid. No matter what you learn from Emily, don't go into your one-man posse routine. Promise me."

I said nothing.

"Call the police. Hell, call them now. If they're there when she shows up, that's perfect. They'll keep you from flipping out. Let them deal with Emily."

"So many people get hurt that way."

"Tough! That's how the big ugly world works."

I said nothing.

"*Promise* me, Conway—"

I clicked off.

When she walked into the room, I still wasn't sure what I was going to do.

CHAPTER FORTY-ONE

Emily said, "Who are you, Hercule Fucking Poirot? Planning to wheedle an abject confession out of me?"

"I don't know who Hercule Poirot is," I said, closing the door behind her.

Emily Saginaw surprised me then: She laughed.

It was an exhausted, nothing's-really-funny, twenty-hours-into-a-twenty-four-hour-drive laugh, but still.

She rubbed her eyes with the heels of her hands. "What now, O Dramatic One? Are you going to call a news conference and explain to the breathless media how you cracked the case? Are you going to ruin the lives of Bert and poor old saggy-tits Betsy Tinker? Am I to be frog-marched past a hundred TV cameras to await the trial of the century?"

"I thought about that," I said, "but it doesn't work. It wipes out the wrong people."

"Those people being?"

"Betsy Tinker, for one. She shouldn't be humiliated just because she got drunk and screwed a guy. And then there's your brother. He's a harmless gasbag. I've known a dozen like him. Got lucky, got rich, thinks it makes him a genius."

"You bet he got lucky," Emily said, bumping a thumb to her chest. "He got me for a sister."

Cork: popped. Good. I made a skeptical face to keep her rolling.

"Bert's a decent front man," she said, looking more than ever like her brother as her eyebrows formed an angry V, "and he could sell iPads to Quakers, that much I'll give him. But for product plans, schedules, targets—anything demanding even a whiff of organization—he is one dim bulb, not to put too fine a point on it. Always has been, always will be."

"Somebody told me you were his secret weapon."

"Bet your sweet ass I was! The plain-Jane sister from Fort Collins. Gal Friday, never much luck with men, never much luck with *life,* just good old Em typing up memos for brilliant Bert."

Push. Keep her rolling, don't let her settle down. "If you were the brains," I said, "how come Bert went belly-up twice before the fence biz worked out?"

It worked. Maybe it worked too well. Maybe something in her head broke. *"Don't you blame those clusterfucks on me!"* she screamed. "*I* tried to bail his ass out! *I* wanted to make nice with that Euro-turd flooring company! *I* begged him not to sign anything without running it past our lawyers! Bert, old high-wide-and-handsome Bert, patted me on the head and did whatever the hell he wanted. Both times, I might add, he was trying to impress broads. God forbid we listen to our sister when we're trying to bed down some sweet little *gash*!"

That was a good-enough segue. "What happened when Savvy Kane rolled into town?" I said.

"Besides Bert thinking with his cock, as usual, and making goo-goo eyes at her? Kane was a tough one to figure out. I'd known all about her, of course, from way back when. She topped the list of possible bimbo eruptions. We were ready to pay her off and send her on her way . . ."

"But?"

"But didn't she shock the hell out of everybody," Emily said, "by being a little sweetheart. Didn't want a thing, she kept claiming."

"The way I heard it, Vernon put her up to all this. She was ready to settle down in Level Cross and be Mrs. Blaine Lee."

"True enough," Emily said, her eyes dancing in a way I didn't like. "But do you know why she had to go along with Vernon? Do you know what his lever was?"

"She slept with him," I said, "and he threatened to tell Blaine, which would have crushed the kid. How'd *you* know that?"

"Vernon and I became partners."

"You and Vernon. You and Shep. Hell, you and your brother. You're a busy gal."

"I spotted him following campaign staff around in his ridiculous SUV with out-of-state plates," Emily said. "Clever like a dancing bear, he was. I had the plate traced and figured out who he was, then introduced myself."

"And told him to switch plates before somebody else figured him out, too."

She nodded. "By then, it was clear not only that Savvy Kane had no plans to blackmail Bert, but that she was ready and willing to interfere with *my* plan. Mine and Shep's. I don't know how or when, but the little twat must have heard us talking, because after a meeting at Betsy Tinker's home, idiot Shep confessed to me that a set of pictures had been lifted from his room."

And stashed under the seat of Blaine's car. "That's when Vernon became useful to you," I said. "You signed him on to get the pics back."

"A task he set about with typical grace and stealth." While Emily spoke, she began to move her feet like she was marching in place. Her shoulders rolled. Her fists clenched and unclenched. I flashed back to the gym in the Framingham house, Bert and Em working out. Remembered how fit she was, how much energy she'd showed that day.

As usual, Randall had been right. Calling in the cops would be the right move.

But it wasn't the move I wanted to make. Not with the woman who helped kill Savvy Kane standing right in front of me.

I felt a pulse in my temple. My breathing sped up. I pictured myself reaching for Emily Saginaw's neck.

That pulse in my temple, the squiggly vein that would be sticking out. An ugly vein. Peripheral vision going away, red mist setting in . . .

I fought it.

I breathed myself out of it. A shrink in a detox taught me how. Long time ago.

Emily Saginaw marched in place, fighting her demons while I fought mine.

I beat mine. For now.

I pulled my cell.

"No!" Emily said, screaming from deep in her throat. Her eyes damn near rolling around in her head now, she whirled, spotted a chair behind her. The chair was no lightweight: stout base, four casters on chrome spokes, steel frame. But she picked it up like it was made of paper, one fist on each of its arms.

She growled, truly *growled,* and began to spin like a discus thrower.

One of the chair's casters whipped past my temple, close enough for me to feel a breeze.

Instinct took over: I hit the deck, rolled beneath the giant surfboard-shaped table. Dropped my phone in the process.

Emily spun once more and let fly the chair. It would've creamed me if I'd still been standing. Instead it flew a full eight feet and crashed, casters first, through the window-wall.

I rolled from beneath the table, knowing I ought to wrap up Emily before she grabbed the next chair.

But stopped.

She had broken like the window.

She slumped against the table, hands over her eyes, sobbing.

Wind-whistle from the window-wall. Big snowflakes coming in.

I watched them while Emily Saginaw sobbed.

I kept an ear cocked. If the volunteers sitting forty feet away had heard the window break, they weren't doing much about it.

"Of all the gin joints," Emily said, huffing a laugh against her tears.

I looked a question at her.

"Don't you see it?" she said. "Shep and I had it nailed. If the next guy Betsy Tinker had decided to bang had been *anybody but Bert*, the election would be in the bag and we'd all be counting down hours til sweet Betsy resigned for unspecified personal reasons."

"And then Bert would be governor."

"Yes."

"And soon he'd be president."

She looked at me from the corner of a bloodshot eye. "You're patronizing me. What else did Shep tell you?"

"Enough," I said. "Everything he knew. Emily?"

She sniffled.

"Bert was never going to be president of the United States."

"Shut up."

"Bert was never going to be governor, either."

"Shut up!" Emily swiveled and hopped as she said it, and then she was sitting on the giant table.

Then she was standing on it.

"Hey," I said.

"Shut up!" she said, kicking one of her shoes at my head. Damn near hit me, too.

She giggled.

More than anything she'd done, the giggle tipped me. It was a five-year-old's sound.

"Hey now," I said, moving toward her like she was a chipmunk I wanted to feed a peanut. "Settle down now." I needed to get close enough to grab an ankle. Jesus, hadn't *anybody* heard the window break? I could use a hand.

"Shut up!" she said in the five-year-old's voice, and launched her other shoe at me. While I ducked, she took two quick steps toward the shattered window-wall, sliding on stocking feet.

Behind Emily, snow blew in and turned to water droplets on the table.

"Climb on down now," I said, "and let's figure this thing out."

"What's to figure?" Emily said in a dreamy voice, looking at nothing. "Tied in the polls, momentum on Wilton's side. Now a murder scandal involving Saginaw's shadowy sister. Bert would lose by ten, by fifteen, by *twenty.*"

I said nothing. Took a short, quiet step to my left, toward her. Then stopped.

She said, "You know what would be lovely, though? You know what would swing the whole thing around?"

"What's that?" Short sidestep. I was getting closer, and Emily was still staring at nothing.

"An outpouring of sympathy," she said. "Such as that which follows an unspeakable tragedy."

"Hush now, and come on down." Sidestep. I was damn close now. I felt snow on the left side of my face. A lunge and a grasp would get her.

"A sister's suicide," she said. "Now *there's* a tragedy. *There's* a reason to vote Tinker-Saginaw."

"It won't do any good. I'll have to tell what I know."

"Why, though? And who would believe you?"

I lunged.

She skipped.

I missed.

The move lit a memory: Me and my mom, boarding a little pontoon boat to tour the Blue Earth River in Mankato. I'd been . . . twelve, maybe? It was after my father left but before I came east to live with him. The pontoon-boat outing was my mom's last try at making us a real—broken, but real—family.

My mom had slipped while stepping from the dock to the boat. I grabbed at her wrist. I whiffed. She went in the drink. At home, we'd laughed about it.

Within a year of the aborted pontoon-boat ride, my mom had been pill-fuzzed and I'd been on a Trailways bus to find my father.

The things that stick in your head are funny.

"I love you, Bert," Emily Saginaw said in a five-year-old's voice. Wispy, lispy. Just beyond my reach.

She stepped through the busted window into snow and wind.

CHAPTER FORTY-TWO

The snow had moved off the Atlantic *fast* and was pounding the city.

I'd slipped from the war room and made for the elevators, had been surprised as hell when nobody stopped me, or even looked up. Had made it to my truck. I would head to Framingham, wait out the snow, and figure out what to tell Wu when he finally hauled me in. Which he would.

It's no secret people in Boston can't drive for shit. But you'd think they could handle a couple inches of snow.

They couldn't. Not in early November, anyway, on a Sunday afternoon. I crawled west on Memorial Drive, creeping around three fender benders before I even hit the bridge that would take me over the Charles River to the Mass Pike. The few people outside who weren't back-ending their fellow motorists had decided it was a snow day. College-kid snowball fights, snow angels, one doofus trying out his cross-country skis. Like that.

Just getting on the Pike took a full half-hour, and my speedometer never topped 45 as I worked west. I passed the time listening to AM radio. When the news hit, they soft-pedaled it. First it was an accident at the Escutcheon. Then it was a possible tragedy. Then it was an unspecified tragedy plus Bert Saginaw halting a speech in Dedham and hustling to his hotel. When I parked in front of Floriano's house, they still hadn't named names.

I killed my truck, rubbed my eyes. I kept seeing Emily Saginaw step over my arm and flutter out the window-wall.

It was full dark with an honest three inches of snow on the ground. Enough snow to cover footprints from an hour ago.

The house was warm inside. But quiet, which was unusual: No sign of Dozen or his sisters fighting and playing.

In the kitchen, Maria sat at a ladder-back chair, sipped coffee, and smoked a Kent. That was weird, too—had I ever seen her seated in the kitchen? Usually she was flitting around between stove and counter, cooking and cleaning at the same time.

"This snow," I said after she nodded at me.

"Yes," Maria said. "Such snow." She looked up, to indicate snow or God or both.

"Floriano out plowing?"

"Yes, plowing." Again with the eyes rolled toward heaven. Maybe she was poking fun at Floriano. With Maria it was hard to tell.

"I'm just waiting out the snow," I said. "Got a drive to make, a long one."

"You go to your room to pack?" she said. *"Acima?"*

"Sí."

I headed for the front of the house and the basement stairs.

Then stopped.

I knew enough Portuguese to get around Framingham, to get around job sites where three-quarters of the workers wore green-and-yellow soccer jerseys.

Acima was upstairs.

Abaixo was downstairs.

Maria knew damn well my room was *abaixo,* not *acima.*

What the hell?

I stopped at the basement door. Shook my head, let go of the handle, stepped farther toward the front hall and the stair landing there.

Then two things happened at once:

Dozen hollered, *"Conway look out look out look out!"*

And something came diving down the stairs at me.

Some*one.*

Vernon Lee.

Maria hadn't been looking to heaven or to God, and she didn't give a rat's ass about the snow. She'd been looking to where Vernon had his hands on her youngest son's throat.

She was trying to warn you. She couldn't say it because Vernon was listening. You get so goddamn stupid when you're tired.

All this flashing through my head as he sailed downward and piled into me, busting us both through the railing at the foot of the stairs. We slammed to the front hall floor. He stood while I tried to get my wits and wind. Vernon Lee: alive as all hell, my size or close to it, greasy gray hair, gray stubble, sweaty face.

In his right fist: an eighteen-inch length of pipe with a 90-degree fitting at one end. The iron fitting would give the weapon some heft. It would make for a nice finish.

I stood as he came at me with a semicontrolled swing of the pipe. I ducked, felt the whoosh, planted my feet, torqued through my hips, hit him in the belly. Between my good stance and the initial adrenaline squirt, I got a lot on it.

Vernon grunted and stepped back, but he didn't go down and he didn't panic. He looked me over a little harder, and then he smiled.

Then he came again with the same swing. *Fake!* my head screamed. But the body does what it does—flinching is almost impossible to prevent. I ducked again just as Vernon pulled the pipe to a halt . . .

. . . and kneed my face, which was now conveniently low.

If he'd connected a little better—if my face or his kneecap had been a half-inch lower or higher—it would've ended there. I would have gone down, and he could have beaten me to death where I lay.

But it was mostly thigh that connected with my mouth and nose.

Blood sprayed. My teeth made a distinct click, and warm blood in my mouth told me I'd bitten my tongue tip something fierce.

I didn't go down. I rocked, staggered, spread my legs like a sumo wrestler—but didn't go down.

Background noise: Maria screaming, Dozen screaming, too, and trying to help me but vised in a headlock by his mother, the headlock impossible to escape, Maria with adrenaline to spare, having been scared shitless a minute ago that Vernon the madman would kill her son.

I took advantage of Vernon's surprise that I was still standing: lunged forward, ducked beneath his pipe, got him in a bear-hug. Held it. Squeezed.

He swung the pipe a few times, but his leverage was gone: The short-armed shots thumped into my back and kidneys, doing no real damage.

I squeezed. Buried my head in Vernon's armpit, kept my chin down and my eyes shut to reduce vulnerability, and squeezed. We tottered back and forth, taking small steps here and there like the world's worst box-stepping dancers, bunching the Oriental rug beneath us.

He wheezed. He squeaked.

I was dead silent. I was focused.

I squeezed.

I heard, *felt,* the last bit of wind leave his lungs. I would squeeze Vernon Lee to death here in Floriano's front hall. I would kill the motherfucker again.

He was a tough man. He was as tough as me. He had to be graying out, had to know he was about done. He had to know he had one last effort in him—if he was lucky.

Vernon had been holding the pipe like a jockey's baton, and it hadn't done him any good. But he was still thinking: He regripped it like a spike ready to be driven.

Then he began banging the back of my head with it. One two three times, quick little shots, bap-bap-bap.

I almost passed out.

Vernon felt me stagger. He liked his new plan. He banged my head again in the exact same spot. The strokes were short, but the fitting at the end of the pipe made for concentrated shots.

At the seventh or eighth impact, my eyes crossed and my grip must have loosened, because Vernon began squirming like a greased otter. He kept the pipe shots coming, always in the same spot at the back of my skull. Then I heard him draw the world's biggest breath, which meant my bear-hug wasn't doing the job anymore.

I was slipping. All I saw was gray. Adrenaline seeped away. Fear seeped in.

I was in trouble. I felt my interlocked fingers slipping from one another, felt myself stagger. Maria and Dozen were still hollering, but they now sounded far away. And still, the short little shots from the pipe, always in the same spot: Bap! Bap! Bap! I needed to change things up. *Now.*

Took the deepest breath I could. Settled my feet, my stance. Willed myself to ignore the pipe-shots a few seconds, adjusted my grip on Vernon's midsection . . .

. . . and threw us both out the stained-glass window.

CHAPTER FORTY-THREE

My ass shattered thirty thousand dollars' worth of glass, and we landed hard on the front porch.

Bonus: During the wipeout, Vernon dropped the length of pipe.

We scrambled to our feet, wide-stanced, no more than a foot and a half apart, and I got my first real look at Vernon since the bear-hug.

He wasn't in any better shape than I was. Breathing like a locomotive, sweat-slick everywhere, bleeding from an eye, an ear, a cheek.

"Moe Coover," I said, and tossed a dumb-ass Sunday punch at him. It was a bad punch that never had a chance, but it was all I had left.

"Which one was that?" he said, blocking the punch with a forearm.

Rage flared at the idea he didn't even know who Moe was. "The old man," I said, panting. "The diaper."

Vernon smiled. "What a way to go."

And there it was: red mist, sweet hot fury.

I marshaled it. I controlled it.

I smiled.

"Savvy Kane," I said.

Vernon panted. "That one I do recall, sir. A touch gullible, you ask me. Agreed to meet me in a goddamn vacant lot 'cause I said I was ready to leave old Bert Saginaw alone! Now why would a fella need an empty construction site for such a declaration?" He shook his head, disgusted.

I balled my fists.

"Not much of a flier, either," Vernon said. "Dropped like a stone, landed all awkward-like. Hoo-eee, believe it."

Then he bull-rushed and head-butted me. It was a good shot in the chest, and he pressed as I backpedaled. After three or four steps, I went back-first through Floriano's porch railing, snapping my head to his driveway. My eyes crossed again with sheer, concentrated pain. One corner of my head was grateful for the cushioning snow that probably spared me a concussion. Another corner was sorry as hell about tearing up my friend's house this way.

But those thoughts came and went as I shook my head to clear it, and I damn near smiled at what replaced them.

Red mist. The full, concentrated dose. No regrets, no reins.

Not much of a flier. Hoo-eee, believe it.

I made it to my feet, staggering some, saw Vernon had done the same. He'd scraped his chin badly in the dive from the porch. A flap of skin the size of three postage stamps dangled. Vernon crouched like a defensive lineman. With his back to the street, he looked like he was set to wise off again.

Until he saw my eyes.

Which were different.

Tunnel vision comes with the mist. Peripheral nonsense vanishes. Your world is dead ahead. Nothing else matters.

Vernon saw this, sensed it. His breath hitched and he straightened his legs a very small amount, raising his center of gravity.

That was when I charged him.

Wanted to get my shoulder into his midsection and lift, but he ducked just quickly enough to force me to grab whatever I could.

Which turned out to be his head.

Which would do just fine.

I got him in an old-fashioned headlock, cinched it tight, spun him.

Floriano's driveway dropped as it neared the street, and the snow made it impossible to even think about stopping.

So I ran us downhill. Vernon was along for the ride, his shoes slipping and slapping as he grabbed at me, trying anything and everything to stop my run.

I wouldn't be stopped.

Red mist will do that.

Tunnel vision. Dead ahead ten yards in the strip of snow-covered grass between the sidewalk and the curb: an elm tree. Two feet around, four stories tall. The street used to be lined with them, but most had been cut down when their roots began busting the sidewalk.

Not this one. This was a good elm. This was an elm with some heft to it. This was an elm to aim at.

I aimed. I picked up speed.

Five more yards.

Sound went away. Any sense of Vernon's 230 or so pounds went away. Everything went away but the sweet hot fury and the chug of my legs, moving hard and well.

Vernon sensed what was coming, twisted like a cat falling toward a swimming pool, pinched my arm, tried everything, tried *anything*.

He was still twisting when I ran his head into the tree at waist level.

Two things happened at once then: Snow shivered from the elm's branches, powdering my head and shoulders, and Vernon became dead weight.

I backed off a foot.

I rammed his head into the tree again.

Red mist. Sweet hot fury.

But it went away. All at once, the way it does. I became aware of Maria and Dozen pulling at me, pleading with me to stop.

I let go of Vernon. He dropped. I damn near did, too.

Then it was quiet, snow muffling everything but my breathing. I hated myself for the way Dozen was looking at me. He'd seen something no kid should see.

"Let's get inside," Maria said, looking up and down the street. No movement, no looky-loo neighbors, no porch lights. At the mouth of the road, a block west, a town snowplow scraped past. That was it.

I thought.

No way was I going inside. No way was I pulling Maria and Floriano into this.

"You two go in," I said, then spoke to Dozen. "You're the man of the house. There's plywood and a circular saw in the basement. Rip a sheet of plywood and get that hole covered." To Maria: "Anybody asks, the damage is from a fight. Your older boys got drunk, had a donnybrook. Okay?"

"Okay, but . . . what you *saying*, Conway? What you *doing*? Is dead body under your feet."

"Go inside."

I pulled my cell and made three calls.

They kept me from thinking about what I'd just done.

CHAPTER FORTY-FOUR

We rolled up to the Blackstone Valley Salvage gate just after nine.

"This it?" Lacross said.

I nodded, climbed out.

He'd been my first call. Caller ID had told him it was me. "Talk to me about Emily Saginaw," he said first thing.

So they were reporting it. They were naming names.

"Later," I'd said. "What are you doing right now?"

"Same as any decent human being. Getting set to watch the Patriots kick the living snot out of the Jets."

"Want to do something else instead?"

"No. What?"

"I'll show you," I'd said, and told him Floriano's address.

Most storms roll into Massachusetts from the southwest. But this one had been an honest nor'easter, pounding in from the Atlantic. Here at Blackstone Valley Salvage, thirty miles from the coast, there was barely an inch of snow.

I stepped to the gray metal box Mikey Guttman had told me about.

He'd been my second call.

"Big favor," I'd said. "Very big, and one you don't want to know about. Think before you say anything. You hang up now, I don't mind. Hanging up is your smartest move."

Then I'd gritted my teeth and hoped. Because if Mikey didn't come through, I was screwed.

"What is it?" he said.

"Access to your yard."

"When?"

"Now. For an hour, maybe two. Like I said, best if you don't know why."

Another long wait.

"You got a good memory?" he finally said.

"Sure."

Then Mikey Guttman had said an eight-digit code. He'd said it once, then hung up.

I punched the code into the keypad on the gray box. The gate rolled open. Lacross drove his Crown Vic inside, killed its headlights. I gestured *wait a sec,* found a fifty-five-gallon drum near the fence, stepped atop it, looked up and down the road. I made myself stand there a full five minutes.

Give Lacross credit: He'd stood over Vernon Lee's dead body, which had still been warm enough to melt the snow that fell on it. He'd looked at the mess that used to be a head.

And all he'd said was, "What do you need?"

"How much do you like that car?" I nodded toward his Crown Vic.

"I paid six hundred and twenty-five bucks for it," he said. "And got ripped off."

That had been the right answer.

In my five minutes atop the drum, no cruiser showed up. Not even a casual swing-by. Everybody was watching the Pats on *Sunday Night Football.*

I jumped down, found the yard's tool storage. Dug out a grinding wheel with a decent-looking blade, hooked it to the air compressor. Fired the compressor. It made a racket, but there wasn't anything I could do about that.

I opened the driver's door for Lacross. "Climb out," I said. He did.

Ten minutes later, all VIN info had been cut from the Crown Vic. I dropped the metal plates, still hot from the grinding wheel, in my pocket. Stowed the tools, nodded Lacross back into the car, climbed in beside him.

I directed him to the back of the yard. To the Granutech crusher Mikey was so proud of.

While the Granutech warmed up, I parked the big car parallel to its maw, fired a propane-powered forklift, backed it into position, and moved its forks to the height I needed. Lacross watched, blowing on his hands and dancing around to fight the cold.

I eased forward. The forks went through the car's right-side windows. When the lift itself touched the car's doors, I raised the forks. Up went two tons of Ford, just like that. I drove the forklift a foot at a time, glancing left and right to make sure I was on target.

Then I lowered the car into the crusher and backed away.

As I got down and stepped to the Granutech's control panel, everything hit me. I had to stop walking. My legs just about gave way.

I fought it.

Then I stopped fighting and relaxed into it.

I went to one knee in snowy mud.

"Sax?" Lacross said.

I said nothing.

Soon the shaking stopped.

I rose. I stepped to the panel.

The big red button, the only one that mattered, was labeled: COMPRESS STAND CLEAR.

I stood clear.

I punched the button.

I compressed.

Half an hour later, after forklifting the Crown Vic—which was by then the size of a fancy refrigerator—to a two-acre pile of other crushed cars, Lacross and I stepped through the gate, punched the code again, and watched the gate roll shut behind us.

Randall was idling away in my F-150.

He'd been my third call.

We climbed in.

Three grown men on a bench seat. Tight fit.

Randall nodded at Lacross, who nodded back, then looked at me a long time. He said nothing. He handed us each a steaming Dunkin' Donuts cup.

I took one. But couldn't get a sip from it: My hand was shaking too much. Randall and Lacross pretended not to notice.

We drove.

Randall worked northeast and said nothing.

Everything was grainy, raw, black and white. Audio hallucinations screwed around with my ears, my head.

"Need to grab a few hours' sleep," I finally said.

"Want me to drop you at Floriano's place?"

"No. Drop him first"—jerking a thumb at Lacross—"then I'll sleep in my truck."

"May I ask why?"

"One more thing to do."

"May I ask what?"

I said nothing.

We drove quietly for a few miles.

"Pull over," I said as we thumped up a sleepy road in Upton. "By that pond."

I looked ahead, looked back, saw nobody, stepped out quickly. Took from my pocket a handful of metal tiles, the VIN plates from Lacross's car.

I threw them hard enough to make my shoulder sing. Threw them sidearm, the way you'd skim a rock. Watched them scatter, watched them plonk into the pond.

"Did I do right?" I said as we pulled away. I was asking both of them, or neither, or myself. Hell, I didn't know who I was asking.

Lacross said nothing.

Randall didn't answer for a long time. "You weren't exactly swamped with good options," he finally said.

When we hit Framingham, the snowfall was over, but the plows and sanders were still working.

"You know what's been bugging me?" Randall said.

"The third set of pics," I said. "Shep's little insurance stash without the red dots."

"Yes! How the hell'd they get to Thomas Wilton's house?"

"Tell him what you told me," I said. Lacross had filled me in on the trip to Blackstone Valley Salvage.

"Wilton has a top-end security cam setup," he said, "but a bunch of clowns manning it. Took me ten minutes reviewing video to spot a man coming out of the hedge and dropping the dirty pics on a patio chair."

"And that man was?"

"That man," Lacross said, "is currently residing in the trunk of my car, which I'm gonna report stolen soon as the game's over."

"Tell him the rest," I said.

"Scituate cops don't get a lot of what you'd call hardcore crime," Lacross said.

Randall looked confused.

"Scituate's where Wilton lives," I said.

"Aha," Randall said.

"The Scituate cops just about peed in their panties," Lacross said, "when one of them took a routine look in a car parked at the harbor and saw the ignition had been busted out."

"The car was stolen two blocks from Betsy Tinker's house," I said.

"So Vernon Lee laid his hands on Shep's set of the pictures somehow," Randall said after thinking it through, "stole a car, made his way down to Scituate, and set them out for Wilton to find?"

"About how I see it," Lacross said.

Randall thought awhile.

"But how? *Why?*" he finally said. "That is, how'd he learn about them in the first place, and why would he take them to Wilton? Where was the profit supposed to be?"

That was for me to answer.

"Margery Lee said it. Vernon was a corruptor, a befouler. Got his kicks screwing up anything and everything that was even a little sweet, a little pure."

"Okay." He stretched the word, needing more.

"Vernon's blackmail play had been toast ever since that day in the parking garage," I said. "Who knows how bad he was hurt. He'd killed Savvy, he'd killed Blaine, and he hadn't been paid a nickel by Emily Saginaw because he hadn't found the pics in Blaine's car. So take the corrupter and befouler bit, and cross them with the wounded-and-cornered-animal bit. I think he turned on Emily, decided to go for the double-cross. He must have known throwing the election to Wilton was the best way to get back at Emily."

Randall nodded. "So he blindly searched Shep's quarters."

"Tinker's house was easy enough to break into," I said. "I proved that."

More nodding. "Then he stole the first car he could and made a beeline for Wilton's place."

"Lashing out," I said.

"Tasmanian devil," Lacross said.

Nobody spoke the rest of the trip.

When Lacross climbed out in the dumpy parking lot of his office-that-was-also-his-apartment, he nodded once and closed the door of my truck. Then he hesitated, turned, gestured at me to roll down the window.

I did.

Lacross stuck his head and right arm through the window and leaned across me. It was an awkward move, and when his long hair drooped I saw the knotty remnant of his ear.

He shook hands with Randall. "You're okay," he said, and pulled himself out of the truck and walked away.

A few minutes later, Randall turned onto Floriano's street. He shut down my truck right behind his own car.

We sat.

Dozen had done a good job fitting plywood to the gap where Vernon and I had destroyed stained glass. He'd also screwed a two-by-four across the busted porch railing. Good for him.

The F-150's engine ticked as it cooled.

"What is it you still need to do?" Randall said.

I said nothing.

He sighed. "Can I help?"

"No."

"When is it enough, Conway?"

I said nothing.

Randall sighed, climbed out, began clearing snow from his Hyundai.

I lay down. Or maybe I fell down.

I was out before the truck got cold enough to bother me. I slept hard.

CHAPTER FORTY-FIVE

It was late Monday afternoon when I rolled into Level Cross.

I'd woken at first light feeling awful.

But I was born to drive. Red Bull, Slim Jims, ibuprofen, and twelve hours took me to the former home of Vernon and Blaine Lee.

And, for a while, Savannah Kane.

Randall had described it well. Raw little ranch house set on a short hill fronting a four-lane road. I had to wait a long time to grab a left turn up the driveway, and the street—nearly a highway—was busy enough so I kept a nervous eye on traffic behind me. Stop to take a left on a road like this, you were a sitting duck for highballing semis.

It had probably been a decent little one-story home, a decent little neighborhood, before they added extra lanes to the road. Now it was wind-scrubbed and achy, a house and lot that would be part of a strip mall in five years max. Somebody had once planted a hedge to shield the lot from cars streaming past, but the hedge had about thrown in the towel.

I rolled up the driveway's short hill, parked in front of the door—the paving carried right to its jamb—and looked around. Yard: grass that didn't look much different from dirt. Ahead: a detached building, a cross between a shed and a one-car garage, painted the same fading yellow as the main house. Next to the shed: a pile of car-related crap, rims and a pair of seats and who knew what else. Parked in front of the shed: a dark-blue Chevy Tahoe, dirty, six or eight years old.

I killed the F-150, heel-rubbed my eyes. My head throbbed. My breath could knock a buzzard off a shit-wagon. I'd spent most of the drive trying to un-see things—Vernon's mushy skull, Moe's face when he told me about being diaper-smothered, Emily Saginaw daintily stepping from a ninth-floor window.

I saw those things still.

Climbed out, stretched, knocked. Sensed and heard a flurry, waited a while. Finally she opened up.

I said, "Miz Lee?"

"Margery," she said, keeping most of herself behind the door. "And you are?"

I told her, reminded her we'd spoken, waited to be asked in.

And waited.

The Southern hospitality I'd known in my racing days was in short supply.

"I've got something for you," I said, looking over her shoulder.

"Well," she said. And stepped aside. Finally.

Looking around the kitchen, I couldn't see that Margery Lee had anything to be ashamed of, house-wise. The place was as tired inside as out—no-color linoleum, a Formica table with only three chairs, duct tape on the arms of the sofa in the parlor to my right—but from the way she'd hidden behind the door, I'd half-expected a hoarder's home full of one-eyed cats and old magazines.

"The state has been coming around," she said, reading my puzzlement. "Child Protective Services."

"I'm not them."

"I know. Now. Please sit." She waved toward the parlor. "I'll get you a drink."

"Okay," I said, but stood instead. Watched.

Margery Lee suited this place. Faded and run-down now, she'd been plain-vanilla pretty once. She was a woman who would've hosted bridge games back when people played bridge.

My mother had loved bridge.

As Margery Lee bent at the waist to pull a Mountain Dew from the yellow-gold fridge, I saw how her jeans, which had already been taken in at the waist, bagged. I saw the crown of her head where her hair had thinned. I saw black moles on her neck that a woman with money would've had removed.

"Oh!" she said when she turned and I was still there. "Would you . . . ?" Motioning again to the parlor.

From outside came the sound of a bouncing basketball.

"Is that Max?" I said. "Savvy's kid?"

"It is."

"I'd like to meet him."

"He's better off outside." She spoke quickly, then must have decided she sounded rude. "He spends more time inside than he ought to, truth be told. I'm sure that's my fault."

"How is he?" I said. "How are *you*?"

"We should really sit," Margery said, and led me to the front room.

There was a picture window here. She looked at my truck, its license plate. "My, Mr. Sax, did you *drive* down?"

"Call me Conway. I don't like flying." What I didn't tell her: I'm on a list. I buy an airline ticket, the Massachusetts Parole Board gets an auto-notice and my parole officer calls me looking for answers. The PO is Luther Swale, Randall's father, and we have an informal long-leash deal. But I didn't want to push him or my luck. So I'd driven, and had removed my FAST LANE transponder so I couldn't be tracked through toll payments.

I sat at one end of the sofa, leaving an armchair for her. But she didn't take it, sat at the other end of the sofa instead. I looked at the chair: It was newer than anything else in the room save a fifty-inch flatscreen.

Aha. Margery Lee had been so scared of Vernon that even now she wouldn't use his chair.

We sat awhile. I sipped Mountain Dew. Margery twisted her hands. This wasn't working out the way I'd expected.

You wanted a sweet auntie type to invite you in for pie. You wanted to talk about Level Cross and the Petty family and racing. You thought someone might pull out a fiddle and propose a sing-along. You thought the whole clan would weep with joy when you opened your wallet. Instead, you're sitting with a ninety-pound ghost who's still terrified of the husband who beat her for forty years.

Shit.

"I want to tell you how sorry I am about your son, ma'am," I said, "and about Max's mother." I shifted my weight, took out my wallet.

"Thank you."

"Tough row. For you. For Max. You've lost a lot."

"More than you know, sir."

I opened the wallet. The checks had been folded willy-nilly, but they were all there. One by one I removed them, smoothed each crease. Checks from Tinker, from Saginaw, from Tinker-Saginaw for Governor. There were four altogether, including the final one from Betsy Tinker, the one for three times the amount of the others.

Pointed at a Bic pen on the table before me. "May I?"

"Of course. What are those, sir?"

"Call me Conway," I said as I signed the checks over to Margery Lee.

Then I straightened them up as best I could—the creases were stubborn—and handed them over. "For Max."

She shuffled through them once. Then twice.

Then she put on the glasses that hung around her neck and shuffled through them again.

Margery Lee kept staring and shuffling, like a Vegas virgin looking at his cards.

I felt embarrassed all of a sudden at my Mister Big act. I didn't want to sit here anymore waiting for gratitude to flow. Instead: stood, turned, looked out the picture window.

"Sir . . . Conway . . . this is three hundred thousand dollars."

"Yes, ma'am."

"Why are politicians giving you this kind of money?"

"Long story. They're legit. Deposit them. The taxes'll be my problem."

"*Why,* Conway? Please stop looking out the window. *Why?*"

I turned. "For Max, like I said . . ."

My hesitation told her there was more. "And?"

"And . . . Miz Lee. Margery. Your husband Vernon won't be coming home, I'm afraid."

She was still for twenty seconds. Outside, traffic streamed.

"Tell me more," Margery finally said.

"He just won't. Trust me."

"Will you tell me how you know this?"

"No."

We stared at each other.

From the backyard came the sound of metal on metal.

"If Max is playing around the car parts," I said, "we ought to keep an eye on him."

"I believe you," she said. At first I thought she was talking about Max.

She wasn't. Fifteen years fell from her face and she smiled, truly *smiled*. "Vernon is gone," she said.

"Yes."

Her shoulders loosened. She looked an inch taller than she had a minute ago. "Never to return," she said.

"Yes."

She had a nice smile.

"Let's introduce you to Maxie," she said, and began to lead me back through the kitchen. Spotting my Mountain Dew can, she swiped it from the side table like it was a jar of piss. "And I'll squeeze some lemonade. Maxie does like his lemonade."

As far as I could tell, Max was a good kid. He had a big bold jaw, like his father. But the eyes were all Savvy: nearly black, smoky, willful. While Margery and I sat on beach chairs he bulldozed around the yard playing with this and that, *atop* this and that, showing off for me, obeying—eventually—his gramma when she warned him away from dangerous piles of junk.

"Are you going to be all right?" I said, looking at my watch.

"He misses his mother," Margery said. "He doesn't say it, but he misses her terribly."

"He's got you."

"Yes." She started to say more. Stopped. Took a deep breath. "He would have me with or without your money, you know. Am I terribly rude to point that out?"

"No. I knew it was true. The money'll help if you use it the right way, and you will."

"Yes," Margery Lee said. "I will."

CHAPTER FORTY-SIX

The sun was rising the next morning when I pulled up at Floriano's. I killed the truck. The absence of engine noise seemed loud. I stared at the steering wheel a few seconds, trying to remember what came next.

The key. You take it out. No, you have to push while you twist it. Like this.

I was that tired. Rubbed my eyes. It'd been a hell of a trip home.

As I stumbled up Floriano's porch steps, a couple of cousins heading to work opened the front door. They took a look at me and began firing questions in both English and Portuguese. I stood on the porch and swayed.

Maria rescued me. Heard the commotion, came out to the porch, shooed the cousins, took my arm, steered me to the basement.

"Cops?" I said, staggering down the steps, glad Maria was guiding me. "Questions? Anything?"

She knew I was talking about Vernon. "Nothing," she said. "Is good. Sleep."

"Vote early and often," I said, giggling. The sound of the giggle scared me.

"Sleep," Maria said.

I did. And how.

Without my pals the poll flunkies, I wouldn't have gotten within fifty yards of the Escutcheon ballroom that night.

It was nine thirty, two hours after my phone's alarm woke me—barely—in Floriano's basement. I'd taken the world's longest, hottest shower, scrambled a half-dozen eggs, washed them down with a quart of orange juice, and dug my only sport coat from my duffel. It smelled like a middle-school gym locker. Oh well.

So here I was for the political wingding.

And a hell of a wingding it'd be, according to news radio. The polls hadn't been closed thirty seconds when the Associated Press and all the networks projected Betsy Tinker as the new governor of Massachusetts, winning something like 53 percent to 46 percent—amazing, the talking heads said, considering the race had been too close to call just a day ago. The last-minute swing could be explained only by sympathy for Bert Saginaw's tragic loss.

Everybody loves a winner, so cops were checking credentials to make sure the hotel's grand ballroom filled only with pols, donors, and volunteers. I milled around until I spotted the boy-genius poll-jockey, the one whose head I'd threatened to bounce off a wall. I approached him. I told him what I needed. He started to speak. He looked in my eyes.

He gave me his badge and lanyard.

In the massive room, the vibe was weird and wild, a frat party crossed with a wedding reception. Classic rock blared, but so did CNN from one huge screen and MSNBC from another. It was a big election night all over the country, but the networks kept coming back to the Tinker-Saginaw fall-and-rise story. And each time they did, the room went nuts. Balloons, a little white-bread dancing, I-love-you-mans here and there as dudes got drunk.

Like that.

Me: stunned, sore, out of place. Hadn't had half the sleep my body needed, so I chugged black coffee and swayed on my feet.

And planned.

Worked my way to the stage, for starters. Eyeballed its wings, figured out where the big winners would make their entrance. Without asking permission, I hopped onstage and walked around, trying to look like a technician. Nobody questioned me. So I walked stage right and stood near a pair of double doors. From what I knew of the hotel layout, this was the place to be.

At ten, the room went extra crazy. I looked up at a giant screen and figured out Thomas Wilton was giving his concession speech. Couldn't hear a word of it. Which was plenty.

I waited. After ten minutes, a state cop poked his head in the double doors, looked both ways, seemed satisfied, and closed the doors. In the room, buzz built.

I moved to the double doors.

Krall came in first, flat triumph on his face.

The triumph went away when he spotted me. It was like he'd hit a glass wall—flunkies on his tail banged right into him.

Then, a pro through and through, he recovered. "Such a day," he said, hands on hips. "Such a . . . *week*. Triumph and tragedy."

"Good title," I said.

"Pardon?"

"For the book you'll write about this clusterfuck."

His face changed. He tugged my forearm, pulled me away from the door. Flunkies came through, bigfooting, telling everyone to clear a path.

"Books are for losers," Krall said. "I'll work til I'm eighty off this campaign, and I'll pull top dollar."

There wasn't much I could say to that.

So I punched him in the kidney as hard as I could.

"Umph," Krall said, sagging.

"You suck blood," I said. "Now you can piss it, too."

"Urph," Krall said.

I stepped close. "If Maria Mendes ever has even a whiff of trouble with the immigration people," I said in his ear, "I will drive to your house and beat you to death."

"Hmph," Krall said.

"They're all waiting for you," I said.

He walked away, I'll give him that. He walked funny, but he walked on stage.

The flunkies had cleared a path for Betsy Tinker. Before she even hit the stage, people spotted her in the wings and went crazy. Cheering, stomping, whistling, chanting. Tinker caught people's eyes, shrugged, made aw-shucks waves . . . the works. She did all the right things. They came naturally to her. Betsy Tinker would be fine.

Shoulders back, she strode to the center of the stage. A bunch of preppy-looking twentysomethings piled in—her kids, had to be—along with a couple of perfect little grandbabies who raised a big *Awwwwwww* from the room.

Krall stood in back, with flunkies and low-rent pols. He didn't look so good.

Finally, Bert Saginaw came through the double doors. He spotted me. I moved toward him. A statie started to block, but Saginaw waved him away and let me pull him to the same corner where I'd punched Krall.

"You're going to be lieutenant governor," I said. Just about had to holler for all the noise.

"I am indeed," he said. "And I want to thank you for your assistance. Wouldn't be here without you, Conway."

He said it like a robot. He was already morphing into a genuine politician.

"My friend Moe once told me something funny about that," I said.

He waited.

I took my time, remembering, making sure I got the line right. "He said if the vice presidency's not worth a bucket of warm piss, what's lieutenant governor of Massachusetts worth?"

Tight smile. "I'm happy to serve any way I can."

"That's good. Because you know what you're going to do?"

"What's that?"

I leaned forward, cupped a hand to his ear. "You're going to do your four years. You're going to be the best goddamn lieutenant governor in the country. You'll cut ribbons when they open strip malls, you'll give Kiwanis speeches every Tuesday, you'll throw out the first pitch at high school baseball games in Gardner."

"Go fuck yourself."

"You'll be second banana. The closest you'll ever come to the spotlight is talking to fourth graders when they take field trips to the State House."

"I believe this conversation is over."

"What you *won't* do," I said, "you won't climb any higher on the ladder. *Ever.* Four years as second banana, grinning and bearing it, and then you say you've had enough. Say you're going back to Saginaw Fence. Hell, say you want to spend more time with your family. Isn't that what they always say?"

"The fuck's this about, Sax?"

"I thought it through," I said. "Had a long drive, figured it out. If I could hurt you worse without hurting Tinker, I would. I'd tell the whole weirdo story about Emily and Shep and Vernon Lee and dirty pictures and red dots and double-crosses and triple-crosses. Time I was finished, even you would be ashamed of yourself."

The chants for Tinker were fragmenting. Everybody on stage was looking our way, impatient for Saginaw. Three staties hovered, waiting for a signal from Saginaw to give me the bum's rush.

The expression that came to his puss was half-smile, half-sneer. "Looks like you've got a problem, Sir Fucking Galahad. See, you can't get me without getting Tinker. So I guess I'll just go ahead and do exactly what I want to do."

"'Fraid not, Saginaw. Lieutenant governor. One term as second banana, and then you're done. With a *girl* for a boss, no less. From what I've learned about you, it's going to be a lousy four years."

"What are you gonna do, though? Tell some reporter a fairy tale? Who'd believe a convicted killer, Sax?"

"They wouldn't believe me," I said. "But they'd believe the pictures."

The smirk vanished. In the hall, momentum was dying. Betsy Tinker looked pissed.

A state cop was walking our way.

"I kept a set," I said. "And I made a few copies. Anything happens to me, the photos go to three separate news organizations." That wasn't true, but I did have a plan: Lacross would get a copy of the photos. Neither of us exactly trusted the other, and neither could release the pics without heavy personal repercussions. It was perfect.

I clapped Bert Saginaw on the shoulder and said, "Go get 'em, Loot."

The crowd gave him a nice hand.

CHAPTER FORTY-SEVEN

I knocked on the door a long time. Felt, rather than heard, hallway footsteps. Then a porch light went on. I took a step back, made myself visible.

Nothing happened for a while.

Then a dead bolt shifted. The door opened four inches.

Charlene looked at me. She said nothing.

"Of the past forty hours," I said, "I spent twenty-four driving."

"You look it."

"You know I think when I drive. I got to think a lot."

She said nothing.

"Can I come in?"

She paused half a beat, then stepped back. She wore a sweatshirt, flannel pants, fluffy slippers.

I stepped into the hall, closed the door behind me.

From the great room, far to my right, came election-coverage sounds.

Charlene folded her arms. "What conclusions did you reach during your drive-a-thon?"

"This was where I wanted to be."

She said nothing.

"This was the *only* place I wanted to be." During the drive, I'd planned to say a lot more. Had put together a pretty good speech.

I couldn't remember any of it.

"You chose a dead girl over me."

"I didn't."

We stood. A light went on in the upstairs hall. Charlene didn't notice—her back was to it.

"In my more reasonable moments," she said, "I know you didn't. But it *feels* like you did."

"It was Barnburner stuff."

"Which you will continue to do."

This was the part I'd feared during the long drive.

"Yes," I said.

"Yes," she said, taking a small step toward me. "You're not the only one who's been thinking. I'm not Martha Stewart. I'm not Henrietta Homemaker."

"You don't have to be."

"My daughters do all right by me. All things considered."

"They do."

Charlene looked up. Her eyes locked mine. "Can we?"

"We can try."

Then it was my turn to take a small step.

And wrap arms around her.

We stood that way a good long while.

I began to shake.

I guess Charlene thought I was crying. "It's okay—" she began. Then: "What's so funny?"

I turned her gently so she could see what I'd already spotted: Sophie's head hanging from the second-floor landing, an upside-down grin plastered to it.

I looked at Charlene looking at her daughter.

Laugh lines.